Never Cheat

a Witch

Edited by
Carol Hightshoe

WolfSinger Publications ❧ Security, Colorado

Acknowledgements

Acts of God © 2022 by Ian Kitley
Skulls on a Shelf © 2022 by Jodi Rizzotto
Better than Gold © 2022 by T.W. Kirchner
Law of Spells © 2022 by Lea Storry
Subscribed © 2022 by Louise Zedda-Sampson
No Age Restrictions © 2022 by Danielle Mikals
Fair Trade © 2022 by Dominick Cancilla
Dream Weaver © 2022 by Wendy Harrison
Can't Be Done © 2022 by Elle Hartford
Dwarves, Donks, and Death © 2022 by Brian MacDonald
Mike and His Three Lives © 2022 by M.A. Lang
Book and Key © 2022 by J.L. Royce
Isabella the Eldridge © 2022 by Frank Montellano
Hex © 2022 by Clark Sodersten
Paper Mage © 2022 by Sandra Unerman
Controlling the Kudzu © 2022 by Bailey Finn
The Friar and the Turnip © 2022 by Christopher Wortley
How to Steal a Spell Book © 2022 by Mirabelle Poppy
The Frog and the Princess © 2022 by Jean Martin
Marigold at Midnight © 2022 by Tyree Campbell
Learning Something Useful © 2022 by Joyce Frohn
Night Work © 2022 by Rose Strickman
Breaking Down a Cursed Sandwich © 2022 by Ray Daley
Payback's a Witch © 2022 by Harriet Phoenix

For permission requests, please contact WolfSinger Publications at:
editor@wolfsingerpubs.com

Cover Art copyright 2022 © Carol Hightshoe

ISBN 978-1-944637-15-6

Printed and bound in the United States of America

TABLE OF CONTENTS

Acts of God

Ian Kitley

No matter how many realities you visit, dimensions you hop, or fae realms annoying princelings kidnap you to; some things are inviolate. And before some smart arse says it, no, I do not mean death and taxes. The former is more a suggestion, one countless zombies, deities, and any idiot sensible enough to include something in their will about tall hills, lightning rods and thunderstorms has ignored since time immemorial. The latter simply leads to uprisings or revolutions anywhere the populace has two brain cells worth rubbing together. What that says about anyone born after the 1700s in my original reality, I don't want to think about.

Now, hold music, on the other hand, that never changes. Whether new-age pop princess trash or medieval string quartets, it's always scratchy and horrible and soul-destroying. I'd suspect Hell of having a hand in the franchises, but the last time Beelzebub and I got drunk, he admitted someone got in before them. Wouldn't tell me who, but I have my suspicions. Anyone capable of selling something sounding like a drowned cat in the middle of an aggressive polka festival as music can't be mortal. It's simply not possible.

"Thank you for holding. We at What's the Worst That Can Happen Insurance value your custom and apologise for the delay. You are number—" I flinched, almost dropping the entire bottle of Wolfsbane into the cookie mix as a screech drowned out my position in the queue. I'd left the phone on the other side of the room after the first several such occurrences, and still it drilled into my brain, scorching my nerves every time. I loved that magic was alive and well in this reality, but whoever's bright idea it was to run communications through it should be turned into a toad. And then cooked.

"—in the queue. If you'd prefer a call-back instead of waiting, press pound and leave your number at the beep. We will endeavour to call you back within twenty-four—" And again with the screeching. That was definitely deliberate. I'd tried that route, and a week later, they still hadn't called. I was guessing the time scale was months, not hours.

"Otherwise, please continue to hold on the line, and a representative will be with you shortly."

I returned to my mixing, checking I'd added the correct quantity of Wolfsbane and humming quietly in an attempt to drown out the caterwauling. No good, but a witch can dream. Surveying the kitchen counters, I took stock of my morning's accomplishments. In the time I'd been on hold, I'd managed enough baked goods to feed a battalion or the typical after-school rush on a weekday. Teresa would appreciate me thinking ahead, but not leaving her to man Trick or Treats, our café and bakery, by herself while I sorted this out. You'd think I'd thrown her to the wolves. Though, come to think of it, the local pack would likely be in today. Did she have enough doggie treats on hand?

"Hello, this is Marcus from WWTCH Insurance. How can I help you today?"

For a moment, I froze, unprepared for an actual human voice to break my reverie. Then I dropped the bowl, scrambled across the room, and snatched up the phone. Good thing it was on mute, or 'Marcus' would have wondered what war had suddenly broken out.

"Hi…Marcus," I wheezed, doing a fine impression of a gasping toad, "I'd like to query a decision…regarding my claim for damages. There appears…to have been a mistake."

"Of course, ma'am. In order to help you, I'll need your name, policy number, and claim identifier code. How about we start with your name?"

I was sure he was reading off a script, but damn if he didn't sound patronising. Some companies, or individuals, had no sense of self-preservation.

"Jemima Beatrix Puddleduck."

You'd think the world opened up and swallowed him whole from the silence emanating across the line. Apparently, my name has that effect on people.

"Sorry, ma'am, I'm not sure I heard correctly. Can you repeat that?"

"Oh, don't worry, you did. My name is Jemima Beatrix Puddleduck. We're a very distinguished coven, despite the name." A name I had no choice in. When you bend reality to the breaking point, you take whatever alias it foists on you.

"Okay, got it. And the rest?"

I rattled off my policy number and claim identifier, having memorised the damn things by now, and the sound of keys tapping provided a much more soothing tune as I waited. Gaze sliding to the opposite wall, or where it should be, I took in the inadvertent view of the garden and midday light. Without the tarpaulins in the way, the breeze was unusually refreshing while I worked.

"Here we are, Ms Puddleduck," Marcus said, choking only slightly on the last. He was doing better than most. "You're claiming the damage to your home was caused by an act of God, correct?"

A smile tugged at the corners of my lips. Diana's bachelorette had been going so well, and the Thor-lookalike stripper turned out to be the hit of the evening. And naturally, what's better than blonde, big and brawny? Why, adding his dark, swarthy and mysterious brother to the mix. Casting and alcohol isn't the best plan, though, and it was only a little my fault I summoned actual incarnations of both Gods in the process. My kitchen's wall was the only real casualty. And the neighbour's prized roses. And the founder's statue in the town square, but no one could prove that.

"Yes, I am. If you check your records, you will find signed affidavits from both Gods in question, and their father, bless his soul, attesting to their guilt. I'd think that proof enough."

More tapping, followed by some more silence. You'd think Marcus was blind to the type of world he lived in. "Um, yes, that seems all in order, ma'am. Unfortunately, your policy doesn't cover those particular circumstances."

I held the phone at arm's length, attempting to send an evil eye curse through it. It didn't work, but I felt better. "I think, Marcus, that if you check part seven, section three, sub-clause C, you'll find I am."

"I see, ma'am, but if you turn to appendix two, definitions of terms, and go to section sixteen, sub-clause D, you'll find your claim does not fit the requirements of 'Act of God'".

Breathing slowly, I made a gesture in the air, materialising the aforementioned policy. Flipping to the relevant spot, I began reading. And then stopped. No. You have got to be kidding me. No one would be so bold.

"Is he serious?"

The gulp was clearly audible. "Deadly, ma'am. And since you signed and accepted all parts of the policy, it is legally binding."

By the time I finished swearing, and I surprised even myself at how long that took, Marcus had thanked me for my custom, informed me not to hesitate to call again if I had further queries, and put the phone down on me, the little coward. The handset slowly arced through the space formerly occupied by my kitchen wall, over the rubble and swampy earth resulting from the burst waterline, to thump gently on the grass beyond. No satisfying smash or anything.

Fuming, I grabbed my mixing bowl and savaged the batter, trying, as Teresa always implored me, to channel my anger productively. I'd channel it productively, all right. Channel it right into some reality-bending, cosmos-breaking, mind-destroying spell to remind the idiots at WWTCH Insurance what sort of clients they really served.

Briefly, I wondered if they'd have treated me differently if they knew my truth, what I was really all about. As previously mentioned, my real name isn't Jemima, but it's what I'm called in this reality, so it's as good a name as any. Yes, this reality. I wasn't born here, and where I was isn't kind to witches of any sort. They tend to start fires when they find us, and other similarly nasty things. So, when my powers left my toys coming to life and replaying scenes from the Exorcist, I wasn't too popular. Good thing those same powers allow me to bend space and time and find a more convenient place to be.

Of course, that comes with a cost and the attention of beings I prefer not to think about, so I try not to go overboard too often. But sometimes, just sometimes, I feel I'm justified to dig deep and let loose with everything I have. Or nearly everything. Volcanic eruptions probably wouldn't do right about now.

I stopped in the middle of a somewhat forceful stir, one which required the reconstitution of my favourite bowl after, a smile spreading slowly across my lips. Teresa wouldn't appreciate that smile. She dislikes it when I get all malicious.

Too bad, I thought as I turned inwards, searching out the strings of the universe I'd need to pull for the spell to work. If Reginald Davis III, CEO of WWTCH, felt comfortable claiming to be a god, why not grant him what he wished for?

~ * ~

The sky was blue, the birds were singing—both of which were

only assumptions due to the special glass of his office windows darkening all colours and shutting out those annoying nature sounds —and for Reginald Davis III, all was good. Not that it couldn't be better, and he'd certainly yell at the heads of department for only exceeding expectations by five percent, but privately, he'd admit they had exceeded *his* expectations.

Turning on his heel, he stepped back to his mahogany desk, the wood gathered from trees surrounding the holiest grove in the country—not the grove itself, obviously—and reread the reports. Profits, and new business, were up, along with claims. But pay-outs were down, and that was what mattered. And in a world in which were-packs required third-party mauling insurance, witches needed malpractice coverage to retain their licences, and the life insurance on vampires was to die for, his success was an abnormality. And that was without taking into account his status as a mere human. Seriously, though, did no one ever read the fine print?

"Mary, ensure no one interrupts me for at least the next hour. There's a special policy I need to review, and I cannot be disturbed," he said into the crystal orb which communicated his wishes anywhere in the building. It was one of his favourite executive toys, almost a personal crystal ball, and he got a thrill out of bossing people around with it.

"Certainly, Mr Davis. No interruptions. Do you need anything before I leave you to it?" His secretary's soft lilt was starting to get on his nerves, and he wondered who else Beings Resources had available. A leprechaun had felt like the right choice a month ago, but all those rainbows in his outer office were beginning to give him headaches. And her paperwork was always a mess.

"No, thank you, Mary. Just some peace and quiet. I'll let you know when I'm available again." So saying, Reginald strode across soft Persian rugs to the special nook in one corner of the room, flicking the switch to banish the glamour usually hiding it from view. Retrieving his favourite scotch and magically infused snuff from their cubby, he collapsed into an old shabby armchair, feet up on a footstool. Ah, the advantages of being king. Or God, as he preferred to style himself.

Sipping slowly, a tingle ran up his neck as the wards protecting WWTCH Insurance headquarters flared for an instant before dying back down. He chuckled, saluting whatever magic-user had attempted retribution. He couldn't understand why they thought he wouldn't take precautions. Sure, the wards didn't stop all magic, but they did stop anything malicious. Who was he to prevent anyone throwing something beneficial his way? It didn't happen often, but not everyone came down with a case of sour grapes.

Another sip of the most excellent drink and a snort of the snuff left him in a lovely haze, and he lay back, letting himself float into the bliss.

Oh, my God! Seriously?

Reginald's left eye twitched at the high-pitched, nasal quality of the exclamation. Had Mary mistakenly conjured the orb back to life while taking a personal call? No, whoever that was, it wasn't her. Completely wrong voice. He'd have been unable to deal with that for even a week.

God, Mom, why do you keep doing this to me?

Okay, who let a little kid loose in the building? Sitting up, Reginald put aside his indulgences and made to return to his desk. He'd told Mary he wasn't to be disturbed.

Goddamn, girl, you're so fine!

For the love of God, pick up your toys right now or no TV for a week!

Palms suddenly slick with sweat grabbed the desk as his step faltered and he stumbled. What the hell? Where was that all coming from? Finally looking at his crystal orb, Reginald saw it was dark, unactivated. These voices weren't coming from there.

Matthew Bartholomew Frasier, so help me God, get your butt down here this instant!

God, Danny, why do you keep doing this to me?

As sure as God made little green...

God bless you.

God is good, God is...

They just kept coming and coming, one after the other, voices raised in every emotion under the sun. Ears metaphorically ringing, Reginald huddled against his desk, head buried between his knees, his own voice attempting to drown them out.

"Shut up! Shut up! Shut! Up!"

No one was listening. Or they simply couldn't hear him. Just as he thought it couldn't get any worse, more voices joined the din, redoubling the noise and drawing out a whimper.

"Got to breathe, got to centre myself, got to find a way

through," he told himself, unable to think of anything over the commotion. Slowly, oh so slowly, he constructed a prism in his thoughts, a space where the voices became little more than a dull hum. Throwing his astral self into it, he breathed a sigh of relief at the comparable silence.

First things first, find out what was going on. Second, find who had done it and make them pay. If he hadn't had all that training in meditation and woo-woo mysticism while his hippy parents dragged him around, this would be unbearable, but his opponent had underestimated him. If they thought this would cripple him, they had another...

God, I wish I could afford that.

As a sudden urge overtook him, Reginald Davis III's eyes flew wide in horror.

Oh no! No, no, no, no, no!

~ * ~

In the outer office, Mary Kelley received an email from her boss instructing her to send a personal check to someone named 'Peaches Donahue'. She didn't know who 'Peaches' was, but accounting could find out. Whoever they were, she must be very important to Mr Davis. Why else would he send her $3000?

~ * ~

"Thank you for your custom, and please come again," I said, beaming as the warlock couple left Trick or Treats. They appeared happy with the birthday cake for their darling demon of a daughter, and satisfied customers meant return business, something we desperately needed. The home kitchen remodel was going well, if expensively, and it shouldn't bite too deeply into our savings, but...

Brushing the thought aside, I turned to the next person in line and blinked. Old Harry, everyone's favourite local veteran and cheerful sidewalk resident, stood there in the first set of clean clothes I'd ever seen him in. Not only that, but he'd apparently had a shave and haircut, too.

"Harry?"

"Hi, Miss Jemima," he said, eyes not quite looking at me as he sidled over. "Sorry for interrupting; I just wanted to give you something."

The something was $50 in crisp, new notes, quickly thrust across the counter. I stared at them, not quite comprehending what was happening. For someone like Harry, that was almost a week's worth of food, if he was careful about it.

Raising my gaze, I realised he was already halfway to the door, having obviously accomplished his mission. Oh no you don't, buster.

"Teresa? Can you take over for a bit? I got a stray I need to help."

Strays were what Teresa called all those whose lives I stuck my nose into. She always said it fondly, without any malice, turning it into a bit of a joke between us, so she'd know what I meant.

"Sure, hon. You go do what you do," my partner in every way that mattered said, bustling out and wiping her hands, hip-checking me lovingly out of the way when she arrived. I didn't need further encouragement.

"Harry, wait up!"

My quarry paused with one hand on the door as I approached, sheepishly turning to face me. It really was him, and for a moment, I just took in the sight, my heart rising at the good times that must have come his way.

"Yes, Miss Jemima?"

"You know you don't need to add the Miss, Harry. Now, you sit down and explain what this is about," I said, waving the bills.

Ducking his head again, the veteran took the closest table to the door, eyeing me like unexploded ordnance. I wasn't that bad. "Just paying you back for all you've done for me, Miss…Jemima."

"Paying me back?"

"Yes, paying you back. I know I owe you far more than that, but it's what I got right now, and if you need help around the shop, all you need do is ask."

Still trying to wrap my head around it, I did what I would normally do and thrust the money back at him. "You don't need to pay me back. I didn't give you that money expecting you to return it or the food expecting payment. Besides, don't you need it?"

His shaking head and crossed arms were nothing compared to the set look of refusal he directed at me. "I owe you, Miss Jemima, and I repay my debts. And, no, I don't need it. I got a house and everything now."

Would the shocks not stop coming? I must have looked like

a landed fish. "What?"

"I got a house."

Even before I said it, I knew it was rude as hell, but I couldn't help myself. "How?"

Suddenly, Harry got all shifty. "I was given it."

"Harry?" I don't use my Mom voice much, especially as I don't have kids of my own, but I'm told I do a good imitation when needed.

"I swear, Miss Jemima. This guy in a suit just walked up to me the other day, gave me keys and a bank card and a bunch of papers saying it was all mine and told me I could have it if I did just one thing. I couldn't believe it, but it's all good. I got myself a lawyer, and he says so."

I stared at him for a full minute as he squirmed in his chair, a nasty suspicion poking at me. I'd kept my ear on recent events, but this was new. Could it be connected?

"And what was the condition for your new wealth, Harry? Don't tell me you've gotten into something criminal."

"No, no, nothing like that. It was really weird, but nothing like that."

"What do you mean by 'weird'?"

"Well," he blushed before continuing, "all I had to do was not say or even think the word—" He quickly grabbed a napkin and a pen from his pocket to scribble the word 'God' for me. "—ever again. I told the man I would love to, but I couldn't promise I would never think it, and he said as long as I didn't do it deliberately, that was enough. And then I signed the paper and felt the magic confirming the deal and he gave me the keys and…" He paused for breath, and I held up a hand.

"So, as long as you never again say…that word, it's all yours?"

He nodded, apparently relieved to have told someone. I could see it in how his shoulders relaxed, a tension I hadn't noticed finally leaving them.

"That's very generous of whoever it was that gave that to you," I said, the grin creeping across my face devilish in its intensity. "Let me get you a pain au chocolat, and you can tell me all about it."

On my way back to the counter, my gaze flicked over the newspaper rack and the day's headlines.

Local CEO's Donation Builds School for the Arts, and variations of it, dominated all the local papers and even some nationals. Davis must have put up a lot of money for this much coverage. In fact, his face beamed out at me from a photo of him cutting a ribbon. I'd seen all this this morning but hadn't paid much attention. It was becoming a bit of a norm for Davis to be in the headlines for his charitable work, much to my previous annoyance.

Now, though, I looked more closely. Behind his smile was a haunted, hunted expression. The expression of a man unable to escape the generosity thrust upon him. And it was all generosity. I knew some people asked God for some truly awful things, but I'd been very clear with my spell. All requests requiring his action would be, at worst, benign.

You wanted to be a God; well, that comes with certain expectations. Just because most of your ilk don't do their job, doesn't mean you're exempt too, I thought, trying not to be too smug. I had done this to teach a lesson, not for personal satisfaction. Not at all.

Pouring Harry and I a coffee to go with our baked goods, I paused a moment to concentrate. I thought I'd made my point. If this continued much longer, it would probably do more harm than good. Who knew how many people would suffer if WWTCH went bankrupt. That would truly answer the question of what was the worst that could happen.

God, listen to me. Rethink your phrasing of acts of Gods, change your policies, and compensate all claims that qualify retroactively for, say, five years, and maybe, just maybe, your life can return to normal. What do you say, God?

Funnily enough, I received a check in the mail a few days later. And the contract for a new policy. I took it to a lawyer friend and got her to go over it with a fine-tooth comb—nothing like getting Rapunzel's great-granddaughter for tasks like that—and you know what she said?

There wasn't a definition for who 'God' was anywhere in it anymore. Seems like even money-grubbing CEOs can learn new tricks.

~ * ~ * ~

Ian Kitley fell down the rabbit hole of genre fiction too many years ago to count and never looked back. When not exploring the beauty our world has to offer, he is lost in a multiverse of imagination, of both his creation and others. Proud to be involved in *"The Inkwell presents"* anthologies as an editor and contributor, his writing can also be found in "*An Election of Words*" from Scout Media.

For anyone wishing to follow his poetic musings, head on over to Twitter and @IanKitley, or @TheInkwellWC for his monthly short stories.

Skulls on a Shelf

Jodi Rizzotto

"Where did you get these?" Sammy gasped when she noticed the row of painted and sequin-covered skulls on my mantle. She reached out to touch one and then pulled back with a grimace. "These look like real human skulls!"

I shrugged. "My friends gave them to me, over the years."

She tipped her head and studied me, no doubt hoping for more explanation.

"Let's get started on your poultice," I said, leading her toward the kitchen. At this stage of our partnership, it was unwise to talk about my skulls. Bad luck for me and usually worse luck for them.

For a moment, my new friend hesitated, and I turned back, wondering if this one too would run out the front door. But then she sighed, shook out her shoulders, and followed me.

Charcoal, my cat and familiar, accused me with her big yellow eyes from her favorite spot curled up on one of the kitchen chairs. Her notched ears flicked twice and then her thoughts appeared in my mind.

Girl is too cheerful. Why do we need her? You got me.

You know why, I thought back at her. Opinionated creature.

My magic compelled me to teach it to others. It didn't want to perish with me in the grave. Sadly, I had no children nor desire to birth any. Neither did I have any younger relatives. Hence, the need pressed into my heart to find an apprentice, an heir to my magic.

Sammy was twenty-three and dissatisfied with her career choice at Walmart. Her family had moved to Texas, and she had no boyfriend. She was young, beautiful, and had many potential years of witchcraft ahead of her.

This time it had to work.

I walked over to the pantry, turning my back on my fluffy grey cat's scorn. "Let's try a headache remedy first." Sammy's face lit up.

She wasn't my first candidate, but certainly the most enthusiastic. I had tried reaching out to young women at our local college. I set up a table on the quad. "Natural Healing Lessons." Most ignored me. They were young and hopeful, racing to the top. They didn't need some old-fashioned women's lore. Some laughed at my stringy long hair and overly mended woolen dress. A few candidates emerged, but none survived their training.

Then I found Sammy on Facebook.

Grabbing a basket, I led her out to my garden and showed her what plants we needed. She filled the basket, and we went inside. We chopped and measured, stirred and simmered. After two hours, when the mixture cooled, we had a thick green paste. I dabbed a tiny portion on her temples.

"That feels refreshing," she said. "You're sure it would take away a headache?"

"Faster than taking pills," I said. "Let's put it in a jar so you can take it home."

Later, we sipped our tea while she wrote up notes about what we did.

"So, you're really a witch," she said. "Are you going to teach me how to ride on a broom?"

I sighed. They always wanted to play with fire, right out of the gate. "Magic doesn't happen if you can't combine herbs correctly. First, you must learn the basics before you can fly off on your broomstick."

Her smile was ear to ear. "Then I'll learn to fly?"

"We'll see."

~ * ~

Weeks turned into months. Sammy spent so much time at my house, I cleaned up the guest room so she could stay over if we worked too late. We discovered we both loved hibiscus tea and cranberry scones. She was a marvelous baker, and my home filled with aromas of cookies and cakes. It felt great to have someone to talk to besides Charcoal.

Charcoal told me she would need more convincing, but she did like it when Sammy scratched her ears. That was practically a glowing recommendation from her.

After Sammy gained consistency in her preparations, it was time to test her potions on live subjects. There were plenty of mice scurrying around in my backyard. I caught them in tiny cages with a summoning spell. Then we fed them potions and recorded the results.

Most potions had harmless effects on the mice, like changing their fur to blue or changing their size. But we also needed to evaluate the poisons. Sammy looked horrified after she fed some to a mouse, and it convulsed, and foam spilled out of its tiny mouth before dying in front of us.

"I know it was only a mouse, but it was a living creature," she protested, wiping her cheek.

"If you needed to get rid of an enemy, it would be smart to know your poison works before you use it," I said in a patient voice. Young people nowadays were a bit too sensitive.

She never looked at me the same way after that.

When I was satisfied Sammy had mastered potions, we moved on to elemental spells. It took hours of practice, but finally she could dry our clothes with a spoken word. One day, she almost caught my house on fire before I summoned water to douse it. Another reason to learn magic from a seasoned professional.

Although Sammy still went to her job at Walmart, most evenings she spent with me. Despite the huge age difference, we got along great. My heart swelled with hope. Finally, a friend I could trust. One thing my magic couldn't produce.

Then one day, Sammy failed to stop by. At first, I didn't think anything was wrong. Maybe she was sick. Maybe she had to work a double shift. I kept checking my phone, but no missed calls or voice-mail. My texts received no reply.

I wanted with all my heart to be wrong, but it appeared my apprentice had ghosted me.

It was a wintery February night, and I huddled under a blanket with Charcoal close to the fireplace. I tried to be content with her rumbling purrs as I scratched her ears. It wasn't the same as sharing my ideas with Sammy. Whispering warnings appeared in my mind.

The next day, Sammy stopped by after work as usual. She walked in the door, unlocking it with the key I gave her. Her hands shook, and she avoided looking at me.

"Where were you yesterday?" I asked.

"It was busy at work." She tucked a strand of her hair behind her ear.

After that awkward non-conversation, we started into her lessons. There was a tiny crack in the wall of our friendship neither of us would confront. But we continued anyway. When she left, I saw her tuck her grimoire under her coat. Usually she kept it at my house. Her face looked conflicted, but I knew it would be the last time she would do magic with me.

My heart dropped like it was made of lead, and no amount of dandelion wine could soothe it. How many times could I endure such cruel rejection?

That night after she left, there was a knock at my door. Charcoal's head popped up from her nap by the fireplace. I peered through the front window to see who was there. Two men in dark suits. Jehovah's Witnesses at this time of night? How annoying. Fortunately, I had a quick spell to get rid of them.

I opened the door.

"May we please speak with Peony Bracken," one of the men said. He was tall, dark skinned, and smelled like lime and spices.

"That's me," I answered. Dread started to creep into my mind.

"May we come in?" the other, shorter pale-skinned man with a military haircut said. He smelled like shaving cream and blood. They stood on my front porch like planted trees. I toyed with the idea of using a wind spell to sweep them away, but part of me was curious to know the purpose of their visit.

"Certainly, gentlemen," I said, opening my door wide. They walked in, glancing everywhere as if they were looking for something. "Would you like tea?"

The shorter man jumped like I had said something shocking. "Oh, no, we don't want to trouble you," he said. He exchanged a look with the other man.

"It's no trouble at all," I said. I wondered if they had heard from someone that I might put poison in their tea.

"We won't be here that long," the taller man said, his deep voice rumbling like a motorcycle.

"Won't you sit down?" I asked, gesturing toward my floral sofa in front of the blazing fire. My thoughts were twitching. Had they found out about the others?

The men perched on the edge of my sofa. When I sat down in my chair, Charcoal jumped up in my lap and spoke into my mind.

These men smell like trouble. Do you want me to scratch them?

Don't fret. I will take care of this, I spoke in my mind back to her. She stretched and yawned, almost falling off my lap.

The taller man's jacket bulged on one side. That wasn't a good sign. "We'd like to ask you about your potions."

I narrowed my eyes. This was about my business, then. But how would they know? My customers were very discrete. Although nowadays witches were not burned at the stake, I still could be blamed for unexplained deaths. When women asked for potions with special purposes, I didn't ask, and they didn't tell.

These men didn't look like police officers. For all their looming menace, they looked like they preferred offices to the streets. They hadn't arrested me yet. I was getting more curious by the moment. "Excuse me, who did you say you worked for?"

Charlotte started to growl quietly.

They both pulled out black id pouches and flashed them at me before I could read them. The taller man answered in his booming voice. "Ma'am, we're not the police. We're from the Bureau for the Prevention of Animal Cruelty. We're following up on a report that you are using mice for lethal experiments without proper authorization."

Flames jumped up in the fireplace. Both men sat back on the sofa. Reflected in the firelight, their stern faces had begun to crack.

Sammy! She ratted on you! Charcoal shouted in my mind.

Not again. I almost couldn't breathe. My student. My friend. Turned me in to the animal cops. I wanted to scream and throw things. But being a seasoned professional, and apart from the fire, I kept my outrage to myself. Clutching both arms of my chair to do so.

I would deal with my apprentice, but first I needed to get rid of these clowns.

"I'm sure you're mistaken," I said in a calm, non-threatening voice. "I love animals! I would never harm them. I've had my cat, Charcoal, for years. I'm sure you'll agree she looks well taken care of."

Could feed me more human meat. Charcoal said in a wheedling voice.

Stop complaining. You can have some stew when the men leave. I assured her.

The taller man reached into his suit jacket, and I stood up quickly, dumping Charcoal on the floor. Spell words gathered on my tongue. But all he pulled out was a small notebook and pen.

"It says here that on February third of this year, you combined nightshade and other plants to make a potion. Then you fed it to a mouse you caught from your backyard," he read.

The spell was already forming in my head. "Wisp of fog, veil of smoke…" I whispered.

"I'm sorry, ma'am. I didn't hear what you said," the shorter man interrupted.

"CAPTURE THOUGHTS, CONFUSE THE MIND!" I shouted.

Silence. I took a restorative breath. That spell used a lot of energy and always made me feel like someone punched me in the stomach.

The two men looked at each other in confusion. I snatched the notebook away from them and tossed it into the fire. They watched me like I was on a television show.

"Tom, why are we in this lady's living room?" the shorter man asked his companion.

"I don't know," the taller one said, shaking his head.

"You were just telling me about how important your work was to the safety of animals. I think you were going to ask me to make a donation or something," I offered. "However, I don't have any extra funds to help you at this time."

"No problem, ma'am. If you would excuse us. We need to get back to work," the shorter man said. They both stood up.

I smiled. "No problem at all, gentlemen. I'll see you to the door."

~ * ~

Unsurprisingly, Sammy never showed up again at my house. So much for her dream of learning to fly. I dragged my cauldron from the garage and set it up on its stand in the fireplace. Then I chopped herbs and steamed them in my Instant Pot.

I never liked her. Charcoal's thoughts intruded.

You never like anyone, I countered.

I like you.

Because I feed you.

Charcoal carefully ignored me and started to lick the inside of her back leg.

When everything was prepared, I drove down to Walmart. I wasn't sure if Sammy's schedule was the same, but there she was in the garden department stacking plastic pots. When she saw me, she dropped the stack, making a loud crash. She looked around and started backing away from me.

"Sammy. You didn't finish your training," I said, following her. "You never learned to fly."

"That's okay. I've been really busy," she said. Her eyes were wide, and her hands shook as she tucked her hair behind her ears. "I don't really think witchcraft is for me. I'm starting college in the fall, and I'll have too much schoolwork to keep it up."

"So, you didn't get squeamish about the mice and call the animal police on me?" I asked, grabbing her arm roughly as she tried to run away. Some of the customers stopped and started to watch us, so I whispered an Ignore Spell and they turned back to their shopping.

All the color drained out of her face. "What did you do with them?"

"Nothing lethal," I said with scorn. My fingers squeezed her arm tighter, and she let out a small yelp of pain. "Do you think I'm that big of a monster?"

She darted her eyes away from me. I had my answer.

"You will come with me now," I said, crushing some herbs under her nose. Her whole body relaxed, and her eyes turned vacant. Without a word, she followed me out of the store and into my car. We drove back to my house in silence.

~ * ~

A few days later, I hot glued the last pink sequin onto my newest treasure. This one I spent extra time painting intricate designs, dots, and whorls over the entire surface. After it was completely dry, I set it in the place of honor on the mantle.

You're gaining quite a collection of those, Charcoal said from my lap. *Itch my ears.*

I'll find my successor. I just need to keep trying. And quit being so demanding.

Meanwhile, I keep these as reminders of my failures. Warnings that I need to choose my companions with care. I sit in my chair, listening to the crackling fire.

Admiring my skulls on the shelf.

~ * ~ * ~

Jodi Rizzotto is a full-time writer and former elementary school teacher living in Southern California. She holds a Master of Teaching degree from California Baptist University, Riverside. After growing up on Tolkien and C.S. Lewis, she writes fantasy because it contains more truth. When she's not writing, she and her husband love exploring back roads in their Jeep and camping at the beach.

She belongs to the Society of Children's Book Writers and Illustrators and the California Writers Club. Her short story "When Magic Failed" appeared in the April 2022 issue of *Analogies and Allegories Magazine*. "The Sea Cave" was featured in the anthology *Magic Portals*. Full publishing credits available on her website.

Connect with Jodi at:
https://www.facebook.com/authorJodiRizzotto
https://twitter.com/rizzotto_jodi
https://www.instagram.com/jrizzotto/
https://jrizzotto.com/

Better than Gold

T. W. Kirchner

Never trust a pirate. A pirate would be the first one to say it, and Captain Hurley Bones often did. The graying sailor had been on enough ships to know it as a fact. He'd been shorted on plunder, stabbed in the leg, bore a scar where a blade cut deep across his chest, and been on both sides of mutiny. Bones longed for the one big treasure so he could hang up his pirate boots, which time had worn the soles of thin.

Bones's black jolly roger had a floppy-eared pup with crossbones underneath. When asked why his entire crew was dogs, the furry kind—not the scurvy ones—his response was the same. "Dogs be trustworthy and loyal. Not bound to the rules of human society. They follow orders and don't mutiny. A better crew cannot be had." Besides, it was one way to keep the plunder all to himself.

Captain Bones failed to mention his pirate dogs, known as the Bones Eight, were only loyal to him. Everyone else needed to beware. His crew could loot a boat without making a sound and escape with the booty quicker than a flash of lightning. Stolen gold and jewelry didn't mean anything to the Bones Eight. Loyalty drove them.

Despite all of Bones' faults, and the list of negatives grew daily, he had a soft spot for dogs. The captain rescued sick and starving cast-offs from the street and nursed them back to health, sharing scraps he could scrounge up. Plundering kept them in soft blankets with warm meals on their tiny boat, the *Pawtail*, which had also been a discarded wreck Bones had repaired. "One man's trash is another man's treasure, and another man's treasure soon be mine."

Early one evening, Bones planned a big job, hoping it was the "one." Word on the seas was that stolen Spanish gold had been hidden aboard the brigantine *Birch Cowpye* docked nearby in the calm Caribbean water. Most people wouldn't have known the dark brigantine by sight. She flew no colors and plundered at night. Bones had already a run-in with that ship and a big score to settle.

Bones addressed his crew before sending them off. "The *Birch Cowpye's* crew be some scurvy dogs...err...thievin' cutthroats.

Their cap'n leaves the ship as soon as she docks, squeezing the last ounce of work outta his crew 'fore they can set foot on dry land. I can't tell you the number of men on board—mostly 'cause you can't count, and neither can I." He gazed over at Turbo who was twisted like a pretzel and licking his belly. Mocha was playing 'bite my face' with Maverick. Bones sighed. "I wish you understood what I was sayin', but even so, I trust you all to get the job done."

While Captain Bones, the getaway driver, readied the *Pawtail* for a quick departure, the dogs went to work. Turbo the terrier was Bones' first rescued pup. His wiry tan fur and round hazel eyes could charm most people like he'd cast a spell upon them. Turbo bounded up to a few of the ship's crew who secured the dock lines. He wagged his tail and gave them his sweetest look. Two of the guys melted, talking baby gibberish to Turbo—the third scowled. "Get outta here ya mangy mutt." The burly sailor released the end of the thick rope and shook his fist at Turbo, trying to scare him off.

"But he's cute for a scruffy lil' thing." A friendly sailor reached out his hand to pet Turbo.

The grumpy sailor swatted it away. "We's got work to do. Leave that flea bag alone."

Turbo hated being call a flea bag, but more importantly, he had to clear the trio from the ship's entrance. When the men turned their backs, Turbo ran up and peed on the grumpy sailor's leg. The warm liquid dripped into the sailor's boot and down to his toes. Turbo gave a low growl, and the chase was on.

"'Elp me catch him, ya idjits!" The pirate's face turned scarlet.

While the three men chased the tiny dog, the rest of the Bones Eight padded up the ship's ramp and slipped past the remaining ship's crew. The *Birch Cowpye* had been out to sea for months, so the crew worked hard to finish their chores, disembark, and go straight to a tavern. A stray dog or two wandering past them on deck was ignored as an inconvenience. Maverick, Wrigley, and Dakota found hiding spots behind barrels on the main deck in case barking and growling were necessary to make the escape while the remaining three followed Fireball's tracking below deck.

If the trio's barking didn't scare people away, they could topple even the sturdiest human. Maverick the red heeler's bark had the effectiveness of nails against a chalkboard. He was all about plowing through objects like a freight train instead of maneuvering around them. Wrigley the gray terrier could bark longer than any dog alive, but he'd be the first to cuddle alongside Bones at night. Dakota the golden retriever was all bark and no bite, but strangers didn't wait around to find out. She was the largest, fluffiest, and most intimidating of the Bones Eight.

Fireball, the tiniest crewman, was a long-eared chiweenie with a fiery attitude. Her pink hound sniffer could detect the slightest scents, especially gold. Even with the putrid stench of sweaty men who hadn't bathed for months, she sniffed her way into the ship's hold. A wooden treasure chest was secured with a metal padlock, which only kept out those with opposable thumbs.

Pepper the blue heeler had never met a stash of treasure she couldn't figure a way into. The speckled black and white dog hopped up on the cedar box and pawed around to find the weakest spot where a slat gave a slight bend. Her canines tore off the first hunk of wood. Like a plush dog toy with a squeaker hidden under the fluff, Pepper destroyed the first slat easily.

Pepper jumped off the chest, and Kona continued the demolition. Wiry Kona could make an eight-foot leap, but her most impressive strength was her ability to chew through wood faster than a beaver and rusty metal as well. She once gnawed through a captain's quarters door single-handed in ten minutes.

Terrier mix Mocha looked on, waiting for her chance. She had many weapons in her arsenal, including strength, agility, and the ability to swim like a dolphin. On her turn, chips and splinters flew in every direction until the chest had a gaping hole.

Mocha jumped in and lifted the tops of the bags so the larger Pepper and Kona could grab hold and pull them out. Each dog took one bag and followed Fireball back up the stairwell to the deck. The sailors had abandoned the ship, except for one scrawny young watchman. As he gazed out into the ocean, the dogs scurried past him with the bags.

"Hey! Dogs, stop!" The man happened to turn at the clinking sound coming from the bags. He drew his cutlass.

Deep throaty growls came from the shadows. Maverick emerged first. His amber eyes locked onto the man, and his pointed ears flattened back. He was joined by Dakota and Wrigley. They bared their fangs, backing the watchman up to the railing.

While the muscle had the situation in hand—or paw—Fireball

sniffed out the ship's head, otherwise known as the bathroom, located above a wooden figurehead. From that spot, the dogs dropped the booty overboard, which landed onto their getaway boat floating directly below.

The furry pirates turned tail and ran, leaving a pale faced and shivering watchman plastered against the railing. Captain Bones sailed away as soon as the Bones Eight jumped off the dock and swam to their ship. Turbo had already dodged the three men, returned to the *Pawtail*, and relaxed on his blanket.

By the light of the full moon and a stiff breeze pushing at the boat's stern, they put a good distance between themselves and the *Birch Cowpye*. Bones suspected the crew wouldn't return to their ship for hours, and by that point, they'd be three sheets to the wind.

Pepper pawed at the captain's leg and stared into his eyes. It was dinnertime. Bones filled eight bowls with scraps from a fisherman's boat for his crew. With a bottle of rum in hand, he sat against the mast pole to celebrate their success. After taking a big swig from the bottle, Bones wiped his mouth on his filthy sleeve. "One for me." He raised the bottle in a toast to his dogs. "And another one for me."

The *Pawtail* floated for another hour on calm water without the captain at the wheel. His crew gobbled down their dinner and picked out a spot to relax while Bones sang sea shanties and drank. Mocha howled along.

"Gather 'round, men…'er dogs." He set down the empty rum bottle. "Let's see what plunder you brought," Bones called out to his crew. The dogs didn't budge. They were curled up and very comfortable. The captain cleared his throat. "Treats for all!"

Sixteen ears stood at attention. Pepper was the first to run over next to him. He gave each one a piece of jerky. "Now for me treat." He dumped over the first stolen sack. Gold coins bounced onto the deck, making his bloodshot eyes light up. He pushed them back in the sack and tied it, which took a while since he was seeing double. He peered into the second sack and grinned from ear to ear. He rubbed his grimy hands together and dumped out the smallest sack. A handful of colorful jewels and a gold crown clinked out. Bones picked up the crown and examined it. The etching around its middle resembled intertwined seaweed. "This be odd. 'Eh, no matter. Should still catch some coin."

"Take your filthy pirate hands off the crown!" A woman

shrieked. She resembled a human, but moonlight shimmered off her scaly body. When Bones didn't comply with her request, her purple eyes narrowed.

The sea creature's sudden appearance startled the dogs, and a barking chorus commenced. Bones rubbed his eyes and took another look.

"Silence!" She yelled while waving her webbed hands in a sweeping motion.

The dogs froze mid-bark—literally. She had turned them into furry statues. Little Fireball's head was tilted back in a baying position.

Bones stumbled forward, clutching the crown. He was too toasted to be afraid. "What did you do to me dogs, witch? Or be it witches?" He squinted. "Is there one or five of you?"

"That's sea witch to you, pirate," she hissed, displaying her long fangs.

"Name's Bones, Madam Sea Witch. I need you to be fixin' my crew if you want this 'ere trinket." He wiped drool from his mouth and put the crown on top of his greasy head. The sea witch cringed.

"Trinket! That's the crown of Ichorn. It was stolen from my people by you insignificant land creatures." Her silvery eyebrows knitted together, puckering the greenish skin of her forehead.

"There be no reason to call names, madam. After all, you be trespassin' on *me* boat. We just acquired this 'ere trinket from someone else. Fix me dogs, and I'll hand it over." He took the crown off and gave her a toothless, lopsided grin.

The salty breeze picked up, swirling the nasty odors of the boat toward the sea witch. Her nose wrinkled. "You foul drooling creature, I could turn you into a fish and take the crown back." She crossed her long, iridescent arms and thrust out her pointy chin.

Rum made Bones more than a bit foolhardy. "Since you haven't already, I be bettin' this 'ere crown won't let ya. Let's test that." He held the crown in front of his face. "I could lick your crown faster than you could cast a spell." His eyes twinkled like a mischievous schoolboy.

Her transparent green skin darkened, and her scaly legs shimmered. "You wouldn't dare."

He stuck out his tongue and held the crown close to his mouth. "Fix me dogs before I count to three." Drool oozed over his lips because he spoke with his tongue sticking out.

The sea creature grimaced. The captain proved more of a challenge than she bargained for. "Sea witches don't obey land creatures."

"One…" His tongue wiggled. "Five…" It almost touched the crown.

The thought of the human's tongue vandalizing an honored item of her people made her scales crawl. "Fine!" She waved her hands.

The dogs could move again, and they darted behind Captain Bones for protection.

Bones was ready to toss over the crown, but even drunk, he didn't trust the sea witch once his bargaining chip was gone. "First, you give me yer word you be leavin' our ship without harmin' any of us."

"I promise not to harm any of you. Now, hand over the crown." She forced a smile, but her fangs were still scary.

The captain made a terrible toss. The crown bounced and rolled. The sea witch stopped it with her webbed toes before it rolled over the edge into the sea. She took a deep, annoyed breath, and coughed from the boat's sour stench. It gave her an idea. "Technically, I can grant you a wish…a favor for a favor." She hoped the drunken pirate screwed up the wish.

He gazed around at his crew. Their sweet faces brought a tear to his inebriated eyes. "I wish I could talk with me dogs, so I'd know'd what they be sayin'."

"You don't want riches or a new boat?" She fanned her nose. The *Pawtail* smelled like rum, pee, and wet dog.

"Nope." Captain wiped his leaky nose on his sleeve.

"I will grant your wish." She mumbled a spell and lifted her palm toward the captain. As promised, Bones could understand his crew perfectly because she'd turned him into a large dog. He looked like a cross between a rabid wolf and a hyena with an oversized head, yellow eyes, and matted black fur. The sea witch huffed. "Your new look suits you. However, you have the power to change back into the vile creature you were by performing a selfless act for humanity." She laughed and jumped overboard, clutching the crown.

Captain Bones looked at his fuzzy paws and wiggled his bushy tail. He was ecstatic. He could run around naked, and nobody cared. He was faster than he ever had been before and could hear amazingly better. He could talk to and understand his crew, just as the sea witch promised. It was the best wish he could've made. He reached the wheel standing on his hind legs, although it didn't respond as crisply to his pawing motion.

Not long after the sea witch's visit, the sky swelled up with black clouds, blocking out the stars. A stiff breeze tore at the mast. He found the one problem with his wish—nobody could furl the sail. Waves splashed over the sides of the tiny boat, and heavy rain pounded her deck. Bones ordered his crew inside the cramped captain's quarters so nobody would wash overboard. When the storm hit with all its fury, the captain and crew were at the mercy of the sea. The sail shredded in the wind and was useless. They huddled together to keep from sliding and for warmth. Without any options, Bones hoped for the best.

Lightning exploded across the dark sky, flashing like a strobe light through the cabin window. Wind howled through the cabin door louder than a chorus of wolves. *Pawtail* pitched and swayed, bumping over vicious waves. Fear gripped the captain and his crew.

The storm raged for hours, but it finally blew past, calming the water, and allowing the boat to float a bit more smoothly. The dogs remained huddled in the cabin until the sea calmed and they finally felt safe enough to sleep.

A loud thud that sounded like the wooden boat had split apart startled everyone awake. Sunshine beamed through the window. Captain pawed at the doorknob until it opened, releasing a rush of seawater and a dank, fishy smell. When the waterfall stopped pouring in, they scrambled on deck. The *Pawtail* had run aground on a white sand beach. Palm trees stood tall among flowering bushes beyond the smooth sand. Bones believed they'd found paradise.

The crew sniffed out the surrounding area. Waterfalls spilled over ledges providing freshwater pools below. Ripe tropical fruit had fallen from the trees for easy pickings. Birds flew from the branches, and small creatures skittered away from them. The scent of humans was present.

Bones and the crew dragged their blankets from the boat and dropped them under a bushy palm tree. The nine dogs worked together to corner and catch fish in shallow water. They had all the basics for survival right at their paws.

After two days in paradise, scantily clad humans showed up on the beach, carrying long spears. The dogs stayed in the shade, watching their every move. Captain Bones couldn't understand anything the humans said because they didn't speak dog or any other language he recognized.

The half dozen islanders were more interested in the boat than the dogs. They climbed aboard and looked inside every nook and cranny. The boat's smell didn't seem to be a deterrent. They removed the three bags of gold and jewels and a bottle of rum.

One of the islanders pointed to the dogs under the tree, and the whole group walked toward them. Humans with spears were very threatening, so Kona, Wrigley, and Maverick started barking, which started the chorus to chime in complete with Fireball's baying and Mocha's howls. The islanders got the message and left without incident.

A few hours later, more islanders returned to the beach. They carried bowls of chopped fish and meat and set them down. From a distance, the people watched the dogs. Fireball caught the whiff of meat first and scurried over. It smelled good and tasted even better. The dogs filled their bellies and returned to the shade. The islanders removed the bowls and left.

This ritual went on every day. The dogs trained the humans to feed them without doing anything special. It was unlike their old home where people chased them away. Bones didn't miss pirating or being human. This was paradise for sure.

One day at sunset, an island girl swam into the surf. Her arms flailed about in a distressed motion. Bones and his crew had been relaxing on their blankets, but the captain realized her distress and swam out to her. Waves pulled the girl underwater, but Bones' strength allowed him to doggie paddle out to her. His strong jaws grabbed hold of the back of her clothing and pulled her head to the surface.

Mocha and Maverick, the two strongest swimmers, assisted Bones in dragging the girl to shore. The dogs surrounded the unconscious islander. Bones shook his body, sending water flying in all directions. He leaned over her and stuck his large nose into her face. Cold droplets from his fur sprinkled onto the girl and made her stir. When she opened her eyes and looked up at his spongy nose and all those furry muzzles crowded around, she screamed and ran off.

Bones was used to that kind of response from women. "She be okay," he said in dog to his crew. "Good work."

A large wave rose from the otherwise calm water. The sea witch emerged amidst the white foam and glided onto the shore. Her feet didn't leave any tracks in the sand. "Well done, pirate. I am surprised. As per our deal, you have saved a human, so you can have your humanity back."

Bones ears pricked up. He didn't want to be human again. He'd have to wear clothes and have manners. Just when he'd found paradise, the sea witch wanted to snatch it away. Before she could cast the spell, Bones peed on her scaly legs.

"You filthy animal," the sea witch said with a snarl. "The deal is off. You deserve to stay like you are." She stormed off into the sea.

Bones and his crew couldn't have been happier. His crew gave him drooly dog kisses and wagged their tails. The captain stretched out on the warm sand with his dogs. He watched the last rays of sunshine shimmer off the ocean and sink below the horizon until only an orange glow remained in the darkening sky. "Trust me. We've got treasure better than gold, men…er dogs."

And they did.

~ * ~ * ~

Although a technical writer by trade, **T.W. Kirchner** loves writing fiction, especially stories with a supernatural element and a furry friend. Along with short stories, Kirchner has several published book series including Reno Red, Dagger & Brimstone, Pirates Off, and The Troubled Souls of Goldie Rich.

A furry member of the Kirchner family is always featured on the author bio page in all her books.

Law of Spells

Lea Storry

Have you ever wondered where the witches went? If they've retreated into the shadows with the warlocks? Have you ever wondered where the sorcerers are in this world of iPhones and computers and airplanes? Well, I'm here to tell you they are still among us. Not hiding. Not keeping quiet. But adapting. Like we all are doing as our world changes every day.

~ * ~

My heart picks up speed while the younger woman in front of me slows her pace. I have 20 minutes to make my flight and it takes 25 to get from security to my international gate. The woman is small, petite, and dressed in a tight pink skirt, pink jacket and blood-red high heels. She wheels three large purple suitcases that thump and bump like toads behind her in the narrow hallway.

I can't get around her. We're in a tiny temporary corridor built to hide the construction going on around us. The woman and her bags are taking up all the space. My hands clench into fists and I clench my green leather briefcase like an axe.

"Excuse me," I call out to the woman.

She glances back at me, long red hair swinging behind her, and then stops, losing her grip on one of the suitcases. It topples over on its side and lands on the gleaming grey tile with a bang.

"Would you move out of my way?" I ask, stepping forward. "Please."

The woman frowns, a grimace that pulls her full lips into a fat upside down U.

"No," she says. "You just broke my vase."

"Huh?"

"You shouted and made me drop my bag," the woman says. "You smashed my vase."

"I didn't shout and I didn't break anything."

"You did."

The woman faces me square on. Her bright blue eyes are the

colour of pool water in the hot summer sun. But her gaze makes me shiver.

"If you packed correctly," I say, breaking her stare, "everything will be fine."

"How kind of you to provide travel advice. It's a tad too late."

"You haven't opened your suitcase," I say, "so you don't know if your vase broke. Unless you're some kind of witch."

I bite my tongue to stop from saying anything more. I don't want to argue. I've got an important meeting to attend and I'm not about to let this bitch get in the way of my promotion.

"Aren't you full of vigour for such a youngster?" the woman says, sticking her strong chin out at me.

"Whatever, lady," I say.

Pushing past her, I get a whiff of something burning. It smells like charred toast. Workers must be welding something behind the temporary wall. I keep my eyes forward despite wanting to see the woman up close. I could swear she's several years younger than me. Botox and plastic surgery can work magic on a face though.

A couple of steps later, I hear a beep from my jacket pocket. I keep walking while I check the text on my phone.

"Great," I mutter to myself. "My flight has been delayed."

There's another message on my cell. Someone airdropped a photo.

"That's weird. Bluetooth is turned off. I'll check it out when I'm at my gate."

Sitting down for the long wait, I finally look at my phone. A picture of a red dot fills my screen. I resize the image and at the bottom are the words:

A piece of advice: always be on red alert.
www.wychwhichwitch.com

I shake my head. Must be some kind of prank. A teenager probably sent this to everyone who was in the vicinity. I passed a school group earlier. Must have been one of them.

I delete the image and bring up a crossword puzzle. The people around me sigh and fidget. I came straight from a long day at the office to the airport. I'm supposed to be on my flight now, on my way from Toronto to Europe. I scheduled enough time to land at the Milan airport, wash up at a hotel, head to my firm's Italian office, sign a document and be on my way again. Despite the delay, the timing should still work. I won't have any time to freshen up but it's par for the course these days. Air travel post-pandemic has been a hassle. Dates, times and gates are constantly changing and don't get me started on the people.

OK. Well, I've started. Gate agents slam down their palms on desks when asked for information. Flight attendants snap at any request, even when I simply ask for water. People sitting beside me on the plane push my elbows off the seat rests and the people in front of me always lean their chair all the way back until my nose is touching the entertainment screen. Then there are those stupid people who think the whole airport belongs to them. Like that woman I ran into a few minutes ago. I'm glad my flying days in coach are almost behind me.

After my meeting, I'll be a partner in my firm. That means perks and many of them, including flying business class. I'm a lawyer specializing in contract negotiation. I'm good, very good, at my job. I'm about to turn 46 and I'm happy with my life. I don't need a partner and kids in order to be fulfilled. A rewarding career is just as satisfying. Besides, I have my cat, Lisa. She doesn't talk back and always agrees with me.

I yawn. It's been a long day. The smell of coffee at the Starbucks across from me wafts over. I breathe it in. I already had my shot of caffeine. Bought a cup at another coffee chain this morning. I try to be good and not drink more than one coffee a day but what the heck, today is sort of a celebration. Besides, since I'll be here another hour, I might as well get a drink. I put my phone in my jacket pocket and walk over to the café.

"Can I start your drink order?" the barista asks.

"I'll have a flat white and a piece of cinnamon cake."

"Want that cake heated up?"

"No thanks."

I reach into my briefcase to get my red suede Louis Vuitton wallet. I pat around for it but can't find it.

"It's in here somewhere," I say to the woman behind the counter.

I open my briefcase as wide as it can go and peer into the dark void. The stainless steel of my laptop gleams under the fluorescent lights. My house keys also glint and a cream-coloured folder looms out of the darkness. I can't see my red wallet.

My cheeks are getting hot, no doubt turning pink.

I pat my all pockets, hoping I might have stashed my wallet there.

Nothing but my phone.

There are now several people behind me, and I can hear the tap, tap, tapping of someone's shoe on the tile floor. I've got to find my wallet. I look in the interior of my briefcase again. Hoping my lost item will appear, like magic, and I can retreat to my chair with a hot drink and a tasty snack.

Nope. Nothing.

"I'm sorry," I say, looking at the barista. "I don't know where my wallet went."

"Hope you find it," she says, moving to the tiny sink behind her and dumping my coffee. It steams as it flows down the drain.

I walk slowly back to my seat. What happened to my wallet? I had it this morning, otherwise, I couldn't have paid for my first coffee. Could I have left my wallet behind in the Uber? I never carry much cash on me, but it is a Louis Vuitton wallet, a coveted item for some people.

My head throbs. It's going to be a pain to replace all of my IDs. I'd better cancel my bank and credit cards. I reach for my phone in my right-hand pocket. It's empty. My cell must be in my other pocket.

It's not.

I jump out of my chair, my head moving quickly left to right, right to left, up and down, down and up.

There's no phone on the seat. No phone under the seat. No phone beside the seat.

"Have you seen a red iPhone?" I ask the man sitting a few seats over.

He shakes his head.

"No."

"Have you seen a red iPhone?" I ask the woman sitting an aisle behind me.

"Sorry," she says while flipping through her own cell.

I know I had it. I swear it was in my jacket only moments ago.

My whole body shakes when I sit down. My hands can barely hold each item I empty out of my green briefcase. Here's the folder with the contract the Milan company must sign. Here's my lipstick in my favourite shade of coral. Here's an unopened pack of white tissues. Here's a fresh pair of blue wool socks and a pair of yellow underwear. I pull out some other travel essentials, stacking everything beside me. However, there's no phone or wallet in the briefcase.

What is going on? How did I lose my phone in five seconds about five steps from the Starbucks counter? Am I going mad? Do I have dementia all of a sudden?

My passport with its gold text is still safely tucked into its compartment in the front of my briefcase. I dump all my items back into the bag and then hug it to my chest. I don't dare put it on the floor in case it disappears too. I have to make sure the contract is signed. If it's not, then I'll lose my partnership for sure.

Thankfully, when my flight boards, everything goes smoothly. I walk onto the plane and soon, we're in the air. I sleep on and off. My dreams are invaded by scenes of hot coffee being poured over phones. I'm glad to land in the morning sunshine in Milan where a vehicle is waiting for me.

At my firm's Italian office, there's a light breakfast and the most delicious espresso waiting in the cavernous board room with a view of the mountains. I quickly cram a croissant into my mouth and barely have time to wipe the crumbs off my face with a white linen serviette when the other team files in.

"Thank you for meeting in person," I say standing up and extending my hand to a man dressed in a sharply pressed navy-blue wool suit. "Shall we begin?"

"Yes, please," he says with a smile.

The CEO and three other people take their chairs. I pull out the cream-coloured folder and pass out copies of the contract.

"You've seen this already, but I am going to go over the parts in red," I say. "There is one line in particular that needs to be addressed starting on page five."

I hear the shuffling of paper and then some more shuffling mixed in with light coughing. The team members trade sideways looks. I sit up straighter in my chair.

"There's nothing marked," the man says, staring at me.

"Oh yes," I say. "I worked on this yesterday. The red is on page five."

"I am on page five. There is no red ink."

I rip the contract out of the CEO's hand and flip it to the

offending paper.

He's correct. There is no red anywhere.

"I, I, I…"

I can't get any other words out. My mouth is as dry as burned toast and my throat feels like it is full of glass shards.

"I, I, I," I repeat.

"Is this a joke?" the CEO asks, looking around the table.

I pour myself a glass of water and then chug it.

"This is a serious matter." The man smooths his orange tie with his palm. "If you cannot get the colour of a group of words correct, I doubt you can do anything for us."

I nod like my hair is on fire.

"Forgive me," I say, croaking like a toad. "I know this sounds ridiculous, but I swear I brought the appropriate contracts."

"You most definitely did not," the CEO says, standing up.

"Please, please," I say, holding up my hands. "There's nothing I can't fix in five minutes. Five minutes. That's all I need."

"Sorry." The man nods to his team. "The deal is off."

The four Italians march out the door, leaving me alone in the large room.

My brain is frozen. It can't comprehend what's happening. My boss is going to shoot me. Worse, she's not going to make me a partner. All my hard work, long hours, vacations I've never taken, they were all supposed to culminate in this one moment, one that would brighten my future with more money, more prestige and more options. Now I have nothing.

I stand up, my legs wobbling. I open the door to the foyer and ask one of my Milan associates to assign me another phone. Then I collapse in a heap on the floor.

~ * ~

I'm a zombie walking through the Milan airport. Despite it being early hours in North America, I had to call my boss. When I told her what happened she did not yell. She did not scream. She did not rant and rave.

"You're fired," was all she said and then hung up on me.

There's nothing I could tell her that would change her mind anyway. I feel like my brain is a soft loaf of bread. Squishy and full of holes. It's all I can do to put one foot in front of the other. It would help if there was a bottle of wine waiting at the gate. Alas, there are only hard chairs and harsh lights.

I flop into a seat. This has been the worst day of my life. Even worse than when I missed the Backstreet Boys concert when I was 14. I sigh. It's almost like I'm cursed. If I believed in that witchy stuff.

Hmmm. That website that was airdropped this morning said something about witches. Oh yeah, www.wychwhichwitch.com. I punch the address into my new phone. The screen goes black and then, there she is. Red hair, pink jacket, red full lips and bright blue eyes. It's the woman from this morning.

"Hello," she says. "Thanks for visiting. I'm Tirzah Louden. If you're here, you must have pissed me off. Well, I'm about to tell you how to get back in my good books.

"It's as easy as abracadabra. Send me one-hundred-thousand dollars through my wychwhichwitch PayPal account. Once I've got the bucks, I'll take off your curse. Can't wait to hear from you. Toodles!"

Toodles? WTF? This is a joke. She's a joke. I'm not giving Tirzah Louden any money. No way. I've got to get home ASAP and away from the lousy people who seem to fill airports.

Mercifully, I don't remember anything about my return flight. Somehow, I manage to stumble my way through it all and arrive at my condo. I unlock the door and my midnight black cat Lisa is waiting for me on the foyer rug. She chirps as she rubs against my leg.

"Hi, baby," I say.

Picking her up, I take off my shoes and wander into the kitchen. I'm hungry but not ravenous. I open the fridge and it's barer than I remember. I love to cook and usually keep a stocked larder unless I get too busy at work to grocery shop. But that hasn't been the case lately.

Putting Lisa on the floor, I open the fridge door as wide as it can go. What's missing? Oh. No ketchup, strawberry jam or red peppers. No pinot noir, tomatoes or pickled beets. All the red foods have been spirited away although some things I would say are more maroon and wine tinted.

What else is gone from my home?

I dash into my bedroom and whip open my closet door. Red shirts and dresses and trousers are gone. In my dresser, any piece of red underwear has disappeared. My cozy red plaid pajamas are nowhere to be found. Am I dreaming? I pinch myself. Ouch! I must be going mad then.

Oh no. My car.

I run to my spot in the parking garage. My vehicle is gone. My 2005 cherry red beater is not here. I sprint to my laptop on my desk and check the dashcam. One second the camera's running and the next, all I see is static dancing before my eyes. My car has vanished. I'm not done paying it off and I bet my car payments haven't gone poof with it.

The stupor I've been wrapped in all day is torn off. I feel naked and cold. Violated. Could Tirzah Louden really have orchestrated these strange heists? How? I don't know what to do. I feel like I should call the police but what do I say?

"Hello officers, a woman put a curse on me. Please send help."

I'm a logical thinker. There are tonnes of stories about witches hexing people but those are stories we tell on Halloween or around the campfire. Lore we tell to scare ourselves. Stories that were told a long, long, long time ago to keep women and minorities in their place. Witches, warlocks, ghosts, and sasquatches do not exist and therefore, don't have a place in today's world.

My phone beeps. It's a text. It's the middle of the night and no one besides my boss has this number. My heart pounds as I open the message. It's a link to another YouTube video. I hold my breath as Tirzah Louden dressed all in red comes into view. She's sitting on a stool on what looks to be an empty stage with blue and pink laser lights waving behind her. It's like a dating video from the 80s. I slowly let my breath out.

"That's right," Tirzah says. "Breath in and out. You know, you should do yoga. You're a very stressed woman. Anyway, by this time, I'm sure you've noticed a few things missing around your apartment."

Tirzah wiggles her butt on the stool.

"This is the fun part," she says. "Yes! You guessed it, I am a witch. I can return your items once we've done our business. Please send me my money by tomorrow at seven a.m. Actually, you know what? Because you've been such a good girl, transfer me ninety-nine-thousand dollars."

"I'm not sending you a damned red cent!" I yell at the screen.

"Then I'll have to start collecting another colour," the woman says. She puts her finger to her chin and looks around the stage.

"Hmmm. How about black? Hug your cat goodbyeeee!"

Tirzah throws her head back, her long red hair swishing behind her, and cackles. The laugh pierces my eardrums. It makes me drop the phone on the floor and back away from it. Lisa looks up at me from the floor, her ears flattened.

The room is spinning. I stick out a hand and touch the wall to ground myself. How is this woman doing all of this? Not the online stuff, duh, but how is she hocus-pocusing away my stuff? Red object by sort-of-red object. I don't have the money she's asking for. I have no one to ask for it either. I definitely won't let her take Lisa. She's my only family.

I shake my head. I must be dreaming. I must be so in shock about losing my job that I've lost my mind. I can't believe I'm actually thinking Tirzah Louden has the power to steal my belongings. I can't believe I'm starting to believe she's a witch.

My eyelids are getting heavy. All the anxiety and worry and disappointment of the last several hours are making me sleepy.

"Snap out of it," I say to myself. "Find the solution to this problem."

There's nothing like a challenge to energize me. Grabbing my laptop out of my briefcase, I sit down on my black couch. Lisa jumps up beside me and settles down for a catnap by my side. Tirzah may claim she has some sort of power over me but she's still flesh and blood and bound by rules and regulations.

I'm a lawyer and one of my skills as a contract negotiator is looking for loopholes. I fill those gaps with long words and obscure legal terms. I'm going to make that bitch crack.

Working my way through online legal texts, I can't find anything that relates to my problem. The bitch is modern, I'll give her that. What she's doing to me is like a form of computer ransom. Except she's not using malware or encryption.

"Hmm," I say to Lisa, patting her soft furry head. "Encryption is kind of a spell. Both are codes."

The witch is using today's technology, with yesterday's incantations, for tomorrow's gains. She's a scammer.

"That's it!" I say, clapping my hands. "I'm going to report her for fraud."

During my first year in law school, I had to study the Criminal Code of Canada. Not all the laws are up to date. Some have been left on the books, forgotten as society grows and develops and leaves certain misconceptions behind. This is the case with Section 365, which states it is illegal to "fraudulently pretend to exercise or to use any kind of witchcraft, sorcery, enchantment or conjuration."

Ha! I've caught her red-handed for a white-collar crime.

"Return my stuff or I'll report you to the police," I text Tirzah. "For fraud."

All of a sudden, my phone starts making a high-pitched wailing sound. The perfect ring tone for a call from a witch.

"Are you sure you want to involve the cops?" a soft voice asks on the other line. "I mean, you did break my vase."

I squeeze the phone in my hand.

"What vase?" I ask through gritted teeth.

"Oh, never mind." Tirzah sighs. "You're wasting my time. Just give me my money."

"Hey!" I say, my voice rising. "You got me fired and I lost everything, including a big paycheque."

"Simmer down. Aren't you a tad bit nervous I might conjure up some fleas to invade your home or do something much, much worse? I'm a witch you know."

"And I'm a lawyer."

"A cheating one at that."

I relax a bit and loosen my hold on the cell.

"Let's talk about you returning my stuff and I won't sue," I say.

I hear Tirzah suck air between her teeth.

"You lawyers and your scare tactics."

"You witches and your hustles."

"Fine," she says. "Meet me tomorrow at one at the Burdock Café."

"See you then."

~ * ~

Arriving at the café after an hour and a half bus ride, I'm slightly fuming. I could have driven here in 20 minutes but the witch stole my car. I'm not looking forward to this meeting and when I spot Tirzah seated in a sunny corner, bile climbs halfway up my throat. The witch is wearing a rib-hugging black dress and those red heels. She means business.

"Let's talk turkey," she says as I slide into the seat across from her.

"Shoot."

"Thing is," Tirzah says, leaning towards me. "I need to know what you know."

"Aren't you the witch?" I ask, leaning away from her and her slightly cigarette-scented breath. "Aren't you supposed to be all-seeing?"

"You're mixing me up with an Argus Panoptes, the many-eyed giant in Greek mythology."

"Oh, sorry."

"Don't apologize. Just get your supernaturals straight."

"All I need to get straight is that you're extorting money from me," I say. "And want to take my cat."

Tirzah puts her hands on the table and clasps them in front of her. Her long pink nails look like claws. Maybe I should have thought this through a little bit, no, a lot bit more.

"Truth is," the witch says, her shoulder drooping. "I'm tired of this game. I'm losing money."

"How is that my fault?"

"Your whole generation is to blame," Tirzah explodes, point-ing a dagger-like fingernail at me. "I've been on this planet for over two hundred years, and I've always been able to scare people. At the beginning, all I had to do was wave a wand. But it's getting harder and harder to make money."

"What's your racket now?"

"I go to the airport, pretend someone breaks something of mine and then take their belongings until they pay up."

"Like you tried to do with me."

"Yeah. It was lucrative until the pandemic struck. Even before that, though, costs were on the rise. You can't imagine how expen-sive it is to rent the warehouse where I put all the stuff I collect. It's robbery! By the way, did you want a coffee? I'm buying."

"Nah, I'm good. Besides, I need to watch my pennies now that I don't have a job."

"That's what I want to talk to you about."

"A job?"

"Yes. Like I said, the world is savvy now. I take someone's things, they buy more. The only thing that truly frightens most people is parting with their money."

"You're asking for a lot," I say.

"I'm getting older, and I don't have the energy for the constant airport hassles and the drain on my powers for nothing. I need a quick bang for my buck."

I look straight into Tirzah's blue eyes. "How do I fit into this then?"

"Be my lawyer. Go over my videos, texts and emails for legal issues. Write me solid contracts so I can avoid the courts. Make sure everything is above board. Make sure I get paid."

"What do I get out of it."

"I'll pay your billable hours at double what you were going to be paid. Plus, you get to keep Lisa."

"You'll give me back my stuff?"

"Every single item. Except maybe those pajamas. The flannel is so warm and cozy. Oh, you'll have to hire your own movers to get your belongings from the warehouse. My spell works only one way: in, not out."

~ * ~

The witches and the warlocks and the sorcerers are still here. They have not disappeared or retreated to the shadows or gone into hiding. They are very much part of our modern world, adapting like all of us. By the way, I've switched to an Android phone.

~ * ~ * ~

Lea Storry owns a writing, editing and publishing business. She's also a published and indie-published author. Lea has no supernatural powers but does consider herself a word witch. She lives in Edmonton, Alberta, Canada, with her husband.

Connect with Lea via:

Our Family Lines website: http://ourfamilylines.ca/

Instagram: www.instagram.com/family_lines/?hl=en

Twitter: https://twitter.com/FamilyLines

Amazon author page: www.amazon.com/Lea-Storry/e/B01CQNZD1O/ref=sr_ntt_srch_lnk_1?qid=14999661 98&sr=8-1

Facebook: www.facebook.com/FamilyLinesStories/

YouTube: www.youtube.com/channel/UClwzQM9ZMMsktCmhG-E-K8A

Goodreads author page:
https://www.goodreads.com/author/show/14250642.Lea_Storry

Subscribed

Louise Zedda-Sampson

The box was unmarked, aside from her name and address, but Rena knew what it was. She'd received the same delivery every month for the last ten years.

"I wonder what's in this one, Mimi?" On a chair by the book-case, Mimi, Rena's black cat, yawned and stretched.

The occult subscription cost a hefty five hundred dollars a month but was worth every cent. Some witches had complained but after the first delivery, which included an invocation to increase wealth, the subscription paid for itself.

Rena rubbed her temples and pulled up the office chair to sit down. If this headache persisted, she wouldn't have time to do the monthly task. The headaches were becoming more frequent and felt like a magic hangover—which was strange because she'd barely been using magic lately. Maybe she could ask the coven to help. They were meeting tonight, so once she'd completed the boxed activity, she would. She hoped this month it wouldn't be too magic intensive. She sat back and closed her eyes, waiting for the pain to recede.

Previous deliveries had included amulets, powerful subterfuge spells—some capable of repelling negative people, casting glamours, and masking enchantments—practical handiwork kits, and chap-books with lessons learned from the Salem Witch Trials. The occult box, almost intuitively, always delivered something new. Her whole coven, the Sisters of Seven (even though there were eight), sub-scribed as a group, each receiving the same order. Afterwards, they'd meet online and talk about their conjuring's, handiwork and invocations.

One of her favourite items sat in the bookcase blinking. She'd had to do some graverobbing to complete the task, unearthing a freshly interred couple by the name of Smith. Taking their heads hadn't bothered her—it was only dead flesh after all—but in case it bothered them, she'd performed a permission ritual beforehand. Once the heads had bubbled and broiled enough on the stovetop (no one used cauldrons anymore) and she'd set them to drain, rubbery lips started flexing, and, after a croaky start, they sang 'Jingle Bells'—in perfect harmony.

Within seconds she'd fixed the awful racket—Christmas carols, eww—and reprogramed. When she dialled into her coven meeting and the sisters heard the Smiths sing 'Start me up', they were in stitches. It was even funnier because Mrs Smith looked like Mick Jagger. Or maybe it was just the lips. Maybe she'd used Botox.

Fond memories. Just the ticket. Rena's headache had retreated.

Rena opened her eyes and commanded the shrunken heads, 'Sing,' and they did. Mimi hissed. Rena was aghast. 'Staying Alive' completely Bee Gees pitch perfect, belted out. Mimi jumped off the chair, fur bristling. Who had reprogramed the Smiths? The only people in the house had been her and Ben. Could the Sisters have done this? And from a distance? She didn't think so because there were protections everywhere, and you'd have to be in close proximity to break them.

Who had tampered with her heads? It really only left—

The front door slammed closed.

—Ben.

"Stop," she said, and the Smiths stopped.

It was one thing for Ben to be interested in her work, but there were strict coven rules about using someone else's magic. Plus, you just don't touch people's things like that.

Rena took a deep breath, requesting the Moon Goddess to share her wisdom. But the only image entering her mind was that bloody nuisance John from next door. He'd been such a pest. Flowers, show tickets, gifts—all of which had gone in the bin—and all the peering through her windows! She'd even caught him hanging around her mailbox. In fact, he'd even taken to signing for her parcels if she was out.

Pests deserved pests. She'd created a major infestation at his house—from a bag of plastic cockroaches. It had been a work of art, really. If it hadn't been successful, she'd considered hopping over to using dark arts, but during the last few months he'd withdrawn his affections. Thank the Goddess for that small mercy.

"Rena," Ben called from the hall. "Where are you?"

Rena wasn't sure how to confront him right now. She did a quick protection sigil with her fingers, but it felt clumsy, panicked.

Like it didn't work. With anger rising, she scooped Mimi up and left her study. But once she stepped out of the office and saw him in the hallway...

...all she could think about was...

Her smile bloomed and she felt a rush of love. *Ben.* She was lucky to have him. They'd met at Houdini's. Lame name for a novelty shop but she'd needed some fake cockroaches—*wasn't she just thinking about this?*—and this was the only place selling them. Ben had served her. *Ben.* She sighed inwardly. His Nick Cave eyes and his messy black hair. He'd helped her out, then asked her out. Then, he'd moved into her house almost straight away.

As Rena walked down the hall, Mimi stiffened. By the time they reached Ben, her claws had dug deeply into Rena's arm. Mimi howled.

"Okay, okay!" Rena dropped the cat. Red lines formed along her forearm.

"Well hello to you, too, you pile of dread," Ben snapped at Mimi.

"Ben," Rena said. "Can't you leave her alone? She needs time to get used to you."

"It's been months. How much longer will it take?" He hung up his jacket, and all Rena could see were his strong arms. "Besides. I moved in with you, not *that.*"

Mimi watched disapprovingly from the rug in front of the door. Ben picked up Rena's scratched arm. "Whoa, these are nasty. Wait here, I'll get something."

Rena rounded on Mimi. "What's the story?" Mimi sat, blinking, cautious, silent. "We'll have words later," Rena said, hearing the cupboard door close in the bathroom.

Ben returned with antiseptic and bandages. "Ouch!" Rena said, as he dabbed the scratch.

"Sorry," Ben said.

"Mimi doesn't usually get upset."

Oh, his hands were so warm. Ben's aftershave smelt like musk.

"I bought you a surprise," Ben said, gesturing to the hallstand where a bunch of black roses and baby's breath sat wrapped in red tissue, tied with a white lace ribbon.

"Oh, my favourites!" she said, looking into his eyes, his gorgeous, deep-blue eyes. He was her goth prince.

"I've finished." He put a bandage on and set the antiseptic aside. His warm hands moved up her forearms then around her to pull her close.

The feeling was electric.

Rena thought about her other favourite subscription item—last month's delivery: the recipe for the Eros tonic. Sex had been good between them before, but this had taken things to a whole new level. After making the first batch, she'd ordered extra, and placed a large backorder for more.

"Let's go find the tonic," Ben said, to which she, of course, agreed.

~ * ~

Several hours later, sated and skin tingling, Rena lay stroking Ben's chest; enjoying playing with the sprinkling of dark hair, and breathing in that after-sex salty-sweat smell. She inhaled deeply. She was just thinking whether they could go again when her roaming fingers ran over something disc-shaped, seemingly on a cord around his neck, but when she looked, there was nothing there.

Ben moved her hand to hold it in his. There was that feeling again. He tilted her chin to face him. "Everything okay?"

Rena nodded. He had the loveliest eyes.

"Why don't you read a bit and relax while I go and do dinner?"

"That's a great idea," she said. Rena kissed him a long, temporary goodbye.

After he left, she picked up her current book *A Tale of Two Witches* and settled in to read, but after about twenty minutes, she was too restless, and a bit bored. The story was meant to be a romance, but it was three quarters done and they hadn't even kissed. She set it aside.

Pulling on an oversized t-shirt from the chair that was always filled with such things, she lay on the rug and reached under the bed to grab her *Necronomicon: 21ˢᵗ Century Condensed Edition*, but it wasn't in the usual place. The book was nearer Ben's side and upside down.

"Rena!" Ben called.

She bumped her head on the bedframe.

"Remember your meeting!"

Oh shit! The meeting was in an hour and she hadn't done the activity. Forgetting the book, she pulled on some tracksuit pants, and ran to her office. The smell of chillied prawns wafted in from the kitchen. It was one of her favourite meals.

When she arrived, however, things were not as she expected. The black roses were in a vase near her laptop. In front of them, everything from the box had been unpacked and spread across the desk. Mimi watched from the window outside, mewling to come in. This was all too much. Mimi was an inside cat, and this was all her stuff. What was—

"I thought you'd be in a hurry," Ben said, appearing from nowhere. "So, I got it all ready for you."

"What's Mimi doing outside, and why—" A broad smile lit up her face. She leaned back on the desk. "Thanks so much, Ben," she said.

"I'll go let Mimi in, shall I?"

"Yes please." She watched him leave and turned to her desk. Oh god. She was going to have to make something. She could barely focus. Since when had she become a sex-starved, submissive school-girl? She was a powerful enchantress, damn it!

Rubbing her temples again, she contemplated ringing the Sisters to cancel. But, she hadn't missed a meeting before and didn't want to now. That left one option.

Taking a deep breath, she pulled out her chair, sat at her desk and read the enclosed brochure.

Dear Daughter of the Moon,

Please find enclosed, one taxidermy kit. We wish you a happy Easter, and have enclosed, yes, you guessed it! A caricature of Jesus Christ with real human skin!

Only kidding. Of course not. It is a fluffy bunny, with all the extra pieces to make him unique and yours.

Please read the instructions carefully, and if all else fails, refer to the additional included instructions. Also, remember, transformation spells need careful preparations, and do not try this on your friends!

Happy handcrafting and bewitching, and have a happy Easter!
Until next month…

Best,
Cordelia
Head of Sales
Coven of the Caring

Rena looked at all the items. A spool of twine. Straw for stuffing. Wire. Glass rabbit eyes, all different colours. A pure-white, flat, fluffy rabbit skin. *Angora,* she thought. A few sachets of powders and oils. An instruction sheet. And underneath that, she found what she was looking for:

CHEAT SHEET
How to magic your way to taxidermy
Ingredients:
a pinch of all-purpose casting powder
a few drops of clove oil
a tablespoon of water
1 black rose petal
3 strands of hair (your own will do)
small section of rabbit fur
a few more drops clove oil
a tablespoon of water
3 fingers of vodka
1 incantation
Instructions:
— *Set taxidermy ingredients apart in a clear space*
— *Mix the first six ingredients in a clay bowl*
— *Drink the vodka*
— *Read the included incantation.*

After reading the instructions, she realised how lucky it was Ben had bought her the roses. Rena grabbed a glass and vodka from the liquor cabinet and closed the door to block out any other distractions. She mixed the ingredients in the special clay bowl, adding three of her long black hairs, and poured three fingers, threw them back, then read the incantation out loud. As she read the last three lines, power thrummed in the air.

Id est simul omnibus,
Ego Impurium!
Transmutes!

But something wasn't right. She felt a pinch, a prod, then…
All went dark.

~ * ~

When she came to, she felt different—inside and out. Everything was foggy, as if her world was filled with cottonwool. She couldn't see or hear, and her body felt numb. Panic welled within. She tried to collect herself, work out what was going on, but she was a tiny spark in a soft and fluffy abyss.

As her consciousness was restored, everything about today came back to her in a rush—the delivery, Mimi's strange reactions, the sex, the Necronomicon, the rushing, the taxidermy kit, everything unpacked—

Why would Ben unpack all the things? And then she knew.

No, it couldn't be.

But she could almost feel it hovering—the magic haze that wasn't hers. One that smelt musky. The headaches had been a magic hangover—just not hers.

Ben? Gentle, loving, passionate, Ben?

In a slideshow, all the pieces came together, even from before today: Ben, pretending to not watch her when he was. Always busy nearby when she had her meetings. Ingredients missing when she thought she'd had plenty. In fact, even from the first time she'd met him, the trace of the enchantment she'd sensed but ignored...

How could she have been so stupid? She should have spotted all these things. But being alone for so long, it had an effect and she'd obviously overlooked a great deal. A lump formed somewhere inside. The betrayal twisting hard. She sank into despair; shrinking, smaller, and felt herself disappearing.

No! She could fix this. She was one of the eight Sisters of Seven! Focusing on the checklist, she regained focus. The best place to start is the beginning. The spell she had read. Rena went through the checklist, reciting the ingredients:

a pinch of all-purpose casting powder
a few drops of clove oil
a tablespoon of water
1 black rose petal
3 strands of hair—
YOUR OWN HAIR WILL DO.

Of course! The black rose petal—something that had touched her heart. Three stands of *her* hair—three being the trinity between the existing, the old and the new.

So, did that mean—

A physical alertness assailed her. She was rigid, but somehow soft. The room came into sharp focus, but almost in two separate screens. She was in the chair in her office, where Mimi had been earlier.

Ben walked in with a plate of chillied prawns, sat down at her desk and began to eat them. He glanced at her, and then above her. "Sing," he said.

Elvis? Yep, a rendition of Heartbreak Hotel. It had been him.

Ben smiled, as if reading her thoughts. "Stop," he told the heads. "So, how does it feel, Rena?"

Feel? She couldn't feel anything. Or speak. Or move. But she had this urge to run, and…these weird cravings for tender, juicy— Carrots!

No!

The air shimmered and Ben changed. He didn't look much like Nick Cave now. Dark hair turned oily light brown. Pale skin freckled. John! Her neighbour!

The full deception hit her hard, betrayal a bitter chaser.

"Ta da!" he said, an aura of smugness surrounding him. "I bet you're surprised."

Somewhere amidst the cotton wool, she felt absolutely ill.

"I really used to love you, Rena. But you were horrible to me. For months. I thought we could get closer if I was someone else. I mean the sex was okay, good even. But the magic. What a rush. Nice touch with the cockroaches, by the way."

He knew. He'd known all the time.

"The magic? I've been watching you for a long time. And those deliveries were quite helpful. I'd just open them, copy everything then reseal the box before you came home. Simple. The one with the face-changing cream especially. It was the game-changer."

Rena remembered that recipe. She'd used it and spent a day as Lady Gaga pretending to be incognito. It had been fun until the Paparazzi found her at the shopping mall. But how—

"It was luck, Rena! I'd just started to work at the shop with my new temporary face when you'd come in! What fortuitous timing! I'd also used a touch of J'Adore, the people pleaser formula. I know, unnecessary with a face like this, but it helped with sales."

Rage and frustration assailed her in equal measure.

"And, helped with you, of course. But once I moved in and found the *Necronomicon*. Ah. It had so much more. Now I don't need the cream, because I have spells."

Tears formed in her glass eyes.

"Now, now. It's for the best. For me anyway." He picked up a tissue and dabbed her eyes. "It's almost time. Let's see how much I've learnt from you." He held the amulet around his neck and muttered the words of power.

Amulet. He needed an amulet. He can't have learnt that much from watching her.

Ego imperium, transmutes!

The room shimmered again.

"Here we go!" Ben said, in her voice—and from her mouth! "Do you think the Sisters will notice?"

Rena hadn't always been happy to see herself in the mirror, but to see Ben wearing her form was something else altogether. But, did he say *transmutes*?

"Just sit tight, fluffy, we can talk some more afterwards."

Ben dialled the Sisters. "It's a shame I couldn't send you away, Rena. But the laws of magic and all that. Need to have you…

…*close for this spell to work*. Yes, she understood. Understood perfectly well.

One by one the Sisters appeared on her laptop screen. During the chat, he even had the audacity to turn the laptop towards her and show them his creation.

"How come yours has a black streak, Rena?" they asked, mentioning the rabbit looked in some ways like its owner.

But Ben dismissed their questions, saying he'd added a little bit of himself, to make it more unique.

"It looks so real!" they said. "Almost alive!"

As the Sisters discussed their own rabbits, something was happening to Ben. His teeth looked a little longer. And were there white whiskers under his nose?

Ben put his hand to his—Rena's—face. "I have to go now, emergency." Ben cut off the meeting. He turned to Rena. "What's happening?"

Rena had a pretty good idea.

Ben's skin became fur, his eyes glassed over. His ears grew long and floppy. He looked just like a were rabbit—the one in Wallace and Gromit came to mind—and then he started to shrink. And this was where she wished she could close her glass eyes. The sound was the opposite of tearing something open—it was the sound of compacting something to fit. Things groaned and squelched and turned inwards. And got smaller, a puddle of blood pooling underneath.

And then…

He was the same size and shape as her, with the identical black streak.

Novice, she thought. Any experienced witch knew a full body transformation required the word *transfomere*!

Ha! And ughh. All the blood. Maybe there was no coming back for Ben. Rena wondered if the Sisters would come to check after the abrupt departure from the meeting. Even if they did, they'd have no idea she was a stuffed rabbit.

Concentrating, she pulled herself deeper, inwards, to her spiritual centre. Calling on the Goddess, she focused on her exterior form, searching for a weakness.

And…there it was.

It was the smallest of sounds. The tiniest of stitches. But eventually it popped.

One down, about a thousand left to go. It would take a while. And once she was out, she could deal with…the pest, even though he was quite contained for now.

In the meantime, however, she could really do with a carrot.

~ * ~ * ~

Louise Zedda-Sampson is an Australian writer, researcher and editor. Louise has edited/co-edited several anthologies and was a AHWA Shadows Awards Finalist for *Trickster's Treats 4: Coming Buried or Not!* [2020]. Her short fiction and articles have appeared in numerous publications in print, online and in peer-reviewed journals, and her horror articles have appeared at This is Horror, Horror Tree and Horror Oasis. Her debut book *Bowl the Maidens Over: Our First Women Cricketers* [2021] examines the Australian women cricketers' first games in the 1870s.

Find Louise at www.louisezeddasampson.com

No Age Restrictions

Danielle Mikals

The children came around often and without any sense of self preservation. They would wander from the far road to the east or through the bit of woods to the north, traipse across the field and lean against the garden fence. Silvia rather enjoyed their company.

"What type is that one?"

She glanced over, followed the line of the child's arm. "Rosemary," she answered. He was frowning almost immediately. No doubt, the rosemary in his mother's garden would be dark green, not a brilliant shade of orange.

"Why is yours different? Is it because you're a witch?"

She cast him a smile. "Yes."

He pondered for a moment before deciding that made sense. He took a few steps towards her and pointed to the next type of plant.

"What type is this one?"

It was a tradition for the children just old enough to wander far afield to make their way to her. They'd visit for a few years before the whispers of their parents made her less friendly in their eyes. More suspicious. Then they would ignore her completely as they aged into adulthood. Then, just as their parents before them, they would fall into the habit of ignoring her completely, seeing her as a distrustful threat, or as a desperate last resort for whatever ailed their lives.

She enjoyed the curious conversations, though. The random queries about her gardens and the small cottage she called her home. Some would ask if her horses transformed into unicorns. The genuine curiosity wouldn't last, but she didn't let that spoil her chance to pass on some knowledge to an eager student, no matter how briefly.

It was a warm day, a few days shy of spring, when Silvia heard soft footsteps approach, stopping on the other side of her garden fence.

"My mom says you have power over the whole world."

She didn't look up from her garden. "If I had power over the whole world, I imagine I would be able to keep trespassers out."

There was a nervous silence. She looked up and gave the girl and soft smile. It put the child at ease, emboldened her to take another step closer, her thin fingers wrapping around the wooden fence. "But you do know magic," she insisted.

"That I do." She sat back, the small plants happy to simply soak in the sunshine between them. "What would you like to ask me about?"

There was clearly some inquiry thrumming on those lips. "I need a spell."

"A spell? But I just said I don't control the world."

"You can control the earth, though," the girl insisted, peering at the garden around her.

"Many people have flourishing gardens."

The girl frowned, the conversation going differently than she expected. "You can control the earth," she said, clearly reciting another person's words. "And I must make a bargain with…regards to that."

"Must you?"

A very adamant nod. The witch studied the girl, the bright eyes, that bit of determination set in her face. Decent shoes and a nice sundress that had less of a feel of the children who usually wandered by. But the eyes stood out; the girl had been by her farm once or twice before, asking about… Yes, asking about the mint and basil.

"What's your name, dear?"

"Muriel."

"Do your parents know you're here?" she asked.

The girl shifted, unsure how to answer. Clearly, she was trying to find the best way to return to the script she'd been told to follow. "Yes."

"And why are you here?"

"I need you to ruin a harvest. Sam Hines. He can't have a good year. His farm needs to fail." The girl was mimicking rather ruthless words.

"And why should I ruin his harvest?"

"Because he's a bad man."

"Is he?" A definite nod and a solemn expression to go with it.

"How do you know?"

"My parents told me." Of course they had. They had told this girl a great many things.

"Does your parent's farm abut his?" Another tiny frown. "Are they next to each other?" she clarified.

"Oh! No. He's across the county. But he is next to my uncle's farm."

A land grab. And they were so cowardly as to use a child to seal the contract?

"What do you offer in exchange?"

"Me." No hesitation.

"You?" Sylvia asked, eyebrow raised. "What would I do with you?"

"You…could use me as an ingredient in one of your spells?"

"I've exhausted my quota on manipulated progeny." That brought on another frown. "Never mind what that means." She sighed, rising from her garden. She wasn't sure which disgusted her more. That bright eagerness to be a pawn or the fact it might be years before Muriel realized how oblivious she had been to her parents having her negotiate her own sale.

"What did your parents tell you about me?"

"That you're powerful. You can control the earth. You know magic. Grandpa says you once destroyed a whole family."

She had. The father had reneged on a bargain struck. Denied it at first and then tried to argue he hadn't understood the terms. It hadn't just been her magic that had risen up to strike them down. She would have settled for the father. But magic had its own impulses and currents. And a deal struck and seen to its conclusion made for very strong magic.

"Does your grandfather know that you're here?"

A swift no from the child. "Mom said not to tell him," she whispered.

A grandfather he may be, but she had no doubt he'd haul his grown child over his knee and beat her ass raw if he knew what she was trying to do with his grandchild.

The family was greedy, ready to start eating their neighbors. Just arrogant enough to believe they could strike without repercussions. She usually enjoyed the chance to reveal the true nature of the world to those foolish enough to believe they'd mastered it.

She looked down at the girl, this bright-eyed innocent who

was about to strike a deal without understanding what it could cost. Had she been less scrupulous, she wouldn't even be hesitating at the chance to strong arm some ridiculous bargain out of the child. Part of her was tempted to deny the child out right and send her on her way. But she knew greed. Those rehearsed words, that bargain, would be recited to the next nearest witch by this child who didn't know better than to do as bid.

The petty power plays of some ascending family were of no interest to her. A curious protégé on the other had...

"Do you remember what that plant is?"

The girl follower her finger, pursed her lips, shifted once, and then gave the correct answer.

It had been a long time since she'd had an apprentice. "Are you clever? Do you wonder how the world works?"

The child nodded, eyes bright. So curious. Wonderfully malleable. Not like the older teens who wanted to learn at her knee with a deliberate craving. A drive for something—revenge, greed, freedom, respect, adoration, fear-spurring them forward. She'd shape no one's craft for some petty ambitions. But a child would be willing to learn for the sake of it.

"I'll make the deal if you will," she decided. "You for the farm of this Sam Hines. Is that agreeable? You wouldn't see you family for years," she warned.

A chewed lip for an answer. Young, but not wholly stupid. Good.

"But I'll miss them. I thought you only needed hair. Or toenails."

"You'll see your family after a few years." If Muriel wanted to see them once the realization came to the fore. "But you want to trade. I ruin your uncle's neighbor's harvest and, afterwards, you come to stay with me. You learn. Do we have a deal?"

The girl's hand was small as she Sylvia took it in her, sealing the bargain.

~ * ~

The farm in question was quite modest. It wouldn't even be some great procurement. Not worth a family risking a child. The problem, she immediately surmised, was that it was boxed in on three sides by her dealmaker's uncle. He wanted the whole swath.

Hardly her concern what the greedy bastard wanted it for.

She waited until well past midnight, walking the edge of the land, feet bare and fingers brushing over branches and the rough bark of tree trunks. She called to it, sang to it. Bidding it to lay dormant, to ignore the warmth of spring, to let the rains slide away and for all the leaves to remain sleeping. The buds would remain closed, the grass limp and dry, as if winter had never moved on.

~ * ~

After the burst of spring, the drag of summer heat, and the riot of fall, there was finally a chill in the air, promising frost on the ground tomorrow. Sylvia rather enjoyed the shift in seasons. She walked down the long drive, arriving at the supposedly impressive house in the late afternoon. A long, wrapping porch and wide front doors demanded attention. She obliged, walking up to knock on the door.

After a moment, Muriel was there, opening the door and blinking those bright eyes up at her. "You came?"

There was an eager note in her question that had Sylvia fighting back a smile. An eager apprentice would be a wonderful change from her solitude. "Did you think I would forget our bargain?" she asked

"I wasn't sure," the girl admitted, a bit shy. "Mom said you wouldn't be able to come for me."

A foolish woman who was about to learn acutely that bargains struck with witches were to be seen to their agreed upon conclusion.

She held out a hand for the girl. That small hand rose up, hesitated. "Can I say goodbye to my folks?"

The witch dropped her hand. "Why not? I'm sure they'll have something interesting to say."

Muriel turned back into the house, the door ajar. Sylvia simply meandered down from the porch, uninterested in the shining fixtures inside. The pea stones kept her company as she waited. There was a brief silence, then raised voices. Then the door opened wide, and a woman stood staring at her. She looked furious. The child was just behind her, watching on with startled eyes.

"What do you think you're doing?" the woman demanded. A strong voice, used to snapping orders and having them obeyed. It would be useless here, in the end.

"Completing a transaction," Sylvia answered civilly. "And I've heard of your brother-in-law's stroke of good fortune. He was able to expand his property just recently?"

A furrowed brow in response. That was where the girl got it from. "Our family's business is none of yours. And you don't have a transaction here."

"Not with you. The deal was between me and Muriel. Shook on it and everything."

"We made no deals with you," the woman denied quickly. "I don't know anything about a deal."

"The one you told me to make." The witch simply raised an expectant brow at her new charge's earnest answer. What next excuse would be trotted out?

At the thin line of her mother's lips, the girl looked between them. Sylvia smiled gently and reached out. "We'll be going now."

The woman took several steps onto her porch. Sylvia assumed they were supposed to be threatening. "My daughter is a child."

"I do have eyes."

"She's a minor!"

So that was the way of it. They thought to escape this bargain on some ridiculous technicality? She could have howled in laughter. Instead, she simply sighed. "Do you imagine I'm a lawyer?" she asked this ridiculous woman who had put words in her daughter's mouth and expected no repercussions. "You wanted me to undo the laws of nature and you think to stay me with the laws of man?"

The woman all but stomped her foot. "Our daughter is a child, and we made no deal with you."

Silvia simply looked to the girl. Explaining anything more to the woman would be a waste of her time and energy. "Come along." It was a slight compulsion that brought the girl down the steps and to her side. Slight, but a deal struck and seen to its conclusion made for very strong magic indeed.

The woman shouted back to the house and a man appeared. He took one look at the scene and marched across the porch. He stared down at Sylvia in a manner she imagined was supposed to be intimidating. "We never made any deal with you," he said.

"As I said to your wife: I know. Neither of you struck a contract with me. Your daughter did."

"My daughter's not going with you!"

"Oh?" She didn't bother to hide her lack of surprise

The father stomped down the stairs, ready to barrel forward and snatch back the lure he'd been so eager to cast into dangerous waters. Then he stopped, bent double, and collapsed on the ground, mouth working as he began to clutch at his throat.

Muriel tried to rush forward, but Sylvia held the child's wrist with the grip of a vise. The young girl looked back, panicked tears about to start falling.

"Do you remember our deal?" Sylvia asked, ever patient. She received a frightened nod. "You'll be coming with me, or should I assume you have reneged?" A deepening of that frown. "That you've lied to me about our contract?"

The girl paused, weighing her options, her obligation. She stopped pulling forward. "I'll go." The words were small. She took a few steps closer, standing next to the witch passively and her father started gulping in air, lungs suddenly working again.

"She's mine," she said to the man on the ground. She looked up the woman standing on the porch steps. "I expect you all recall what happens to those who try to interfere with a bargain struck."

The man was glaring at her, red faced, with spittle on his lips and chin. His wife was leaning against the railing with a knuckle white grip. Neither of them spoke.

"I told you." The solemn voice came from inside the house. "I told you not to deal in magic and you didn't listen."

The man was older than the two before her, more grey hair than dark. There was a hunch to his back, one borne of work. A curl to his hands that spoke of a skill performed over decades. He set a hard glare at his daughter and son-in-law. There was a burning hatred there.

"You never listen," he said.

He walked slowly down the stairs, old knees making the journey uneven. He gave the witch a hard look, but he had a soft expression when he bent down to his granddaughter

"Be a good girl. Listen, to what you're told, and when you're older come to my house, darling." He glanced once at the witch, the threat there something Sylvia respected: he'd see his granddaughter again no matter what she said or did. Then he was focused again on his grandchild. He kissed her forehead. "When you understand what happened here, just leave it to lie, okay? Don't bother with your parents."

She frowned. "Why wouldn't I want to see them?"

He simply sighed and straightened as much as he could. "She's a bright girl," he said, pride in the short sentence.

"I wouldn't have use for her if she wasn't."

His frown wasn't one of confusion, but of anger. Yes, she approved of this one.

"I'll treat her well," Sylvia assured him gently. "In a few years you'll see for yourself." Then she looked down at her new apprentice.

"Come," she said. "You've much to learn." She squeezed the girl's hand and led her away.

~ * ~ * ~

Danielle Mikals works at the AOK Library at the University of Maryland, Baltimore County. She contributed to *Hunger For Awe: Love This Anthology of Poetry and Teach*. Write: A Writing Teachers' Literary Journal. She has been published online in 805lit in January 2022.

Fair Trade

Dominick Cancilla

Catherine asked the stupidest question imaginable: "How are things going?"

It was three days since the baby—*her* baby—had been still-born, and Janelle continued having trouble feeling anything but numb. She sat at her kitchen table, thinking blank thoughts, and slowly stirring a spoon through a cup of coffee that must have long ago cooled to the temperature of the room. It must be shock. It must be denial. But it just felt like nothing.

"I don't know," Janelle answered. "I don't feel like I know anything. I don't even know who I am right now. I think back to last week, and my memory is of a woman who isn't anyone I recognize anymore."

"I'm sorry," Catherine said. "I thought you could use some company but—is it too soon? If you'd rather not talk, that's okay. Or if you want to talk about something else."

The baby was all Janelle wanted to talk about, and it was the one thing she didn't want to talk about at all. She wanted to be alone but couldn't stand to be. After the stillbirth but while Janelle was still recovering in the hospital, Catherine had let herself into Janelle's apartment and removed the crib, the changing table, the boxes of diapers—everything that, when unopened, had been first a promise and then a blight. Janelle hated Catherine for the intrusion and loved her for the pain that intrusion had swept away.

"No," Janelle said. "It's okay. I'm just—I don't know what to do, you know?"

"You've got time, at least," Catherine said. Which was true. Janelle had arranged for maternity leave, so switching it to sick and bereavement leave was no hardship for work, since they already had a temporary covering for her.

For a minute, then two, they sat in silence interrupted only by the occasional ding of Janelle's spoon against the side of her panda mug. There should be a baby crying. There should be bustle and fussing, laughing about his look the first time he was put in the bath, ridiculous joy at changing a diaper. Instead, it was silent. As silent as Jeremy had been at the moment of his birth.

"I want to feel something," Janelle said, breaking the stillness. "I want to be binge-eating depressed. I want to wail and slam my fists into the walls. I want to scream at God for bringing me here." She looked Catherine in the eye for the first time in what may have been an hour. "Why can't I?"

Catherine looked down at her mug, unable to bear Janelle's gaze. "I don't know," she said. "Everyone handles things in their own way."

"I don't think I'm handling it at all."

Catherine sighed, apparently steeling herself. "Look," she said, "there's something I was thinking about."

A little worried about where this was leading, Janelle waited for Catherine to continue.

"You know Roberta? Keith's sister?"

The stirring of Janelle's hand ceased abruptly. "I don't want anything to do with him or his family."

"I know, I know," Catherine said. "But this isn't about him. Hear me out."

Janelle almost got up and left the room. Here was something she had feelings about.

She'd only dated Keith for a few weeks, and they'd had a nasty breakup after she discovered she was pregnant. They'd been together just long enough for him to borrow a couple of things she certainly would never see again and for her to discover his supposedly deep-seated religious feelings somehow came with an uncomfortably strong pro-abortion streak.

During the pregnancy she'd tried repeatedly to get him to commit to supporting the baby financially. Good luck with that.

Janelle kept her seat, recognizing her impulsive anger was nothing Catherine deserved.

"You never met his family, right?" Catherine asked.

Janelle shook her head.

"Okay. Well, Roberta's boyfriend is a driver for a limousine company. A month or so ago, he had a really bad accident when a jack failed, and a car fell on him. He ended up losing his hand."

Janelle frowned. What made Catherine think she wanted to hear this?

"He thought that was pretty much it. You can't be a high-class driver with just one hand, can you? Well, Thursday I saw in the newspaper he had been arrested for shooting a police officer—he grabbed the cop's gun during a traffic stop or something—and there was a picture of him. In the picture, he had two hands."

"So he didn't really lose a hand."

"No, he did. Roberta comes into my shop all the time and a few weeks ago she came in with him and I saw the stump. It was covered in bandages, but still a stump. You couldn't have hidden a hand in there."

"They reattached it."

Catherine shook her head. "No. There was too much damage. Anyway, in the picture there were no stitches, and there'd have to be stitches. It made no sense, right? So yesterday Roberta comes into the shop, and we got to talking. She was still really mad at him for getting arrested. He'd never done anything like that before, and she said she's shelled out ten thousand dollars to get him his hand back. Ten thousand dollars!"

Janelle shook her head again. "There's no way. Keith's family doesn't have any money. They're all broke."

Broke enough there was no way Keith could cover childcare without ruining him financially at least. He'd said he thought he could scrape up enough just this once to pay half for an abortion, but that was the extent of it. Janelle had long ago resigned herself to being an unsupported single mother.

"Are you kidding?" Catherine said. "They're loaded. His dad's a stockbroker. The point is, Roberta says she found this woman who can do, as she put it, 'certain things.' That sounds weird, right? Certain things? Well, for ten thousand dollars from Roberta and some kind of promise from her boyfriend, the guy wakes up the next morning with his hand back. Just like that! Then he goes and uses his newly restored hand to shoot a cop and probably get himself sent to jail for life. What an idiot."

"No," Janelle said. "That doesn't make any sense. You can't just give someone their hand back."

"I can't," Catherine said. "You can't. But, apparently, someone can. And maybe she can do something for you."

~ * ~

Keith was going slowly insane. Just three days into an enforced celibacy and he was about ready to start stabbing people at random just to give his frustration somewhere to go. The bar was warm, but he was sweating like he was in a sauna. The ice in the drink he'd forgotten he was holding was almost melted, and the bartender kept giving him odd looks, like he thought Keith was going to start trouble.

He couldn't believe he'd agreed to this.

When Roberta told him about Louis getting his hand back, he's assumed she was nuts. But then he saw the guy and there the hand was, good as new. Five fingers don't lie.

Louis and Keith had knocked back a few and Louis told him the whole story. There was this woman—kind of hot, but with an icicle vibe—who could apparently make things happen. It wasn't a "you get three wishes" situation, but more of a straight business transaction. You gave her some money and you exchanged promises. In Louis' case, her promise had been that he'd have his hand back, and his promise was that five times, for five minutes, the hand wouldn't be his.

"What the hell does that mean?" Keith had asked.

Louis had admitted he didn't know.

Now, after seeing the news, Keith thought he did.

At the time, though, this had sounded like the answer to his prayers. He couldn't have a baby in his life. If the girl had been able to prove it was his, he'd have to either take off or spend his life paying through the nose for the thing. Morality fanatic that he was, Dad would definitely cut him off, too. Couldn't have the other rich assholes knowing he had a bastard grandson.

Keith had gotten Roberta to help him contact the woman and they'd made a deal. Her price had been $30,000, which was a hell of a lot, but considering the hole it would get him out of if it worked, it had seemed worth it. Along with the money, she'd asked Keith to swear to her he wouldn't even attempt to have sex for one year. If he would promise that, on pain of forfeiting his money, then Janelle's unborn financial burden was as good as dead.

It hadn't even taken a day for him to sell some of the stocks in his portfolio from Dad and bring the woman the cash.

~ * ~

Janelle had to be out of her mind.

"She doesn't use a phone," Catherine had said, "but you take one of her cards and follow the instructions on it. What can it hurt?"

What can it hurt to let yourself hope when there's nothing to hope for? What can it hurt to try insanity when reality has so thoroughly let you down?

The business card was blank white on one side. On the other side, it was black with white letters that read simply, "Write what you need, then burn."

Janelle said she'd think about it, but the moment Catherine left, she went to the kitchen drawer to get a pen. This wasn't a lottery ticket you held on to for a few days so you could dream pleasant dreams of riches before checking the numbers to verify you were still broke. Any delay was just time spent dwelling on the possibility of the impossible, and false hope was a growing wound.

She put the card on the cutting board and wrote on the white side, "I want my baby." Then she turned on the stove's burner and dropped the card into the flame. There was a flash and a knock, and in the next moment the card was gone.

Janelle turned off the burner. It took her a moment to realize someone was knocking on the door.

The woman at the door was thin, white, and young—barely past 21 if Janelle had her guess. She wore jeans and a blouse unbuttoned just enough to hint at the lack of a bra. "I'm Melissa," the woman said with an oddly disturbing smile. "Shall we talk about Jeremy?"

Like it was the most natural thing in the world, Janelle let Melissa in, sat with her on the couch, and talked.

"What would you give to have your baby back?" Melissa asked, cutting right to the chase.

"Anything," Janelle said. What else could she say?

"Good," Melissa said. "Here's how this works. I need ten thousand dollars from you. It doesn't have to be cash. You have jewelry from your mother that's worth about that, and it would be sufficient. The only other thing I'd need from you is something you've had close contact with since before Jeremy was conceived and a promise."

"What kind of promise?" Janelle asked.

"That's the key," Melissa said. "The baby will be a great benefit, so it must be balanced with a great sorrow. In short, someone must suffer. It won't be Jeremy and it doesn't have to be you, but it could be. For example, would you trade Jeremy's life for the lives of two other children?

"No!" Janelle nearly shouted, so reflexively horrified she burst out with the word before she even realized she'd done it.

"I don't mean you'd have to kill anyone. They could be the children of strangers. Two women you'll never know will wake to find their child dead beside them. Would you allow that to save Jeremy?"

Janelle shook her head. "No. Never." Even if she didn't raise a hand herself, she'd feel the guilt. Why would she wish the pain of losing a child on another woman when she knew how deeply it hurt?

"Then what if I took something from you. What if you had Jeremy but could never love him. You'd never feel what a mother is supposed to feel."

"And he'd never have a mother's love," Janelle said.

"But he'd be alive," Melissa added.

This was a far more difficult proposition to turn down. If she was without love for her child, the suffering would be all her own, wouldn't it? But how would that affect her baby? Growing up with just one parent, and that a mother who didn't love him? What if she had other children and loved them in a way Jeremy could never be loved? What would it do to him?

"I can't," Janelle said. "I can't do either of those things. Is there something I could give that would just be from me? You could take an arm. You could take an eye."

"A noble sacrifice wouldn't fit the bill. You would look at the trade as a fair one—an arm or eye for a child—and there wouldn't be sufficient suffering. I suppose we could bend the rules a little and have Jeremy crippled. You'd have to live your life with the guilt of knowing it was something you'd inflicted on him, but I suppose you'd never agree to that either, would you."

"No," Janelle said.

"You'd rather suffer the loss of your baby the rest of your life than cause an innocent harm, is that it?"

Janelle nodded. Her eyes had begun to tear up.

"Well," Mellissa said, standing up. "That's unusual. I think we're done here. I'll let myself out."

And she did.

Janelle broke into violent, wracking sobs. She'd actually allowed herself, just for a minute, to hope. There was no reason to, but she'd let herself cling to the chance of a miracle, and the loss of that ridiculous hope was crushing. For the first time in days, Janelle could feel, and it felt like the world was smashing down upon her.

~ * ~

It was official: Keith couldn't keep his promise. Then again, why should he?

It had only taken one drink to help set his mind straight. The baby was already dead. If he broke his promise, what were the consequences? He'd lose his money, sure, but so what? He'd already lost it.

What the hell was he doing driving himself crazy doing something he didn't even need to do? And besides, odds were, the whole thing was a coincidence and a scam. The woman who'd taken his money had laughed all the way to the bank just lucked out the baby'd been born dead. She'd probably already skipped town with his cash.

Heck with this.

Keith got up from the bar and had a look around. There was a brunette at a table by herself. Nothing to write home about, but then it wasn't writing about her that he wanted to do. He bet himself he could have her back at his place within the hour.

Straightening his shirt and putting on his most charming look, Keith walked over to her table. "Excuse me, gorgeous," he said. Then his phone rang.

Keith ignored it.

"So, I was thinking," Keith continued, "that a beautiful woman like you—" The phone should have gone to voicemail but instead was ringing on and on, looping through the first bits of an old Rod Stewart song. "Just a sec," he said, holding up a finger with one hand and retrieving the phone with the other.

The woman was looking at him like he was an idiot.

As soon as Keith had the phone out, it stopped ringing. A text message from an unknown number showed on the lock screen: "That's an attempt" was all it said.

What the hell did that mean?

Then the phone rang again, and this time the screen showed who was calling. It was his father. "Oh, shit," Keith said aloud.

~ * ~

Janelle's cell phone was ringing in the kitchen. She focused on the distraction to push back her tears and went to find it.

The phone was on the kitchen table where she and Catherine had been talking. As Janelle picked it up, she absently noticed Catherine's coffee mug was still there, but Janelle's panda mug was not. Where had that gone? Like it mattered.

Janelle answered the phone. "Hello," she said, voice cracking.

"Ms. Kane?"

"Speaking."

"This is St. Paul's Hospital."

There was a fist clenching in Janelle's stomach. "Yes?"

"It's about your baby. I don't know any other way to put it, so I'm just going to come out and say it. It's a miracle, Ms. Kane. It's an honest to God miracle."

~ * ~ * ~

Dominick Cancilla lives in Santa Monica, California with various lizards and his wife, author Deborah Markus. Melissa, the supernatural protagonist in the short story included here, also appears his novels *Tomorrow's Journal* and *Revenant Savior*.

ÒRΕΑΜ WEAVER

Wendy Harrison

Lucinda Darling's feet danced across the treadles on the loom, tracking the beat of the Black Sabbath music coming from the turntable on the other side of the studio. The fabric she wove absorbed the soul of the sound, and she was always careful to match the music to the needs of her customers.

Two kinds of people shopped for her handwoven goods, the ones who admired the beauty of the fabric for its own sake and those who knew about the added ingredient. Although they didn't drown witches anymore, Lucinda was cautious and offered her magical services only to those she trusted to keep them secret.

Lucinda created different powers in the cloth for each person who ordered it. For one, it could be the strength they needed to get through a personal tragedy. For another, it could be the patience they required in dealing with a failing parent. And for some, it could be the capacity for righteous rage at being mistreated. Lucinda didn't charge extra for the special orders. It was her calling, her ministry. She was, in all respects but one, a good witch.

The bell over the door to the studio jingled. She heard the tinkling sound even with the pounding bass of the music rattling the windows.

"Hi, Tabitha," she said without looking up from the rising and falling shafts on the loom until the sudden silence got her attention.

Her best friend was next to the turntable, moving the arm off the vinyl disk. "That's Detective Elias to you."

"Only if you're here on official business." Lucinda kept weaving as she hummed to the missing music.

"It's official, all right. A noise complaint."

"Out here?" Lucinda pointed to the wall of windows that ran along the back of the spacious studio, exposing a panoramic view of the river. "Are the dolphins upset with me?"

"If not, they should be. And poor Minerva." Tabitha walked to the other side of the room where an owl sat on a tree branch in a large cage, its dark eyes blinking at her. "Bird abuse is a crime, you know."

"She doesn't mind. It's quiet in the cage."

"A sound block spell?"

"Of course. You don't think I'd disturb her with Black Sabbath, do you?"

Minerva winked at Tabitha and went back to sleep.

"Do you have time for a tea break?"

Lucinda stretched her arms over her head. "Sure do. I need to move around a little."

She stood and walked to the corner of the room where she kept the teas and mugs. She filled the kettle and put it on the stove. Once it was ready, she added Dream Magic tea leaves, her own special blend.

They sat at the counter and watched the river as they sipped. "So, what's new in cop land?" Lucinda enjoyed the stories of mayhem and mishaps Tabitha saw every day. There were always tales to tell. It was Florida, after all. However, the two women didn't consider their hidden status as witches to be part of the peculiarities of the local population.

"There've been some break-ins along the river," Tabitha said. "Whoever it is has been searching for something. They left behind valuables, money, jewelry. Not a typical burglar at all. No prints left behind. Even the houses with security cameras were a bust. None of them showed a thing."

Lucinda sipped her tea. "Maybe it's kids, making a mess for fun."

"The cameras?"

"Don't they all know how to hack into things these days?"

Tabitha didn't look convinced. "Maybe you should start locking your door."

Lucinda snorted into her tea. "I have Minerva. And Wanda." She reached into the pocket of the large apron she wore when she was weaving and pulled out a wand, which was carved from Evergreen wood and topped with the image of an owl who looked like Minerva.

"Be careful with that thing." Tabitha raised her hand, which began to glow.

As she tucked Wanda back inside her pocket, Lucinda said, "Relax. I only use her for good. You know that. My mother would come back to haunt me if I did anything else. But don't worry about me. Only a fool would take me on with Wanda close at hand."

When Tabitha left, Lucinda went back to the loom, but she had trouble settling into the meditative state that usually took over when she wove. The story of the mysterious burglar unsettled her. She knew to trust her intuition, but try as she might, she couldn't pinpoint what was bothering her. Giving up on the weaving and Black Sabbath, she thought a walk along the river might help.

Slipping binoculars around her neck, she headed along the well-worn path along the grassy bank. She looked across the flowing river to a small island, surrounded by tangled mangroves with tall palm trees in the center. It was a favorite resting and nesting place for seabirds, whose calls echoed across to her. Lucinda stopped and raised the binoculars to get a closer look at the egrets and ibises in the thick tall growth.

"Screech, screech!"

It was Minerva, back at the house, sounding the alarm. It always seemed odd to Lucinda that people associated a feathery "hoo hoo" sound with owls when most of them made a very different noise. Minerva's voice could be terrifying coming out of the darkness, but it was unusual for her to be heard during daylight.

Turning, Lucinda aimed her binoculars at the house some distance from her. She didn't see anything but started to run, checking to be sure she still had Wanda in her pocket. When she reached the house, she tugged the sliding glass door open.

"Minerva," she called. The bird quieted but her feathers remained ruffled, puffing her up to almost double her size. Relieved the owl was unharmed, Lucinda's eyes darted around the large room. A movement caught her attention. Her hand dove into her apron pocket and closed around Wanda. She turned to where she thought she had seen something. Or someone. The swaying of the dreamcatcher caught her eye. A delicate blend of bamboo and feathers, it hung over the front door, but there shouldn't have been a breeze inside the studio to set it swaying. Lucinda walked over to the door and saw it was ajar.

"I know I closed it when Tabitha left." She pulled it shut and walked to Minerva's cage. "What happened?"

Minerva stared at her and muttered.

"I can't understand you." It wasn't the first time, more likely the hundredth, that Lucinda was unable to communicate with her companion. She was never sure if it was deliberate on Minerva's part or a failing on hers, but she had learned she couldn't always count on Minerva to share her thoughts.

"All right," Lucinda said and raised Wanda to restore the sound block broken by Minerva's cries. "Get some sleep."

The next day, Lucinda started on a new weaving project, this one for a young woman who was looking for love. No Black Sabbath for this one. Puccini's "O mio, babbino caro" floated through the air. You didn't have to speak Italian to feel the romance in the room. It was one of Minerva's favorites, so Lucinda had suspended the sound block spell for her and hoped she wouldn't be tempted to sing along. They didn't call them screech owls for nothing. But Minerva was content to close her eyes and sway on her perch in time to the music. Moments before the end of the aria, Lucinda felt a change in the air. She looked toward the cage where the owl had opened her eyes and begun to mumble.

Lucinda felt a chill. It was the same sound Minerva had made in reaction to the open front door. She stood and slid away from the bench. Facing the door, she wrapped her hand around Wanda but kept her hidden. A man stood in the doorway. He was tall, with dark hair and hazel eyes the color of the river. His white teeth sparkled as he smiled at Lucinda.

"I wasn't sure if I should knock. This is the Dream Weaver Studio, isn't it?"

"It is. Can I help you?"

He stepped inside and began to close the door.

"Screech, screech."

He jumped at the sound and took his hand off the door.

"You can leave it open." Lucinda walked over to him and held out her hand. "I'm Lucinda Darling. This is my studio." She gestured toward the cage. "And this is Minerva."

He took her hand. "I'm Simon Gamboa, and I'm looking for a gift for my mother. Something handmade. Something she won't find anywhere else."

Lucinda kept her left hand low where Simon wouldn't see her signal toward the cage. Minerva got the message but showed her disapproval by turning her back to Lucinda.

They walked around the studio as Lucinda showed Simon the

samples of her work she displayed for the tourists. He stopped at a silk scarf. The pattern in the sparkling fabric was a cascade of shades of green with a barely discernible repeating image of a brown owl scattered through it. Most of the time, Lucinda had to point it out for customers to see, but Simon immediately spotted it.

"Minerva, I presume?" When Lucinda nodded, Simon moved closer to her and reached out to touch the fabric. She could feel his fingers through the silk and dropped the scarf. They both reached for it.

"I have it," she told him and picked it up from the floor. She couldn't understand what was wrong with her, but she knew she needed him to leave.

"I'll take it," he said.

Welcoming the excuse to move away from him, Lucinda walked to the worktable by the windows. "Would you like it gift wrapped?" When he nodded, she turned to the roll of shiny paper with the Dream Weaver Studio logo printed on it. She folded the scarf into a box, wrapped it, and tied a final sparkling ribbon on it. She told him the price, and he reached into his pocket for his wallet. Instead of the expected credit card, he pulled out a one-hundred-dollar bill, the amount on the tag attached to the scarf.

"Thank you. I hope your mother likes it."

She walked him to the door but didn't miss his rapid inspection of the large space. When he hesitated at the threshold, she reached around him to grab the doorknob. "Goodbye, Mr. Gamboa." He nodded and smiled.

"I hope we run into each other again. Maybe next time without your bodyguard."

The sound block didn't stop Minerva from hearing what sounded like a threat to her mistress. She began screeching again. Simon laughed but quickened his pace down the path away from the studio.

Lucinda closed and locked the door before she picked up her cellphone. "Tabitha?" Lucinda used all her strength to steady her voice. "I had a visitor." She rushed through a description of her encounter with Simon. "There was something off about him. Even Minerva knew."

"Too good looking?" Tabitha knew her friend was rarely affected by mortal men. The occasional warlock, maybe, but not a mere mortal.

"This isn't funny." Lucinda's voice rose. "I'm telling you; he was looking for something. And I don't mean a scarf for his mother. He was checking the place out."

"Okay. I'll tell you what. Come down to the station, and I'll have someone put together an Identikit. We'll see if he looks familiar to anyone."

Lucinda took off her apron and got her purse. "I'll be back soon," she called to Minerva who began to screech as the door closed behind her. "Now you want to talk?" No broomsticks during daylight so Lucinda hopped on her motorbike, jammed a helmet over her flyaway hair, and headed to the police station in downtown Porta Larga.

The station was busy, and Lucinda began to have second thoughts about the alarm she had raised. If Tabitha hadn't mentioned the burglaries, would she have been so concerned about the man who had raised her heart rate? How serious had Minerva been, with her screeching and mumbling? Maybe she was only in a bad mood and wanted Lucinda to be in one too. It wouldn't be the first time.

She sat on a hard wooden bench in the hallway outside the room where the Identikit computer was being used. After waiting for half an hour, she stood and walked to Tabitha's desk in the detective area.

"Still waiting?"

"Give me some paper and a couple of pencils," Lucinda said.

Tabitha smiled. "Do it yourself?" She pulled a large pad out of her desk drawer and added a handful of sharpened pencils. "Knock yourself out."

Lucinda sat in the empty chair next to the desk and went to work. Fifteen minutes later, she held up the pad. "This is him. This is Simon Gamboa."

Tabitha whistled. "I sure hope he isn't the burglar. He's too pretty to be in a cage."

"I won't tell Minerva you said that."

Lowering her voice, Tabitha said, "Are you sure he's not one of us?"

"Absolutely. I would know." At least, she thought she would. This whole thing had thrown her off balance.

"Why don't you go back to the studio and get some work

done? I'll call you if we come up with anything. And this time, lock the doors."

As Lucinda approached her house, it struck her she had left her apron behind with Wanda in the pocket. "Oh no, no." She knew what she would find when she opened the door.

Minerva was flying loose around the house, screeching at Lucinda who rushed over to where she had put the apron. She pushed her hand into the front pocket. Nothing. Nothing was there. How could she have let this happen? Wanda had been handed down through four generations of witches. How could she be the one to lose her?

"Minerva. Stop. Settle down. We have to talk." The owl slowed her frantic flight around the room and returned to the branch in her cage. She began to chatter.

"No more mumbling. You have to tell me. Was it Simon? The man who was here earlier?"

Minerva stared at her and blinked once, a silent yes. "Did he hurt Wanda?" Two blinks. "Do you know where he went?" Two blinks again. "Was he one of us? Did I miss it?" Two blinks.

That was good news and bad news at the same time. Good news because if Simon was mortal, he wouldn't know how to make use of Wanda's powers. Bad news because if he got frustrated with her, he might try to destroy her. Lucinda wasn't sure how much power the wand would be able to muster without her personal witch there.

"We're going to fix this. I promise. First, we have to find Simon."

Before she could come up with a plan, her phone rang. The caller ID said UNKNOWN. "Simon?"

She heard him chuckle, a deep sound that might have weakened her knees if she had heard it before he stole her wand.

"Got it in one. How did you make out at the police station?"

"What do you want?"

"I already have it. I've been searching for the witch I kept hearing rumors about. The one with special powers. I could use some of those powers myself. I was hoping to find a way to become invisible. It would be so helpful in my chosen career."

"Thief?"

He laughed again. "That's harsh. Let's say I relieve people of their excess baggage." When she didn't answer, he added, "I was hoping you would show me how it works."

"How what works?" If she kept him talking, she might be able to hear something in the background that would help her find him.

"Don't be coy. The magic wand."

"If I refuse?"

He was silent for a moment. "That would be a mistake unless, of course, this piece of wood is fireproof."

"I'll help you. Just don't hurt her."

Now he was laughing. "Her? This keeps getting better. I promise I'll return her if you help me pull off one more job."

"I need to think. Call me tomorrow morning." She disconnected the call. In that moment of silence when she had threatened to refuse him, she had heard what she needed.

The more she thought about what he had done, the angrier she became. She could feel lightning bursts of rage tearing through her body. Lucinda was a good witch, but only until she was betrayed, when she became a very dangerous witch indeed. Then she was capable of setting aside everything she had been taught about using her powers for good. Who decides what is good and what is bad? Her mother had always told her she would know, but what she knew in this moment was that recovering Wanda and punishing Simon would be good by any definition.

Across town from where Lucinda lived, there was a camp with vacation rental cottages called Happy Palms. Most of the housing was empty during the scorching off-season, when Florida lost its charm for most tourists. A bell tower sat in the center of the property. It rang the hour from seven in the morning until seven in the evening. During the moment of silence on the phone, Lucinda counted the sound of the bells ringing six o'clock. Simon had to be in one of the cottages.

She wished she could ask Tabitha to come with her, but Tabitha was able to become part of law enforcement because she could match her status as a good witch with her job. She would never be able to carve out an exception like Lucinda was planning.

It was a long wait, but at midnight, Lucinda left the house, leaving the door open, with instructions for Minerva, who bobbed her head in excitement. Lucinda would've preferred being able to travel through the darkness on her broomstick, but she didn't want to risk being noticed by someone having a late night out.

When she was close enough to the entrance to Happy Palms, she pulled off to the side of the road into a stand of trees where her motorbike wouldn't be spotted. Gliding toward the cottages, she began to focus on Wanda. Looking in the windows of one vacant cottage after another, she came to one that showed signs of use, with a car out front. Lucinda peered through the front window and saw a small pulsing light. It was Wanda. Everything else was dark and quiet.

Lucinda tried the window. It was locked. Touching it lightly with her forefinger, she heard it click. The window slid open. Lucinda looked into the room and saw Wanda rise from the desk drawer where Simon had hidden her. The wand flew into her hand. She stood there, in front of the open window, taking a moment for gratitude for the return of her companion. Was she still angry enough to go through with the rest of her plan? Yes, she certainly was.

Lucinda used Wanda's power to lift a glass table from the middle of the room up to the ceiling, and let it crash to the floor. As she expected, Simon came stumbling into the room, barely awake, but stopping in time to avoid the broken glass. Lucinda saw him look toward the desk with its open drawer. He cursed and then saw her at the window. Before he could move, Lucinda raised Wanda and said, "Bad luck to your soul, and mouse you be."

A look of horror crossed Simon's no longer handsome face as he began to shrink. It took only a minute for the transformation spell to be complete. He stayed frozen in place, a sleek gray creature with a long tail and white whiskers.

Lucinda stepped away from the open window and waited. It wasn't long before she heard the sound she was waiting for.

"Screech, screech!"

~ * ~ * ~

Wendy Harrison is a retired prosecutor who turned to short mystery fiction during the pandemic. Her stories have been published in numerous anthologies including *Peace, Love & Crime, Autumn Noir, CRIMEUCOPIA: Tales from the Back Porch, The Big Fang, Gargoylicon,* and *Death of a Bad Neighbour.* She lives in Florida where she spends her time writing, weaving and waiting in vain for cooler weather.

CAN'T BE DONE

Elle Hartford

It was midnight on the darkest night of the year when Trent decided to confront the witch at last.

This wasn't a particularly good idea. The witch was far more powerful than he was—a fact he knew well. In fact, no one in Belville knew the witch better than Trent did. And that was just one of the reasons the task had fallen to him.

Trent had served the town of Belville for a few years now, and he felt a sense of responsibility to it, that special kind of responsibility that comes unexpectedly simply because it's the first. He'd never felt tied to any other place. He'd hardly felt welcome anywhere else, least of all in school, where he learned about plants and healing and, mostly, how to survive by simply getting by. But now that he'd spent years in Belville—*how had that happened? Where did the years go?* he wondered—tending people's injuries and giving them tonics to ease their colds, he felt it was time to take a stand. He knew it in his bones.

Even if a part of him would rather *not* know.

But in Belville, there wasn't much room for hiding from things that needed to be known. That was the problem with living in such a magical land; sometimes, it seemed the mountains themselves had a will, and even the forest was full of judgment. All the town residents—be they witch or human, ogre or fairy, young or old, knew there was no escaping destiny.

Even if that destiny was scary.

And Trent wasn't above admitting when he was scared. On the contrary, Trent believed very firmly in honesty at all times—and in leaving the world better than he found it. This new quest fit into both of those beliefs. He couldn't avoid it, and it needed to be done. He had to face the witch.

The witch was known simply as Saki. She might have been young, but at times she seemed impossibly old, like a matriarch who makes her own time—or perhaps, like an evil queen. She hadn't been in town as long as Trent had, but she had a sort of insidious power, the kind that convinces people not to ask too many questions. Trent had seen how she'd influenced and manipulated the lives around her. The lives *he'd* been charged with taking care of.

Yes, it was definitely time to do something. The only problem was the witch was almost never alone. And she was *always* watching.

Hence the plan to strike at midnight.

Trent shivered. The town of Belville was nestled high in the mountains, and even on a good night, it wasn't very warm. He longed for the security of his little hut with its roaring fire.

But this has to be done, he reminded himself firmly. *The sooner the better. I've already put it off for too long. Even if I don't want to do it for me—which I do!—I've got to do it for the others. They've been asking, after all.*

They had, indeed, been asking. The bookseller, the baker, even the lady who ran the tavern and ought to have been far too busy to take an interest in what he did—or didn't—do. In the little community, there weren't too many leaders to turn to. There were more gossips than anything else. And gossips, while very useful in reporting action, were not so helpful in actually getting anything *done*.

The town alchemist had been helpful, though. Using her knowledge of ancient science and metals and minerals he'd never even heard of, she'd made Trent a special box.

And that was what the entire evening hinged upon.

I've got a trick up my sleeve, Trent reminded himself, stoking the fires of his courage. *There's no way this can fail. All I have to do is see it through.*

With his hand clenched around the magic box in his coat pocket, Trent left the serenity of the town's smoking chimneys and silent streets behind. Without another thought—without *allowing* himself another thought—he turned his steps toward the forest.

To think too much now would only mean he lost his mettle.

And besides, he wasn't entirely sure the witch couldn't hear his thoughts.

Trent had planned everything very carefully, in part so he *wouldn't* have to think. He knew the minute she saw the box, she would know what it was. Not even an alchemist could fool a really powerful witch, after all. That's why he had to keep it hidden until the last moment, and then to disguise it, if at all possible. It was his secret weapon, and he had to use it carefully. If the witch figured out what he was up to, it would be all over before it began.

She met him at the edge of the forest.

"Quite a night for secrets," she said, starlight glinting off pearly teeth. The darkness hid her hands, her clothes. The bats overhead chittered in chorus.

Trent didn't answer. He didn't have to; the witch knew what to do.

This was the great danger of the witch, of course. She always knew more than anyone else—and she wasn't afraid to use her knowledge. This was what scared him. He wasn't sure, even now, what there was about himself to be known. What would she take an interest in, or use to her benefit? The dirt from the garden under his fingernails, the look in his bright eyes, the way his breath shook? What little clue would give him away? He never knew until she struck.

But tonight she did not strike immediately. That day, in town, he had challenged her knowledge of the stars. So now to settle the question of who was more familiar with the heavens, she led him down the forest path, up the mountain. It was a familiar trail, and his feet followed it easily. But he had never walked it before in such darkness, with such a secret in his heart. Even the tall pines and firs around them seemed to lean in curiously. And—were those eyes, staring out from behind the gooseberry bush?

Trent reminded himself not to think.

Higher, and higher still they climbed. The wild forest gave way to the wilder mountain side, and the gentle slope became rocky cliffs. Then it was cliffs on top of cliffs, and the air was thin, but full of danger. To slip or trip would be certain doom. The little town so far below, like a sleeping child, would not be able to save him if he fell. Or if he was *pushed*.

Trent shuddered.

Above the unlikely pair, clouds parted. In the cold night sky, the stars twinkled like they, too, were in on the secret. Was it written on his forehead, in his messy hair, in the way his hand never left his pocket?

The higher he went, the more he relied upon that box. Luckily for Trent, the town alchemist had never failed him—not once.

Trent and the witch reached a flat spot, a resting place where the trail gathered its breath before it turned and leapt up the rest of the mountain like a scared hart. The witch's face was cool and satisfied. She would not make them hike up any farther. The trial would take place here, where the massive boulders framed a view of the town, the constellations, and the peaks beyond painted in swathes of dark blue and black.

The witch said nothing—not yet.

Trent's tired fingers clutched tighter.

Is it time? Do I make my move first?

No—he had missed the moment. The witch turned, and so did he, so they stood together. Side by side, they looked up into the night. And they ignored the emptiness just beyond their feet.

But still, Trent could hardly catch his breath.

It was his own lack of breath that gave him the idea. *Surely,* he thought—because he'd forgotten he shouldn't be thinking—*surely, even witches like Saki get tired when scaling mountains, too.* And tiredness was a kind of weakness, wasn't it—and wasn't weakness exactly what he needed? A *vulnerability,* as the witch herself had so often said?

Trent didn't have as much knowledge as she did, but he did have some magic of his own. He shuffled the secret box out of his pocket and held it behind his back. Quickly, quietly, he conjured it into the right shape—the shape of a goblet.

A goblet which could hold thirst-quenching water after a strenuous hike.

Or, perhaps, something else.

Resolute and not thinking once more, Trent held the goblet out to the witch.

"Would you like a drink?" he asked.

Her white hair glinted like steel in the dark, and her eyes were just as sharp. "I have no need of it," she said, and her gaze slid over him before it slid away, back to the stars.

Oh boy, Trent worried. *This might be more serious than I imagined. She didn't really resent my comment about her knowledge of the stars that much, did she? What if she's thinking up a spell to get me eaten by Ursa Major, or Draco, or something even worse?*

He cleared his throat and acted with more immediacy. The goblet disappeared behind his back. In a flash, he had a new plan. A better plan? He couldn't be sure—he was back to not thinking.

"Here, then," he said, extending his hand once more. "How about a snack while you're stargazing? Something to sustain you."

The witch barely glanced at the fine little cake on the plate he'd conjured up. "No need for that, either," she said, her attention still focused up.

Focused, like someone silently brewing up a spell.

Trent dropped the magic box in his haste. He fell to his feet at once, and came back up after another hurried, whispered spell of his own. This time he held out a flower.

Well, it *looked* like a flower, anyway.

"Here," he said, a bit desperately. "Have you ever seen something like this up here before?"

The witch turned to look at him this time, her boots scraping on the rock. Her face, he thought, held traces of pity. She didn't even answer his question. She simply held him with her gaze.

On the plus side, though, she was no longer staring at the sky like she might call down a celestial bear or dragon.

"Trent," she began, in unsettlingly formal tones. "You know what you said was unforgivably rude. I only put up with it this long so we could come up here...where there are fewer witnesses."

Great, Trent thought. *This is it.*

Trent mumbled something, but even he wasn't sure what it was. He was staring at the ground. Surely, *somehow,* he could still make the plan work...

"...and I wanted to give you an opportunity to explain yourself," the witch was saying, in the tone of someone who knows exactly what explanation they require, and is giving you a chance to play along with their game.

But Trent was still staring at the ground. *Three,* he was thinking. *I tried three times already. But nothing worked...this is the last time I let them talk me into anything down at the tavern, that's for sure...*

"Trent," the witch sighed, at last, "what are you looking at?"

And without meaning to—without even seeing anything but the rock at his feet—Trent held out the palm-sized box.

It was his chance.

She *gave* him his chance?

This thought startled Trent out of his non-thinking spell. He lifted his head, finally. The witch held the little box in her hands. The conjuring tricks of before had faded, of course. Now, the box looked precisely like the rocks Trent had stared at underfoot.

But it held a secret. The rock beneath the witch's fingertips was hollow, a geode—the kind of ingenuity only an alchemist could think of. The witch's pale fingers sought a hinge—most geodes don't have them, but then, most geodes don't come from alchemists and magic-makers, do they? And so the witch opened the box, exactly as Trent had intended all along. The moment had come.

But there was nothing there.

Trent blinked. This, he realized, had *not* been part of the plan. *Am I falling? Did I trip? Did I drop it? Was my magic too much? Oh, what have I gotten myself into?*

"Trent," the witch said again. And when her voice didn't do the trick, a twinkling flash of light caught his attention.

She flourished her hand at him—her left hand, on which she now wore a diamond ring.

~ * ~

The stars, the mountain, the town, the night—it all swirled back into place, this time colored by Trent's relief.

"You know you can't trick me," Saki said, her voice full of amusement. "I know you too well. I was totally on to you this entire time."

Trent's knees buckled. Suddenly impervious to the cold, he sat on the nearest rock and wiped a hand over his face, pushing back his hair. "In that case," he said, when he finally found his voice, "why'd you have to wait until the very last minute rather than going along with it?"

"Come on," she said lightly, taking a seat beside him, leaning in close. "You're a witch yourself, and you still can't guess? How well do you really know your fiancé?"

Even as the words left her mouth, he understood. Trent laughed aloud. "Fourth time's the charm," he said, quoting his beloved partner in looking after Belville, Saki.

"Exactly." Saki grinned at him, her slim white bob shaking in the starlight as she nodded. He put his arm around her, and for a moment, silence reigned.

Saki admired her ring.

And, seeing this, Trent broke. "I'd like to see *you* try to propose to someone who's not only magic and really important to you, but also the greatest matchmaker Belville's ever seen," he muttered rebelliously, still shaking out the last of his nerves. Saki only chuckled. Even though she was so good at reading people, she could be modest, too, and she knew when less was actually more. Trent went on, "Can you believe we're really going to get married?"

"Yes," the witch answered, playing with the empty geode box. "Because I can see how hard we're both trying to get there. I think it's beautiful," she continued, after a moment. "*If*, of course, you can get past the goofy magic and excuses."

At her teasing, Trent coughed. "Well, I didn't know exactly what to do. You're so much better at this stuff than me. But I had to try."

"I know." Saki took his free hand, and her ring winked starlight at them both. "Just make sure that from now on, you try to work with me, rather than trying to trick me. Because you ought to know that *that* simply can't be done."

~ * ~ * ~

Elle Hartford adores cozy mysteries, fairy tales, and above all, learning new things. As a historian and educator, she believes in the value of stories as a mirror for complicated realities. She currently lives in New Jersey with a grumpy tortoise and a three-legged cat.

Find more stories of Trent and his friends at ellehartford.com. And while you're there, sign up for Elle's newsletter to get bonus material, behind-the-scenes sneak peeks, and terrible jokes!

Dwarves, Donks and Death

Brian MacDonald

Dwarves loved muscle cars. Rory imagined one of the little guys from Lord of the Rings bombing around in a sweet cherry red Mustang. How would they drive? Were they even tall enough to see over the dashboard? And how would they use the pedals?

And yet.

Would the magical world's greatest builders ignore cars? Would the masters of metalwork and gears just say, "Nah. We're short." And walk away singing "Hi Ho Hi Ho" to go dig in the dirt for jewels?

No.

Rory figured it was because people clearly had some racist Dwarf stuff in their heads. It wasn't really their fault. Walt Disney was bound to have done some damage to their psyches with his pro-elf leanings. If anyone wanted to, they could work on that though. Just get their hands on some good Norse stuff to read. Maybe a decent little retelling of "The Wager of the Gods"? Fun stuff about the forging of the magic boat, Sklidbladnir.

But, she digressed.

Dwarves loved muscle cars. And that was why Rory and her husband, Francis, were in Dunn's auto body in East Somerville chatting at the front desk about getting the muffler on the Beast fixed. Well, it was one of the reasons. Dunn's did great work. They could be a little pricey unless you knew how to haggle. Which she did. But the kid in the polo shirt was annoying her.

"Five hundred dollars for the muffler? That's way too much."

It's not just the muffler, Ma'am. We have to look at the whole exhaust system. Just from a quick look, I can tell the muffler was dragging quite a ways. That could have pulled things out of place," The counter-guy with his crisp blue polo shirt and well-trimmed haircut explained with a kind smile. He was good.

"It wasn't dragging very long. We taped it up as soon as we

noticed."

"I'm sure you did." He smiled. Then he turned to Francis with a sheepish smirk, "Somebody didn't notice immediately tho, huh, Sir? I mean, the scuff burns show it dragged a bit." Oh. Bad move.

"Dude." Francis crossed his arms and frowned. "She's talking to you. I'm just here to drive and deal with assholes."

Polo shirt didn't even flinch. Not bad.

"So. You were explaining to my beautiful wife why you wanna screw us on the work?"

"I was just saying that…" And, now he was stumbling.

"Oh. I heard ya." Francis pointed a thumb at Rory sitting next to him. "Pretty ladies like eye contact when you speak to them." He turned to wink and smirk at Rory. "Smart pretty ladies demand it. Right, hun?

Rory smiled at her husband. Francis was so sweet when he was aggressively protective. "I do like eye contact, love."

Polo turned to her, trying to take control back with a professional smile. It probably worked a lot with the ladies. Travis was pretty in an "I wear a polo shirt and have a sharp haircut, but I work at a garage and have tattoos so you know I'm safe-dirty fun" sort of way. Rory was not impressed.

"So. Ma'am, what I was saying was…"

"I think I need to speak to your manager."

"I'm sure that we can…"

"No? Fine." Rory picked up her oversized purse from the counter, threw the straps over her shoulder, and turned on her heel. "Francis, dear, it looks like we're going to Sullivan's."

"Oh good. They have better coffee. These guys just have shitty Keurig pods." Her husband lumbered two steps to the front door and held it open for her to walk through.

"Is there a problem Ma'am?" another lower voice rumbled from behind Rory. She turned slowly, making sure to keep her eyes at typical eye level. No need to tip off she was expecting a dwarf to be speaking to her.

It's a good thing she did too. Because the dwarf she saw wasn't a little one and he sure as hell wasn't small. Rory expected the well-groomed and plaited beard and long hair. She expected the broad shoulders. She expected the solid build and musculature. She did not expect him to be six inches taller than her five foot two.

That may be typical size (or small compared to her six-foot-five Francis) but to a dwarf that was gigantic.

"Mr. Dunn? I was just…" Polo stammered.

"It's no problem, Travis." Dunn soothed "I just came out to get you. The damn printer is doing that thing again. Can you pop back to the office and fix it for me?"

Travis of the polo shirt took off like he was being chased with an axe. Which he probably would be after Rory was done here. She almost felt bad for him.

"Travis is a good kid. Kinda green with the front desk, but he's fantastic with the computers." Dunn held up the reading glasses that hung around his neck from intricate golden granny chains, breathed on them, and rubbed them on his steel blue Dunn's auto body polo shirt. "And he can see where all the wires go for the printer. My old eyes here can't."

"I'm so glad you have a good use for him."

Dunn harrumphed knowingly.

"So, Ms…"

"Mrs. Murphy. Mrs. Rory Murphy, if you please." Rory placed her bag back on the front desk. "And this is my husband, Francis."

The hidden smirk under his beard changed slowly as his eyes sharpened a bit on Rory. They were iron black with tiny flecks of gold. Unusual for your typical Somervillian, but more common for a mountain dwarf of Germanic descent.

"You're not here for a muffler are you, Mrs. Murphy?"

"Oh, I'd like a muffler. The car sounds a fright right now." She tilted her head and smiled sweetly at him. "But what I'd really like to talk to you about is the Sixty-Seven Dodge Charger you have in the chop shop at the back of your garage. Avocado green. Burnt orange flames. Looks like a seventies kitchen vomited on a muscle car?"

His eyes hardened. The iron became coal.

"It belongs to…a…Mr. Davis…" Rory turned to Francis, "Thrombottle, I believe."

Francis squinted a second as if he needed to hand-sort the information in his brain. Which he honestly might have. "Thrombottle. Yeah." He chewed his lip thoughtfully. And then his eyes lit up. "Davis Thrombottle. Market analyst. In his thirties. Drinks scotch like he knows what he's buying but doesn't know peat from smoke. Kind of a prick but he didn't deserve to get scammed."

Dunn sat down on the stool at the desk and leaned on his elbows. "If I knew of anything like that, I'd say it was all done legally. With paperwork. Signatures." Dwarves knew contracts. They were raised practically from birth to read and understand the most subtle nuances in massive ledgers of paperwork.

"I'd expect nothing else, Mr. Duneyrr." Rory used his true name. His eyes hardened more. The coal became obsidian. "That said, I believe we can both agree the means by which you acquired the car in question was…unconventional? I mean, playing Fates for pink slips?"

For the unacquainted, Fates was a fairly simple but daunting game. Imagine if the Pokemon players of the nineties got interested in Magic. Possibly they started with Magic the Gathering and then wondered if it truly existed? Maybe some went looking into it and discovered they had an inclination towards using it. Then, they learned about the Tarot. They learned how to make predictions. And then? Two of them got competitive. The idiots decided to read their own fates with the cards. Competitively. And they made rules to gauge who had the best fate and the worst.

Fates was basically the bastard child of a coked-out hookup threesome between Magic the Gathering, Russian Roulette, and Tarot. Rory wasn't a fan.

"Mr. Thrombottle has requested that I return his car for him. He feels cheated."

"Cheated by fate?" Duneyrr sneered. "That would be his problem then, wouldn't it?"

"Oh absolutely. The Fates must have had a greater plan. That's why he sent me. They must want me to test your fate with my own."

The massive dwarf threw back his head with a thunderous laugh. His body shook so hard he almost fell off his stool. When he finished, he leaned forward, wiping tears from his eyes. "And what exactly do you intend to bet me?" He gave her a long, lewd stare. "You're cute enough, but I like my girls with a bit more…" He grabbed the air to form large breasts. "A bit more meat on them."

If Rory hadn't shot her husband a death glare, Francis would have hit him squarely in the face and then with anything in the room not nailed down. Instead, he loudly cracked his knuckles

"Francis, be a dear and give me the car keys?"

"Wha-huh? Sure..." He fished the keys out of his pocket and handed them to Rory. She immediately placed them on the counter.

"Nineteen Seventy-Five Caprice Classic. All original. Interior. Body. V-8 Engine." Rory smiled knowingly. She could hear the air leave Francis.

"And why would I want that piece of crap?" Duneyrr's eyes flicked in the direction of the car and snapped back. He was interested.

"You can't street race that Charger. It's worth too much. But the Caprice? Well, you can Donk race that can't you?"

Dwarves loved muscle cars. And they loved street racing. But, what they *really* loved was Donk racing. Late Seventies and Eighties era blocky cars. Big, shiny rectangles of pure metallic muscle. And the Caprice Classic was king in Donk racing.

Duneyrr stared daggers through her for a solid thirty seconds. Then he grabbed the keys and barked, "Travis! Get your ass in here. Bring the boys. We got a Donk to check." A minute later polo boy was back with a squad of dwarves in Dunn's garage coveralls. Dunn threw the keys to Travis. "I want it priced for work. You have five minutes."

"I'm going too." Francis followed. "You scratch my baby and I'll put you in the ground." He whistled merrily as he followed them.

A dwarf shot him a look and muttered, "Asshole."

"What? We don't whistle while we work? Too soon?" He winked at Rory and smirked.

Five minutes later, Duneyrr had his Tarot deck out on the desk. The cards were old, ornate pressed, and painted metal. French design, but clearly dwarven.

The rules were simple. Three cards for each player. Each player drew one card from wherever in the deck they wanted. Reshuffled. The other player drew. They repeated until both had three cards. Best fate won.

Duneyrr closed his eyes. He put his hand on the deck and fanned it out. Then, he tapped the one he wanted and flipped it.

The Emperor.

Good card.

Forceful.

Leader.

It fit.

Rory picked up the cards and shuffled them, running them through her hands to check for inconsistencies. The deck was marked. She knew that. And after she touched them, she knew how. They had barely noticeable dents on them, almost a braille for fingers that knew them. Which she didn't. Yet.

Rory fanned them out on the table, running her fingers over them slowly. He wanted to play with Magic? She could do that. Rory was a Druid. The last one in the world, as far as she knew. She and her husband were Murphy's Law Investigations. They helped people with things nobody could understand…monsters in the bathroom, murderous mermaids, and even a vampire clown in an amusement park. She handled the Magic. Francis handled the hitting things. Neither of them was fond of anyone using magic to hurt or exploit others.

She stared at the cards, letting her eyes unfocus. Slowly, the picture on the backs of the cards slid from a dwarf holding an axe and a hammer to a haze of colors. And then, as she waited, golden threads showed up in the haze. They led from the cards to all over the room in all directions. Some led behind her to the street. Others led to the garage. But. Many of them led to Duneyrr. Those were his choices. Every time he used a card it made a connection. And Rory could read connections. She was a Druid. It's what they did.

Rory saw all the connections from the cards. He had some favorites. But one? He stayed away from that one. He never touched it. She reached out, and ran her fingers over it, memorizing the dents. It was hers. Then Rory flipped it over.

Death.

The worst card.

Change.

Inevitability.

Duneyrr laughed. "Shit start, Mrs. Murphy. I hope you don't mind losing your car."

He reshuffled and pulled his next card.

The King of Pentacles.

Minor card.

The Money-maker.

Rory reshuffled. Pulled a card.

Death.

Again.

Her inevitable was near.

Her change was a failure.

Two death cards in a row was the worst pull in the game.

Almost nothing could save her.

The dwarf chuckled. Rory was having a horrible run of luck. He reshuffled and pulled a card.

The Magician.

Best card in the game.

The creator.

His Fate was to be a creator of wealth.

He would lead forcefully.

Damn good Fate.

"Tell me something, Mr. Duneyrr," Rory questioned as she reshuffled the cards one last time, "Are these cards truly magical?"

"In what way, Mrs. Murphy?" The dwarf leaned back, beaming a wicked smile.

"Well, do they actually give us the Fates? Because yours is rather lovely. And mine seems…worrisome."

"The cards have never lied to me." Duneyrr gave a condescending smirk-frown. "If you're worried about your last card, you can just give up. You'll lose the car, but hey at least you'll live."

"Hmm." Rory tilted her head and tapped her lips with a knuckle. "That is a decent deal. Perhaps you'll consider my counter proposal?

Rory pulled another card out of the deck. She did not flip it up this time.

She laid it face down on the desk and pushed it to Duneyrr.

"Tell you what. I'll give you one chance. You can give up right now and give me the Charger."

"Or?' Duneyrr leaned forward, staring hard at Rory. "What're you going to do?"

"Or I flip this card." Rory tapped the top of the card with her fingernail. It made a tiny metallic clinking noise.

"So what? Every card in that deck will give me the win," the Dwarf growled. "Hell. Most of them may kill you."

"All but one. If it's another Death card, *you* fail, right? That's the best hand in the game."

"Well…yeah…but…"

"And if the cards actually give fates, *you* would die, right?"

"I suppose…" The Dwarf leaned closer. He snuck glances at the card. Rory wasn't supposed to notice. She did.

"So. Give up or I flip the card." Rory crossed her arms and stepped back from the desk.

"Lady, you're nuts," Duneyrr growled. "I have a damn good hand. And yours sucks."

Rory said nothing.

"There's no way you could win."

Rory smiled calmly.

"DAMNIT!" Duneyrr pounded the table and brushed his cards to the floor. "Fine. You win. You crazy bitch!"

"Aww! You're so mad you mispronounced my title. Try it again. Witch. I prefer Druid, but I'll take Witch from people who aren't that bright."

"Shut up. You won. Show me the card."

Rory flipped the last card.

Death.

Three Deaths was the best hand in the game.

It trumped everything.

Her inevitable change was failure.

And it was his.

She was delivering his failure.

His jaw dropped. "You cheated." He mumbled accusingly.

"I'd say you played a game with clearly marked cards and couldn't win," Rory smirked. Maybe not her classiest move, but he didn't deserve class. "I'll take the Charger if you please."

He growled and reached for both sets of car keys.

"Oh no. Keep the Caprice here. We still need that muffler done. It would suck if everyone you cheated learned about those cards—now wouldn't it?"

~ * ~ * ~

Brian MacDonald writes in the earnest hope his words can bring joy and comfort like the books of his youth brought him. He has returned to writing after a twenty-plus-year hiatus filled with teaching Intensive Special Education in both private and public schools in Massachusetts. His years with his students have informed his worldview and taught him to take nothing for granted as well as to see the beauty in the chaos swirling in our minute-to-minute struggles in life. Brian's work often includes elements of fantasy and science fiction as well as humor and fisticuffs. Brian would like to state he disagrees with Conan. While he agrees crushing one's enemies and hearing the lamentation of their loved ones is indeed enjoyable, Brian is absolutely certain "Homemade Calzone" night at the MacDonald house with his wife, sons, and reruns of Leverage is the best thing in life.

Brian has been published in the House of Loki anthology, "Ghosts, Ghouls, and Ghastly Creatures." His characters, Francis and Rory will return in Knight Writing Press' soon-to-be-released anthology "Mermaidens."

Mike and His Three Lives

M. A. Lang

"God!"

"Yes? Mike? What do you want this time? Oh, Jesus!"

"Yes, Dad?"

"Check it out, it's this guy again!"

Mike picked himself up off the ground and shakily got to his feet. He hovered and wavered and promptly vomited—or he would have had he been alive. The feeling was still there, the queasy sensation of burning bile that came up from your stomach and hovered at the bottom of your throat until it exited your mouth.

"Eww, gross, Mike."

Mike turned and stumbled over something in the road. It was him, or what was left of him. Sure, he looked different than last time, when he found himself at the bottom of Blindside Bluff after a night of hard partying, or the time before that when he found himself underneath the ice of Lake Lastman, after an unfortunate attempt at ice fishing while stoned. This time, he got drunk and didn't see the car that was honking its horn. He didn't remember the brakes squealing or really feel the thud as he was thrown into the bushes.

He blinked at his body. He couldn't get used to it. It always hurt for the next week. *That old witch didn't tell me that was how it was going to be.*

"Mike, what did you do this time?" God hovered above the street to look disapprovingly at the scene.

"Really, Mike? Drunkenness?" God sighed. "At least you didn't take anybody out with you."

Mike glanced up. "Sorry, Big Guy."

"Last time I told you to be careful, remember?" He, The Big Guy, sighed. "You really are making it hard to plan a schedule. I'd prefer to meet people at their appointed time. I keep moving other people's appointments to make room for your unexpected appearances and departures. Mrs. McCarthy was supposed to die yesterday. Her family is going to think some miracle is occurring, what with her still hanging around."

Mike screwed up his features. "Sorry—it's just that I got these extra chances and all."

"Listen, Mike, do me a solid and not die for the next month or so, okay? The Pope is breathing down my neck about some stuff, and he always seems to take up so much of my time, right after all those crazy fundamentalists who continually misinterpret my message; I'm *always* cleaning up their mess."

"Okie dokie, Big Guy, I'll do my best!"

Mike's soul floated home. His body followed and he spent the next day and half on his couch nursing the biggest hangover the world had ever seen.

~ * ~

Mike pulled himself up to look at his reflection in the bathroom mirror. He grimaced. A third red dot burned its way into his forehead, right outside his hairline. A reminder of how many times and how many were left. *How many were left? What'd she say?* Mike's head pounded. Maybe he would remember. Coffee…where was it? It was one good thing about being alive.

Mike stood by his coffee maker, listening as it brewed its magic beans. Magic…as he stood there, he recalled the events that led him up to this rare moment of reflection. There was something important he needed to remember. Something he couldn't mess up this time. Someone, someone he needed to pay attention to. Maybe his teachers and parents were right all along. Had the time for personal responsibility finally come? He shuddered as all the details came back to the surface.

~ * ~

Coming back from Derek's that night, Mike hadn't expected to get lost on that dark road in the woods. He knew the way, but he'd smoked some funny stuff, and half of his brain was foggy. The other half was worried about running into a cop. He ended up making a wrong turn and his junky little car wedged itself firmly in a muddy, rutted track. Mike cursed and sweated as he tried to push his car out of the hole. His feet slipped and he was splattered with mud.

"Come on! Come on!" His car remained firmly stuck.

He barely remembered stepping back, stumbling, and then rolling down an embankment. He did unfortunately remember landing on a log and the sudden pain of a sharp, pointy stick thrusting itself into his chest. The next thing he remembered, after regretting his last choice of words, was the rough beams of small wooden hut.

"Ouch!" He had tried to get up, but a sharp pain in his chest made him quickly reverse course.

His eyes darted back and forth. "Is this Hell? I was expecting a lot more flames and demons."

"Nope, ain't heaven, either." A scratchy voice spoke from somewhere to his right.

"Purgatory, then?"

"You Catholic or something?"

"Err…no…"

A small, scrawny woman walked over. "Still Earth. Disappointed?"

"Um, no…oww…" Mike tried to get up again. "No, I'm quite relieved. I thought I'd died."

"You did."

"What?"

"That's what usually happens when sharp objects poke you in the heart. And I ain't talking metaphorically."

Mike took as deep a breath as he could manage and raised himself on his elbows. "Then how am I alive? Are you a doctor?"

"Yep! A *witch* doctor!" The old woman threw her head back and laughed uproariously at her own joke. She leveled her head and looked directly at Mike. "But seriously, I saved your life."

Mike rubbed his head. "Thank you. I'm so glad you found me." He glanced around awkwardly and rubbed the back of his neck. "Listen, I'm practically broke. You're the first doctor I've seen in years, but I can probably find some way to pay you."

The old woman waved him off. "Young man, think nothing of it."

"Seriously?"

The old woman moved closer to him, as if ready to divulge a

deep, dark secret. A strange glint of amusement danced in her eyes. "Young man, I'm sorry I did not have a chance to obtain your consent beforehand, but desperate times call for desperate measures! You were also dead, so there's that little fact. You see, I've been looking for an opportunity to irk some rather powerful people. People who always doubt me. It just so happens you came along at the right time!"

Mike's eyes widened in alarm. "Who are these people and how powerful are they?"

The old woman ticked off a list on her fingers. "God, that kid of his, Satan, the Grim Reaper..."

"What!" Mike rose higher on his elbows.

"Oh relax, boy!" The old witch pulled up a stool that suddenly appeared, sat, and composed her face into a look of utter thoughtfulness. She sighed, then continued. "You see, these, well, I guess we traditionally see them as men," she rolled her eyes, "these *fellows* just won't give me my due. You see, bringing people back from the dead is my specialty. This really grinds their gears, though." She laughed. "Men and their fragile egos! Oh, you should see them every time I meddle in their plans!"

"Wait—do they all talk to each other or something?"

"They're more like frenemies, really. Old Grimmy says he's just the messenger, though, makes his deliveries and lets the 'higher pay grades' sort out all the rest."

She sighed. "Anyway, I'm getting off track. You see, I'm always trying to convince them I would free up so much of their time if they had less newly dead people to deal with. Sure, they can take care of all the old people or those expecting or wanting the end to come. I tell them, 'Leave to me all those who still want a chance, or just do something dumb.'" She looked pointedly at Mike.

Mike drifted off. She slapped his face. "Boy, you still with me?"

"Huh?" Mike's thoughts returned. "Yes, yes, something about dead people."

"You! You, as a formerly dead person!"

Mike rallied once again. "I'm guessing God and his cronies don't like your ideas."

The old woman smirked. "You're not as dim as I thought. No! In fact, they do *not* like my plan. That damn glass ceiling is hard to break, you know. A little more power, that's all I ask. Is that such an unreasonable thing in exchange for making their jobs a bit easier?"

Mike shrugged.

"Anyway, at the last meeting…" She held up a hand when she saw Mike was about to interject. "There's no time for further explanations, boy! As I was saying, at the last meeting, I once again discussed my plan, and once again the top brass scoffed. Well, witches get things done. I wasn't going to wait for them anymore. Besides," she rubbed her hands with glee, "I knew I would derive endless amusement from their frustration. And guess what? I was right!"

"So…that's why you saved me? To annoy the higher ups?"

The old woman grabbed Mike's cheek. "Who's my smart boy! Yes! And to demonstrate my skills, of course! Perhaps one day, they will come to their senses and grant me what I am owed!" The old woman mumbled some words and sharply clapped her hands.

"Okay, boy, here's how this works! You can't die, okay, at least not for a while. You've got three more chances."

"Cats get nine lives."

"Cats are smaller and, well, not exactly simpler, just…smaller …use their brains for the important things in life. Now, boy, focus! Three—you've got three more chances to die and then live again. After that, well, I can only do so much, I'm sure God's friend ole' Pete has been told about you. I'd make sure you're ready to meet 'im when you mean to."

"You could put in a good word for me, though, right?"

"You're missing my point!" She sighed. "Anyway, each time you die, a small red dot will burn its way into your forehead. This will help you keep track of your brushes with death. *Don't* forget how many times you have! So, how many times do you have?"

"Three."

"Right, how many times?"

"Three."

~ * ~

Steam wafted up from a cup of coffee as Mike traced his fingers over the burns on his head.

"Crap!" He jumped up. He wasn't ready, not by half. Three times, three burns on his forehead. There would be no going back to beg that witch for more chances. Who knows what she would do? He'd possibly spend the rest of his life continually getting lost in the woods again and again in an endlessly repeating cycle. He paced around his apartment. *You're a damn fool, Mike. You've gotten more chances at life than most people will ever have, and you've blown them all.*

He sat down on his couch. His head pounded.

"Hey Mike, you look troubled, what's up?"

Mike looked toward the ceiling. "I've got a major headache, Big Guy."

"Eh…sorry to hear about that. I thought it would be a good design element, you know. Keep people on the path of moderation." He chuckled. "Guess it doesn't always work consistently."

Mike grunted.

"So, I just finished my weekly meeting, Mike, and I can't help but notice that you seem to have finished your free trial of immortality. I must say, you went through it remarkably quickly. What did you think of it?"

"That I shouldn't have told Derek about it."

"Hmm…so it's his fault?"

Mike winced as he jerked his head up. "Come on, Big Guy, save me the guilt trip. I just remembered I've burned through all my chances." He sighed. "Say, listen, I'm not quite, you know, ready. Think you can give me, say, several more decades? I don't think that witch lady is too keen on any more handouts."

"She's a tough customer, that one. She did seem pleased with herself though when she told us of your encounter." The Big Guy paused. "Maybe I don't give her enough credit—she seems to know her stuff."

"I wouldn't cross her," Mike said.

The Big Guy chuckled. "She does like to conjure up a frightful image for herself. Anyway, back to you—the remainder of your lifespan is now in your hands. Are you going to take better care of yourself?"

"Gonna stop hanging out with Derek."

~ * ~

Mike slowly drove down a rutted path. He carefully picked his way down a wooded hill, skirting around a log with a sharp stick covered in dried blood. He walked into the woods, searching back and forth for a dwelling of some sort. He eventually came upon an old powerhouse adjacent to an abandoned oil rig. Its roof had caved in. Mike peered in at the lone window. The interior contained an old stool, broken bits of rusted equipment, and a table.

"What the…could this be…how'd she…?" Mike's thoughts trailed off.

Mike walked around the woods for another half an hour, unsure of what exactly he was looking for, but saw nothing to indicate anyone had recently been living in the area. He walked back to his car, treading the same careful path back up the hill. He traced his fingers along his forehead. Three scabby bumps nested right outside his hairline.

~ * ~

His joints creaked and ached. Mike looked at his reflection in the mirror. He traced his fingers along his forehead. Three faded pink patches peeked through thin, wrinkled skin and marked off the area where his hairline had been. After brewing some coffee, he shuffled his way over to his recliner and slowly sat down. His old joints creaked again in protest. His head pounded.

"Hey Mike, you look tired. What's up?"

Mike looked toward the ceiling. "My old bones ache, Big Guy, but I guess I got what I wanted, been able to put some miles on them, after all."

"Well done, Mike. So, I just finished my weekly meeting. Your, er, 'savior' asked how you were doing."

"Yeah, I went looking for her a few times over the years. I could never find her, though. How is she?"

"Oh, fine."

"Hey, I've been wondering about something."

"Okay."

"That old woman said she wanted to be granted what she was owed. Did you guys ever give it to her?"

A deep chuckle gently rattled the pictures on the wall. "I know what story she sold you, but truth is, she has always had want she wants. As we discussed, she is an imposing character, who does not easily take 'no' for an answer. She has been doling out her gifts since, well, forever. Some people, just, er, use her gifts more quickly than others. There are a few people I've watched for *centuries*. Drives me nuts, but what are you going to do?"

"Umm…" Mike never got the chance to finish his thought.

"Hey, Mike, it's been good talking to you. Don't forget your appointment."

Mike closed his eyes.

"Ouch!" He got up. A bright light blinded him.

A small, scrawny woman walked over.

"Hey, I've been looking for you!"

"Hurry up, boy!" She slapped his face. She looked the same as she had all those years ago. "You have a one o'clock with Peter, and he does not appreciate tardiness!".

~ * ~ * ~

M. A. Lang lives in Western New York State. In addition to her writing, she is also a photographer, self-styled yogi, mandolinist, banjo picker, and liberal rabble-rouser. She has had writing published in *Baily's Beads, Literary Yard, Quail Bell Magazine, cc&d, Page & Spine, Zoetic Press, You & Me, Silent Spark Press,* and *Quarantales* (an anthology published by Impulsive Walrus Books). Her work is also found on the blogs of Clawfoot Press, Writers for Recovery, and Atlas Obscura. More of her writing can be found at https://giftfromthesea.wordpress.com/ and she can be reached via @MALangCreative1 on Twitter and by searching for M.A. Lang Creative on Facebook.

Book and Key

J. L. Royce

Thomas held up the worn, leather-bound volume. "I got the Bible here, but where's the dang *key*?"

The children crouched in the maid's stifling quarters high in the back of the plantation house. Eleanora, pawing through Cissy's small trunk, nodded. "That's good, keep looking—try, oh, her jewelry box."

"She's got no jewelry box, silly—she's a *servant*," he said.

"Well, she shouldn't have a *Bible* either." It was, after all, against the law to teach slaves to read and write. But the housemaid Cissy had learned her letters in the islands, before arriving in South Carolina.

The only ventilation in the windowless room was the transom above the closed door. Thomas wiped his forehead and turned to a rough-hewn cabinet in the corner. Finding it locked, he worked his penknife into the latch to lift the simple mechanism and open it.

"Got it!" he exclaimed, and held up a large iron key, a length of string tied to its bow.

"Quiet! Want them to hear you in the kitchen?"

"But what's this—she's got a picture of Poppa. Why keep it locked away?"

A daguerreotype sat on the top shelf of the crude cabinet, encircled by a wreath of dry flowers, candle stubs on either side. Below was a shallow clay dish, stained brownish-red and smelling of incense. Bundles of dried plants adorned it, unrecognizable symbols scrawled in charcoal around them.

Thomas stared at a lock of hair, tied on the frame with a bit of ribbon: two sorts, intermingled—fair and straight, like his father's, and curling umber, like...

"Come on, we don't have all day!"

Peering deeper, Thomas reached into the cabinet, withdrawing a pair of cloth bands. The photo tipped and clattered noisily to the floor.

"What did I say?" Eleanora hissed.

Picking up the picture, he hastily laid it face-down on the shelf.

"Here's what she tied up the Good Book with." He waved the frilly lace in the air.

"Don't touch those—they're *lady's* things!"

Eleanora grabbed the garters from Thomas and studied them—and her brother—with suspicion. She returned to the trunk, and with a cry shook out a delicate nightgown.

"What's that black thief doing with this! It's—it *was* Momma's." Their mother was three years gone, dead in childbirth along with their baby brother.

"Ugly old crow…"

"She ain't ugly," Thomas protested, "*or* old."

The slender Creole who folded their clothes and served them their meals often smiled with affection at the boy who so resembled his handsome father. She wasn't like Pearl, their wet nurse and nanny, always fussing about and chattering. Thomas liked the way Cissy walked, and the way she smelled when she bent close at table. She wasn't Momma, but…

"I think she may be sick, or tired," he said. Lately, the maid had seemed listless, not her cheerful self.

Eleanora ignored the comment, holding up a bone white, thin-waisted corset. "She's got no business wearing Momma's things…"

Reminded of his mother, Thomas felt the familiar pain.

He'd heard stories in town, from men who'd survived the battlefield. Soldiers returning maimed from the war might point at the neatly pinned, empty sleeve or pants leg and speak of their lingering pain, the ghostly ache of a missing limb, gone but *not* gone.

Thomas thought he understood that pain, like he was part of her, still.

"We're going to ask about Momma, yes?"

It was the only reason he'd told Eleanora. Why else reveal he'd been eavesdropping on the young maid in her room, except to share the Creole's use of the Book and key.

"We'll see how it goes with simple questions."

"How's this work, anyway?" he asked, fingering the corset.

Eleanora snatched it away. "It's nothing you need to be asking about!" She returned it and the other items to the trunk and closed it.

"Let's get started. What did you see, exactly, when Cissy did it?"

"She had the cabinet open—I couldn't see what was inside,

though—and she was sittin' in front of it, cross-legged, in Momma's nightshirt."

Thomas recalled the queer, candlelit scene: the Creole in gauzy fabric, hair a dark cloud about her head, swaying and murmuring insistently, eyes half-shut.

"I guess she was prayin' from the Good Book. Then she put the key inside, bound it up—she took those garters, off'n her legs…" He paused as that odd excitement returned.

"And?" Eleanora demanded.

"Uh, she read first," Thomas said. "But what passage do we use?"

She looked at the edge of the Bible and saw several indentations. One seemed especially deep, so she opened to a key-shaped impression where a passage had been marked in ink.

"Yes—this would do," she said.

Eleanora placed the black iron key into the depression, closing it, the bow and string emerging from the top.

"*I'll* bind it," she said, frowning at her brother.

Thomas watched her wrap a garter around the middle of the heavy volume. "She kept them on her legs—why'd she have 'em—"

"That's enough!" With some difficulty, Eleanora pulled the other garter around the Bible's length.

"It'll be heavy, so be strong and *don't* drop it," his sister warned, handing him one end of the looped string. "Or maybe I should tie it to the cabinet knob like you say Cissy did…"

"I won't drop it!" Thomas protested. He did not want to miss the chance to ask questions.

They sat down on the worn rag rug, cross-legged, as he had seen the Creole do. Together they lifted the Bible by the string. The key slipped slightly but held.

"Now recite the passage," Eleanora whispered.

"What? I don't remember…"

Eleanora rolled her eyes. Better versed in the Scriptures, she slowly intoned the Psalm, so Thomas could follow along.

"*Save me from all them that persecute me,*" Thomas stumbled along, "*and deliver me; lest he tear my soul like a lion…*"

By the time they'd finished, the book stopped turning.

"Now what do we do?" Thomas asked. "It's gettin' heavy…"

"We ask questions, of course, and it turns—or doesn't. Go

ahead—try an easy question."

Thomas considered, then said, "Am I gonna join the Army, and be a hero of the Confederacy, like Poppa?"

They stared expectantly, but nothing happened.

"That's a *no*," Eleanora declared. "Don't feel bad—you won't be old enough to join up for at least five years, and the Confederacy will *certainly* have won by then. My turn."

She took a slow breath, so eager and reluctant at the same time.

"Will I marry and have children?"

Thomas groaned, but to his surprise, the heavy book took a quarter turn before stopping.

"Well! *Yes*, I'd say," Eleanora declared.

"You *made* it move."

"Did not! Your turn."

Thomas frowned, wishing to ask about his mother, then brightened and spoke.

"My birthday—will Poppa come home for my birthday?"

The Bible swung strongly a full turn, then back half-way.

"That's a *yes*, ain't it?" Thomas asked. It had been several months since their father had left.

"I *guess* so," Eleanora replied, frowning. "Or maybe it's a *yes, but…*"

"But *what?*" he complained.

"I don't—" she began, then stopped, raising a finger. Her eyebrows went up.

Thomas heard it too: slow footsteps on the back staircase leading up from the scullery.

"Come on!" the girl whispered.

She pulled the garters from the Bible and thrust them back into the cabinet, closing it as quietly as she could. Thomas blew out the candle, and she placed it and the Bible back on top of the trunk.

Eleanora took her brother's hand and scuttered out of the room, roughly pulling him along, as a shadow crawled up the wall behind the narrow staircase. She pulled the door shut behind them, grimacing at the click.

"What do we do?" Thomas pleaded, crouching behind his sister. He glanced around the short hall: no other exit and the other few doors were all shut.

Cissy rounded the last steps and came face to face with them.

She stood blinking.

The caramel glow of her skin seemed washed out, and a sheen of sweat stained the scarf restraining her heavy hair.

"What—what you children doing here?" the servant mumbled, wiping her hands nervously on her white linen apron.

Eleanora put her fists on her slim hips. "I heard Aunt Luella say the silver looked *dull* last night. I thought you *might* like to know before you *catch* it."

The woman before them clutched the fabric of her apron, then released it. She ducked her head, with a slight bend of the knee.

"Thank you, Ma'am. I do appreciate it," she murmured.

Cissy noticed the towheaded boy and smiled. "Young Master, are you hidin' behind your sister's skirts?"

"Not *hidin'*, Cissy—just…standin' around."

Improvising, he tugged his sister's sleeve. "*Now* can we go back to playing?"

"Come along, then," Eleanora sighed, and walked haughtily past the Creole, tightly gripping her brother's hand.

Thomas slipped past Cissy, inhaling involuntarily and looking up. Her full lips were smiling at him, but her eyes were creased in pain. Before he could ask why Eleanora was pulling him down the stairs.

~ * ~

The afternoon weather was tropical. Surrounding the house, sweltering fields stretched to the horizon. Slaves labored still, with more long hours left before their day was done. And beyond that, the swampy wilderness remained, impenetrable and dangerous, as it had flourished for thousands of years.

On the riverside porch of the stately mansion, brother and sister relived their adventure. They relaxed in the cool draft from the river that had given *Belle Brise* its name. Eleanora idly moved to and fro in her rocker, contemplative. Thomas, however, remained agitated, rocking the old porch swing so violently his sister feared he would tear the chains right out of the porch's sky-blue ceiling.

"How many days until my birthday?" he wondered aloud.

Eleanora had been considering how to soften the blow. Their Father's company was in Virginia, seeing considerable action, and unlikely to be making any birthday visits.

"*Weeks*, not days." She considered. "Thirteen, or thereabouts, I think—now, we don't know quite what it was telling us—"

Eleanora broke off as a brawny figure sauntered around the corner. Jedidiah, the plantation driver, slowed as he noticed them. Powerful and ruthless, he inspired fear in the other slaves. Staring at them just long enough to make his opinion of the children clear, he slouched on.

When their father was barely a man, directing the clearing of swampland for more rice planting, Jed had stepped between his young Master and an alligator lurking in the fetid waters. It cost the slave several fingers but gained him the family's notice. Soon he became the Master's strong right-hand man, controlling the three score field slaves.

Eleanora had heard of Big Jed's cruelty in maintaining discipline from her aunts. She watched in disapproving silence until he rounded the back corner of the house and disappeared.

"I don't know *what* the Bible was saying when it moved both ways. Just what did you see when Cissy did it?"

Eleanora had never asked Thomas *why* he had been spying on the Creole servant in her quarters. She didn't want to embarrass him. Cissy was a slave, after all, and children were curious.

"Well, she was sittin' on the floor, like I said, wearin' nothing but that shift. She did some chanting, swaying, then settled down real still and asked it things—questions, but I couldn't understand her talk, it wasn't proper English."

"Questions, you say…young Master?"

The rumbling voice startled them into silence. Big Jed stepped back into sight, from where he had been listening. When neither child replied, he advanced on them, one booted foot on the lowest porch step. He continued in a low growl.

"Y'all know, with Master gone away to fight the Yankees, it falls on these shoulders to protect his kith and kin." He advanced another step, stretching his mangled left hand along the banister towards them.

"And not all threats come at ye as clear as a gun, or whip…"

"Cissy meant no harm," Thomas blurted. "She has his picture, with flowers."

"There you are!"

Before Eleanora could react, the screen door flew open, and

Cissy burst out of the parlor.

"What did you do—"

Cissy froze, eyes round, at the sight of Big Jed. His cruel smile was not a comforting sight.

"Here she is! I'm thinkin' you and I should go someplace and talk about just what you been doin'."

"No!" She turned on the children.

"Did you use the Book and key? What did you *see*?"

"*Hoodoo!*" Big Jed growled. He crossed the porch in one stride and gripped the Creole's wrist in his good hand. "Witch-woman!"

Eleanora stared at Cissy. "Hoodoo magic?" She paled. "You did something to Poppa?"

"Go on," Jed chuckled, "tell 'em what you been *doin'* to Poppa."

"No!" Cissy protested, "not *hoodoo*—*Obeah*—*good* magic, to *protect* him."

Her comely face twisted in a pained expression, not entirely due to Jed's grip on her arm.

"I love Ephraim," she sobbed, speaking the name no slave was permitted to use.

Big Jed laughed.

"And he loves you, oh my—*loves* the way you howl like a wildcat when he does ye! I heard the noises, last summer, from his sleepin' porch." The large head bobbed. "Oh, yes'm…"

With her free hand, Cissy slapped him, hard. Her captor sneered.

Struggling against Jed, she asked, "Quick—*what did it tell you?*"

"I'm to marry," Eleanora offered.

"And Poppa's comin' home, for my birthday!" Thomas declared.

Cissy started, shaking her head. "No!"

Jed twisted her wrist. "What you done, *witch?*"

"I've protected him, watched over him, with the Book and key, and things I learnt as a girl. Nature demands a balance—I've been sufferin' the consequences. But if I don't undo the damage…"

Big Jed grabbed her by the shoulders and shook her like a doll.

Cissy stared up into his cunning face. "Let me set things right," she pleaded. "Then I'll do anything you want…"

A slow smile spread across his face. "Oh, I know you will…"

Cissy sought to escape again. With one back-handed blow,

Jed sent her sprawling on the porch at the children's feet, where she lay, dazed.

He faced them.

"Young Mistress, you tell your Aunts that I caught this'un in a serious offense—threatening the Master of Belle Brise—and I'll deal with her like any other troublesome slave."

Bending down, he casually lifted the limp body and slung her over his shoulder.

"The Master may be needin' a new upstairs maid, to do him *service*."

He slouched off down the dusty road, towards the cluster of mean huts housing the field slaves, carrying the woman and softly whistling to himself.

~ * ~

Eleanora and Thomas rescued their father's picture from Cissy's room before another servant tossed her meager effects into a gunny sack and removed them. She found the key worked the lock of their father's bedroom, and troubled by this knowledge, left it there, on his desk.

They glimpsed Cissy from time to time, bent over in the rice fields, working the crop in the brutal heat, but she ignored them. Months later, as summer waned, they saw her rise and stretch, revealing a belly swollen with child. Expression dull, Cissy returned to her labor.

Thomas's birthday drew near. The adults prepared to celebrate the birthday of the Master's only son. Thomas persisted in his claim his father would join the festivities.

A week before the event, a rider approached, tall and uniformed, on a roan stallion. The appearance elicited curiosity and a buzz of activity. Thomas ran out to meet him but was disappointed to see it was not his father, but another Confederate officer.

The grim-faced man dismounted and let Thomas take his reins.

"Young man." The soldier acknowledged him with a nod, but his eyes held no pleasure at the sight, and he sought out the Master's sisters.

Then a keening cry of distress filled the hall of the splendid house. The officer returned, hat in hand, and gestured to the butler.

Thomas and Eleanora, standing nearby, listened.

"The field hospital did what they could for him, but he didn't wake up from his coma." Lieutenant Jenkins stood, uncomfortable dealing with civilians and their emotional lability.

"The hospital in Charleston is better," the officer continued, "but there's little they can do. I felt Ephraim should come home—perhaps the familiar sights and people…"

The elderly Negro arranged for a cart to fetch the Master of Belle Brise home.

~ * ~

It would be the night their childhood was snatched from Eleanora and Thomas.

Servants converted the front parlor into a sick room, windows darkened with heavy drapes. Eleanora reluctantly assumed the role of caregiver, organizing her father's place, his sisters too grief-stricken to cope. Dealing with the military, the doctors, and the servants, she realized their adult treatment of her was a burden, not a privilege.

The silent figure of the comatose man lying in the parlor overshadowed any thoughts of celebration for Thomas's birthday. Finding himself ignored by the adults and his preoccupied sister, it was a welcome diversion when he encountered Cissy one evening.

Thomas was wandering the grounds, chasing fireflies but with little enthusiasm, when he heard a whispered hiss from the bushes edging the lawn. Investigating, he found the slave crouched out of sight there.

"Why, Cissy—what are you doin'—"

Eyes wide and glowing in the twilight, she raised a long finger before her lips. "Quiet now, please, young Master!"

He sat cross-legged next to her, slapping at mosquitoes. Cissy smelled of the rice fields and her hard labor.

"Hullo." Thomas had never seen a pregnant woman up close. He gawped at Cissy's unwashed body, ungainly belly, and swollen breasts.

"Never wanted none of this to happen, you see," the Creole began. "And I don't know as I can make it right. But I mean to try."

"How?"

She gently reached out to touch Thomas's arm—nails cracked and rimed with dirt, skin rough from labor. She withdrew it immediately, looking abashed.

"Take me to Ephraim—so I can pray for him."

"I don't think you can come into the big house no more," Thomas warned.

Cissy's face grew determined. "What about his *child*?"

"'course *I* belong—"

She grabbed Thomas's hand and lay it where the dress stretched taut over her abdomen. The flesh felt hot through the threadbare garment, and hard as a melon. Embarrassed, he tried to tug free but she would not release him.

"This! This is *his*!" Tears glistening, Cissy released his hand and wrapped her arms around herself, sobbing.

Thomas thought of his father, of the little time they had spent together. The man was never unkind, but also never idle. After losing his wife, the plantation owner had thrown himself into managing his property. His sisters staged dances, brought the ladies of the county to present themselves; but he showed no interest in finding a new bride. The war, and his departure for Virginia, had put an end to the matter.

Now, Thomas realized, Cissy had been hovering nearby, kind to Thomas…kind to Father…

Thomas stood, chin outthrust. "You want to help him?"

Cissy nodded.

"Come around the back, by the root cellar, and wait at the top of the stairs. I'll fetch you when it's clear. Don't come out 'till I do!"

She clutched his hand. "Thank you…Thomas."

He departed for the side porch door, Cissy creeping behind, stealthily weaving from tree to tree in the twilit yard. Neither saw a figure hulking in the shadows behind the riverside gazebo, watching them, and following.

~ * ~

Eleanora was seated at her father's side, a small black missal opened. Her fair ringlets curled around her face as she bent over her prayer book, lips moving silently. Thomas thought her nearly asleep, her head drifting lower. Their old nanny, Pearl, sat in a corner of the parlor, preoccupied with darning some staff clothing.

"Oh! Thomas…" Eleanora blinked at her brother, startled

from her dozing. She ran a hand over her forehead, damp with perspiration from the oppressive warmth of the closed room. Pearl looked up and studied the boy, eyes narrowed. Having mostly raised the lad, she acknowledged him with a polite nod but suspicious gaze.

"Can't we open the windows?" Thomas complained.

"No!" Eleanora stood, peering down at their father. "The river vapors could do him a harm."

Thomas joined her. The man lay on his back, face gray and expressionless, eyes closed, breath a shallow whisper. The bandaged head no longer bled from the blow he had received on the battlefield. A falling shell had killed his beloved mount, throwing the officer to the ground where he was found stunned and unresponsive—as he remained.

Thomas examined his sister with a sidelong glance. "You been crying again, Ellie?"

His sister was momentarily speechless at his attentive concern.

"I suppose." She drew a kerchief from her sleeve and dabbed at her eyes in the mannered fashion of their aunts.

"And you been here mostly all day?"

She nodded.

"Why don't you take a rest? I can set with Father." He motioned for the missal. "I can practice my reading."

Eleanora gave him a wan smile. "I could use a rest." She looked inquiringly at the servant.

Pearl's face conveyed her pleased surprise at Thomas's gallant offer. "I ain't goin' nowhere, Miz. Young Master's right—time for you to take a rest. You'll need your strength for the coming days…"

With bowed head, Eleanora gathered her skirts and drifted away, mounting the broad staircase to her bedroom.

Pearl's expression grew wily, and Thomas gnawed his lip.

"Master Thomas." She nodded at the chair Eleanora had occupied. "You want to set next to the Master, don'tcha?"

The son made his way over to sit in the bedside chair.

Pearl returned to her needlework, leaving Thomas to fidget with the missal.

"Any time you're ready…" The look on her face made it clear she wondered what mischief had brought him here.

Fearing Cissy would lose her patience and burst in, he spoke. "Pearl…do you believe Father loves all his children? Like

God loves us all?"

Her gaze rose from her work as she reconsidered him. "Why of course your Papa loves y'all."

"And he'd want to *be* with his children, wouldn't he?"

Her expression softened. "This has been hard on you, hasn't it? Your Mama dyin', the Master goin' off to war. You're probably wonderin' what will happen to you and Miz Eleanora if Master was to remarry, or…"

Thomas made up his mind. Leaping up, he tossed the missal on the chair and strode off to the back of the house. Pearl shook her head in bemusement, though it was nothing like the surprise she felt when he returned, with the Creole in tow.

The former maid wore the stained homespun clothes of a field slave, in stark contrast to Pearl's tidy uniform.

"Master Thomas!" Pearl's voice was an urgent whisper. "You'll be gettin' poor Cissy in all kinds of trouble…"

The objection trailed off as Pearl's eyes traveled from Cissy's pregnant belly to the man lying in silence on the sickbed.

"No…" She shook her head. "I don't know what this girl been tellin' you—"

Cissy tore her gaze from the man on the bed and strode over to the old servant. "Get out, and don't say anything. You know what I can do…"

Wide-eyed, Pearl's nose wrinkled at the unwashed smell of hard labor. Heaving herself out of the chair, she clutched her work in one hand, fetching out a simple cross hanging around her neck.

Cissy laughed, though there was no humor in her voice. "I know the Good Book very well, and its uses."

She raised the sack she carried. "If you'll be on your way, I'll see what I can do for the Master, here." She sat at Ephraim's side and opened it.

Pearl bustled away, glaring back at the boy. "Get out, young Thomas! Go!"

But he remained, fascinated by the items Cissy withdrew: sprays of dried flowers and herbs, desiccated parts of animals, and crudely made candles of cloudy fat. Last she removed a knife, with a crudely carved wooden handle but long and honed to a sharp point, which Cissy laid upon her lap.

"What's all this for?"

Cissy arranged the items around the sick man, beckoning Thomas to light the candles from one of the slender tapers nearby. She caressed his father's cheek.

"Living in this house, I looked away from my people and their ways." Cissy seemed calm now, dark eyes beautiful in the candlelight. "Going into the fields, I returned to them, and their needs, and their ways. I practiced my Obeah—and learned much."

Thomas stood by her side, gazing at the pallid face on the pillow.

"Your father was kind, though you may not have reckoned it." Her arm came around Thomas's narrow shoulders. He ignored the odor of stale sweat as Cissy drew him into her embrace.

"There was no talkin' him out of volunteering, it being his 'duty' and all, though I pleaded, on my knees… I worked my Obeah to protect him—but the *loa*…"

"Is that what y'all do in the woods—pray to these *loa*?"

Cissy answered in a rush. "We call them to come visit us, and they *ride* us, tell us what they need, and we give it, to get their favors. Though I did *none* of that before, when I was in the house—just my prayers and questions. But now, for this…"

She studied Thomas. "What would you do, to see him made whole again? What wouldn't you give? I've asked myself that…"

Her callused finger tested the knife's honed edge. "There's a balance to be kept, and when the balance was lost, that fool Jed interfering, we lost the Master. But we can make things right if we restore the balance…"

"Like for like, that's what we must offer. My people have gone to summon the *loa*; he will be here to heal. And when he arrives—"

A figure detached itself from the shadows. Cissy lapsed into stunned silence, staring at this darkness carved from the darkness that ensnared the house and tried to swallow even this sick room.

"What?" The deep voice carried a note of amusement. "What will *he* do?"

It was Jed—not the man, but his form. He erupted in laughter.

"What? Afraid we'll be interrupted? They quake in their beds, the unbelievers."

Thomas knew the field boss mocked the *hoodoo* practitioners. And the boy sensed this was *not* the help Cissy had summoned.

The visitor stretched out his arms, turning them, admiring

the ripple of muscles.

"Magnificent, isn't it? This fool was spying on my people, in the woods, when their summons called to us. And I found him waiting like a lamb. Yes, a mighty warrior, this one could have been."

Cissy was wide-eyed. "You...are Kalfu? The Gatekeeper? I called for healing. Why—"

"The Crossroads is *mine*, and when the call came, *I* responded." The being sounded petulant. "Do you *deny* me, child?"

The figure drew near, face flushed with fiery blood beneath ebony skin.

"No, lord!"

Kalfu stepped over to the bedside. "This is the one under your protection, daughter?"

Cissy nodded, mute, the knife clutched in her hand.

"I call for payment! You have protected this unbeliever—" he gestured at the sickbed "—and now he must pay the price."

"I offer like for like," Cissy pleaded.

Kalfu stared at her with smoldering red eyes, then shifted its gaze to the towheaded lad, so similar to his father.

"*This* is the exchange?" he sneered. "Soul for soul? Your man is a warrior, washed in blood and pain, and has the souls of many on his hands. This boy is a mere *innocent*."

Cissy spoke boldly. "Do you accept this man's flesh and blood in payment, or do you *lie* to your faithful believers?"

The red eyes flashed in anger at her bold accusation. "You *dare*..."

Thomas tried to squirm out of Cissy's grasp, even biting her arm, but she maintained her hold as she pronounced, "Like for like!"

The *loa* relaxed, laughing at Thomas's struggles. "He has the father's spirit. Very well; flesh and blood of the man's seed will restore him. I declare it so!"

Cissy turned to the shocked boy, relaxing her grip.

"I am sorry; this world is not for me or mine."

She closed her eyes, squeezing out tears, and gripping the blade double-handed, plunged it into her belly.

"What?" thundered the *loa*. "*You* are not—"

"The baby!" Thomas cried. "She killed their baby!"

A groan emerged from his father, rising in volume, even as his body arched and his eyes fluttered open. Blinking, he struggled to rise.

The *loa* Kalfu laughed. "A clever bargain, daughter—though it cost you your life."

Seeing Cissy slumped by his side, bleeding, the Master of Belle Brise summoned the strength to climb off the bed and kneel by her side.

"*Mon bien-aimé,*" he whispered, removing the knife and embracing her.

Cissy's eyes fluttered open, face alight with the fleeting pleasure of seeing him restored. "Ephraim, my love…"

Then they closed, never to reopen.

"Master?" The rumbling voice was subservient. "What…"

Jed, restored, stumbled over to them.

"It's all *that* one's fault!" Thomas declared. He grabbed the knife from his father's weak grip, and stabbed the field boss, striking up beneath the ribs and piercing the heart.

Jed rocked and fell, the blood of tormented and tormenter mingling on the floor.

The household, freed of their enchantment, rushed in to find the Master of Belle Brise and his son, grieving over the body of a slave, in a scene of murderous revenge.

~ * ~ * ~

J. L. Royce is an author of science fiction, the macabre, and whatever else strikes him. He lives in the northern reaches of the American Midwest, exploring the wilderness without and within. His work appears in *Allegory, Fifth Di, Fireside, Ghostlight, Love Letters to Poe, Lovecraftiana, Mysterion, parABnormal, Sci Phi, Strange Aeon, Utopia, Wyldblood,* etc. He is a member of HWA and GLAHW. Some of his anthologized stories may be found at: www.jlroyce.com.

Isabella the Eldridge

Frank Montellano

I no longer bothered picking my steps carefully. There was no reason. My boots were stained beyond recognition. The entire place stunk to high heaven, me included, and no one else cared what they looked like.

This was the Bottom Market, a place of last resort populated by the lowest of the low, the dregs of society cast off from every other city. Anything could be found here, if one looked hard enough. Of course, anything found here would be broken, damaged beyond repair, and worthless.

That's exactly what I was looking for.

And yet, even in this lowliest of places, I had to go down-stream to find her. Amidst the waste, slop, and vile run-off, wrapped up in old rags, looking like nothing more than another pile of refuse. The Old Blind Woman. They say she gave up her sight to punish someone who wronged her. A last, desperate trick. What-ever the truth was, it was plain to see she was a witch with nothing left to lose.

I crouched down beside her. A rat screeched nearby, annoyed at my presence no doubt. "Megarith?"

The pile of rags shifted. Moved. Muffled, a coarse voice whispered, "She needed the babe. Powerful magic in a babe."

"What?" I asked.

"You were about to ask me what she needed the baby for. Or have we reached that part yet?" The Old Blind Woman yawned, stretched. "Dark magic." She unfolded her legs and lifted a rag off her head. I saw the stories were true. Deep scars surrounded empty sockets. What a mess. The patchy remains of her thick eyebrows danced like hairy warts as she grimaced and scrunched her face. "After being roasted in an oven, together with a few other savories, and then ground to powder and ashes, she would use the material in certain spells and potions." She sounded as if she recited a treasured family recipe for pot roast. "Or she could have wanted to transform the baby into something else." A wrinkled hand reached up and wiped the drool from the corner of her mouth.

I fell back on my butt, stunned.

The rat chittered and squeaked.

"Yes. He should know better. Never cheat a witch," she cackled. "They will make you rue the day and the night for the rest of your short, pitiful, life. Trust me, I should know."

"My name is Josef. I need your help," I said. "I don't have much—"

The witch cackled. "I don't want your money!" She gestured around her. "Does it look like I care about money?"

"Well, what can I offer you?"

"Come closer."

I inched forward, within reach of the witch's questing arms. The rat disappeared under her, and at least one lump moved around under her layers of rags.

Her arms found my shoulders as a rat peeked out from the folds of her hood. I slapped her hand away before it reached my face. Disappointed, the witch felt along my arms. She sniffed, though how she could smell anything besides the decay and rot around her I had no idea.

"Cursed. Yes." Her hands felt along my chest, then lower. "Her touch is wrapped around—" I slapped her hands away as they sought to probe between my legs. She cackled. "You asked what you could offer me." She cackled again, and I swore briefly as the rat seemed to whisper in her ear. "Which is dearer to you, young man, your eyes or your manhood?"

I let her seeking hands touch my face. I tried not to shake. "Will you help me?"

"Yes," she whispered, her fingers playing lightly across my green eyes. "Oh yes, I will help you."

~ * ~

That evening, Megarith bathed in a mixture of wilted skunk-weed and rancid flaxseed oil. She cut off her long, stringy hair and threw it into a fire along with all of her rags. She cried as she murdered three large rats, her familiars, killed without ceremony, without blessings or curses over their remains. "I know who has cursed your family. Do not speak her name in my presence or I will have taken these steps for naught."

I watched in silent disgust as she devoured her meal.

Megarith did not speak again until the last tail was gone. "She must not catch wind of me until it is too late. Any magic I use before the final battle will be subtle and limited, used only to hide from her. Do not expect anything more."

We rode north in my father's wagon. I swore when a wheel cracked and broke a day out from the village. The horses neighed and tried to rear against the weight of their harness.

"Hush!" Megarith warned me. She snapped three small bones in half and spat over crossed fingers. "I already told you! I can't stop her if she hears us coming."

"It's the curse!" I tried to gain control of the horses and myself. Too much had been lost already because of the witch and her damn curse.

"Do not draw attention to yourself."

I released the horses to find their way home and pushed the wagon off the trail. Megarith grunted and snorted like a pig in heat and soon enough a brace of boars obliterated any sign of our passage as they rummaged nearby.

We walked the rest of the way to my village, following the river instead of the road. Megarith flung handfuls of river water into the air and wove the fog thicker around us, adding to the morning fog already on the fields. Minor magic she told me, using the local water and only adding to what was already present.

Megarith pulled me into the cold water. "Empty your mind and think only of the river, let it carry your thoughts away. Think only of the water, of the mist." She held me there, with only my face above the surface. Above me, she scrunched her eye sockets closed and the scars on her forehead and cheeks reminded me of how the water ran at a low waterfall north of town my mother used to take me to as a child. I closed my eyes and let my mind empty. I felt the water carry away all my worries, all my desires, everything. When we crawled onto the bank, Megarith was the one who led the way. My mind was blank. We rolled in with the fog, over the low stone wall, between the homes, staying close to the river and out of the forest. "Good. She does not realize I am here. Stay away from the tree in the village center," Megarith whispered. "I can feel her presence there."

A wolf howl shocked me back into the present. My eyes

watered at the sight of my village. All the doors were locked and barred where they used to be open and inviting. Families cowered in their homes, fearful of strangers. Of anyone. Our cattle died in the pastures, the fields were overgrown and untended. The winter would be a hard one this year; if we lived that long. Our last chance was Megarith. The only witch who would help us. I know, because I had pleaded with them all.

Isabella the Eldridge had made our lives a living hell.

~ * ~

Howls and screams echoed through the village. I turned to Megarith, to tell her those torturous sounds came from Isabella's pet, a large gray wolf that transformed into a man on occasion, but her mutilated face was contorted in such pain and passion I held my breath.

"Gebhard von Blü—I shall not say his entire name." She spat on the ground. "I would curse him again! He is the one I gave up my eyes for, gave them to a taloned devil who promised to make Geb suffer like no other for all eternity. Every time he changes during his immortal existence, every time the curse manifests, it causes him unbearable pain and it is still not enough!"

We hid behind the church and watched as limbs twisted and the creature writhed into a man shape underneath the large oak at the village center.

The wolf-man's voice rang out. "Village people! My mistress commands me to repeat her claim every month until she is satisfied. Hear my message! You have betrayed Isabella the Eldridge. She has sheltered you all these years and yet you cheated her out of her due! This is your penance, to suffer my tooth and my claw until you make things right between you and your protector. She demands the next first-born male as part of the bargain she made with your elders. Until then, you are doomed by her curse for breaking your oaths! Your crops will suffer, your herds will suffer, you will suffer! You cannot hide under the cross forever!" He sniffed the air, his head turning to the left and right as if sensing a new scent, or perhaps an old one.

"We gave her the child! My child!" I heard my older sister scream from the front steps of the village church. "She took my baby!"

"Lies!" the wolf-man snarled. "No matter how many times said, a lie is still a lie! The child was marked! A first-born male of each generation was part of the price for your protection. One who knew not of the Redeemer!"

"We cannot do as she demands," my father said. "The witch asks too much! We cannot give her another child."

"You must, or I will kill you all! And then I will carve the unborn from your wooo—" His last word merged with a howl as the wolf-man twisted painfully and cavorted through his change. The tortured wolf loped off, headed north, over the stone bridge and through the forest back to his mistress.

~ * ~

I guided Megarith into the town hall, next to the church. Despite the sacrifices she had made, no matter what she had done to hide her powers, I feared what would happen if the witch stepped on hallowed ground, both to her and to our last bastion against Isabella.

I lit the sconces and waited for the villagers to join us. I glanced at the woodcuts on the walls. The panels told the history of our people. The two nearest scenes showed the caravan of wagons fleeing from the constant wars in our homeland and our first encounter with Isabella the Eldridge at the edge of her forest.

Megarith's fingers danced over the woodcut forms and figures while I explained. "My grandfather told me of how he hid under his mother's skirt when a haggard figure with long black hair screamed down from the sky on a broom. Yes, that's her up there. All thin, covered in browns and greens, she looked like a living extension of the forest portrayed underneath her, a nightmare made from muddy leaf and swaying stick is how he described her. If we only knew then how true that was! The witch demanded to know what they were doing in her lands. Lightning shot out of her fingertips, and she called the river to rage and rise in its banks. The elders pleaded with her. That's them on their hands and knees, begging for a safe place to call home. They swore mighty oaths on all they held dear to never cause harm by word or deed."

Villagers entered the hall. I heard the comforting sound of my grandfather's wooden leg tapping on the floor. He gets around pretty well, having lost the leg as a child when his home was raided in the old country. A few coughs and hacks told me Megarith still reeked despite our recent rinse in the river.

"The next panel shows Isa-I mean the witch-agreeing to give us sanctuary in exchange for a share of the year's bounty to be sent north to her by wagon at the end of each harvest. She raised her arms and spoke to the nearby trees. On her command, the giant oaks of her forest uprooted themselves and lumbered away, mighty giants swaying side to side as they left behind a pockmarked plain that became our fields. One tree, there in the middle, remained behind and became the center of our village. The rest of the trees still guard the borders of our village and crops today." A crowd of the remaining villagers surrounded us. I hugged my sister and father.

"I never knew where she settled after our fight," Megarith said, dropping her hands. "Oh yes, witches fight. We swear oaths of sisterhood and gather together in coven under our mother the moon, but we all desire to gather power to ourselves, taking it from whomever we can, including our own mothers, sisters, and yes, even our daughters." A shaky hand tapped her chin as she turned around.

The others gasped when they saw her face.

"Megarith the Blind is her name," I said, making the introductions. "Treat her well. She is the only witch who was willing to help us in our plight."

More woodcuts adorned the walls, but I had no desire to describe them. They showed the making of the stone bridge across the river, the annual caravan of tribute riding through the forest to Isabella's enchanted treehouse, and the spreading of the village to the southern fields and pastures. In all of them but the first, Isabella was portrayed as a shield against the world beyond the forest. Would the next woodcut show us feeding an innocent newborn to the witch in exchange for this protection?

"I am of the second generation to live under the aegis of the witch. My uncle was given over to her before I was born. The witch was in the village for his harvest birth, whether by coincidence or foresight is unknown, but she chewed through the cord herself and flew off with him. He has no Christian name. We were not told of this frightful requirement of our protection. That even the first male child of each generation, born during the harvest time, was to be given to her as tribute."

One of the elders cried out, "We did not know!"

"Can you stop her?" another asked. "Our village dies with us if you cannot."

Megarith caused a stir as she wandered among the gathering. She stopped near Rene and Judith, huddled together, the only women showing. They carried bundles of sadness instead of joy, yet they were our only hope to satisfy the witch's demands if Megarith could not help us.

"Girls," the witch whispered. Both women broke down crying in relief.

Megarith continued walking around. Her fingers drifted through the air, her eyeless sockets and mutilated features turned this way and that, searching for something. She stopped in front of Rachael, our pastor's sister and one of the most devout members of the church. "You."

Rachael stood there, brave. Her only sign of nervousness was the shaking hand that reached up and grasped the cross around her neck. "I cannot be pregnant. It is impossible."

Megarith's hands felt along Rachael's solid frame. "I have already been promised eyes. What are you willing to give up to end the curse?"

Unflinching under that eyeless interrogation, Rachel responded without hesitation. "Anything you ask."

Megarith shook her head. "Don't be too quick to answer. You may regret your choice once you hear the price. Come, walk with me a moment." The witch held out her arm and Rachael guided her to an empty corner of the hall.

Megarith whispered something in Rachael's ear.

"No!" Rachael cried out. "You cannot ask that of me!" The woman ran and found her brother, falling into his arms with a sob.

"Woman," Megarith said, "I do ask that of you, and I may yet demand more if I am to fool your so-called protector and break her curse. Others may need to step forward as well, if we are to succeed."

My grandfather clacked his wooden leg against the oak floorboards with an air of determination. "We will all do whatever is needed to save our beloved village. Have no fear, witch."

~ * ~

I drove the wagon north, as I had for many a year. Grandfather was beside me, keeping me company. Megarith was in the carriage cradling a swaddled piglet, along with Rachel, whose constant prayers mixed oddly with the squeals of the pig, making them sound almost like an infant's cries. The wagon's interior was covered with scrawls. Small poppets hung inside the doors on either side. Both were meant to blur or stop any seeing that Isabella might use to determine who rode the path to her forest home.

I wondered who God would listen to, Rachael or the pig? Would He hear either of them through the devious scrawls and protective dolls? I did not pray anymore. My faith had left me during my long hunt for another evil to help us against Isabella. The powers of good had failed us against the evil of the witch.

I was ten the first time I rode with the tribute north. My father sent me along with one of our largest hogs after the harvest was done and the weather grew too cold for crops to grow. My mother was sad to see Muddy go. She gave the hog more mind than me! But we knew it was for the best. With these gifts our families would stay safe. And I would be back in a week.

On that first ride I was with the animals in one of the last wagons, eager to see the home of the witch! Our protector! The wagons took us further into the ancient forest than I had ever been, but I was unafraid back then. I remember the excitement I felt in seeing the staves that marked the forest trail as the witch's path. Today I looked at those same markers with fevered apprehension. Would Isabella discover our intentions before we reached the treehouse?

We were a full day into the journey north when I caught a glimpse of swift movement on the left side of the path, the side of death and darkness. A gray blur dashed between the trees.

"We've got company!" I shouted. Isabella's wolf familiar came alongside of us and leapt ahead, blocking the path. He threw back his head and released a bone-chilling howl. I yanked back on the reins but there was no need. The horses came to an immediate halt.

The forest around us was as silent as death. From the carriage I heard Rachael praying, more frantic than before. Of the pig I heard nothing, but what sounded like the cries of a newborn rang through the air, desperate and needy.

My grandfather tapped his cane on the footboard. "Move aside! We have business with your mistress!"

The wolf paced back and forth in front of us. He snarled and growled but did not attack. Was Isabella looking through his eyes? Every moment with the wolf was a chance for our plan to fail!

My grandfather spoke, loud and clear. "We come on behalf of the village elders with the tribute. Mother and babe are in the carriage. Let us pass I say!"

I shook, unsure what to do. Megarith had talked at length with Rachel and my grandfather last night, but not me. I was just the driver she said. Saliva dripped from the wolf's mouth. One bite of those powerful jaws could easily rip out the throat from the horses or any of the human passengers.

My grandfather tapped his cane again. "Come! See for yourself if you don't believe me."

The wolf trotted around the wagon. He jumped up on the side of the carriage and looked inside before returning to the front of the wagon. Stretching, Gebhard went through the pain of shifting into human form. It felt odd knowing his name. He had always just been the witch's familiar.

"I smell a mother, a babe, and innocence," he said. The wolf-man smiled. "Ah, and an unblessed soul as well. Excellent! But something is amiss." The wolf-man breathed in, trying to sense what bothered him. "There is something else." The wolf-man approached the wagon, unafraid of me, my grandfather, or the contents of the carriage. Even in human form he could easily overpower us.

He swung open the carriage door.

"Gebhard von Blücher!" Megarith shouted. The horses reared in fear and neighed!

The wolf-man staggered back, so shocked at the unexpected sight of Megarith's damaged, eyeless face that hair sprouted across his back and talons burst from his fingertips.

Several things happened at once. The witch blew some powdery substance into the wolf-man's face, causing him to sneeze violently and convulse even more than he already was because of the transformation. At the same time, my grandfather rose up and jumped down on top of the flailing wolf-man, impaling him with his leg and his cane! Where the wood penetrated Gebhard's arm and leg, he stayed human. The rest of his body sprouted fur and continued changing into a wolf.

"Quickly!" Megarith urged my grandfather. "Stick your arm in his mouth! You must taste of his fangs and his blood before he dies!"

My grandfather, out of breath, removed one hand from his cane and reached down.

Gebhard growled, trapped in a state of half-man, half-wolf, and rolled, his muscular wolf jaws biting down on my grandfather's right shoulder.

I cried out and jumped down to join the fight.

"No!" Megarith shouted. "Get back and handle the horses! Your grandfather must do this on his own!"

I grabbed the harness and steadied the horses as my grandfather and the wolf-man tumbled in the leaves and debris on the forest floor. Blood covered them both. Gebhard was still trapped mid-change, some magic woven by Megarith. But his head was fully wolf. My grandfather's strikes blinded the wolf on one side already, but the wolf did not need to see to find his target.

As they slammed into a tree trunk, my grandfather raised his cane. Something extraordinary guided his hand and he stabbed the wolf-man through the heart. Gebhard yelped and life fled his mangled body.

But the fight had destroyed my grandfather as well. I could see the life ebbing from him, same as the wolf-man. My grandfather smacked his lips and tried to talk. Nothing came out but blood. Then he started to shake.

"Grandfather!" Right before my eyes, his wounds closed and white fur blossomed across his frail, shaking body. A few moments later, a three-legged white wolf sat there, wagging its tail weakly. I caught a glimpse of my grandfather in its eyes before it turned and limped away.

What was left of my grandfather disappeared into the forest.

Megarith climbed down from the carriage. "I told you others had to step forward if we are to succeed. Your grandfather volunteered. Someone had to take Gebhard's place so the witch would remain unaware. If she seeks her familiar, she will feel his presence." Megarith felt along the ground for the half-wolf, half-man corpse.

Rachael, the swaddled pig in her arms, poked her head out of the carriage and immediately threw up. I did not blame her. She closed the carriage door.

I did not hear what Megarith whispered to the wolf-man's remains, but it seemed tender and caring in some way. I believe she would have cried if she had the ability. She pulled my grandfather's cane out of the body. His wooden leg was still embedded. "Here," Megarith said, holding out the blood-covered cane. "He wanted you to have it. If you meet him again, stab him through the heart with this. It is enchanted. End his suffering."

I brushed away tears, wishing I had no eyes to cry with. Would I have the strength to kill my own grandfather? When would this curse end? What more would we have to do before this nightmare was over? I picked up a handful of leaves and wiped the cane clean of blood before helping Megarith back into the carriage.

"Yaw!" I called out to the horses, and we continued toward Isabella's enchanted treehouse.

~ * ~

After a further days' ride, we reached the large glade near the dark heart of the forest. I stared at the towering tree in the distance where Isabella the Eldridge lived. This glade was the only way to her enchanted treehouse. Driving the horses in a circle, I watched as the witch tree shifted along the forest canopy surrounding the glade, similar to how a rainbow moves with the view and stays out of reach.

I stopped the horses and opened the carriage door. Rachel handed me the pig and then stepped down from the carriage. She helped Megarith down while I looked around the glade.

"Josef. Rachael. Walk along either side of me. Tell me when her tree stops moving."

We walked in widening circles as Megarith worked her magic. Isabella's home kept pace, moving along the tree-covered horizon with us. We stopped and sat in the grass after a few hours.

"Okay, now what?"

"Josef, when you have come here before, how did you approach her tree?"

"The caravan master walked to the shaded end of the glade and held up an old staff gifted to the village at its founding. The trees would uproot and shuffle, opening the way to the witch's dwelling. At the end of the way was the witch tree."

"She is a tricky one. Where is the staff?"

"It's back at the village!" I threw up my hands in disgust. "We can't use it. She would know in an instant we were here. I thought you had a plan to sneak in!"

"I do!" Megarith insisted. "Rachael, guide me to the edge of the glade."

All four of us, including the pig, walked toward the trees. The enchanted treehouse danced along the horizon.

"Josef, get your grandfather's cane."

I went to the wagon and grabbed it. I handed it to Megarith, wondering what she wanted with such a precious reminder of my grandfather.

She ran her hands along its length, and I noticed runes lightly carved into the wood. Another piece of witchcraft. That must be what made the difference in the battle earlier. Megarith's fingers found some remaining hair and a bit of blood. "When you traveled here before, was Gebhard ever waiting for you in the glade?"

"Yes, sometimes in wolf form and sometimes in man form."

"And during those times, was the way to the treehouse already open?"

"Yes, I think it was, now that you mention it."

"Then your grandfather has one more bit of aid to give us. It's time for my last tricks." She nodded to Rachael and then slowly waved the cane around. The blind witch followed its pull and we followed her. As we walked, the pig cried, sounding just like a baby. My eyes watered and when I looked again, there was a baby boy in Rachael's arms, swaddled tight. More witchcraft!

Meg advanced toward the tree line and murmured while holding the cane above her head.

The trees danced out of our way.

~ * ~

The forest was eerily quiet as we followed the grassy path to the witch tree. I gazed up along its massive trunk, straining my neck and eyes to catch any sign of the witch. It was the largest tree I had ever seen and the sight of it never ceased to amaze me. The branches above shifted and moved with the wind and wildlife, at least I hoped that's what caused the limbs to creak and sway. I shivered at the notion this towering monstrosity of a tree could move on its own. It took an hour to walk around the tree. I know this because that is exactly what I did one year when I was younger and dumber while others placed the tribute under its spacious shade.

This was no time to go looking around though. We went straight for the huge break at the base of the trunk. No one from the village had ever been inside. I could vaguely make out wooden steps. There was no sign of Isabella anywhere.

A ragged wolf howl sounded off in the distance.

"She knows."

I scanned the skies. "There!" I pointed at the witch on her broom, barely the size of a swallow, before realizing it was only for my eyes. Megarith was blind and Rachael had settled on the grass, her gaze only for the package in her arms. She was crying, though I knew not why.

Another howl.

"Josef. When the witch arrives, present the babe to her. Whatever you do, do not look at Rachael or me. Do not lie, but you may be evasive. Above all, try to keep me out of your thoughts. Think back to the river and empty your mind." Megarith went and sat behind Rachael, their backs against each other. She looped a rope around them both and mirrored Rachael's form. She whispered her spells and Megarith disappeared behind Rachael.

I took a deep breath and faced the witch. I could not think of the peaceful river but hate for what happened to my grandfather filled my thoughts as I stood in the shade of the witch tree. Perhaps the witch would believe my hate for her was due to the curse. I did not care.

Isabella the Eldridge landed her broom on the grass some yards away.

~ * ~

As a child, I grew up at the edge of the forest, all smiles and wonder, feeling safe under the witch's watchful eye. The village spread on either side of the river, with a strong stone bridge connecting the two halves. My people, who only ever wanted to live in peace, put aside their weapons and tilled the virgin soil. A wagon was sent back toward the old country to share the news of a safe place to settle. My grandfather told me how lucky I was to be living in such blessed times. He kissed the cross that hung around his neck and tapped his wooden leg with his cane.

I never saw the witch closely as I learned my chores and duties. But I knew her name, everyone in the village knew her name. Isabella the Eldridge. Our protector. I kept a look out for her. The only warning I would get is when the birds on the pasture fence would take wing as she flew by. At those times I would run all pell-mell, hoping to catch a closer glimpse or at least follow where she was going before I reached the fence at the end of the field. On full moons it was easy to catch her silhouette as she kept an eye on her forest.

Now, Isabella the Eldridge stood in front of me. Tall, slim, barefoot, unnaturally young and more beautiful than I ever imagined. She wore a dark green robe, fastened about her waist with a vine. Straight black hair fell past her elbows. I wanted to hate her. I did hate her.

"Well, well," she said. "What do we have here?"

"I am Josef, from the village on the edge of your woods. I have come with the tribute, so you may lift the curse plaguing my people." I felt something rustling around my feet but my eyes would not leave the enchanting image before me.

The witch looked over at Rachael, sitting on the ground off to the side behind me. "Who is she?"

"Rachael, the pastor's sister. She spends her days in service to the church."

"Married?"

"No."

"Scandalous! And in her arms?"

I tried to keep my voice steady. "We call him Piglet. He has no Christian name yet."

At this, Isabella smiled. "Oh, and from such a steadfast member of the church! I understand why her thoughts are filled with prayers, so miserable yet willing to give the child up. He must be delightfully filled with sin." I could almost see her drool. "Bring him to me."

I felt myself obeying her command without a thought, but I fell, my feet held fast by vines thrusting up from the grass.

"Never mind," she said, smiling at my predicament. "I will get him myself."

I was able to turn enough to follow the witch as she headed toward Rachael. Of Megarith, there was no sign. Had she fled? But there was something unusual about Rachael. When I moved my head, she moved as well, dancing a bit like a rainbow. Megarith!

Isabella turned and stared at me. "What are you thinking

about?"

I bent down and tore at the vines. "I don't like to be tied up!" I said, clearing my mind of any other thoughts but freedom.

"Not so fast, Josef from the village. I know you were involved with my wolf. What did you do to him?"

"Nothing!" I spat.

"Well, no matter. He is on his way here now. I will ask him myself."

She turned back to Rachael, whose image danced away from her. "Ah, just like my tree. Such a simple trick will not stop me. But who is behind it?" The witch snapped her fingers and the illusion disappeared. Isabella reached down and took the bundle from Rachael's arms.

"Ah, finally! Young, innocent, and not promised to anyone yet! Do you know what magics I was able to perform with the last tribute? Do you have any idea what I can do with this one?"

"Lift the curse!"

"In time, in time." She spun around with the bundle in her arms.

I tried not to smile.

Isabella turned my way. "Why are you so happy?"

It was too late, the rope around Rachael was untied and Megarith appeared. Faintly, a trio of small spirits danced around her body.

"Hello Isabella."

~ * ~

On the day of my nephew's birth, screams rang out from my older sister's house. Her husband stood on the porch and defended their home with a pitchfork from the elders standing outside. I wondered what all the fuss was about. I assumed the baby had passed and would need buried, as this was a not uncommon occurrence but still a sad event. I rode toward the staging grounds to help with the rest of the loading for the trip north. The harvest was over, and it was near time to give Isabella her due. Father was on the road and stopped me. He said I was to take our wagon and depart before the caravan, loaded with a very special cargo.

I returned home and gathered a few supplies for the trip. What cargo couldn't wait? I wondered. My father arrived with his parents.

Grandmother cradled a bundle which coughed and cried. He was alive! My nephew was yet unnamed, as everyone had been busy bringing in the harvest. Curiosity raged in me as to why they deserved a personal meeting with the witch. It was not my place to ask though. Spare cloths, a jug of milk and a hollow cow horn joined the other supplies. Grandmother climbed into the wagon first, me and my grandfather on each side, and then the baby was handed up to her. I helped my grandfather in next, his remaining knee giving him some trouble. I wondered where my sister was, flashing back to earlier with her husband, the pitchfork, and the elders.

My sister wailed, but we left without any incident.

Near the bridge, the sound of my grandfather's cane tapping on the wagon got my attention. He asked for a short delay so they could relieve themselves before advancing into the forest. Daylight was quickly fading and I was eager to be off, but my grandparents brooked no argument. I pulled the wagon off to the side and assisted my grandparents in the slow process of getting down from the wagon. I stayed with the horse. A short while later, I heard the baby cry. My grandparents returned with my nephew and we continued on.

With only one wagon, the journey north was lonely and shrouded in a thick silence broken by occasional hungry wails. The rocking motion of the wagon kept the baby asleep for the most part. We slept on the trail in the wagon, safe from the dangers of the forest as long as we stayed on the path marked by the staves.

We reached the glade without incident. It was only then I realized I did not have the staff to open the final path to the witch tree! The caravan master had it!

"What's wrong?" my grandfather called out.

I got down and told him.

"Nothing to worry about. We are expected."

Sure enough, the witch's familiar entered the glade. The great gray wolf sniffed around the wagon and howled. Trees uprooted and moved aside. I guided the wagon toward the witch tree but the wolf blocked the trail. His growling made it clear only my grandmother and the babe were to proceed. The grown men had come as far as they were going to come on this trip. We gave my grandmother and nephew a hug. We watched as she walked down the tree-lined path to the witch tree. Above, Isabella appeared on the horizon. She came in fast, flying in a downward spiral and eventually landing somewhere in the upper branches of her home.

I wheeled the wagon around and left the glade on the way back to the village. Behind us, clouds gathered and thunder rumbled.

"Let's put some distance between us and the witch," my grandfather said, noting the darkening sky. There was a look in his eye. Something told me it would be wise to follow his advice.

"Hee-yaw!" I said and cracked the reins.

Lightning struck nearby and spooked the horse. I tried my best to control her, but she foamed at the mouth, eyes wild with fear. The rear wagon wheels fell off and we jumped. Lightning struck the horse dead! We ran along the path.

"You go on!" my grandfather told me as he limped as fast as he could.

I slowed and stayed by his side. "I'm not leaving you!"

The lightning struck the staves on either side. I pushed my grandfather off the path and followed behind him. We ran blindly, getting lost in the forest proper. It kept us alive. Rain and lightning fell all around but nothing more.

There was no doubt Isabella the Eldridge was furious. I did not know the cause but knew it had something to do with my nephew. We returned to the village, unsure of what we would find. It was too late though. Our fields were flooded, our homes destroyed. My people dead or scattered. Even the caravan wagons were overturned and emptied.

Bats flew overhead and into houses as I searched for survivors. I found my sister and others, but many of the elders were dead.

Howling somewhere nearby signaled the witch's familiar. He ran into our ruined village, snarling and growling around the oak at the village center, his fur matted from the rain. His eyes flashed yellow. The wolf growled and struggled through his change.

"Village people! Your tribute is not accepted!"

I looked at my grandfather. "You baptized the baby?"

"Your grandmother's idea."

Isabella screeched out of the sky. She came in on a lightning bolt and thunder blast, striking in the village center next to her familiar. We tried to cover our eyes, shield ourselves from her curses, but we were powerless. For too long we had lived under her protection. We were without defenses.

~ * ~

I covered Rachael's body with my own as the witch war waged around us. Even with our eyes closed, we were blinded by the constant lightning. We backed away. I had to drag Rachael, who was stunned or out of her mind. Although there was nothing I could do, I had to know who was winning.

Megarith was surrounded, attacked on all sides by vines from the ground. Isabella was batting at unseen things in the air around her. Lightning was still striking with frequency, though none seemed to be hitting Megarith. The witch tree was on fire. It looked like they were both losing.

I slapped Rachael, bringing her back to the present. We retreated down the path toward the glade and the wagon.

I turned back to see Isabella mount her broom and take to the sky. Smoke was heavy in the air from the fires.

I heard Megarith shout. "Scout! Fang! Fur! Bring her back down!"

I thought I couldn't get more scared, but then I saw the witch tree sway.

"Run!" I screamed. We ran.

The white wolf that used to be my grandfather ran past us toward the battle.

"Grandfather!"

He turned and growled, blocking the path exactly like Gebhard did when he stopped us as we dropped off my nephew and caused all this mess.

I took my grandfather's advice once again and ran away.

I reached the wagon first and helped Rachael into the carriage. We rode the witch path back to the village. The staves on either side of the trail had fallen over.

We do not know what happened between the witches, who won between Isabella the Eldridge and Megarith the Blind, but we have not seen either one since. The glade and the witch tree cannot be found.

The price was high to rid us of the curse. Grandfather's humanity, Rachael's eternal soul, and the final price has yet to be paid. I promised Megarith my eyes in return for her help, and if I learned anything from all this, it's that one should never cheat a witch. I will be here if she ever comes to collect her due.

~ * ~ * ~

Born in Southern California, **Frank Montellano** has worked (in no particular order) as a movie projectionist, media specialist, sailor, aircraft electrician, teacher, security guard, Kmart employee, vice-principal, and traveling stuffed animal salesman.

He possesses sea stories aplenty, having retired as a chief after 24 years in the U.S. Navy. He's been around the world and crossed the equator (on land and sea) several times during his naval career, serving two tours on the flight deck of the USS Abraham Lincoln. He also served as part of NATO forces in Afghanistan, as well as being deployed to various spots in Africa, Germany, Indonesia, Italy, Japan, South Korea, Spain, and the Middle East.

He has a bachelor's and master's degree, both in education. He loves to enrich young minds and has taught everything from 4-12 grade in California and Louisiana classrooms for over 20 years. His first day teaching in a classroom was on 9/11, although he did not take that as a sign of things to come.

He is married, living in Louisiana with his amazing wife, and has four children who fill him with pride and joy every single day. His hobbies include photography, writing, reading comic books and graphic novels, and eating his wife's cooking. His favorite authors include Roger Zelazny and Neil Gaiman. More information, stories, and photos can be found online on various social media sites.

hex

Clark Sodersten

The old wizard's eyes were sharp. They darted back and forth, covering every move Jaren made. Especially they watched his hands.

Watching to make sure Jaren didn't steal anything that was a part of him. A loose hair, flaked skin, even a bit of toenail or something his saliva had touched. He was very careful, this one. He never left his home, not for any reason. Everything was brought to him. He didn't want to be hexed. He didn't want anyone to have power over him. Yet he expected the villagers to give him that same power over them, trusting him to use it for good.

And they did, because they needed his help, needed it desperately. And because they knew him; he was not a native, but he'd been here for decades, and mostly he'd used his power for good.

Mostly.

The old man had reason for his caution. There were no other wizards in this town, but there were in other towns not so far away. He wanted nothing of his to fall into their hands, lest they be hired to curse him—for he was not without enemies, and he knew it. Like most wizards, he also hid his origins so no one could track down anything he might have left behind in his childhood.

Jaren bowed slightly at the door. There was a chair there, for visitors, with a small table before it, then two meters of open, scrubbed stone floor between the chair and the closest of the wizard's own furnishings. No one came any closer than the chair, and so far the wizard had not offered Jaren even that.

The wizard was an old man, no one knew how old. He'd been in the village sixty years, but he looked hardly older now than he had then. He must be well over a hundred, perhaps even two. Such things were possible for wizards, though the secrets of longevity were among those they wouldn't share with others. Little details like that were the reason wizards might be welcomed to a town; but were never loved.

Whatever his true age, he looked to be middle aged—but the middle age of a merchant, scholar, or gentleman, not the harsher middle age of a farmer or laborer. Like Jaren, who was young and strong still but with a face more pocked and lined and weathered than the wizard's. The wizard's hair, which he cut short, had gone gray, but his face was unlined and his brown eyes undimmed. He had strong, sharply etched features with an especially large nose and ears. He was generally thin, though there was a little flab to his face. His eyes were always slightly bloodshot, the whites a little yellowish.

He didn't look particularly muscular, but he didn't need muscle. His house was well defended. Jaren knew Hollie's brother Shen and his friends had tried to break in here at night, not long after she died. They'd never made it inside the house. Something they'd touched on the outside made them fall down with seizures, foaming at the mouth.

The wizard had said nothing when their kin had come to claim the bodies, and they'd said nothing to him.

Shen had been stupid. Nobody in this town made excuses for the stupid. Jaren had loved Hollie as much as any of her brothers had, maybe more, but he wasn't stupid enough to try and invade the house of a wizard.

"What do you want?" the wizard asked. His voice was rough, quavering slightly. It sounded older than he looked, and the tone suggested the wizard's mood was especially prickly today.

Jaren looked around the at walls and swallowed. There were books, bottles of liquids, vials of things that were hard to see but were probably hair or skin samples, carefully labeled but too far away for Jaren to read. Some larger glass containers, some containing what looked like slime, others small, live reptiles. It was said the slime was sometimes used by wizards to create their cures, and both that and the reptiles to make poisons—very likely whatever it was that killed Shen and his friends had been made inside some lizard the wizard had hexed.

Otherwise the room was furnished simply but well. People paid handsomely to escape death, and there were so many deadly diseases in these days after the fall. Sometimes a healer could be of use, but with the knowledge of the ancient doctors long gone, many times only a wizard's help would do. So the furnishings were well-made and comfortable; two large, deep armchairs, two walls lined with bookshelves, a metal-topped bench on which stood equipment both chemical and mechanical. Two doors leading out, one certainly to a rare, functioning indoor privy and the other probably to a kitchen. In one corner an old but solidly built bed. Probably the very bed where—but Jaren didn't want to think about that.

Jaren pulled out a small glass vial, an old one from the days before the fall, the kind the wizard himself used and very few people could make anymore. In it was a single gray hair.

The wizard's eyes focused on it briefly. "Whose is it, and why?" he asked.

"It is Hared's." Jaren looked at the wizard under lowered brows. "Hollie's father."

There was a long silence at the mention of the girl. The two men stared at each other, but neither made any remark about her. It was, as the ancient and nearly forgotten expression said, the elephant in the room.

Did the wizard know Jaren had loved Hollie? Jaren thought probably not. Certainly the old man would know who was married to whom and who was son of whom, after all these years in town. Jaren doubted he knew about relationships which hadn't yet been formalized. The wizard had so little contact with the villagers— business, and nothing else.

Jaren wasn't sure how much it would matter. It might make the wizard more suspicious, but he was already suspicious of everyone, all the time. The old man couldn't stop helping people just because he was suspicious of them; he needed the money and at least a modicum of goodwill to live in the town—and after what had happened to Hollie the goodwill needed shoring. Helping her father might be a way to do that.

Nobody had ever believed Hollie's attraction to the wizard had been natural, especially since it was well known he had samples from her after her wasting sickness of the year before. As for the disease that killed her a few months after their relationship—killed her so quickly, so suddenly no one would have had time to ask the wizard's help even had her parents still trusted him—only a handful believed *that* had been natural, and even those thought she had succumbed to grief and humiliation.

Certainly the girl who'd come out of the wizard's house that day hadn't been the Hollie Jaren knew. Not the Hollie who laughed easily, who found joy in even the simplest things, who always seemed to experience everything as if it was new to her. That Hollie was dead when she came out that door, even before the disease killed her body.

The wizard cleared his throat. "I have been given to understand Hared wishes no further congress with me, neither he nor his family. Why does he now send me this by way of another?"

Jaren licked his lips. Even talking to the wizard made him feel impure, and he had trouble controlling his anger long enough to say his piece. But he'd made a vow to help Hollie's father, and he took his vows seriously. "He didn't. I took it secretly. If he knew I'd brought it to you, he would surely curse me. But without your help, he will die. Will you refuse to help him, because he bears you a grudge? He won't pay you, but my father will. They have been friends from youth. You'll get your money."

"I bear no man any grudge, whatever they feel about me. I am willing to treat him, but with only a hair I can't know what disease he has. A saliva or mucous sample would have been better. And how will you administer the treatment to him, if he is unwilling?"

Jaren noted the wizard had still not asked him to sit, not even with a gesture. Jaren had no wish to, in any case. "I don't think the disease is a problem. It's the Hacking Disease; Mater says the symptoms are very clear. Do you need to know more than that to cure him?"

"If the symptoms are clear, that should be sufficient."

Jaren nodded. "As for giving it to him, I know that's a problem. I'd hoped you might be able to solve it. Is there no way to give a man a cure without him knowing it?"

The wizard's eyes left off their watch of Jaren's hands to dart to his face. "It is possible, but I will have to meditate on how it might be best done. Leave the sample, and return tomorrow. You know my usual terms?"

Jaren nodded. "I will bring half of the payment with me tomorrow."

The wizard gave a languid nod, his eyes half closed. Jaren bowed and left, careful to touch only the handle of the door as he closed it, and that with his sleeve over his hand. The vial remained on the small table where Jaren had left it.

~ * ~

The wizard whistled tunelessly as he put the hair into the gene sequencer. It was hard to whistle well with false teeth, but teeth were one of the few things he couldn't make last much beyond their normal span; the enamel couldn't be regenerated. Teeth were tough and lasted a long time if you took care of your gums, but not for two centuries.

Having fed in the sample, he let the sequencer do its work. He was going to have to find someplace to get it serviced soon, that and some of his other equipment. The sequencer's results weren't as reliable as they once were, and with every use there was a risk it would stop completely. Much of the memory had gone bad, so it was no longer possible to store the sequences of the villagers, he had to get a new sample every time to sequence for the working memory.

He'd been reluctant to go to a maintainer, though. Every century, even every decade, replacement parts and materials were getting harder to find and more expensive. Many of them couldn't be manufactured anymore, not since the collapse of industrial society. It was increasingly necessary to recycle or rework both parts and materials. No one fully understood how the equipment worked anymore. For both wizards and maintainers these were secrets jealously kept, handed down to only the must trusted, loyal, and able of apprentices, and no one person knew everything.

It wasn't just the cost of servicing that worried him, though. A prudent wizard kept enough saved by for the inevitable costs. What made him tired just to think of it; was the move. Maintainers were few and scattered. Finding one meant leaving his house. Once outside he was vulnerable. The human body was messy; it was always sloughing off pieces, especially hair and skin. No matter how careful you were you couldn't be sure something might not be left behind once you went outside, and then—there were always unscrupulous wizards who were willing to create diseases as well as cures, deadly diseases tailored to a specific person and their genetic code. He'd done it himself.

Once outside you were vulnerable. But only if they knew where you were or who you were. It would take time to get a sample to another wizard and have a disease designed, and by then he'd be long gone. Unfortunately, it meant, if he had maintenance done, he'd never be able to come back to this town. He'd have to take everything with him, find a new town that had no wizard, build up a new reputation. He was older than he looked, and the idea made him weary.

Still, it might be time to leave this town for other reasons. There was too much hostility after that last incident, trust was too much eroded. That business with Hared's daughter had been stupid, stupid, but it had been a long time since he'd had a woman, and he'd been smitten with her from the first time they'd brought her to him. Infatuated, stupidly infatuated.

Altogether it was time to move on, hard as that was. Get all his equipment gone over. But first he'd solve this Hared problem. He didn't want the man inciting people to attack him when he left his house; outside the protection of his walls people would be less afraid of him. And perhaps he would do a few more treatments after that one—he needed more money if he was to travel and then establish himself in a new place. A few more months, perhaps, and he would leave.

He moved over to the rest of his equipment and began to prepare it.

~ * ~

"Here is what you must do, if you don't wish him to realize you have administered the cure." The wizard had left on the table for Jaren not a vial or flask, but a bulb—Jaren had thought at first it was made of animal bladder, but when he picked it up he realized it was old-fashioned rubber, or perhaps some form of rubbery plastic. "Take care with it," the wizard said. "When you visit Hared, take off the small white stopper, leaving an opening. Then you need only squeeze the bulb. You need not be especially close to him, but you should be at least in the same room, and the hole should be pointed in the direction of his sickbed. The closer you are, the better, but I have made a—well, you wouldn't understand the technical term, but the cure should remain floating in the air for some time. There should be enough for at least some of it to reach him. Can you do that?"

"I can," Jaren said. He placed the bag with half of the payment on the table. "Thank you, sir. How soon should we expect improvement?"

"Since you are not dosing him directly it will not act as quickly as it otherwise would, but you should notice improvement within a few days. If he is not cured, or nearly so, in a week, come back to me—if possible, with a better sample."

Jaren nodded and left, careful as always not to touch anything he didn't have to.

He walked toward the town—the wizard lived a bit outside it—thinking. How much could they trust the wizard's actions? Jaren had spoken to people who had known this wizard for decades, and he had studied the man as well as he could. The wizard knew Hared was the center of those who spoke against him, and he was sure the wizard would want to get rid of that opposition.

Of course he might instead want to cure Hared, so Hollie's father would be beholden to him. But since the cure was to be secret the wizard couldn't be sure Jaren would ever tell Hared, or anyone else, where the cure had come from. On the other hand, if the cure killed Hared, the wizard could be certain Jaren would tell everyone about it, and opposition would harden. Killing Hared would be taking a risk.

So how would he act?

Jaren was almost sure—almost—that whatever was in the bulb would make Haren better at first, quite likely even be designed to cure the Hack. But there would be something else in there, something which would delay, incubate, then kill suddenly, after Haren appeared to be cured. That way Hared would be gone, but no one could be sure the wizard had done it.

Jaren was almost sure, but not quite. Who could enter the mind of a wizard?

He had to make up his mind what to do with the bulb.

~ * ~

A week later Jaren returned with another bag, the final payment. As he bowed at the doorway, he spoke. "Thank you, sir. Hared is up again, almost entirely cured. I thank you for putting aside your quarrels and helping him." He looked up at the wizard. "I am willing to tell him now of what you did for him. Would you wish me to?"

The wizard considered this. "I think perhaps not," he said at last. "It may do more harm than good."

Jaren nodded. His mind was made up. He moved the bag full of coin toward the table. The stopperless bulb he held beneath it, the opening pointed toward the wizard, but in such a way the old man could not see it. It was probably a needless precaution, the wizard wouldn't be afraid of it anyway since whatever hex was in it would have been designed only for Hared. But just in case he kept it hidden until the last moment.

Then he dropped the bulb, still facing the wizard, and dropped the weight of the bag of money atop it. The bag was heavy and sank nearly to the table, flattening the bulb. He couldn't see if anything came out of it. Whatever came out would in any case be invisible.

Jaren placed the stopper beside it. "Oh, I have returned your rubber bladder as well, in case you should need it for a similar case."

The wizard nodded. Jaren saw no trace of suspicion in his eyes, or at least no more than usual. "I thank you," the man said. "These are not so easy to find anymore."

Jaren left, careful of what he touched.

~ * ~

Hared sat at the table in his kitchen, his once-strong face haggard and sorrowful. He looked up as Jaren came in.

"It's done," Jaren said. "I don't think he suspected anything, and from what little I've found out about wizardry, it may not matter; depending on what he did, he may not be able to cure himself, even if he knows he's infected."

Hared nodded. He talked rarely these days, but this time he stood and squeezed Jaren's hand.

One gray hair. One single, solitary gray hair.

After the wizard had taken Hollie he'd made her bathe, scrub herself down completely. She'd told her father that before she died, though she'd been little willing to discuss the event. Then the wizard had cast her out of his house naked, humiliating her because he feared some trace of him might remain on her clothes.

There had been single gray hair still on her naked body, in a place where the wizard hadn't found it—Hollie's father hadn't wanted to tell Jaren where. One solitary hair to be the seed of the wizard's own destruction.

~ * ~

The wizard died two weeks later. Probably they wouldn't have known when it happened had they not been watching the house closely, waiting, hoping, uncertain. The old man might not have been infected, he might have been suspicious and applied a cure to himself, it might not have worked.

But the wizard was dead. Jaren had noticed the stillness in the house, He went in, careful to touch only the handle of the door, which was not barred.

The wizard lay on the floor, his teeth clenched and his body rigid, as if he had died in some final seizure. Jaren nodded to himself and went out. Then he laid wood all along the outside of the house and set fire to it. The scent of the smoke wafted into the village, and then Hared came, and Jaren's parents, and others in ones and twos and at last in families, to watch the house burn. The house and, had they but known it, irreplaceable equipment probably worth more than all else in the village put together.

The whole village came to watch the fire, silently, somberly. They could not have known what he and Hared had done, yet their presence felt like support. He watched with them, and thought of Hollie.

~ * ~ * ~

Clark Sodersten grew up in Hawaii but now lives in Spain, where he ended up after twenty years in the Air Force. He is now a stay-at-home father taking care of three kids, while his wife works full time to pay the bills. He writes stories when the kids go to school.

Paper Mage

Sandra Unerman

Ashie ran hard towards the Mage's house, one arm clamped to steady the satchel at her side. She was afraid of jostling her purchases, but she was too late to keep to a safer pace. Once inside the back door, she turned towards the kitchen, to check the packages before she delivered them. But she did not get the chance.

"Come here, girl," the Paper Mage called, from the door of his workroom.

Every time she left the house, Ashie found it harder to face him on her return. She could not expect to live long, if he realised what she was up to, even though her hopes of success were starvation thin. When she was with him, she could sink into the identity of a mere servant, anxious only to do his bidding. But when she arrived each morning or returned from an errand, she had to fight the desire to escape, to let down her friends and abandon the task she had undertaken. Now she walked into the room with her head bent, so the Mage could not see her face. She took out the tiny parcels for inspection: crushed insects, roots of woad, stone chips, and other ingredients to be compounded into paints. They seemed unharmed by her run.

"What took you so long?" the Mage asked.

It was a question Ashie did not want to answer. If she told any lies, he would find them out. "I stayed to talk to the old man's apprentices. I lost track of the time."

"Talk?" The Mage's legs stiffened, as he turned towards her. "What did you talk about?"

Ashie kept her glance down to his beautiful, embroidered boots. "Nothing much. Just friendly gossip." She had asked the lads about the preparations the Mage had ordered, in case there was anything in them to help her understand his achievements. But for all she had learned, he used nothing different from the ordinary.

"Gossip about what?"

Ashie shrugged. "What kind of work they do. Is their Master an easy one?"

"He'd never take you on, failed apprentice mage, failed apprentice scribe. Be glad of the work I give you and keep your mind on doing as you're told."

Twice Ashie had shown enough talent to be taken on as an apprentice, despite her childhood in poverty. Twice she had been thrown out by her master, because of her insistence on experiments and her peculiar, sideways methods. Since then, she had taught herself. She did not know what magic was within her capacity nowadays but not enough to withstand the Paper Mage, if he made up his mind to destroy her.

~ * ~

The reception room was not large, but it was richly decorated. The ceiling was painted with a pattern of golden lions, the windows covered by curtains embroidered with hunting scenes in gold and green. The walls were crammed with portraits, framed and unframed, some full length, others no more than a head and shoulders. They stared out, mostly men, young and old, with a few women scattered among them. They wore the kind of clothes Ashie had only seen as a passer-by in the street; when grand folk walked in parade. Even if the Paper Mage had not shown them off as his best work, she would have known they had all been painted by the same person. Their expressions all bore the same traces of puzzlement.

The Mage took his place at a lectern carved with more lions and pointed Ashie to a small, plain desk. "Stand there and write down the words you hear spoken. And say nothing." This was what he needed her for. Household servants he could replace easily enough but no trained scribes would risk the dangers of his service these days. Only Ashie, who could no longer survive on her own, or so she had made him believe.

The first visitor was a burly man in a fur trimmed coat. He took off his hat in an elaborate bow to the Mage. "Master Baugrain, what an honour to see you," he said.

The Mage merely nodded in acknowledgement. "Lord Milbone, I've heard about your brother. I can understand why you are interested in a portrait of him."

"Excellent." Lord Milbone seemed relieved to be taken so quickly to the point.

"When can I meet him?"

That made the man uncomfortable. "Is that necessary? You've often seen him about."

"Seeing is not looking. I need a good stare at him, not long but thorough."

From where she was placed, Ashie had her chance to stare at the Mage's side view, without attracting his attention. He did not trouble with fancy clothes, apart from the boots. His plain grey jacket and trousers showed off his height and sharp, lean face. His thick-lashed eyes never seemed to blink.

Lord Milbone fidgeted. "I'm not sure what I can arrange. Perhaps you can attend some of the civic events next months, where he's bound to turn up."

"Or not, at any one of them. I have no time to waste on that kind of chance."

"But—" Lord Milbone said. "But the portrait must be a surprise. How can I invite him to my house, after what he did, even if I don't tell him you're coming?"

Ashie wrote it all down, as she had been instructed. Both men would have a record of the words they had spoken and none of the implications. Everyone in the city knew what happened, when the Paper Mage took a commission, usually at an enormous fee. As the portrait was painted, the subject grew feeble and dizzy. When it was finished, the spirit drained out of the person to leave nothing but a shrunken body. A body that lay in a trance for years, until it crumbled away.

Nobody knew the secret of the Mage's art. Nobody ever accused him outright, because they were afraid he might turn his attentions to them. People paid great fees to other mages to defend them or to try to undo the spells, without any success. Those who had tried to assassinate him, in the early years of his success, had died themselves instead. So, there was no purpose in all the coyness that Ashie could understand. Maybe it allowed the Mage and his clients to avoid facing the truth of their deeds, even in their own minds.

"You must exercise more ingenuity than that," the Mage said. "Find an excuse for an invitation and send me word. And make it soon. I am eager to earn my fee."

After Lord Milbone had gone, Ashie had no time to tidy her desk. A woman strode into the room, chased by a worried servant, who failed to bar her way.

"What have you done to my son, you abomination?" The woman planted herself in front of the Mage, who bowed, as if she had paid him a compliment.

"Good morning, Lady Glasspin." He shooed away the servant. "I did not expect to see you today.'

"Is his picture here?" The lady's clothes were not as elaborate as Lord Milbone's but just as grand, dark blue brocade and a velvet hat. Her face was shiny with sweat and she glared at the Mage, as though unafraid of his scrutiny.

"One of my best efforts," he said. "Do you wish me to have it framed?" He walked over to a small picture pinned to the wall. It showed the back of a young man and his face, as he looked over his shoulder; a bright-eyed lad with a curly smile.

"I wish you to restore him to me." Lady Glasspin lowered her voice. "I don't care how much the Rufflin Clan have paid you, I'll double it."

"My dear lady." The Mage returned to his lectern and folded his hands across the top.

"Whatever it takes. Another portrait, with more costly paints and expensive cantrips? I'll pay you to undertake 'em."

"You misunderstand the nature of my art." The Mage did not smile but there was satisfaction in his voice. "Commission another master to make such a picture, if you wish."

"That's no good," Lady Glasspin said. "You know how often that's been tried and the money wasted. Or spells uttered to take the power out of the pictures here and nothing changes. You're the only one who can help, or I wouldn't have come to you."

"I'm flattered. But the portraits are the pride of my heart. I would not change one touch for a dragon's hoard of treasure."

"I don't care about the picture." Lady Glasspin's hands clawed at her sides. "You are full of cunning and power, the greatest mage in the city. Accept a commission to bring my son back, however you choose. I'll swear it has nothing to do with the picture, if you wish."

"That would certainly be a novel commission. But fruitless. And think of the damage to my reputation."

"Think what an enemy I will become, if you refuse me," Lady Glasspin said and now the Mage did smile.

"Then I would have to become an enemy of yours. How

would that help your son?"

The lady's shoulders sagged and her head dropped. Ashie thought she would fall but slowly, she straightened up. "I'll find a way to change your mind," she said and marched out.

The Mage turned at once to scowl at Ashie. "What have you written?"

"What was said, just as you told me."

"Not her. I never told you to write her down." He strode over to her. "Let me see."

Ashie was surprised into a full stare at his face, as she picked up the papers to give to him. He did not seem to notice. He ran his glance down her scribbles, while she took her chance to study him. He looked younger than he sounded, his skin smooth and rosy, his teeth white and full between his parted lips. Small creases, fine as paper cuts, showed round his heavy-lidded eyes and full mouth.

He did not take long to read Ashie's notes. He had trained as a scribe himself and must remember the shorthand well. She dropped her gaze at once when he glanced up. "You're not quite a fool," he said. "Nevertheless—" He tore the page where she had moved from her first report to the second and handed her the top part, along with the previous pages. "You may transcribe that into the day book. I'll dispose of the rest myself."

~ * ~

Three large portfolios sat on a table in the workroom, each bound in black leather filmed over with grey mould. Ashie could not tell which had been opened most recently. She fingered the laces that held them shut and sensed the spells twisted into them. She reckoned she could sneak past those but not without leaving traces.

"What are you doing?" The Mage walked into the room and stood uncomfortably close as she turned round. He must have left his dinner early.

"Stretching my hands," she said. "They get cramped with writing in the day book."

The Mage did not back away. "You could do that without moving from your place. What are you doing over here?"

Ashie had no space to step backwards. "This leather's soft and cold. It soothes my skin."

"I never gave you leave to wander round in here. I never gave you leave to touch my books. Don't look at them."

"Why not?" She knew that was a mistake as soon as she uttered the words. She risked a glance up at the Mage's face and that too was a mistake. The anger she expected to see was held back by a sharp attention, a devouring alertness, as though to spread out her soul for examination. He had never touched her, yet. But he was the stronger in body as well as in magecraft. If he seized hold of her, she had no weapon to use against him.

"Don't question me," he said, and she dropped her gaze to his feet once more.

"No, sir," she said, and he sniffed.

"Go back to your place and stay there."

~ * ~

Late that evening, Ashie returned to the derelict hut she called home. She lived alone but she was not surprised to see a light inside. Her friend Josh squatted in there, with a small lantern.

"At last!" He sprang to his feet. "What kept you so late?"

"Work." Ashie's back ached and her hands were stiff. She folded herself down onto the bundle of sacks she used as a bed. "You shouldn't have waited."

"I was worried." Josh hunkered down opposite her. "What has he done to you?"

"Nothing yet. But I can't think straight when I'm with him."

"Please, Ashie, be careful." Josh's scowl loomed through the lamplight. "Remember Pogo."

"What else am I doing there?" Ashie thought about unwrapping the threadbare shawls which served her as a coat and decided she was too tired to bother.

"Have you found his picture?" This was what Josh had come to ask.

"The Mage doesn't leave any of the finished portraits lying about. The ones that aren't on the walls are shut into big books, where I can't get at them."

"It must be there." Josh rocked backwards and forwards. "He's limp on his bed like a rag puppet. Nobody else could have done that to him."

"What would you do with the picture, if I could sneak it out of there?"

"Whatever you say. I came to you because of the things you've done for us, after the Big'uns said you were no good."

"I am no good, for doing things their way." Since her former masters had thrown her out, Ashie had earned a scant living from those who could not afford the services of a proper mage. Not that they paid her in coin, mostly, but they shared food, scavenged clothes and anything else they could manage. The Paper Mage ought to be out of her reach, by all common sense. But she had been unable to resist the challenge, when Josh asked for her help, for the love of meddling, as much as for friendship's sake. She had known Pogo for years, a small meek lad who had been stricken down, when he offended the Mage. "If I touch Pogo's picture, the Mage will know it."

"Isn't there anything else you've found out?" Josh asked. "Some weakness we could betray to another mage or a clue to help them undo his spells?"

"The other mages are too frightened to try." Ashie had seen that when they came to visit.

"I don't want you destroyed as well, Ashie," Josh said. "Maybe you should forget about the picture and leave the Mage now."

"Too late," Ashie said. If she stayed with the Mage, anything she did might make him more doubtful still about her. But if she left him, his suspicions would blaze up immediately. "I need to have a go at him before he has a go at me."

"What can you do?"

"I don't know yet."

Josh opened his mouth and she yawned at him. "Go away, Josh. I'm too tired to argue."

He went still for a moment and then leaned over to push a small flask into her hands. "I've brought you a nip of firewater. Don't try anything, before we talk again."

When he was gone, Ashie sniffed at the flask but did not drink. "I can't wait any longer," she whispered, although nobody was within earshot. Another day in the Mage's house and she would give in to despair, like everyone else around him. And more talk would achieve nothing, except perhaps to draw Josh into danger as well.

Pogo's offence had been to admire one of the portraits so much he spoke to it constantly. Ashie had hoped to learn more by her own observations and maybe she had, but the Mage was too wary to give much away, even to the servants he despised. "Not the paints nor the brushes but the looking. And he utters no spell aloud, so I'll have to make up my own." She sat upright. "Dawn tomorrow," she said, tucked the flask away and lay down to sleep.'

~ * ~

The morning was a bright one. Ashie sat at the door of her hut, with a pot of ink she had made herself and a bunch of crow quills. The Mage's portraits were mostly done on fine parchment, despite his name, but she had only a grubby blank of cheap paper, scavenged from the back of a grocer's shop. She was fasting, which was her custom before any difficult enterprise.

"I know you," she muttered, her eyes half-closed. "From the greasy curls tucked into your hat to the points of your boots, which rub blisters into your toes." Pictures were Baugrain's medium, but words were hers. She wrote each down with care. "I know the twitch of your shoulders when you are impatient and the tuck to your lips when you feel smug."

The physical description came first, in the most precise words she could find. Her hand ached but her mind remained fresh and clear. Then she began on what she had learned of his spirit. "You must have hated the first person you drained into a picture. Were you their apprentice? Was that who taught you to hate everyone you cannot bully?"

This was harder. Ashie felt every word drag on her own spirit, until she had to fight to persist, to describe all her observations of the Mage's behaviour. "Eyes on guard," she wrote. "So fierce that whatever they once protected has withered into nothing."

By now, she could hardly shape the letters on the paper, and she still had the turn in the spell to accomplish. "No need for guards in here," she wrote, as painfully as if she pushed a cart uphill. When she used up all the space on both sides of her paper, she turned the page on its side, to go crossways over the lines she had already put down. "Nobody to annoy you or challenge your powers. Let yourself flow into the words and you'll never have to prove your superiority again."

She felt the change, the shift that passed through her hands, although it was not one she could touch or see. But she did not know whether she had done enough. As she struggled for more words, the pen dropped from her fingers and she fainted.

~ * ~

"Ashie! Ashie, wake up." That was Josh's voice and Josh's hard grip on her ankle. Ashie's head hurt but she knew who she was and where she was, as soon as she opened her eyes. She sat up and Josh let go. "I told you to wait," he said.

She could not spare him any attention yet. "Hold on," she said and scrambled to the nearest patch of weeds. There she vomited, although she had little in her gut to throw up, wiped her mouth and went back to sit opposite Josh. He offered her the firewater, which she pushed away. "Water," she croaked and sipped at the cup her fetched for her.

"What have you done?" he asked, both excited and horrified.

"Not sure. What's happened?" Ashie drank more water and began to feel alive.

"The Paper Mage is sprawled flat, knocked out like Pogo and the others. Bennie in his kitchen told old Puffbill, who told me."

"That's a start." Ashie felt relief rather than triumph. "What's happened to the people he painted?"

"Nothing." Josh grimaced. "They're the same as before."

She was not surprised. "More to do, then." She wished she did not feel so washed out. "We'll have to search for Pogo's picture, before we can try the next thing."

"They won't let us in." Josh hunched forward. "I was afraid you were inside, so I went there first. The house is full of mages from all over the city and grand folk desperate to get at the portraits. I sneaked in long enough to hear them row over what to do next. But someone's bully boys threw me out, as soon as they spotted me."

"What kind of row?"

"One loudmouth reckons the Mage's death will break the spells. He was ready to knife him where he lay, except the others were afraid it wouldn't work. Someone else wanted to set fire to one of the pictures, to break the spell but they couldn't decide which one to try."

"They'll pick on someone like Pogo, if they think of it." Ashie took hold of the hut door to pull herself to her feet. "We'd better find his picture first."

Josh reached out to steady her. "I told you: they won't let us in. Or worse, if anyone recognises you."

"Then we'll go to somebody they won't keep out."

~ * ~

They found Lady Glasspin in her front hall, ready to set off for the Mage's house. One of Josh's cronies let them in through the kitchen and Ashie scuttled towards the sound of the lady's voice, before anyone could stop her.

"Don't go without us," she called.

"You?" Lady Glasspin stared. "You're his clerk. Did he send you here?"

"Yesterday I was his clerk." Ashie decided not to explain too much. "He doesn't need one anymore."

"What are you doing in my house? Is that kitchen thief with you?"

Josh was at Ashie's side, with a loaf of fine bread under his arm. "I'm her friend," he said. "She needs to eat, or she'll be too feeble to tell you what you need to hear."

Now that she had come to a halt, Ashie did feel shaky and weak. She leaned against the wall and let Josh feed her pinches of bread from the middle of the loaf.

"Leave them alone," Lady Glasspin said, when servants reached out to grab the two of them. "And, bring the girl a cup of small ale, before she chokes." She watched in silence, until Ashie pushed upright, with a mumbled thank you. "You'd better have more to offer me than thanks. What have you come to tell me?"

Ashie swallowed hard. "Take us to the Mage's house and I'll show you how to bring back your son."

"Tell me now!" Lady Glasspin took two steps forward and her hands crooked into claws.

"It won't work here." Ashie did not flinch. "We have to be in front of his picture. And we should hurry, before anybody else does anything stupid."

~ * ~

The hall and reception room were crowded with well-dressed people, just as Josh had described. Nobody obstructed Lady Glasspin. She refused several offers to show her to the Mage's bedchamber, where he lay now. "I don't care what he looks like, so long as he doesn't wake up." Ashie kept her hands down by her sides, so as not to hint at the paper squashed under her breast wrappings. Nobody here was likely to suspect what she had done but she would rather not give them an excuse to search her.

The picture of Lady Glasspin's son was in the same place on the wall. "Look at him hard," Ashie told her. "Sing aloud to him; tell him stories and rhymes. Remind him of his loves and adventures."

"Do you think I haven't done all that, hour after hour?" Lady Glasspin snarled and seized hold of Ashie's shoulders.

"With his body," Ashie snarled back. "His spirit is here. You have to call him back here."

The grip loosened. "Can you be sure of that?"

Ashie would not lie but dared not give the true answer; that she was sure of nothing. But she had been right so far. She said, "Ask the mages if they have any better plans."

Lady Glasspin turned to the picture. "You hated baby rhymes. Even before you could speak, you demanded to hear street songs with unsuitable words. Maybe a rhyme will rouse you into yells of complaint."

Her whisper was harsh but steady. "Five fingers, five toes, two eyes and a nose." She did not pause when Ashie crept away to the workroom, with Josh in tow.

They found the portfolios already open, their contents scattered across the floor. Other people were searching for faces they recognised but they let Josh and Ashie join in. Everyone was still busy, when Lady Glasspin gave a loud shout.

In the reception room, the young man's portrait had faded and smudged. It looked as though it had been painted in grey wash. "What's happened?" Lady Glasspin seized Ashie's arm and this time, her grip could not be dislodged.

"Let's go and see." Ashie was eager herself to know the answer.

Halfway down the street, they met a woman, who ran towards them. "He's woken up," she called. "My lady, he's awake and talking. Grumbles about a voice in his dreams but he knows his name. My lady, come and speak to him."

Later that day, Josh and Ashie found the picture of Pogo, crumpled and discarded in a corner. By then, people had heard of Lady Glasspin's achievement and had stripped the Mage's house of portraits to work on, beside the bodies to which they belonged. Josh rounded up Pogo's friends to gather round his body, beside Ashie's hut and exhort him back to life. Ashie fell asleep before they succeeded but nobody minded. "You've done enough," Josh said, as he settled her into her bundle of sacks.

She woke twice that night, once at the shouts when Pogo woke up and again, later, when the paper under her breast contorted into hot crumbs. She dug out the remains and tucked them under her sack, before she fell asleep again. In the morning, Josh came to tell her the Mage's house had been burned down. His body was found in the remains, stabbed through the heart. The killer remained unknown.

~ * ~ * ~

Sandra Unerman's historical fantasy novels, *Spellhaven* and *Ghosts and Exiles* are published by Mirror World. Her short stories have appeared in a number of venues, including *BFS Horizons* and *Mirror Dance* magazine. She writes articles for the British Science Fiction Association and the British Fantasy Society. She lives in London, UK, and is a member of Clockhouse London Writers. She has recently completed an MA in Folklore Studies at the University of Hertfordshire.

CONTROLLING

The Kudzu

Bailey Finn

My family has served Woodsburrow for as long as I can remember. My father solved the very first murder case over 262 years ago. Since then, our growing town has seen ten judges, sixty prosecutors, and about thirty-five defense attorneys.

I have stayed here to serve everyone who has served Woodsburrow. I was here with my father when the courthouse was built. He insisted positions of power were the best places to protect the innocent and hide from the hunts. I grew to agree with his sentiment and to care for the town and its people, so I continued to serve even after his passing. Every few decades I change my name and appearance to keep people from becoming suspicious and to blend in.

There aren't many monster hunts anymore, but there are still plenty of individuals who would see justice maligned. So, I remain. It is my honor to keep evil at bay and preserve the hope of the town.

The Public Defender's Office has always rehired me. With generations of experience, it's easy to compete in any field, including law. It also gives me an edge when it comes to understanding legal precedent, making me one of the region's leading defense attorneys. This time, with the name Mari Lynn, I have been part of the Public Defender's Office for two years.

The town is small and so is our courthouse. Judge Ryan Vigil is the presiding judge. The current prosecutor, Andrea Martin, is also quite talented. She gives me a refreshing challenge whenever I go against her in trial.

Today I had a meeting with Lilyanna Watts, my current defendant in a murder case, as well as a later meeting with Judge Ryan and Andrea. However, the morning was peaceful, and I decided to walk the property while waiting for Lilyanna's appointment. I strolled through the halls toward the exit with confidence and a click-clack of my wedges. I still wore my signature black. Apparently, it's 'in'.

Cerbie, my familiar and delightfully rambunctious mutt, was on the courthouse steps. He stretched from his napping position and sat up. Woodsburrow is small enough people still don't mind animals on public properties like they do in the larger cities. Cerbie barked and I returned his greeting with a pat on the head.

"Come on boy, let's take a lap." He followed me as we walked the perimeter sidewalk. The courthouse and surrounding botanical gardens were being taken over by kudzu. The vines, while enchanting to look at, only survived by choking the life out of their various hosts. I had tried pruning it back myself, but the weed still spread like wildfire. I looked around to be sure no one was within sight and held out my hand to will the infestation to recede, even just a little. Today, I only managed to bring it back an inch or two.

"Mari!" A familiar voice called. It was Dennis Clowry, the latest security hire. He was a little naïve, but he was always eager to serve where he could. I turned to face him. He was wearing his usual ear-to-ear grin. I didn't think he had seen the plants recede, but it was best to distract him regardless.

"Oh hey, Dennis, what's up?"

His ears turned the color of his red hair. "Well truth be told, I just arrived. It looks like everyone inside is looking for you. They asked me to help find you. You'd better get in there." He hooked his thumb in the direction of the double doors.

"Oh, that's odd. I don't have a meeting for another hour. Thanks, Dennis!" I waved goodbye while breaking into a jog-sprint towards the entrance. Cerbie followed and it wasn't long before I literally ran into Judge Vigil himself. He stifled a grunt before taking a deep breath.

"Oh my gosh, your Honor, are you alright?" I caught my balance and made sure neither of us dropped anything.

"Quite alright, just watch where you're going in the future." Judge Vigil's tone was icy and insistent. "Please join me in my office, Ms. Lynn."

Ryan was generally a nice person, but the furrow of his brow suggested he was uncharacteristically stressed and apparently upset. We met Andrea along the way and went into his office together. Judge Vigil shut the door. He almost never shut the door.

"Is everything alright sir?"

"No. However, I must say, I have heard some troubling news." He glanced over at the deputy standing in the far corner.

"Sir?" Judge Vigil returned his attention to Andrea and I. Andrea remained quiet; her eyes locked on him.

"I received word evidence has gone missing in the Lilyanna Watts case."

I clenched my fist and tried to keep my composure. "What?"

"As the investigating officer," the deputy stepped forward, "I stopped by evidence this morning to do an inventory." He paused for a second. "I received an anonymous call saying the gun and other items had been removed from evidence."

"Who was the last person to sign for the evidence?" Andrea asked.

"According to the evidence clerk—it was Mari Lynn," the deputy said.

Judge Vigil pinched the bridge of his nose. "That doesn't exactly bode well, but it doesn't convict you either. I'm waiting for a copy of the security tapes."

"Yes, your honor, but what about Ms. Watts? We have a meeting scheduled for this afternoon."

Judge Vigil thought a moment, "I don't see a reason to frighten her yet. If we find a criminal element, we will update her, but keep the appointment, for now, to keep the case on track."

I nodded and Andrea excused herself as we were both dismissed. I headed back to my office with Cerbie and shut the door. "Okay Cerbie, I need you to find that missing evidence, start here in the building, but search the whole town if you must. Request help from the Coven too, we may need their assistance."

Cerbie barked in reply, I opened the door for him, and he bolted out to begin his mission.

Covens exist to ensure no one is falsely accused and convicted for something they didn't do. I knew I would need them if someone was playing dirty.

I'd also need to be ready to stop the culprit from leaving the building until the Coven could assist. I opened the middle drawer of my desk and pulled out a few vials of liquid and powders. The selection of ingredients I had was lacking due to the confined space, however, I was glad I had anything at all. It was amazing what could pass as 'naturalist' these days; I had the growing popularity of essential oils to thank for that.

The sage and lavender were from my garden, of course. A handful of each and I was ready to make a truth-telling serum and a mild paralysis potion. All I needed now was something to brew it with. The cast iron and stock pot at home would have been preferable, but the break room kettle would do. With any luck, I could prepare the potions and still be able to search the property with the others before Lilyanna arrived.

I took a deep breath and carried the herbs to the break room. Someone must've just made tea because hot water was still in the kettle. As I dropped the ingredients into two travel mugs to let them steep, Dennis came barreling through the door. This time he wasn't wearing a grin.

"Mari! We have the security tape and Judge Vigil wants to review it with both you and Andrea present." He didn't wait for me to answer as he ran down the hall.

"Right!" I sealed the mugs, set them in my bag, and dashed after Dennis to Judge Vigil's office. Andrea was already there. I was surprised the deputy wasn't still there. Hopefully, that was good news and the evidence had been recovered. Yet, the queasiness in my stomach told me otherwise.

"Alright, that's everyone." Dennis shut the door. Judge Vigil clicked a remote to play a video on the TV. It showed a woman walking through the evidence room. She paused when she came to the shelf with three boxes on it Each one labeled with the name of the victim and the case number on it. After opening the boxes and removing the gun and some other items, she turned and glanced up at the camera. It was Lilyanna Watts.

"With this new evidence, I will entertain a motion from the prosecution to amend the charging documents to include tampering with evidence to her charges." Judge Vigil said glancing at Andrea.

"Now wait just a minute, sir. That doesn't prove Lilyanna was the one to take the evidence."

Judge Vigil just stared at me.

"Mari, are you serious?"

I didn't like the smirk I saw on Andrea's face when she asked the question. And, of course I couldn't explain how easy it would be for someone to appear as someone else using magic.

"Look Mari." Judge Vigil pointed at the TV. "Ms. Watts is on camera and that also means she may have used someone's card to get in. I have no choice but to take you off the case until we know how she got in that room. The sheriff has already been notified and deputies are picking up Ms. Watts up now. Dennis will escort you home."

"What about the evidence clerk?"

"Deputies are talking to the clerk who was supposed to be on duty at that time."

I felt Dennis grasp my shoulder. "I'm sorry Mari, let's go." Dennis's tone was more compassionate than the others.

"Y-yeah. Okay." I let Dennis take me to his car.

As he shut the car door and started the engine, I thought I might have a better chance of asking for his help one on one.

"Dennis, can you take me to Ms. Watts instead? You could supervise us at the station. I have to talk with her."

"Mari…"

He sounded exasperated but willing. I just had to push him a little more.

"Please, it's important. You believe me, don't you?"

Dennis hung his head with an audible sigh and took a wrong turn, left instead of right at the intersection, and rolled up in front of the Sheriff's Office.

"Dennis, you truly are the best!" I hugged his neck as he took the key out of the ignition.

"Yeah, well. Just don't make me regret this." He warned before a small grin returned to his face. I strode up the stairs and into the station. Dennis followed close behind. Judge Vigil must not have told the authorities I was off the case, because it seemed to make perfect sense to them Ms. Watts' attorney would come to see her.

They brought her to a small interview room. When she saw me, she sank into her chair, relieved.

"Oh, Mari, thank God. I don't know what's happening. I told them I wasn't going to talk about anything until I spoke with you."

"There's a video of you stealing evidence. I want to know why."

Her body trembled and she broke out in a cold sweat.

"I-I can't."

"This is serious."

She didn't answer but had the look of someone being burned at the stake.

"Lilyanna…if you are covering for someone, they could do this to others, and it needs to stop."

"They threatened me. They threatened you. I can't." She retreated further into her shoulders. I was just about to try a different approach when one of the deputies came in.

"Hey, Judge Vigil says you are under house arrest and being investigated. I'm afraid I'll have to have you step out and ask you two some questions."

Dennis' face paled, I took his arm and ran like hell. I got him to his car before taking off on foot. He drove off like a mad man in what I chose to believe was an attempt to buy me time. Bless him, he was the best.

When I arrived home, several patrol cars were out front, and my door was open. I crept around back to my garden shed. It was dark enough I could fly now, and I needed to get back to the courthouse to find out who had the evidence. Cerbie appeared behind me, gathering, and taking shape from the shadows.

"Hey buddy, things aren't great right now. Do you have good news?" I whispered.

His eyes glowed and the shadows around the remaining lights of my back porch danced and took on the shape of the gun—in Judge Vigil's office.

"Okay, tell the Coven I need their help. Have them meet me at the courthouse." I grabbed my shovel. The shovel wasn't as aerodynamic as my broom, but it was a whopper in a fight. I checked the potions in my bag to make sure they were still sealed and took off on the shovel. Cerbie kept up with me, disappearing and reappearing as he used the streetlight shadows below me.

I landed by the front doors of the courthouse. It was dark and empty. Although it was now covered in crime scene tape, there were no deputies on guard. They had probably been called out to search for me after the ruckus I had caused. Based on the number of cars in front of my house, they might still be searching there.

I stepped over the barrier and climbed the stairs before unlocking the door. I thought I would have to do the same for Judge Vigil's office, but his office door was ajar. On his desk was a gun. I stepped inside and reached for it. On the other side was Judge Vigil, bleeding out.

"Ryan!" I stopped myself from touching the gun, dropped

my shovel and knelt to give him first aid as best I could. As I applied pressure to his chest a creeping, sinking thought came into my head. If he was still bleeding, and the evidence he was looking for was still on his desk then the culprit must still be in his office too.

"An…And…" Judge Vigil struggled to speak, and I shushed him. I took a piece of my clothing and tied it over the wound as tight as I could. In the corner of my eye, I just barely saw a shadow move and rolled with the judge before a silver sword came down at us.

Andrea's voice broke the silence, "You're early, I wasn't going to get rid of you until you were charged as an accessory to Lilyanna Watts."

I set Judge Vigil down gently and scrambled to unscrew one of the traveling mugs, praying it was the paralysis one. "What the hell? Why are you of all people doing this?"

"Why does it matter? You'll be gone in a moment." Andrea lunged for me, and I splashed the contents of the mug at her, rolling away once more. She pursued me, which told me everything I needed to know about which concoction I had used. At least the truth potion would make her more cooperative to questioning.

"Tell me why!" I commanded.

"Because I know you, *witch*. My family has trained to find and hunt the likes of you for generations. Your witchcraft has tainted this city. No, a city built on witches was never pure! I'll take you and your vassals down so we can rebuild it from scratch!"

She came at me again and I dove for my shovel and used it to block her blade. I felt a deep rage. One I had never felt before, pure loathing. I had thought the hunters were gone. How could someone contain such hate?

"You would sacrifice innocent people"? I growled. She went in for another strike. The sword broke my shovel and drove into my shoulder.

"Of course, I will do whatever it takes for my cause!"

"You and me both." I used my free arm to splash the correct potion on her. She plunged her blade deeper into my shoulder before her movements stopped. I screamed as I pulled the blade out. It hurt like hell. I used my entire body weight to ram her, and we both came tumbling down. I had just staggered to my feet when twelve cloaked figures arrived—the Coven.

"Who—who are they?" Andrea's voice cracked. Her eyes

darted around but she still couldn't move an inch.

"Come on Andrea, I'd think you, of all people, would recognize a jury when you saw one."

~ * ~

Six weeks later, Judge Vigil had a gnarly scar but was stable and recovering. He didn't remember anything after Andrea attacked and I first tried to stop the bleeding. This may have been for the best considering not even I know what the Coven did to Andrea.

The people of Woodsburrow looked for her, naturally, but when the gun turned up with her fingerprints on it and Ms. Watts and the evidence clerk testified to having been blackmailed by her, most folks concluded she was a fugitive on the run, somewhere out of state. My name was cleared. Dennis and Ms. Watts received clean slates, too. Many had started to believe Andrea was the murderer as well. Although, there was no real evidence to prove it.

It was about two or three months before a replacement prosecutor arrived. I met with him outside the courthouse.

"Pleasure to meet you, I'm Mari Lynn, the public defender for Woodsburrow."

"Pleasure's all mine, the name's Val. I just moved from East City. Wow, that kudzu sure is taking over the courthouse something fierce." He clasped my hand with both of his and shook it with gusto.

I smiled. "Yes, but we've been working to get it under control. Hopefully, together as a team, you and I can take the courthouse back entirely."

~ * ~ * ~

Bailey Finn is a speculative fiction author who enjoys paranormal adventures and mysteries. She works full time in crisis intervention helping families through the worst of times. When Bailey is not helping those in need, she enjoys ballroom dancing and getting the gang together for a round of tabletop gaming.

Bailey resides in Colorado Springs and is a member of Pikes Peak Writers where she is always happy to connect with fellow authors and readers, as well as dancers and gamers.

The Friar and the Turnip

Christopher Wortley

HANOVER—TUESDAY EVENING

Anna was blocking the aisle. The supermarket was crowded, and people were struggling to get by. She smiled and apologised as she tried to juggle a bag over one arm and a basket over the other, whilst pressing her phone to an ear. She was trying to hear her boss over the noise.

"Sorry, say again, Hemming. It's a bit busy in here." She listened once more. "Where? In a cave?"

Anna was tired and in no mood for this. It had been a long day and all she wanted to do was to get back home to her little flat and peel off her shoes. She'd found them online, advertised as super-comfy. They were anything but.

"Anna, are you still there?"

"Yes, sorry, go ahead."

As far as she could tell, Hemming was saying some cavers had broken through a thin wall of rock into an unexplored cavern, somewhere up in the hills to the south. And they'd found a bunch of kids. Foreign kids. And no sign of any adults.

"Yes, I know I'm the one on call tonight, Hemming, but you've seen my caseload. Can't someone else—"

"Okay, okay. Where are they now? Send me a link."

She took the phone from her ear and looked at the map. "You've got to be kidding," she said to herself.

A few minutes later she was in the car park. She threw her shopping in the boot and got into the driver's seat. She was too tired to worry if this was all an elaborate joke. *I'm no work-experience girl,* she thought to herself. *If Hemming is having a laugh, I'll get him sacked.* She put the car in gear and set off for Hamelin.

THE TOWN HALL—WEDNESDAY MORNING

Anna sat in a small room, high up in the old town hall. It was mid-morning. The windows were open, providing a welcome breeze. Around the table were five councillors who, together, made up the Emergency Subcommittee of Hamelin Town Council. Anna had been introduced to everyone a few minutes earlier. Clockwise from her sat Klaus Müller—Social Services, Günter Zimmermann—Treasurer, Stefan Schwarzkopf—Culture, Heritage and Tourism, Ursula Kloetsch—Mayor, and Petra Rosenbauer—Education. Anna vaguely knew Klaus and Petra through work. The others were new to her.

She was feeling a little self-conscious, partly because of the situation but also because she'd convinced herself she smelt to high heaven. She'd been up all night with no change of clothes. She thought she saw Stefan sniffing the air experimentally. She threw him an apologetic look. She hoped for an understanding smile but what came back was something more like a leer. She wouldn't be putting him on her Christmas card list any time soon.

"Please, Anna, go on," the mayor said.

Ursula was a practised Chair. Her body language was non-threatening and her tone was neutral. Unlike Klaus, who was constantly fiddling with a pen or a paperclip, she sat motionless, an island of black and white couture in a stormy sea. Her hair fell in curls. Each had its own allocated position on her shoulders.

"They spent the night in the school, but we'll need to find proper accommodation for them from tonight," Anna said.

"What have they said? What have they told you?" Petra asked.

"We're still trying to figure out what language they speak. It's a bit like German but at the same time, it's not. Sometimes they use words that sound like English or even Swedish. But the good news is they're learning German fast. Even in the few hours since they woke up, we've been communicating better. I'm sure we'll get to the bottom of it all soon."

"And you have no idea where they came from?" Ursula asked.

"Not yet."

"I've been checking all the schools," Petra offered. "Nobody's missing." Petra was pleased to be able to contribute something to the group, instead of listening to the others. She was finding it awkward, being in the same room as Stefan. It was hard trying not to catch his eye. How on earth had she got herself into this ridiculous situation; a tawdry affair with Stefan? What had possessed her? She wished she could go back to doing her old job, teaching English to college students.

"They must have some ID or something?" she said to Anna.

"No, nothing."

"Some clues from their clothes, perhaps?"

"Their clothes are…" Anna hesitated, "peculiar, to say the least."

"We must be very careful," Klaus said. "We don't know what's happened to them. Whatever it is, it might have been very traumatic. We might be dealing with abuse." Klaus was a little put out Hanover had moved in on his patch so quickly. Still, he had to admit his team couldn't possibly have dealt with this all on their own.

"I agree," Anna said. "We're trying to take it slow. Not pressuring them at all. But I have to say, they don't appear to be distressed, just curious. Curious about everything. Especially TV. That's what they're doing now, watching TV."

"What are they watching?" Stefan asked. "Lord of the Flies?"

"Poor taste, Stefan," Ursula said, sharply.

"They like Disney films," Anna said. "Cinderella went down very well last night."

"Well, they must belong somewhere," Klaus said. "There must be a police report or something. A dozen kids can't—"

"Fourteen, in fact. Aged from four to twelve. And, they've told us their names." Anna passed Klaus a piece of paper. He passed it on to Günter, who passed it on to Stefan, who laughed.

"Someone's put them up to this. 'Hartmud', 'Mengot', 'Chunegund'. These are names off gravestones or something, like something out of the Middle Ages."

Out of the corner of her eye, Petra thought she saw something. No? Yes? There it was again. An elephant. And he was waving his trunk at her.

"What about me," the elephant appeared to be saying. "Will someone please talk about me?"

With considerable effort, Petra pushed the illusion from her mind. But, of course, he was still there: the elephant in the room. Nobody wanted to address him, with his long, grey trunk and his big, grey ears. Petra noticed his tattoos: 'Famous' and 'Legend'. One word on each ear.

There was a knock at the door.

"Come in," Ursula said.

"This gentleman says he has information about the children," the clerk said.

A tall man was shown in. He was sombre and assured. His face carried no greeting and his manner was cold. Apart from that, there was little to remark on. Except his clothes, which were pied. Red and yellow. But nobody said anything. In Hamelin, everyone was used to seeing people dressed like this, so it usually went without comment. Nonetheless, Petra did notice the elephant was waving his trunk more wildly, now.

"Sit down, Herr…?" the mayor said.

The stranger sat down at the end of the table, a little way away from everyone else.

"Now, I understand…" Ursula trailed off.

The man had a finger to his lips. Then he spoke for the first time. "Listen."

"To what?" Ursula asked, in her best non-challenging voice.

"Just listen. What can you hear?" He then pointed at Petra. "You. Tell me everything you can hear."

Petra found herself on familiar ground. She sometimes played this game at home, late at night, as she was trying to get to sleep. She would lie still, next to her husband, trying hard not to think about Stefan, lying in his bed, next to his wife. And she would play the listening game. The idea was this: even when everything seems to be quiet, there are always ten distinct things to be heard. You have to count them. She listened now. She could hear Günter's insides churning. His unreliable indigestion was infamous. She wouldn't mention that.

"I can hear us all breathing, I can hear the clock on the wall, I can hear Klaus's chair creak as he shifts about in it. And outside, I can hear traffic and a plane and people chattering. And someone laughing."

"Yes, that's it," the stranger said, "laughter. It's very precious."

There was a moment's hush. Had the stranger said something profound? The Emergency Subcommittee of Hamelin Town Council wasn't sure.

Ursula broke the silence.

"Yes, quite. Now, please tell us. What do you know about the children?"

"They're mine," the stranger said, simply.

"What do you mean? In what sense are they yours?"

"Maybe he's their father," Stefan said with a smirk. "In which case, he's been a very busy boy." He winked at Petra, who giggled. She immediately wished she hadn't. There was something about this whole extra-marital affair thing that was making her behave like a teenager.

Klaus witnessed the smirk and the giggle. It fuelled his suspicions there was something going on between the two of them. Klaus thought of himself as a decent kind of bloke. He was polite and friendly, and, as far as he knew, he was liked by his colleagues. But there was something about Stefan that wound him up; something that made him want to lash out. And here was yet another reason to dislike the guy: if Petra must have an affair, why choose Stefan, for Christ's sake? Oh, sure, he was the light and soul of the party. But couldn't she see he was really an oafish boar? *If you're going to cheat, why not cheat with me?* he wanted to say to her. But he held his tongue.

Ursula was talking again.

"Are you their social worker, perhaps—"

Klaus wasn't having that. "Ursula, does he look like a social worker?"

"Not all social workers have to look like you, Klaus," Stefan said.

Ursula pressed on. "But you work with children, yes? Fräulein Hoffman, here, is from Hannover. She also works with—"

But the stranger interrupted her. And what he said next left nobody in any doubt about his take on the whole children-in-the-cave situation.

"They are mine. I took them…in lieu of my one thousand guilders."

Petra thought the elephant looked relieved. He could relax now. Everyone had got the message.

"Oh, great," Klaus said sarcastically. "It was only a matter of time till one of you lot showed up."

"And I want them back."

"Stefan, will you tell this lovie to skedaddle."

"Why me?" Stefan said.

"Well, he's one of yours, isn't he? One of your re-enactors."

"Nope. Never seen him before."

"Well, that's even worse. He's a wannabe re-enactor."

"Well, he does look the part, I'll give you that," Stefan said. "Maybe you're right. Maybe I should, indeed, sign him up and put him on the roster."

Anna remembered bringing her niece to Hamelin a couple of years back, to see the story acted out. *The chap who played the piper that Sunday wasn't nearly as convincing as this man,* she thought.

"Look, this isn't a bloody screen test." Klaus was in full flow. "Nobody's dishing out Oscars. We've got a job to do, but instead, here we are, playing a part. I've told you before, Stefan, in the eyes of the world, this town is nothing but a big joke. I've just about had—"

"All right, Klaus, keep your hair on," Stefan said. He said it in English. He liked to pepper his conversation with English phrases. He'd managed to seduce Petra with some choice quotes from Shakespeare and Seamus Heaney. And his English aphorisms always went down well at the various tourism seminars and heritage symposia that filled his diary. What's more, if it meant he could needle Klaus at the same time then that was a nice bonus.

But Klaus wasn't to be put down. Not this time. "You know what? You're half the trouble, Stefan. Turning us all into circus performers. One day, somebody is going to do something amazing, right here in Hamelin. Maybe invent the elixir of life: a bloody miracle cure for everything. But nobody is going to give a damn. We'll still be known for just one thing. Him!" He pointed an accusing finger at the stranger.

"Gentlemen, can we please get back to the matter in hand." Ursula tried to regain control.

"Exactly," Klaus said fuming. "Here we are, in the middle of an honest-to-goodness crisis, and what are we doing? We're listening to an out of work actor who thinks he can just pop on some fancy-dress and barge in here without—"

He stopped. The stranger was slowly and deliberately taking a pipe from his left sleeve. There was silence as he laid it gently on the table. It was a simple thing: a thin piece of wood with holes down its length.

"Well, *quelle* surprise!" Klaus was trying to play Stefan at his own game, throwing in some French. He glanced as Petra. She didn't appear to have noticed.

"You." This time the stranger pointed at Klaus. "What crisis do the Bürgers of Hamlin face?"

"The children, of course. Your children!"

"Ah yes. My children. I must warn you. If you do not return them immediately, there will be consequences."

The stranger patted his pipe. The gesture reminded Ursula of the evil Emperor, in Episode VI.

"Consequences? This is ridiculous," Klaus said. "This joker needs to—"

"I never joke. I have no sense of humour."

"Well, you're having a good old laugh at our expense, now!"

Stefan weighed in. "I applaud you, fine fellow. You've got the costume just right. The joker in the pack, eh? Ha ha. But you're probably right about the sense of humour thing. I can't see you doing too well on the stand-up circuit. I'd stick to tragedies, if I were you."

"Yes, and while we're handing out career advice," Klaus said, "here's another piece of advice. Why don't you stick your tooter up your bloody—"

"Klaus, please," Ursula interjected.

Klaus was getting quite agitated. Anna tried to calm things down. She recognised challenging behaviour when she saw it. She'd taken a course. She knew what to do. She must first address the disruptive element, in this case, the stranger.

"Herr Piper. We are not comfortable with nasty threats. If you can't play nicely, we'll have to take your pipe away."

Ursula raised her eyes to heaven. Some of her curls slipped their moorings.

It was only then Anna remembered her course had been focussed on eight-year-olds. Goodness, she needed to get some sleep. She took another swig of coffee.

"I want them back, all fourteen of them," the stranger said calmly.

"Just a minute. How did you know how many…" Anna was startled. "That's not common—"

"Gertrud, Lugard, Chunegund, Methild…"

"And how on earth do you know their names? Frau Kloetsch, I must protest. Somebody has been leaking sensitive information and—"

"Enough!" Ursula had really had enough. She nodded at Günter. He understood and picked up the desk phone to call security. "We've wasted enough time-"

"You're not going to give me the children?"

"Of course not."

"In that case, Bürgers of Hamelin, you leave me no choice."

THE PIPES ARE CALLING

The stranger raised his pipe to his lips and blew. Nobody knew what to expect. Perhaps a tune, so beautiful it could lure sailors to their deaths. In fact, what came out was rather disappointing: a thin, reedy sound, with an unexceptional melody.

Where was security? Ursula looked at Günter but he shook his head.

"Phone's dead," he said. Ursula picked up her own phone, but it too was dead.

Klaus decided it was time for action. He got up and started to move towards the piper. But as he got close, his knees inexplicably buckled beneath him. Meanwhile, Petra was at the door, rattling the handle. It was locked. She banged on the door, but nobody came. She banged harder but the sound of the banging was now being drowned out by two new sounds: one was that of a strong wind that had whipped up from nowhere. It was all around them, swirling and gusting, as if they were caught in a squall at the bottom of a canyon. The other sound was more terrifying: an insistent squeaking. It came from the rats. There were rats everywhere: on the floor, on the window ledge, on the table, nibbling at the biscuits.

Günter screamed. Anna screamed. Petra looked down, and she screamed. Two rats were tearing at her handbag, biting through the leather, trying to get at her chocolate bar, the one she bought every day, the one she regretted buying every day. And then there was an additional noise: a rattling. It was the cupboard on the wall. Its doors were shaking and knocking. Then, with great force, they burst open and yet more rats came streaming out. And these weren't small rats. Oh no. These were huge rats, with scary, pink eyes and long, lank tails that flicked about as their owners scurried this way and that. Three rats started to climb Stefan's trouser leg. Stefan screamed.

Ursula found herself backed up against the window. Outside,

she heard more shouts and screams. She looked down at the street below. The trees were swaying wildly in the wind. Ursula didn't remember anything about a wind, but maybe the piper had spent the last 700 years perfecting new tricks? Her attention was caught by the road surface. Why was it moving? Then she realised it had become a living carpet, a river of rats: brown rats, black rats and the occasional white rat. Across the street, the cheese man had barricaded himself inside his shop as rats piled up against the door. Nearby, a woman snatched up her baby. A moment later, his pram was full of toothy, whiskery invaders.

The piper stopped playing for a moment, but the wind didn't stop. And the squeaks didn't stop. And the screaming didn't stop.

"Now, we are even," he said.

"No, wait, please. I'm very sorry if we didn't take you seriously." The mayor's voice was raised above the noise of the wind. "Please. The rats. You've made your point. Take them back."

"The rats are yours. I am merely returning them to you." He blew a few more notes, as if he were spinning plates, keeping the wind howling, keeping the rats scurrying. Then he got up to go.

"But we don't want them. Please. Take them back. Get rid of them."

"Get rid of them? Really?"

"Yes!"

"And what will you pay me?"

"Payment. Yes, of course." Ursula gave Günter a pleading look. "Günter?"

The piper went back to his playing. The treasurer looked at his laptop. There was a big brown rat on the keyboard, sitting on its haunches. It stared straight back at him. Eyeballing him. Daring him. It seemed to be saying, "Come on, if you think you're brave enough."

This is my moment to be heroic, Günter thought. Gathering strength, he didn't know he had, he wrapped his sleeve around his hand and then, with one, fluid movement he swept the rat aside, snatched up his laptop and held it up close to his face. As he summoned up a spreadsheet, he felt a wave of calm come over him. Spreadsheets had that effect on him.

"I suppose we could tap into the contingency fund," he said, "but it's supposed to be reserved for a rainy day."

"It doesn't get much rainier than this," Stefan shouted, as he batted wildly at the rats closing in on his crotch.

Ursula spoke in a commanding voice, "Günter, as Mayor of Hamelin, I officially declare this to be a rainy day. Please release the money. All of it."

"All of it?"

A group of four rats stood on their hind legs on the window-sill. They were squeaking in harmony like some ghastly, ratty, barber-shop quartet. And from down below came the sound of an angry voter, stamping his foot in vain as hundreds of rodents rushed around him, happily ducking and weaving. Rats were not Ursula's worst nightmare, angry voters were.

"All of it," she said.

"Very well. Herr Piper, we can offer you one hundred and twenty thousand Euros."

The piper stopped playing for a moment.

"What's that in guilders?"

"Hmm. Well, allowing for inflation…let's see…it was twelve eighty-four, I believe…and then, of course, the Euro…Jan nineteen ninety-nine…"

"Günter!" the mayor shouted.

"Good heavens," Günter said, "it comes to exactly one thousand guilders."

"Payable immediately?"

"Yes."

"Very well."

The piper stopped playing. But the wind kept on howling.

"Come on, come on! What are you waiting for?" Anna shouted.

The stranger was looking at his pipe. "I'm trying to get it in reverse. I don't usually…"

"For pity's sake," Petra said.

"Ah, got it." He moved a little lever on one side and started playing again. It was the same tune but it felt different, somehow. And then, finally, the wind stopped. And the squeaking stopped. And it was all over. The rats were gone. Everyone collapsed onto their seats.

The piper also sat down. He put his pipe back on the table. Then he took off his pied hat, turned it upside down and laid it beside his pipe before pushing it in front of Günter.

"One thousand guilders, please."

Everyone looked at the mayor. Anna was impressed at how quickly Ursula had recovered her poise. Her curls were all back in place. Had she really managed to touch up her lipstick already?

"Well, Herr...whatever," Ursula said calmly. "Naturally, any payment will have to go through the Accounts Committee. Then we'll have to take a vote in full council. I'll have a word with—"

"You said 'immediately'. You will honour your contract, here and now."

"Well, I'm sure we can work something out. But I should point out that when you say 'contract', there's nothing actually in writing." Ursula was looking smug. Too smug for the piper's liking, who went to pick up his pipe again. But Stefan got there first. He grabbed it and, with great theatre, snapped it in two.

"Hah! Put that in your pipe and smoke it!"

The piper looked blank. "It's a pun. It's a pun, in English!" It was Stefan's turn to look smug.

"Ah, yes. A joke. Very precious. Perhaps, even more precious than gold." The piper was silent for a moment. Then he said, "Ladies and gentlemen, this is what you must sacrifice. I will take from you your sense of humour, in lieu of my guilders."

Nobody understood, but they watched and waited to see what would happen. The piper got up and then, very deliberately, he reached into his right sleeve and withdrew his spare pipe.

"Damn!" Stefan said.

The piper started to play again and, sure enough, the wind started up again. Everyone jumped up on the table, looking round to see from which way the rats would come. Klaus took hold of Petra's hand but found no comfort. Petra took hold of Stefan's hand and also found no comfort. Günter took hold of Ursula's hand and found an unexpected thrill. They all braced themselves.

But the rats didn't come. Instead, inexplicably, everyone started laughing. They laughed loudly. They laughed uncontrollably. Their faces were pictures of joyous pleasure: chuckling, hooting, guffawing. It was a happy sound. But it didn't last. Soon, these laughing faces started to peel off. They became blue, ghostly, laughing heads, torn from their hosts like rubber masks. They floated towards the piper, gathering around him like cartoon birds around a dazed coyote. The humans they left behind were completely sombre; completely humourless.

Then, yet more blue, laughing faces came flying through the window. The townsfolk were having their senses of humour ripped from them as well. The piper turned to the door, which flew open of its own accord. He walked down the stairs and out into the street, followed by all the translucent, laughing heads. Outside he was joined by thousands more ghostly, giggling visages and they all followed him out of town.

He was last seen walking into the hills, chuckling to himself.

EPILOGUE

That was a few years ago, now. The children were all okay. They were housed with foster families and they soon settled into twenty-first century life. Curiously, they were spared the fate of all the other townsfolk. From then on, it was only they who liked to have a laugh and to tell a joke. Needless to say, they spent a lot of time in each other's company. They found everyone else to be terribly boring: functional, but mirthless.

As the next generation was born and grew up, it was left to the cave children, who were young adults by this time, to slowly reintroduce laughter back into the community. But, of course, mediaeval humour is an acquired taste. Have you heard the one about the friar and the turnip?

~ * ~ * ~

Christopher Wortley is a full-time songwriter and part-time writer of prose.

In the *speculative fiction* genre, he is the winner of the Secret Attic Short Story Competition #16 (**JustLikeMe**), and his short story, **Big Porky Pies**, was recently published by *Audio Arcadia* in their compilation, *An Eclectic Mix, Volume Eleven*.

His first full length novel, **Stone Dead**, is now available. A murder mystery—set in Stonehenge, 2,300 BC—where secular and religious power collide, and a reluctant female investigator must solve the puzzle of the young acolyte's murder in time to avert another.

As an established songwriter (published by *DWB Music Ltd*), Christopher writes pop songs—mostly k-pop and j-pop—occasionally hitting the Number One spots in Japan and Korea. He also writes for Eurovision, which brings its own excitements. For the stage, Christopher writes musicals including **Act Your Age,** a full-

length musical farce (published by *Stage Scripts*).
Christopher lives in England

how to Steal a Spell Book

Mirabelle Poppy

Koschei brought his teacup to his lips once more, breathing in the fragrant steam. The liquid soothed his throat, tasting of mint. Gently, he placed the cup back down on its saucer and gazed out the window at a landscape of rolling hills. The wildflowers were in full bloom, dotting the hills with shades of yellow and pink. What a lovely morning. It would be even lovelier if his secretary wasn't making so much noise.

A loud thump drew his attention to the ceiling. Koschei put the saucer on the mahogany table. So much for a quiet morning. He'd better go make sure all her body parts were still intact.

With a sigh, Koschei stood up from his cushioned chair and conjured the spiral staircase once more. Said staircase was an assortment of old wooden floorboards with no railing for support. One would simply have to pray they didn't fall on their way up. Even if they did (as Kinga had done many times), Koschei could simply patch them up again. Koschei had planned on building a regular staircase, but casting a simple telekinetic spell was easier. Building things was a pain and for all his knowledge of thaumaturgy, Koschei could never master construction spells. Who needed them anyhow? Such things should be left for mortals to mull over.

Now, where was that girl?

"Kinga!" he called.

"I'm okay," she replied. "I just fell from the ladder."

Just? If it weren't for Koschei, all of these falls would've certainly resulted in her death.

Koschei followed the sound of her voice down the sunlit corridors of his home. There was hardly a speck of dust to be seen. Cleaning spells. Yes, cleaning spells were quite possibly his favorites. Kinga called him boring for having such dull spells as his favorites, but after a lifetime of creating spells for the sole purpose of using them on a battlefield, such trivial things were delights for Koschei.

He reached the door to his study. At the beginning, he'd tried to keep Kinga out of the more secretive parts of his home, but he'd soon found that was quite impossible. Kinga could go for days and days and weeks and months complaining about it. Not even a silencing spell could keep Kinga from voicing her opinions on the matter. And with the preservation of his mental health in mind, Koschei let her have her way.

She was too foolish to do anything with the information in these rooms anyhow.

Kinga was bent over picking up books when he entered. Her neon green dress stood out in the dull colors of the room. Her hair was tied into a ponytail with a ribbon (also neon green) and fell over her shoulder as she created a pile of books in her arms. The ladder had returned to its place leaning against the grand oak bookshelf. The windows opened wide into the valleys and hills, as a cool breeze shook through the sheer pink curtains. The first time Kinga had seen his office, she'd been disappointed. *"So dull!"* she'd said. *"You'd think you were nothing more than a common nobleman."*

Koschei had reasoned that he was, in fact, a nobleman, but that fell on deaf ears as Kinga continued to critique his home's interior design. The shelves took up too much space, the rug—expensive, hand-woven, 100% unicorn wool—was ugly, and the paintings that took up the rest of the walls were in poor taste.

Tch.

Of course, any lingering irritation in Koschei faded away upon seeing the rather large gash across the girl's forehead. Crimson blood, so unlike his, dripped down from the top of her forehead to the edge of her black eyebrow. Her eyes were as green as her dress today.

"Haven't I told you to be more careful?" His thumb hovered over Kinga's brow, and slowly, the skin began to stitch itself back together.

"At least a thousand times now, sir," Kinga said. Her high-pitched voice always tilted a bit on the word 'sir', as if she fully intended to mock him with it.

"Then how come you haven't taken my advice?"

"Because your advice is boring, sir."

He was not boring. He was practical. These mortals had no

idea how fragile they were.

With a snap of his fingers, the books scattered on the floor lifted themselves up as if beckoned by a strong wind, rising in the air until they found their proper place on the bookshelves once more. Orderly, just as Koschei preferred.

"I must write to the King soon, so take your stationary and meet me here by noon," Koschei said. "For now, I must attend to the local gnome population."

"Wreaking havoc again, are they?"

"They seem to be good for little else." Koschei sighed. They were so snappy, too. He meant it quite literally. Those little devils had obscenely sharp teeth. He nearly got a finger bitten off last time.

"I'll just stay here then," Kinga said, glancing about the room. "I'm sure I'll find something to do."

"Don't break anything this time."

"I won't."

~ * ~

Naïveté hadn't been what Kinga had expected of an ancient thaumaturge, but she supposed the man had been locked away from society for the better part of three centuries. With Koschei gone, she was free to continue her search.

Kinga passed through the corridor, humming a tune as she took the path to the library. How long had it been now? Six months? Six months spent looking for that damned spell book of his. It took long enough for him to let her into these secretive corners of his quaint, little home. Searching for it while pretending to be looking for nothing had proven itself even more difficult. Had Koschei been any wiser, he would've found her out long ago. Thankfully, she had stumbled upon a fool. A fool with a tender heart.

She came to a stop at the doors to the library. They were made of an enchanted, cold iron. Anyone without permission to enter would be caught with a sudden chill, passing from their hand to the rest of their bodies, as if ice had burrowed into their flesh and frozen their veins.

When Kinga placed her hand on the ring of the door, she felt nothing but the metal beneath her fingers. Smooth and slightly cool, as it absorbed some of the warmth of her flesh. They creaked open, hinges scraping. The room on the other side was domed and made entirely of honey-colored wood.

It smelled a bit like the inside of her father's shop. Like wood shavings and pine needles. Shelves lined the walls, a shade darker than the ceiling and floor. Thousands of books were kept here, under lock and key. One of them was Koschei's spell book. She'd gone through most of the library's collection. All that was left was the section closest to the windows. Large, stained-glass windows that dappled the room in splashes of colored light. They didn't make reading the books any easier.

Kinga kneeled down, scanning the shelves. Meanwhile, doubt began to gnaw on her heart. If it was not here, what would she do? Koschei always went into this room when he needed to consult his spell book: An unassuming leather volume with gold embellishments, larger than it appeared on the outside. She'd only caught glimpses of it here and there whenever Koschei ran into a problem requiring a spell he couldn't remember. There could be a million spells cast on it to keep thieves at bay. Still, Kinga had no choice. She needed power. She needed a miracle.

That was why she would not feel sorry for the old man, nor would she ever give up on coveting his power. She'd either find the damn book, or her dear fiancé would find her. Either way, she was cornered.

She had nothing to fear. The book was tucked behind several others and hidden from view. Kinga reached for it. Gingerly, she gripped the book, waiting for a curse to be placed upon her. Nothing happened. It was heavy in her hands, but felt like any other leather book otherwise. Gold vines were wrapped around it.

Kinga stood up, heart pounding in her ears. Was this an illusion? Was it real? Would it burst into flames as soon as she left the premises? She hugged the book to her chest.

No turning back now. Turning back was never an option. Not since she left the mansion and came here to beg Koschei for a place to stay.

That would all be over soon. She'd never have to fear anything ever again. Not the Duke. Not the King. Not their armies or their wrath. Not even death.

~ * ~

Koschei returned at sundown with a mark on his arm in the

shape of a gnome's teeth. They hadn't managed to break the skin, but it still hurt like hell. He rolled one of his shoulders. What a pain. He never would've moved here if he had known they had such a problem with the local gnome population.

He was halfway home when a scent like cinnamon filled the air. Another pair of footsteps joined his on the dirt path. There were two of them between the pine trees now. Dragon leather boots? And a confident gait that grated on his nerves. Koschei let his arms fall to his sides, as his mood soured further.

"Valentin," Koschei said. "Don't you have better things to do?"

Valentin towered over Koschei (he was unnaturally tall, you see), his black cloak trailing behind him. His hair, almost as dark as Kinga's, was braided down his back. Valentin gave Koschei an unassuming smile, although he knew from experience Valentin had only mischief on his mind. Those brown eyes were always twinkling at the prospect of one scheme or another.

"Someone has to check in on you from time to time, old friend," Valentin said. "Make sure you're still alive."

"I'm immortal."

"No one is ever completely immortal, Koschei." Valentin took Koschei's arm and pulled him closer. With his other hand, he brushed over the bite mark the gnome had left. Everyone's thaumaturgy felt a little bit different. Valentin's felt like sunlight in a meadow, or alternatively, a fire waiting to swallow you whole. He was a warrior first and foremost, after all. A moment later, the bite mark had disappeared, leaving only pale skin beneath Valentin's touch.

"Hard as we might try," Valentin whispered. He gave Koschei a pointed gaze. Sometimes Koschei thought Valentin still worried about him. Him and his obsession with deathlessness.

"That was a long time ago," Koschei murmured. He twisted his arm away and walked further down the path. "I suppose you're planning to worm your way into dinner."

Koschei followed behind him. "Don't mind if I do."

"I do mind." He minded a lot, actually. Koschei hated all reminders of his life before this little house in the middle of the forest. Sometimes he thought the memories might drive him a little mad.

They reached the house soon after, leaving the pine forest behind them, and Koschei walked up the stone steps to the door.

Kinga must be bored out of her mind. He had meant to be back by noon, and now the sun was already sinking beneath the horizon.

"Kinga," he called as the two of them entered the house. There was no answer.

"Who is Kinga?" Valentin asked. He hung his black cloak on the coat rack near the door and placed his shoes in the neat line on the doormat. Kinga had called that boring and ugly as well. Koschei stared at the shoes for a moment longer. Something was wrong.

Her shoes were gone. Kinga's shoes were gone.

"Kinga!" Koschei ran up the stairs, with Valentin following close behind. Perhaps she was sleeping? But the shoes, the shoes. A walk, then?

In the back of his mind, he knew that was not true. He'd seen it in her face every time she looked out the window for a second too long. As if she was waiting for someone. Koschei had never asked what she was so afraid of. Why would he? Neither of them had anything to fear here.

He should've asked. He should've helped her properly. Koschei's heart tightened. He was so sick of losing people. Sick to death of it. So sick he felt he could vomit his insides out at any moment.

He opened the door to his office, where she should've been. There was only the rustling of papers in the wind, and a room painted orange and dusty pink from the fading sun.

"Koschei." Valentin put his hands on his shoulders, like he had whenever Koschei's emotions got the better of him during their days as friends and partners. A comforting gesture, but it had only ever made Koschei more anxious. It felt like Valentin was trying to pin him down.

"The library," Koschei said. She'd always spent her evenings there, poring over old books. He nearly tripped over his feet in his haste to leave his office. Valentin seemed exhausted already, growing more confused by the minute. There could not be even a second wasted, however.

Koschei snapped his fingers as he stepped into the library and the torches lit themselves. He crossed the room to the shelf where he kept his spell book hidden. He pulled out one book, then another, and another. Where had it gone? Koschei turned his gaze up to the thousands of books around him. This had been where he'd always left it. He felt at a loss. What had always been his had now been stolen from him.

"It's gone," he breathed.

"What's gone?" Valentin asked, crossing his arms.

"My spell book." Koschei stood up on shaky legs. Suddenly, all those nights Kinga had spent in the library made sense. Seeking knowledge, she'd claimed! She'd been looking for the damn book this entire time. "She took my spell book."

He had thought she was a fool. As it turned out, he was the foolish one. Koschei ran a hand through his red hair. Somehow, amidst all his irritation, Koschei could not help but be impressed. No one had ever stolen from him before.

"Should we go after her?" Valentin asked. "Whoever she is. You still haven't told me, by the way. Nice to see you're as accommodating as ever."

"Yes. All my life's work is there, after all," Koschei said, nodding to himself. They were both safe then. Kinga and his spell book, that is. "Not that she'll be able to use any of it."

"Why not?"

"Because I put a spell on it, obviously." He wasn't a complete idiot, just a partial one.

~ * ~

Kinga slammed the book closed and then dropped her head onto the volume with a groan. She couldn't read a single word. Why? She had only ever saw Koschei write in Merchiean. It must be a spell. That was why it was all blurry.

Well, that's what you get for trying to steal from the ancient thaumaturge.

"Oh, shut up," Kinga mumbled. She wrapped her hands behind her head as if to shield it from further verbal attacks, though she knew it was all her own mind's doing.

This wouldn't have happened if Koschei hadn't been so stubborn about taking on apprentices. He'd left her with no choice. Yes, there had been no other choice. Kinga glanced out the window, her anger fizzling out into exhaustion. There were soldiers from the King's army staying in the inn across from hers. She could see them lighting lanterns outside and bringing out pints of beer to drink themselves silly with. They weren't good for much else other than drinking and terrorizing the locals. She'd have to move on soon, lest they realize she shared the same green eyes as the Duke's betrothed.

Kinga leaned back in the chair with a sigh and gave the book a seething glare. Perhaps the words would decide to make sense if they got scared. No such luck. Another burst of anger welled up inside her, and she tossed the book toward the opposite wall, which wasn't very far in her decrepit, little room. She waited to hear a satisfying thump as it hit the floor. The universe wouldn't even give her that.

Kinga twisted around to see who had interrupted her late-night musings. The man straightened, book in hand, face in shadows.

"I thought you'd treat my possession better, at least. Even if you had stolen it."

Koschei. She could see him clearly now: Red hair, blue eyes, a flawless complexion (no doubt due to the spells she could not read), and his body clothed in a simple white dress shirt and black slacks. How dreadfully boring his fashion sense was. Some things never changed, she supposed.

"You can have it back," Kinga said, crossing her arms, hoping her nerves did not show. "It's all gibberish anyway."

"Gibberish to you." Koschei flipped through the pages with his slender fingers. "Thieves aren't allowed to know my secrets."

Kinga huffed. "No one is allowed to know your secrets, sir. Though they might make better use of them than you."

Koschei snapped the book closed in his hand. He drew closer to her, until he could lean against the side of her desk. In the candlelight, he looked almost gentle. "Alright then. How would you use the power my teachings would give you?"

Keep the Duke away. Leave this wretched kingdom. Who knew what else? How could anyone possibly now what they'd do with so much power until it was within their grasp.

"Who are you so afraid of, that you'd steal from the most powerful thaumaturge in the world?" Koschei asked.

"Second most powerful!" A familiar voice rang, deeper than Koschei's, but gentler somehow. There was someone on the other side of the door.

Koschei rolled his eyes. "Shut up, Valentin."

"I only speak the truth, darling!"

Kinga tipped her head to the side. "Darling?"

"Ignore him." Koschei sighed, rubbing the bridge of his nose.

"He's an imbecile, that's all."

Kinga glanced at the door once more, before bringing her attention back to Koschei. No matter how many times she looked at him, he really wasn't very frightening at all. They said he'd killed thousands at war. The Koschei she knew had trouble hurting common houseflies and spiders.

"I was in an unhappy engagement," Kinga said, "to a stupidly powerful man. So I went to another stupidly powerful man and stole his spell book. Are you satisfied, sir?"

"The Duke of Mikowa is your husband?" Koschei asked.

"Betrothed."

"Well then," Koschei said. "I have no choice."

Kinga froze. Of course. He was like anyone else in this kingdom. Even Koschei wouldn't go against the Duke of Mikowa. Everyone just gave that devil what he wanted. What else were they to do with an army like the Duke's poised at their throats?

"Now I'm afraid I must teach you thaumaturgy."

What?

On the other side of the door, she could hear Koschei's friend cackling away. *He's going to teach me? Despite everything?*

"But I stole from you."

Koschei nodded, putting a finger to his chin. "I was quite impressed by that. You're a skilled actress, truly. I thought you were a complete and utter fool."

"I thought you didn't take apprentices." Kinga gave him a suspicious look. Perhaps this was some kind of trap by the Duke?

"I don't," Koschei said. "In fact, I quite despise it."

"Then why?"

Koschei smiled, placing his hands behind his back. "Because, we're friends."

He's gone mad.

~ * ~ * ~

Mirabelle Poppy lives and works in the Midwest, with plans to go into librarianship in the near future. In her spare time, she reads and writes novels, along with the occasional short story. In the rare moments where you won't catch her reading or writing, she is off planning big dreams, watching her favorite dramas, and taking hikes through the wilderness.

The Frog and
The Princess

Jean Martin

In bygone days there was a prince, Prince Bertrand of Willifarrenen, who was handsome, and charming, and full of himself, as princes so often are.

His serene highness had a great many family connections, so he had no great trouble getting into Highthrone University, as a Regal Studies major.

He was popular with his fellow students. He pledged the best fraternity. He went to all the best parties. Which was one of many reasons why his class work was anything but the best. Another reason being—the prince was not what anyone would call intelligent.

But he was good looking, and charming, so he had no trouble getting other people to assist him with his work, so he could pass his exams, and maintain a decent grade point average.

Especially after he met Esmeralda. Esmeralda was majoring in sorcery, one of the top students in her year. She was taking graduate level incantations classes. But she was young, and young women are sometimes distracted by charming princes.

Bertrand never told her she was beautiful. Because she wasn't, really, her nose was just a little too long, and her mouth a little too wide, to be a real beauty. But she was tall and slender. Her hair was black as the midnight sky, and her black eyes sparkled like stars.

She had been turning heads since she was seventeen, and she thought it possible the prince's head had been turned too.

Especially when he told her she was striking.

Esmeralda, while gifted, was also young and inexperienced. She thought it might be nice to be a royal. She could do a lot of good as a queen, of course, and she rather liked the prospect of brocaded gowns and emerald tiaras.

So, she spent way too much of her time, getting Prince Bertrand through his classes. She practically wrote his term papers.

She stayed up with him helping him study for exams. Her own grades suffered because of her efforts. But the prince was so handsome, and so charming, and he bought her dinners at the best restaurants, so she helped him more than she should have, and he was going to graduate near the top of his class.

As their senior year came to an end, Esmeralda began to hope. She began to imagine a royal equerry coming to her dorm room with an heirloom ring on a cushion, or perhaps in an ebony box, and a letter, written on the prince's elegant hand, and sealed with his royal seal. "Esmeralda, oh, dear love of my heart, will you honor me…"

Or, perhaps he might ride up to her on his white horse, which he kept in the college stable, and sweep her up into the saddle and carry her off.

She was concerned when he took Princess Clarinda of East Gloffingham to the winter ball. Princess Clarinda was quite possibly the loveliest princess in all the seven kingdoms, with golden hair, skin like fresh cream, and a truly impressive figure.

She was quite certainly the dimmest royal ever to attend Highthrone University. It was well known she had failed Scepter 101, the only student ever to have done so, and she would have flunked out long ago, if her father had not been a big name alumnus, who had paid for the new alchemy lab.

Esmeralda could not imagine Prince Bertrand having any real interest in such a spectacularly unintelligent girl. She assumed it was some sort of diplomatic thing, involving trade agreements or treaties.

She had great expectations when the prince asked her to dinner at Chateau Fey the best restaurant in town.

He picked her up in his carriage drawn by four white horses. He was wearing his finest jerkin.

They drove to the best restaurant in town, where, of course, they had the best table in the house, and the finest wines. Their supper was of the best, including the restaurant's famous fairy cakes.

Esmeralda looked for rings in her wine glass.

She got a very expensive dinner, a gold chain set with peridots, and a certificate of thanks from the prince's father King Norman the fifth.

"You're a smart lady." Prince Bertrande smiled a big, phony smile. "You knew all along, that there was never anything serious between us. I mean you were a big help and all. But well, you know how it is. I'm going to ask Clarinda to marry me at the graduation ball."

Esmeralda wasn't sure if she wanted to cry or set fire to his pants.

"I hope you'll be at the wedding. It should be quite an affair." Prince Bertrand looked smug, and somewhat relieved, as though he'd gotten a disagreeable task out of the way.

Esmeralda realized all his smiles, and his compliments, and expressions of affection had been fake. The charming Prince Bertrand had taken advantage of her. She did not like being taken advantage of.

She allowed him to take her back to the dorm, and then as soon as the equerries weren't looking, she pulled her wand out of her purse, and turned him into a frog.

She put her wand and the squirming amphibian back in her bag and carried them up to her room.

The prince had ditched his equerries before and he was not always good about showing up for class, so it was a while before he was missed. But, in due time, word went out throughout the land that Prince Bertrand had vanished. Equerries, footmen, couriers, and halberdiers were sent off in search of him. They would seek through every corner of the seven kingdoms. But he could not be found.

For his highness was living in a large jar half full of water, and dining on cockroaches from Esmeralda's dorm room.

There he stayed, until the day after commencement, when she took him with her to her homeland, and released him into a convenient lake. There he spent his days eating flies, crickets and minnows, while avoiding waterfowl, snakes, and other, larger, frogs.

Until, he remembered, how the spell could be broken. All he needed was a princess who would kiss him.

He tried speaking. It wasn't easy, since he was, now a frog, and his mouth wasn't quite like a human's. But he could say, "I'm a prince. Kiss me and I shall make you my bride."

Though he was still hoping to marry Princess Clarinda.

His new voice gave him confidence. Now all he needed to do was find a princess.

So, he hopped out of the pond, and followed a stream to a

river, and followed the river, to a large city, where there was, indeed, a palace, built beside the river, with a lovely garden by the water's side, where, surely, there must be princesses, amusing themselves, gathering sweet smelling flowers, and dreaming of the princes who would ask for their hands.

So, the prince hopped onto the riverbank, and into the garden, where he found a cool, damp place, where he could eat flies and wait for a princess to come by.

He waited most of the day, before going back to the river, because frogs can't stay out of the water too long.

But he was back the next day, where he did, indeed see a princess. Not particularly fair. Her hair was brown, and she had freckles, a pug nose, and not much figure to speak of. But she was wearing a silken gown embroidered in gold, and surrounded by an entourage of waiting women, men at arms and page boys. So, she was a princess, and he was in no position to be picky.

He hopped out onto the garden path, and, before he could speak, a lady in waiting screamed, and tried to squash him.

He leaped back to the river, wondering what he would have to do to avoid being squashed. Because he knew, royals were, almost never alone, especially princesses, as they had to be protected from bandits, bad barons, and dragons.

But, every day, he hopped into the garden, and sat in a damp, shady spot, eating insects and waiting for the princess to be out with, perhaps, just one waiting woman, or, perhaps, by herself.

It finally happened, early one morning, the princess, her name was Delia, slipped away from her old nurse, her governess, her guards and her waiting women, and went walking in the garden alone to do some thinking.

Truth to tell, Delia didn't like being a princess. She never had. There wasn't a lot to do, besides wear expensive clothes, and wait for some prince to come along and marry her. She never had any privacy. She never did anything really interesting. Mostly what she did was embroider and try to look winsome. She wasn't good at either. All in all, it was a very dull existence, and she had been wondering, for years, how she could get away.

Then the prince hopped out onto the path, and began, "I am a prince. If you kiss me, I shall make you…"

"Holy cow! A talking frog!" Princess Delia said before he

could finish. "Say something else froggie!"

"I am a prince," he said again. "Prince Bertrand of the kingdom of Willifarrenen. If you will kiss me, I will…"

"Wow!" Princess Delia scooped Prince Bertrand up, and held him in both hands.

"You're squeezing me," Prince Bertrand wheezed. "Kiss me, dammit, so I can be a prince again!"

"You really know what you're saying." Princess Delia was amazed.

"Yes! I'm Prince Bertrand of Willifarrenen. A wicked sorceress cast a spell on me and turned me into a frog. If you kiss me, I shall make you my bride, and…"

"Yeah, right" Princess Delia said, thoughtfully. "Come with me, your highness."

She carried him toward the palace, where, Prince Bertrand, assumed she would kiss him. He would be arrayed in royal robes, given fine food, feted by the king and queen, before being given a fine horse and a retinue of men at arms, and sent home to his parents who pined for him.

That was not what happened.

Instead, Princess Delia found a large jar in the kitchen, and filled it half full of water, and put Prince Bertrand in that.

Then she slipped up to her chamber and put a few of her jewels and her small store of coins into a velvet bag.

She slipped, quietly, down to the servant's quarters, where there was a housemaid who was nearly her size and was not yet awake and at her work. She took the housemaid's dress, leaving two gold coins to pay for it.

She found a large basket in the larder, and put the bag with the jewels, a loaf of bread, some cheese and two apples in it, along with Prince Bertrand in his jar.

"What the hell are you doing?" Prince Bertrand demanded.

"You'll see," Princess Delia said.

She took off her fine brocaded gown and donned the housemaid's well-worn linsey wolsey dress.

She slipped down to the garden, again, to the river, to the part of the wall where there was a gate with a lock that could be picked, easily with a hair pin.

She was out the gate in a minute. In a few more minutes she

made her way down to the river side. There she waved down a bargeman, and was on her way to Wallford Town, and the famous Wallford Town Fair.

She arrived just before sunset. There she found a room at an inn, a length of cloth and a pot of paint. That night, she painted a banner, SEE FROSCHLING THE TALKING FROG, THREE PFENNIGS.

The next day, she took her banner, and Bertrand, in his jar, and set up outside the inn.

She hung up her banner, and, not surprisingly, people came up to see the talking frog. But Prince Bertrand sat, silent, in his jar, staring at the crowd, and glaring at Delia.

People laughed, which wasn't such a bad thing. People asked for their money back, which was.

In due time, the crowd diminished, and Delia picked up the prince and squeezed him, just hard enough. "Talk!" she said.

"Won't!" the frog said.

"Yes you will!" Delia said, squeezing him a little more.

"Why should I?" Prince Bertrand demanded.

"Because if you don't," Delia said sweetly, "I will take you up to the roof, and leave you there, where you will either dry up and die, or be eaten by a bird. But if you do, I'll give you all the minnows, and crickets you can eat, and a nice big bowl to live in, your alleged royal highness."

"But if you kiss me," Prince Bertrand said. "I'd wed you, and make you my queen, and…"

"One, I don't believe you." Delia said. "Two, I don't want to be your queen or anyone else's. Being a royal is boring. I want to get out and see the world, and right now you're going to help me do that, but only if you talk, understand."

Prince Bertrand, as I have said, was not very bright, but he understood.

"What do you want me to say?" he asked.

"Anything you like," Delia said.

Bertrand smiled, as much as a frog can smile. For he had had an idea. A way to be sure he'd be kissed and home before the next sunset.

The next day, as the crowd gathered, and paid their pfennigs, he swore. He cursed. He used inappropriate language. He was lewd. He was crude. He was vulgar.

He was ridiculously popular.

People crowded around to hear the frog shouting profanities, vulgarities and obscenities. They laughed and laughed when he made some crude comment about a man's hat or a lady's figure. Nobody had heard a frog talk before, and they had, certainly, never heard one swear. Prince Bertrand was a huge hit.

By the fair's end, Delia had made enough money to buy a handsome caravan, and have it painted with large, green frogs. She also bought Prince Bertrand a fine, large porcelain bowl with an attractive porcelain castle inside, for him to live in.

She watched him, carefully, to make sure he didn't hop away, and make sure nobody grabbed him, or squeezed him too hard.

She also made sure he had clean water to swim in, and plenty of minnows and crickets.

They traveled from fair to fair, Delia in her caravan and Froschling her famous, foul-mouthed frog, in his handsome porcelain bowl.

Delia enjoyed the fair life, the crowds and the music, the peasants, the merchants, the tradesmen and the nobles, who were all only too happy to pay to hear Prince Bertrand use crude and vulgar language.

As she traveled, she heard stories of Prince Bertrand of Willifarrenen, who had disappeared from Highthrone University shortly before he was due to graduate.

His doting parents, and his beloved Princess Clarinda were searching everywhere for him. It was believed he might have been abducted by an evil sorcerer, or possibly turned to stone by a basilisk.

A large reward was offered for his return.

Delia wondered if her talking frog might, actually, be a prince.

At the end of the season, she had a chest full of gold, so it was she came to the Kingdom of East Gloffingham, where there was a great fair at city of West Heffingam. She and Prince Bertrand set up, and Prince Bertrand swore like a sailor. Which was much admired in West Heffingham, it being a port city.

At the end of the day, Delia left Prince Bertrand in his bowl, in her caravan, with three fat minnows, and went to speak to several sea captains, who had recently come from far off lands with rare and fine treasures.

She wrangled, she bargained, she haggled, and she got good

prices, on some very pricey goods.

By the time the fair ended, Delia had a load of fine silks, crystal goblets, orient pearls, and other very expensive and desirable things, including a small, and very handsome gilded cage, meant for a rare bird.

Their caravan was very crowded, and Prince Bertrand wasn't at all pleased about it.

But, the woman who would spend the next six years as Delia the Peddler was quite happy as she made her way to the capital city.

She put on her finest attire and put Prince Bertrand in the gilded cage.

He found it uncomfortable. But he kept quiet, when she asked him to remember roofs and hungry birds.

It took a good deal of talking and a fair amount of bribery for Delia to get in to see Princess Clarinda. It was quite true that several waiting women and the princess's duenna shrieked when she produced the frog in its gilded cage. But, in due time the shrieking stopped, and Prince Bertrand was able to say, "Clarinda! It's me, Prince Bertrand! Kiss me and make me human again! I pray you, at once!"

Princess Clarinda didn't stop to think. (In fact she rarely stopped to think.) She simply scooped the frog out of his cage and kissed him. A minute later there was Prince Bertrand, looking somewhat the worse for wear, standing before her in the all together.

The princess and the ladies in waiting, and the princess's duenna all shrieked some more, while an equerry wrapped Prince Bertrand in his coat and took him off to an elegantly appointed chamber, where he enjoyed a bath, and a dinner that wasn't minnows or crickets. He was provided with several elegant suits of clothes, and in due time restored to the bosom of his family.

Meanwhile the king's chancellor questioned the peddler woman, who explained she had found the frog while watering her horse in a pond nearby and brought it to the castle.

The king's chancellor rewarded her with several bags of gold and sent her on her way.

Prince Bertrand considered having Esmeralda locked in the dankest dungeon he could find and sending Delia back to her parents. But that would have meant letting the world know he had been Froschling the foul-mouthed frog.

It was a part of his life he preferred to forget.

Anyway, Delia had left the palace grounds as fast as she could. She'd had enough of courts, courtiers, equerries, and everything else connected with being a royal.

She went off to see the world. She traveled the length and breadth of the seven kingdoms and met all manner of people and saw and did all manner of things, until she got tired of travel and bought a handsome farm. She married a handsome farmer, who owned the farm next door. Together they raised fine cattle, fine horses and very intelligent children.

Prince Bertrand married Princess Clarinda. Together, they were good looking, charming, and almost completely useless.

In due time, they became king and queen, and, fortunately, found a chancellor who could talk them out of all the hare-brained ideas they had, and run things for them. Since neither of them was capable of planning a picnic, let alone ruling a kingdom.

Esmeralda, the sorceress, became one of the most powerful and successful enchantresses in all the seven kingdoms. She freed Princess Elfrida of Effingham from the sleeping curse placed on her by a gang of evil fairies. She found Prince Godfrey of Gallimaufry, who had been stolen by his wicked uncle, and hidden among shepherds. Most wonderful of all, she broke the curse of Lord Litchfield, and freed the kingdom of Glacemore from a plague of zombies.

Along the way, she met a very attractive knight, who always treated her with the utmost respect and never took advantage of her, or anyone else. In due time, though his family objected at first, they were married, and did, indeed, live happily ever after. Though, she would often tell her daughters, before you meet your handsome prince, you may have to make a frog or two.

~ * ~ * ~

Jean Martin has a BS degree in Journalism from Ohio University and has been laughing about it for longer than she cares to admit. She lives, at present, in McKeesport, Pennsylvania, with an orange tabby cat named Samwise, who likes bagpipe music.

If you, for some strange reason, like this story. You can find her story "The Sun Makes the Wheels Go" in last year's PARSEC Triangulations. Ms. Martin is a shameless self-promoter.

Marigold at Midnight

Tyree Campbell

For Marigold Tallgrass there was something outré about having to descend three steps to enter the cottage after crossing the threshold. Above her the open rafters, ripe with webs and insect carcasses, only added to the otherness. The cottage could not have pleased her more.

She stood her carrybag on the dusty floor and took out five hurricane lanterns, chosen for their deep candle wells because the flames risked igniting the dust. These she placed strategically in the front room, so they formed the points of a pentagram. One by one she lit them with long matches. At first the flames flickered. Shadows appeared to move at the periphery of the room and enhanced the ambience. Presently the flames steadied, and the shadows stilled once more. Standing in the center of the pentagram, Marigold clapped her hands three times. The sharp reports echoed throughout the empty house and cautioned demons their mistress was home from her long absence.

"Athwart," she called out.

There was no response, not even telepathic.

Well, she couldn't blame her familiar for being snooty. Not since birth had they been separated for so long. She pulled a soft leather pouch from her carrybag and loosened the drawstrings.

"I brought you some dried, honey-dipped locusts," she called out, a melodic, teasing summons.

Still not a sound came from within the cottage. The silence weighed on her heart.

"Maybe I should give them to Coralie," she muttered, tightening the strings. "Her raccoon will eat almost anything."

Wait.

A shadow edged low along the hallway wall and paused at the entrance to the front room as if in anticipation.

You could have left sooner.

The tone was heavy with accusation. "Yes," Marigold admitted. "I could have woven a spell and opened the cell door at any time. But I would have had to stay on the move, forever, as an escaped convict. This way, I served my sentence, and now I'm free." She sighed. "I missed you, Athwart."

The mottled brown coatimundi padded into the front room. *Let's see those locusts.*

She placed three on the antique coffee table, and Athwart leaped onto the sofa. After settling herself, she picked up one between her front paws, sniffed it, and purred with satisfaction.

"I thought you'd like those," Marigold said, as she took her carrybag to the bedroom and unloaded the clothing into the hamper. "They're almost as good as the food in jail."

Next time, don't interfere.

"I know, I know. But the poor man's coffee was cold." She returned to the front room. "I just used too strong a spell, and the cup fell onto his lap, and he testified I deliberately spilled it on him."

Thirty days.

"I'm sorry. But it was only twenty. Good behavior, you see."

A second locust went down crunching. *It seemed like thirty.*

Marigold wanted to cry. "Oh, don't go on at me, Athwart. I said I was sorry." She forced herself to brighten as she sat down beside the coatimundi and stroked her back. "Did we have any visitors?"

Two seagulls. And Baywindow showed up.

Marigold laughed. "Belinda. What did she want?"

A miracle.

Marigold sat up straight. "Uh-oh. That sounds like trouble."

It is. Are there any more?

"Not until you tell me what she wanted."

There's a man she likes. She wants to be thinner.

"That sounds like a Stephen King story. Well, I can do it, but I don't know whether I should. Tonight's the night, you know."

I know.

"You sound dubious."

Do I? I'll wager that's because I am dubious. Marigold, a massive adjustment such as the one you're planning is bound to have repercussions. To say nothing of concussions. Didn't that jail sentence teach you anything?

"This cannot possibly harm anyone, Athwart. Why are you always so negative?"

Thus my name.

"All I want to do is help people learn how to get along."

Do-gooder. I would like more of those locusts, if you think you can emerge long enough from your saccharine dreams to place some more on the table.

Smiling tolerantly, she complied. "And it has to be done at midnight."

Why this midnight?

She ruffled the fur at the top of Athwart's head. "Because it's the full moon, silly."

Marigold closed her eyes and sensed the time—Greenwich Mean, adjusted to local. Four hours and twenty-seven minutes to go. Plenty of time. After a nudge to Athwart to follow her, she went out the dinette door to the deck that opened onto the rugged Pacific coastline south of Carmel, forty yards away and ten yards below. She crossed her arms on the railing and leaned forward, relaxed. The sun was an hour from its nightly immersion. Sometimes she pretended she could hear it hiss as it touched the ocean at the horizon. Presently her chest rose and fell in a sad sigh. She wished there were someone to whom she might describe the sunset—or better yet, to share one with.

Marigold Tallgrass was hardly the sort of stereotype one might conjure upon hearing the word "witch." No hooked nose and chin, no cackle, not for her. To be sure, now and then she did use a broom for transportation—avoiding the TSA and the inevitable questions about the unusual objects in her carrybag; eyes of newt, for one—and she did employ a cauldron on occasion, albeit mostly for a homemade soup both she and Athwart enjoyed. She was tall and slender—she liked to think of it as willowy—with hair now flaxen due to a spell—next week, umber! Her face, the fine pale white of *statuario* marble, took on a fresh glow after each shower, as if the loofa allowed her to polish her skin. Her eyes, for the moment, were pearl-gray. A spell to change the color? She considered: what accessorized with umber hair? Green, perhaps. She had not had green eyes for over a century. Yes…this time a jade green. Or maybe serpentine. So many colors, and so little time…

Athwart was staring up at her. She lifted the coatimundi up onto the railing. "Better?" she asked.

Her familiar tightly clutched the railing. *You can fly. I cannot.*
"Just look at the sunset."
I see black and white. Rods only. You promised me cones. You said you knew a spell.
"I do know a spell. And I did promise. Please wait a little longer, my friend."
I'll just be right here, grousing. Are you going to change clothes?
She was wearing black jeans and an aqua pullover, her gentle contours only vaguely evident under them, and black loafers. A long gauze skirt afterwards, she thought. Mauve, with a purple peasant blouse.
Peasants come in all colors.
Marigold chuckled. "Ah…the sky is turning."
It is all fifty shades of gray to me.
"Not for long."
She placed a sheet of yellowed parchment on the railing and summoned an inked nib to her slender fingers. The numbers came to her, a string of binary code she had conjured and memorized during her most recent incarceration. It related to technological deprivation, something others in the cells had experienced, though not herself. A word had also come to her, not out of nowhere, but from a cellmate: interconnectedness. At first the word meant nothing to Marigold. The more she thought about it—and in that cell she had ample time to think—the more she decided it meant far more than the selective definition usually attributed to it. It was in the very nature of things—of existence itself—that everything is connected. It had very little to do with "six degrees of separation."

The oxygen she exhaled fifteen times a minute traveled to some other entity, some other life form: her cellmate, a butterfly, the head of lettuce growing in the fields outside Salinas, the goose migrating to or from Manitoba, and so on. The herring a man on a German boat caught in the Baltic Sea went to a woman in a cannery on shore who cleaned them and gave them to another man for smoking, from which point the smoked herring went to the canning process, involving a machine designed and manufactured by other men and women…somewhere—men and women who probably opened the tins and ate the smoked herring. That, that was interconnectedness. In one way or another, everything on the planet—including the very planet itself—was involved with every other thing.

This, then, was the source of her powers. The source of her (she smiled at this) sorcery. She, and so very few others on the planet, recognized this. She, and she alone—or so she thought—knew what now had to be done. Because there was another kind of interconnectedness, a technological one, and it was destroying humanity.

The solution had come to Marigold in a flash—the way all good ideas come. The imposition of it would be hard on people at first, but people had endured and even thrived under such conditions. She considered relationships. Social media were no place to make friends. You needed to hear each other's words, not read them. Reading eliminated timbre and tone, accent and cadence. Eyes spoke volumes without so much as a consonant. And touch. My stars, touch! So she'd had her flash.

She tittered at the memory. "Eureka."

Athwart sneered. *You no smell-a so good yourself.*

The code was long, with many a winding turn that led to who knew where or when…but Marigold had engaged a memory spell that allowed her to recall it exactly, precisely, at any time. This was a Good Thing, as the trouble a misplaced 1 or 0 might cause…she shuddered to think. As in all spells, precision was required. The attraction spell she had cast on Gerrold Teasnake back in eighth grade even now, two centuries later, continued unabated, and his advances had been rejected by more than 32,500 girls and women. It was worse than being a small-press writer. And the spell had been intended to make *her* attractive to *him*. She sighed at the memory, and thought, *the best plans of mice and men to get laid…*

Athwart's tail rose. *That's not the right quote.*

"It is for me, my friend." She gazed out at the sunset. Red sky at night, sailor's delight. She'd known a few sailors, now and then. Even Captain James Cook, before he became the main course at the *Honolulu Snack & Hula.* The spell she'd cast on him served him right; dinner and a drink had been okay, but what he'd assumed would follow—not okay. And there was that problem with those growths on his toes…

Invited by nightfall, the stars came out, igniting in turns. Even this late in February, bits of the winter constellations took shape. A glimpse of Sirius, the Dog Star. Above her, dependable Arcturus. And Vega, poised to become the North Star in ten more millennia. She wondered whether she would be around to see that. There were longevity spells…but there was also a price.

Marigold snapped her fingers, and a spark formed that hovered just over her shoulder, allowing her to see the parchment and what she inscribed on it. Athwart blinked and turned her face away.

Ones and zeroes she began to print, clearly and carefully, on the parchment. The ink did not run; but dried immediately. The code was much too long to fit across the parchment, or even across thirty of them, so she doubled it back in the ancient Linear B style, left to right for the odd-numbered lines, right to left for the evens, thus creating one continuous sequence. Small she printed; each numeral no larger than an eleven-point. Even with that size, she used up the entire sheet, leaving but a quarter inch or so all around. At twenty minutes to midnight, she inscribed the last 1.

Light from the full moon overwhelmed that from the stars like cosmetic foundation over freckles: the stars were present, but no longer visible. The spark she had created still lurked over her shoulder, awaiting any further bidding she might have for it. Athwart, bored, had gone inside to watch a culinary show involving unusual foods. Marigold looked up. The Man in the Moon seemed to wink at her, knowing what she was about.

Eight minutes. Six. Three.

Marigold laid a Palmetto on the railing and enabled it. The clock in the top right corner confirmed the accuracy of her own time forecast. Two minutes and twenty-seven seconds and counting down. The monitor also showed the date, with the month and year. It also indicated she had no messages pending.

So what else is new?

She draped the parchment over the railing. The spell required the light from the sun to ignite the parchment, even though the ignition had to be performed at midnight. The Moon reflected sunlight. From a pocket of her jeans she withdrew a magnifying glass. She turned the handle this way and that until the lens formed a tight spot of light. She waited.

Fifty-seven seconds.

She drew a full breath and held it for a couple beats before she expelled it. Thus relaxed, she steadied the glass in her hand. Time counted, unabated. The people of the world would wake up to better lives as they had to connect to one another in real time. Her gift to them. They would never know who had bestowed it on them, but that scarcely mattered to Marigold.

Thirty seconds. She aimed the dot of light at the parchment. Heat accumulated. Fifteen. A dark dot began to form on the parchment. Eight. The dot began to emit wisps of smoke. Four. One. The dot burst into flame.

The parchment burned. Marigold studied the Palmetto monitor. Nothing was happening there. Her heart lurched. Something was wrong. A zero? A one? Or did she have to wait until the entire parchment was ashes?

Ye goddesses…

C'mon, she urged the Palmetto and the flames. C'mon. I can save the world…

Plus thirty-two seconds. The parchment was ash. On the monitor, time kept on running without pause into the future. She stared at it in disbelief. Nothing had changed.

Nothing.

The stars held to their courses; the Moon man still watched her—perhaps with a sardonic smile now. A breeze blew. Waves frothed in the distant ocean. And all personal communication devices on the planet still operated. She had failed. She shed a tear, and another. Failure left her without even the strength to dry her cheeks. Blinking formed more tears.

I was so sure…

Loneliness set in, adding to her inability to change anything in the world. It would continue on, oblivious to her efforts, to her hopes. She had no friends to console her. Well, maybe one.

"Athwart," she called.

A man emerged onto the deck. Taller than Marigold, he had a shock of loose yellow hair and eyes like Venus in the morning. He was older, and he was naked. He was grizzled and gorgeous and had a sour expression on his face. "I can't believe you fed me locusts," he said. "Don't you have anything better to give me?"

She did.

~ * ~ * ~

Tyree Campbell is a retired U.S. Army translator with over a hundred stories published, including two dozen novels and sixteen novellas in his repertory so far. He also developed and writes the Bombay Sapphire superheroine series for Pro Se Press.

He is kept in reasonable shape by two husky mixes, Coda and Laika, and by the watering needs of everything from carrots to bok choi. He just finished the penultimate draft of a novel whose setting is the Mohorovicic discontinuity between the Earth's crust and mantle.

Learning Something

Useful

Joyce Frohn

"There's someone coming." Baba Yaga said, standing in the doorway of the house. Vasilisa nodded and finished throwing grain to the chickens. "You take care of him."

Vasilisa smiled. "You think I'm ready?" She wiped her hands on her linen dress and slipped on a pair of straw clogs.

Yaga's smile was grim. "I hope so." She started to close the door of the house. "Because I'm not going to be."

"How did you know—" Vasilisa went quiet when she realized the door was firmly shut. A sudden gust of wind brought her a stale odor. Vasilisa realized how Yaga had known someone was coming and why she didn't want to get involved. Or maybe it was that she just didn't care enough to take time from breaking in the hut's newest pair of legs. Vasilisa turned to look at the dirt path coming from the village. She was shocked. A handsome prince in a suit of armor on a prancing white stallion was coming up the path. By the smell he hadn't bathed in a long time and the sour smell was mixed with a spicy odor she knew came from magic.

She stood tall, trying to look impressive and wishing she had a cleaner dress. Behind her the chicken legs of the house were scratching in the dirt. From inside she could hear Yaga thumping around trying to calm the legs down. The horse stopped with a snort as it came level with the skull topped fence.

The rider looked up at the chicken legged house which was now scratching one leg with another. She heard Yaga cursing at the new legs. His eyes were wide. "This is the house of Baba Yaga?"

"Yes. But she is busy. I am Vasilisa, her apprentice. I can help you."

He stared, although whether at the jerky movement of the chicken-legged hut or at her shabby dress she didn't know. She shrugged and pointed to the legs, covering nerves with seeming calm. "It always takes a few weeks to break in a new pair of legs." She tried to make it seem a perfectly ordinary thing.

Just then a window flew open. Baba Yaga stuck her head out. She could hear the knight's gasp as he saw Baba Yaga's face. Between the long nose and the sharp chin; Yaga's face was a bit of a shock but the fact the hint of smile showed her sharp-edged fangs didn't help. "You can fly in the mortar and pestle. Take this kit." She tossed a pack basket out the window. Vasilisa caught it and put the straps on her shoulders. She hoped it had food and a clean dress in it. "And take Cat before I step on it." She tossed the black and white cat out the window. Vasilisa tried to grab him but he twisted in mid-air and landed on his feet beside her, flicking the red ribbon on his tail in her face as he walked to the man-sized mortar behind the hut.

"But I haven't even said what my problem was," the knight managed to say.

"You're not the first idiot in a cursed suit of armor." Yaga slammed the window shut. Then she opened it a little, "Who's the target?"

And that made everything make sense. Vasilisa had heard of men being given a suit armor and sent against an enemy and not being told before they couldn't take the armor off until the job was done.

The man gulped and stared. "Hurry up or I'll come out and make you into a replacement lantern," she said with a snarl.

The man glanced at the skulls mounted on the fence. And stammered out. "Koschei the Deathless."

Yaga giggled. "This would be fun but—" Just then the feet started to walk in a circle. "I have to take it for a run to calm it down. Take off."

"Right." Vasilisa turned to the man and pointed to the path. "Go down the hill and take the path to the left. I'll meet you at the lake. We can camp there for the night and can go over the details then."

The man nodded. He was having trouble holding back his steed.

"Hurry," Cat yelled from the pestle.

Vasilisa glanced over her shoulder to see the chicken feet coming closer.

His eyes widened and his horse galloped out of view.

She bolted for the mortar and jumped in, pulling the pestle sharply upward. In seconds she was soaring above the trees watching the chicken-legged house crashing over the fence sending the chickens scattering. She heard Yaga yelling, "I hate roosters."

Vasilisa pulled the mortar up higher. She flinched as Cat climbed up on her shoulder. "Be careful. This is a thin dress."

"Yaga doesn't mind."

Vasilisa rolled her eyes. "Her skin is tough as leather." She flew in an ever-widening circle.

"Shouldn't you go find that knight? You're not supposed to just be flying around."

"Party pooper." She pulled his tail a bit. "Tattle Tail."

She swooped down over the road and spotted the knight. She wanted to wave but it took both hands to move the pestle. She thought of diving over him but the way his horse was snorting, it wouldn't have been a good idea. She zoomed over the lake. "This is the best thing." She couldn't keep from smiling.

She flew on toward the lake and circled it. "No sign of Koschei. He must be at his cabin."

It took her only a few minutes to find a nice soft patch of grass by the lake and near the road. It took the knight almost an hour to join her. By that time she was going through the pack Yaga had thrown to her.

After the knight dismounted, he tended to his horse and walked to Vasilisa's side. "I'm afraid I didn't introduce myself earlier but—ah—"

Vasilisa nodded. "You were wise to leave quickly."

The knight shrugged and looked at the ground. "Some say that isn't wisdom but cowardice." He paused and Vasilisa understood he was no warrior and when she got a better look at his face she could see he was young. He put his hand out and she took it. No sword calluses, just a lot of dirt. "I'm Aleksandr Pertokov, a prince of Moscow."

Cat stood on his back legs and looked at him. "Which prince? What are you, a third son?"

He stared at Cat. "It talks."

Vasilisa nodded. "Baba Yaga's world took me a while to get used to, too. He's not very polite. But I do need to know all you know about this curse."

Aleksandr nodded and settled himself on the grass. Vasilisa tried to make sitting downwind of him seem casual. Up close the odor was bad. He shrugged. "I guess it began when this girl's father caught me in her bedroom—"

Cat stretched and yawned. "And why didn't he make you marry the girl? You must be a third son or worse."

"She was already engaged to a Czar's son."

Vasilisa raised an eyebrow. "You're lucky to be alive."

He nodded and sighed. "I said I would do anything. But how was I to know? He said all I had to do was attack an old wizard. It was after I had the suit of armer on that he told me to kill Koschei the Deathless." He slumped down.

Vasilisa nodded. This was bad. "So did you try to kill him once and—"

He shook his head. "I'm a city boy. I had no idea where to find him until someone said to ask Baba Yaga. It took me three weeks to find her." He looked very young and panicked.

"So, why Koschei?"

"Because he seduced the girl's mother years ago, disguised as a knight." Aleksandr shrugged. "Or tried to seduce her…" His voice trailed off.

Vasilisa nodded. Like mother, like daughter. But she didn't blame either of the women, it could be hard to put up with a man you didn't know; who you had been married to in childhood. "How did he curse her?"

Aleksandr shrugged. "I didn't ask too many questions." She glanced at him with a raised eyebrow. "There was a sword at my throat."

Vasilisa tried to look wise, but she was feeling her heart flutter at little. "I need to know the exact words of the spell and it would be good to know what kind of spell was on the mother."

"He gave me this sword and said it had to shed Koschei's heart's blood and—"

Vasilisa grinned. "This will be so easy." She reached down and ruffled Cat's ears. Aleksandr looked puzzled and hurt. She hastily explained. "Koschei can't be killed by ordinary ways. And he loves to demonstrate it. All we have to do is wait for someone to come to him for help and you stab Koschei; he gets up unhurt; his supplicant is impressed. Koschei gets twice his usual fee. You get the curse lifted. Everyone is happy."

Aleksandr reached for her arm. Vasilisa twisted away. She didn't want those greasy hands touching her. He looked hurt.

"Have you tried, washing?"

"How can I? I can't get this armor off."

Vasilisa pawed through the pack Yaga had given her. Sure enough there was a small bag inside. She really needed this one. She pulled out a sponge, washcloth, comb and gourd of soap. "Get your boots off and wade into the lake. Use these and you might get some of the smell off." She handed him the soap and sponge. She laid the washcloth on the ground. "I'll leave this towel for you to use when you come out."

Vasilisa checked the bag as soon as he was in the lake. Sure enough the little stick and the cloth were there. She spread the cloth on the ground and whispered, "Cloth, we are hungry." Then she lit a fire. She was glad Aleksandr hadn't seen her using flint and steel. Yaga still hadn't taught her how to light a fire with magic. Cat settled next to her, sniffing the milk-pot. "Go tell our prince supper is served." Cat meowed in protest but headed to the lake.

Soon Aleksandr was coming up. He sniffed the air, hungrily. "I thought you'd like it if I had a meal ready. I didn't know what food you had," Vasilisa said. That was good soap; the smell was almost gone. Cat was already eating the fish and licking his paws. Soon he was curled up asleep on the cloth.

He gasped and dropped to the other side of the blanket. He took the tea she offered him and grabbed a hunk of dark bread with the other hand. He smiled. "I spent the last of my money on grain for my horse. I'm responsible for getting myself in trouble but he's innocent."

She nodded and put a bowl of kasha and some bread aside. "He'll like this, too. Could you gather firewood?" She also put some milk and a bit of fish aside.

After they finished eating, she waited until Aleksandr took the food to the horse. She tapped the cloth and said, "Thank you, cloth." The food disappeared and she pulled the cloth out from under Cat. He grumbled and walked to the fire. She blew on the basket and began the growing spell. She was opening a few bits of the weaving to make a window on one side, when Aleksandr came back with an armload of firewood. "It's small and rough but..."

She took a small bit of pride in the shocked look on his face. She walked over to make a window on his side.

"Now if you'll make a circle of stones for the fire right outside the doorway, we should be snug enough." Aleksandr had his back turned to her while he was building a fire circle. She took the towel, laid it on the floor and pulled it to cover the rough floor. She pulled the tablecloth into a curtain down the middle. Cat stalked into the building and curled up in a corner. Vasilisa took out the washcloth and shook it out until it was the size of a blanket and blew it into a quilt. "You have blankets for yourself?"

"Of course, but if you need them…" He said as he finished the fire circle. He gasped again as he saw the rich red carpet on the floor of the cabin with a purple curtain in the middle and the blue down quilt on one side.

She smiled at him. "I'm fine. I don't mind sleeping rough."

He took a breath. "I'll go and get my blankets. We should get some sleep." Vasilisa smiled and nodded.

She walked over to the fire she had made and picked up a smoldering stick from it. She walked to the new fire pit, laid the stick down and whistled. She smiled as the fire leaped into the pit. She gathered an armload of twigs and blew them larger and then said the doubling charm until there was a large pile of wood by the fire pit. "That should be enough wood. I'm sure Aleksandr doesn't mind feeding the fire." She yawned, magic was tiring. She looked out at the sunset, slipped out of her dress, kicked off her shoes and settled herself under the quilt.

She woke to Cat walking on her face and chanting, "Wake up, wake up. I'm hungry."

She rolled over. "I left you some milk and fish, let me sleep."

Cat pawed at her ear. "I ate them in the night."

Vasilisa rubbed her eyes and pulled her dress on. "I'll get breakfast as soon as I've had a wash. Besides the cloth can't feed us until we take it down." She paused, listening to the even breathing from the other side of the curtain. "And he's still asleep." She stepped into her shoes, shrank her quilt back to a washcloth and picked up the gourd of soap and comb. She smiled at the small pile of wood and added some more wood to the well banked fire. He was good at taking care things and was kind to animals, a good prince.

When she was coming back from the creek, Aleksandr was

coming to it. She smiled at him and handed him the washcloth and soap. She took the cloth down, shook it back to its original size and spread it by the fire. "Cloth, we are hungry." She was spreading butter on the bread and putting the teapot on the fire when Aleksandr came up.

He dropped down and started eating. "I'll never get used to this."

She wrapped smoked fish in a cloth. Cat reached a paw toward it. She slapped his paw with a finger. "That's for Missy." Aleksandr raised an eyebrow as a question. She held the fish close as she said, "Missy is Koschei's cat." She sighed. "If he's been drinking—" She sucked her breath in. "Let's just say it's best to check with her to see if he's up to having company."

Cat rubbed his head against her body. "Missy will be so glad to have that." When they finished eating, Aleksandr picked up his blankets. Vasilisa drew a map for him. "If you follow the river as it leaves the lake, you'll come to where it splits. Take the right fork and you'll see a small wooden cabin on the other side of the river. Wait for me on this side of the river, it's deep."

"Yes, I'll wait for you there." She waited until he was behind the bend in the road. She took a cup from her bag and held it above the fire. She spoke a few words and water came flowing out onto the fire. She waited until she was sure the fire was out.

Cat tried to grab the bag of fish. "I'll carry that. You know I'll make sure it gets to Missy."

Vasalia grabbed the bag from his mouth. "That can go in my pack." When she had everything shrunk down and packed it back in her basket, Cat tried to climb in. She pulled him out and carried him to the pestle by the scruff of his neck. "Behave yourself."

She had been waiting for Aleksandr for an hour when he rode up. His horse was lathered from running. Aleksandr smiled at her but rubbed down his horse before tying it to a small tree. She rubbed Cat's head, "A true prince always takes care of his animals and people." She stepped out of the mortar and leaned the pestle against it. She took out the washcloth and put one edge at the riverbank. "Drink."

Aleksandr came up to her. "How are we going get across." He stared as the water flowed into the washcloth.

Cat wandered along the riverbank. "Missy," he called.

Vasilisa smiled at a tiger-striped cat. "In a minute." She glanced at the water level, dropping fast. When the river was only ankle deep, she walked over with Cat riding on her shoulder. She reached a hand back toward Aleksandr, "It's safe." He gingerly walked through the low water.

Cat jumped out of the basket with the smoked fish in his mouth and ran up to the striped cat. He was purring as he dropped the fish. "A good time?" He tried rubbing against her head.

Missy was devouring the fish but raised her head. "No." She rubbed her eyes with a paw. "Koschei is dead. Yesterday he spilled something and it hit him and..."

Aleksandr stared at the small white cabin and screamed. "No. How? He can't die. I have to...I have to..."

"Koschei the deathless was also Koschei the careless and Koschei the Illiterate," Vasilisa began. "If we hurry, there'll still be some blood in his heart." She started leading him to the house. "Be careful. Even dead, he's dangerous."

Aleksandr nodded and drew his sword.

"Don't go through the door! It'll be booby-trapped." Vasilisa reached for him as he ran through. There was a crash, a billow of purple smoke and Vasilisa stopped.

"Aleksandr?" she called. She looked down and saw the edge of his mail tunic. She grabbed it and pulled. It began to fall apart. "Aleksandr!" she yelled as she pulled on the tunic. As the mail broke into a pile of rust, she saw movement inside it. "Don't worry. Baba Yaga can fix anything he did." She reached into the thrashing pile. There was something small, a purple toad with a jewel in its head. "Is that you, Aleksandr?"

The toad nodded.

She wrapped her hands around him and hurried toward where the two cats had been. "Missy? Can you..." She paused and watched a tiger give Cat a last lick on the face before walking away.

Cat looked up at her, whiskers drooping. "His spells on her were already fading."

Vasilisa held out the toad. "We have to get back to Baba Yaga as fast as possible. This is Aleksandr."

Cat leaped the small stream. "That's your problem." She followed him over, pausing to pick up the washcloth which was no larger than it had been. She twisted the edges together and wrung out a river. She shook it dry and dropped it in her pack basket. She walked to the mortar. "We should be home in a few hours." She looked at the horse. "We just have to figure out how to get his horse back. That's easy."

"Easy. Right." Cat said.

It was two days later Vasilisa walked up to the skull topped fence leading the horse. She tied it to the fence. Yaga opened a window. "What took you so long? Missy sent word through the bears."

"The horse couldn't stand to be near the mortar so I've been leading him a bit and then going back for the mortar." Yaga shook her head and whistled. Vasilisa saw the mortar and pestle fly back to its normal place. Cat jumped out and leaped though a window into the house.

"You need to practice charming animals or at least riding them. So you got nothing done?"

"Not quite." Vasilisa drew a small cage of willow branches from the ground.

Baba Yaga ran down the ladder. "It's beautiful. I didn't know Koschei could do something so…" She reached out for the cage. "If I study it enough; I'm sure I can duplicate it." She reached a finger through the bars and stroked the toad's back. "You're beautiful. We'll take good care of you."

Vasilisa shook her head and pulled the cage back. "You have to reverse the spell; that's Aleksandr. He hit a booby trap."

"So we lost a booby and gained something wonderful."

"He's a prince."

"Russia has many princes and no purple jeweled toads. So we keep the toad."

"But he was human."

"Russia has enough of those, too."

Vasilisa pulled the cage close. "Just take the enchantments off of him."

Yaga sighed. "I will but you might regret it. And I still prefer toads to men." She held her hands over the cage and began to chant. Light came from her hands and enveloped the cage. Vasilisa had to shut her eyes.

When she could open them, a skinny, ragged man was sitting on the ground on the broken remains of the cage. She stared at him for several minutes. He slowly rose and took the reins of the horse.

He stared at the ground and sighed. "I never meant to lie to you. I'm a prince...but—" Yaga snarled at him and jumped back into the house.

Vasilisa shook her head as he took the horse's reins. She watched him ride away and climbed the ladder. "You're right; I need to study more."

~ * ~ * ~

Joyce Frohn has stories out in two current anthologies, "Dark Cheer: Cryptids Emerging" and "Crunchy With Chocolate". She became a published writer after graduating from college with a biology degree. She understands that's normal. She shares a house with a very supportive husband, a college-student daughter, two cats, a gecko, a guinea pig and a lot of neglected housework. She would like to thank the monsters under her bed.

Night Work

Rose Strickman

He had parked some distance away, at the end of the long drive, and crunched up the gravel through the insect-buzzing woods. The front porch was brightly lit, encased in mosquito netting. A woman sat inside, bent over dark fabric piled on a table. Her hand rose, a needle flashing in her fingers.

There came a soft mew, startling him. On the front step, a small black cat, near invisible in the darkness, detached itself and entered the porch through a cat flap. It leaped onto the woman's lap, and she looked up, needle suspended, pale eyes bright in the night.

He straightened, pulling his suit into order, before marching to the front steps. "Hello?" he called. "Are you Jenna Marten?"

She said nothing, merely looking at him with wide eyes through the mosquito netting.

"I'm Patrick Roth," he said, raising his voice slightly. "May I come in? I'm here to discuss the proposition."

After a moment, she nodded. Patrick ascended the steps and swung open the door.

Inside, the porch was warm on this summer night, with a slight breeze blowing through. The woman didn't rise to greet him, but sat in her wicker chair, the cat a black velvet bundle in her lap. Her sewing project lay spread over the table: a black coat on which she was embroidering white roses, glinting with little sparkling beads.

"That's a nice design." She inclined her head in acknowledgement. He indicated the other chair. "May I sit down?"

She nodded, and he sat. She made one last stitch before sticking the needle into the fabric and carefully folding her project into a large basket she placed beside her chair.

"You *are* Jenna Marten?" Another nod. Patrick shifted and cleared his throat. "Well, you weren't easy to find, Ms. Marten. You didn't respond to any of our messages." He shifted some more. "You look, uh, different than I expected." Patrick had been envisioning either an old crone with wild white hair and a crazed cackle, or a voluptuous vixen with masses of black curls, sparkling black eyes

~ 213 ~

and full red lips. But Jenna was small and skinny, dressed in tired old shorts and a ragged t-shirt, with fine, light-brown hair and unremarkable blue eyes. Her features were sharp, and she seemed younger than her twenty-something years.

Jenna said nothing to this. Patrick had the impression she could have waited there all night in perfect silence.

"I hope I didn't disturb you. We were told we'd have a better chance of finding you awake at night. And at the—ah—dark of the moon, you didn't leave your house. So much."

"Who?" Her voice was soft and scratchy, and so unexpected Patrick jumped a little.

"I'm sorry?"

"Who told you?" Though quiet, her voice was insistent.

"Robin Oakwood. He said you were old associates."

Her lips parted in a soundless laugh, and she shook her head ruefully. One hand rose to scratch the cat's ears.

When it became clear she wasn't going to furnish him with more details, Patrick continued, "I'd like to discuss a very interesting proposition with you, Ms. Marten." He leaned forward, only to hesitate. "Ah—we are alone?"

"Only my parents," she said in that soft voice. "They won't wake."

"You live with your parents?"

She stared at him.

"Right. None of my business. Anyway, Ms. Marten, I come as a representative of the Pecks campaign. John Pecks, as you know, is running for state Senator and I think we can all agree he is the best man for the job. And now *you*, Ms. Marten, have a chance to help—"

"What does he want?" Her voice was as calm and quiet as ever, cutting across Patrick's spiel.

"He wants to win the election," Patrick said at last.

Jenna sat back, stroking her cat. It half-closed its eyes in pleasure, purring. Patrick concealed a shudder. He hated cats, almost as much as Pecks himself did.

"We—the Pecks campaign—would like to hire your—your specialized services. Basically, Ms. Marten, we would like to pay you to ensure John Pecks wins the election. I'm authorized to offer you a considerable amount of money, Ms. Marten, upward of one million dollars. If you can guarantee Pecks will win."

She seemed to consider this. Then she shook her head.

"Two million? We *do* have some very generous donors—"

"Not the money." Jenna shook her head again. "Can't guarantee Pecks will win. Too complicated." She made an eloquent gesture, as if gathering scraps out of the air. "The election. Too much going on. Too many people. No spell could control all that."

Patrick shifted uncomfortably at the mention of a *spell*. He still didn't like to think of it that way. Still, he was encouraged: she seemed to be bargaining. "There must be something you can do. Robin had such good things to say about your work—"

She let out a soft, contemptuous noise, rolling her eyes. In her lap, the cat glared at Patrick through supercilious slits.

Patrick gave it an unloving look. "Is there anything you can do, Ms. Marten?"

"Maybe." She paused. "Don't usually do this kind of work."

Enough of the velvet glove, Patrick decided: it was time for the iron fist. "Robin said you might say that." He fished around his pocket. "He said if you did, I was to show you this."

He placed the clay bead, strung on a long cord of leather, on the table. Jenna froze at the sight of it. So did the cat, staring with wide eyes.

"Does this mean anything to you?" Patrick eventually asked.

Jenna gave a single, stiff nod. She reached out to take the bead, stuffing it away out of sight in her own pocket. "How much money?"

Victory. Patrick hid a smile as they progressed to the real negotiations.

~ * ~

"She wants *me* to go see *her*?" Pecks scowled in his luxurious office overlooking the city skyline.

"I told you she wouldn't come here." Robin Oakwood lounged on one of the leather sofas. He was as annoyingly well-dressed and good-looking as ever, Patrick noted with a surge of irritation: his sheet of long black hair, his bright green eyes, framed by curling lashes, startling against his flawless, dusky skin. Robin had proven himself highly useful to Pecks' campaign, but Patrick had never warmed to him. He was just too handsome, with too much mocking humor hidden behind those slanting eyes.

"Jenna never comes into the city," Robin continued, the familiar note of laughter ringing in his musical voice. "Not if she can possibly help it."

"Well, she can help it this time!" Pecks stood and paced to the window. As always, Patrick admired him in motion: for such a short, thin man, he moved with great conviction, every gesture filled with authority. That was power for you. "I don't have time to go gallivanting around the backwoods—"

"Jenna's services *are* highly specialized," Robin said, interrupting Pecks as only he dared to do. "Very rare, and very valuable. Not to mention her powers are much stronger out in, as you put it, the backwoods. You'll get better value for your money if you meet her on her terms."

"I thought you said you could make her cooperate." Patrick folded his arms and scowled at Robin. "I thought you could call in a favor she owes you."

"True," Robin said. "I can make her cooperate. But for her spell to actually work, there must be an exchange of some kind, by money or some other medium. That's how her kind of magic operates."

"Spell," Pecks grumbled. "*Magic.* We don't even know what this girl can do!"

"Jenna is a woman, not a girl." Robin's eyes gleamed. "And trust me: she can do a great deal."

"Oh, really?" Pecks' lips twitched at the thought of what *else* a woman could do. Still, he gave Robin a satisfyingly sour glance. "She'd better, Oakwood, after all the trouble she's putting me through. *And* the amount she's charging."

Robin smiled, slow and beautiful. "Oh," he said, "don't worry about *that.* You'll get magic aplenty, I guarantee."

~ * ~

Two weeks later, on the day before the full moon, Pecks and his two aides set out.

On Robin's advice, they traveled incognito into the countryside, though Pecks protested at the lost campaigning opportunity ("Rural voters love me!"). They also left behind most of Pecks' entourage, reducing the party to Patrick, Robin and Pecks himself. They drove out to the small town near Jenna's isolated house, the windows of the car tinted, Pecks and Robin invisible in back while Patrick drove.

They arrived in the mellow glow of a summer afternoon and parked the car in a public lot. Pecks remained hidden in the vehicle while Patrick and Robin went out to forage for dinner. Robin seemed pleased with the little town: he straightened, looking around with shining eyes, and drew deep breaths, smiling brilliantly. "What are you so happy about?" Patrick demanded in irritation.

"I enjoy this place." Robin gave a fond glance at the late afternoon sun, the leafy riverside park and brick buildings. "And I like being out of the city."

"I suppose it *is* pretty around here," Patrick said grudgingly. He half-glanced over his shoulder at the car they'd left parked on the other side of the bridge, beyond the shallow, gurgling river.

Robin correctly interpreted his look. "Don't worry," he said. "Pecks won't wander off."

"Of course not!" Patrick said, too hastily. "It's just…he gets bored."

"That he does." Robin shrugged. "But he won't wander. Not this time."

Patrick was still wondering in alarm whether Robin had locked Pecks in the car, even as they brought back tacos and drinks. By this time, the summer dusk was settling over the town, casting a purple twilight along the river and dim shadows between the buildings, through which locals darted like fish. Overhead, the first few stars appeared. It was a beautiful evening, but the gathering darkness, combined with their errand tonight, gave Patrick a strange shiver.

"So what now?" Pecks asked through a mouthful of taco.

Robin swallowed. "Now, when we've finished eating, we go meet Jenna at the appointed location."

"We don't need to pick her up or anything?" Patrick sipped a Coke.

Robin shook his head. "She'll make her own way there."

"Can you believe this!" Pecks exploded suddenly, glaring into his smartphone. "That Woodley bitch's polls are up!" A vein popped in his forehead. "It's all about visiting those hospitals. Kissing babies—"

"After tonight, the election will be a foregone conclusion," Robin said. Patrick raised an eyebrow at him: Jenna had said the exact opposite, and Robin knew it. Robin ignored him with utter serenity, patting Pecks on the wrist. "Just wait."

Pecks relaxed, lowering his phone. "I hate that cow," he muttered in a savage undertone. "I just hope this Jenna of yours has something to defeat her." He closed his teeth on his taco.

Something flashed in Robin's eyes, but he lowered his lashes before Patrick could catch it.

When they had finished eating, they set out again.

Out of town they wove, and along curving country lanes, while other cars flashed in blazes of headlights and the huge full moon sailed overhead between trees and mountaintops. The lights of houses and farms soon fell away as they pushed deeper into the forests. Pecks growled in dismay when the asphalt gave way to gravel and dirt. "We're almost there, sir," Patrick assured him. He'd checked it out a week earlier and plugged the coordinates into the map app on his phone. Though now the phone seemed to be malfunctioning, the computer's voice becoming tinny and the screen flickering before suddenly going blank.

"Dammit," Patrick muttered, shaking his phone. Well, he was sure he could find the place again. He spotted a familiar-looking stump, the remains of a tree blasted by lightning, and sped up.

They parked at the edge of the road and got out, Pecks grumbling and adjusting his tie, Robin as assured as ever. Indeed, he seemed even happier out here in the woods, grinning up at bats as they swooped overhead, and setting off into the grassy verge even before Patrick got out the flashlight.

"She'd better have something good after all this," Pecks muttered as they wound down the path, toward the voice of the invisible dark stream. "This is like something out of a horror movie." He swatted at mosquitoes.

"Oh, she will." Robin's cheerful voice floated back as they tramped across the rickety wooden bridge. Another turn of the path, and the ruin of the ancient mill came into view.

It had been well constructed, this mill. Even though the great wheel was gone, along with the roof and every floor, window and door, the stone structure itself remained, a perfect hollow shell. Someone was sitting in one of the empty windows, a pale blur in the darkness. She lifted her head at their approach, and Patrick recognized Jenna. The cat, he saw with relief, was nowhere in evidence.

"Ms. Marten!" he called. "How'd you—we didn't see your car."

She said nothing to this, but pushed herself out of the window frame and strolled around to the empty doorway, beckoning them after her.

Inside, the ruin loomed tall and ominous in the beam of Patrick's flashlight. Leaves piled up against the walls. In a corner, something scuttled. Patrick jumped, heart thudding, and scowled at Robin's smirk.

"Hello!" Setting aside his disgust at his surroundings, Pecks advanced on Jenna with his widest campaign smile, holding out his hand. "You must be Jenna Marten. I'm John Pecks, Senatorial candidate. Nice to meet you!"

Jenna looked at his hand, unsmiling, and made no move to take it. Awkwardly, he lowered his arm.

"I was told your, ah, special talents might help me win," he said. "You will of course be amply compensated…" He trailed off as Jenna began walking around him, studying him as though he was a rather unimpressive piece of statuary.

Jenna completed her orbit. "Hmmm." She shot a narrow-eyed look at Robin, who smiled.

Pecks tried again. "I understand you have certain specialized skills, Ms. Marten, which could increase my chances—"

"Quiet." Jenna's soft voice cut through the air like a knife.

A muscle worked in Pecks' jaw, but he fell silent. Patrick stepped closer, standing by Pecks protectively. He glared at Jenna, who ignored him. She took Pecks' right hand, peering closely at the palm; then stepped closer, to stare into his eyes with a deep frown.

After a long moment, she stepped back, sighing. She gave Robin another sour glance and shook her head. Robin just grinned, bright and sharp in the night.

"So—can you do anything?" Patrick's voice was perhaps a trifle higher than usual.

"Yeah," Pecks said. "What did you see there, little lady?" He tried his best campaigning grin on her again, but under these circumstances, it fell flat.

"Can't guarantee you'll win," Jenna whispered like a sigh of wind. "But I can make people more likely to vote for you."

Pecks smiled again. "That's all I need. Voters already love me, you know."

Jenna had already turned away. Humming an odd little tune under her breath, she wandered around the ruin, occasionally bending down to pluck something from the ground. Flowers, Patrick saw: bright summer flowers hidden among the dead leaves, glowing between Jenna's hands. How could flowers grow inside this dark old mill?

Still humming, she turned back to Pecks, hands moving, weaving a long chain out of the flowers, spilling down toward the earth. Taking up the completed chain, she stood directly before him.

"Hold out your hands." Slowly, Pecks did so. Jenna began that melodious hum again, a strange, dreamy tune, as she wound the flower chain around Pecks' wrists and then around her own.

Pecks gave a laugh that didn't entirely hide his nervousness. "What's this going to do?"

"Charm," Robin said as Jenna continued composedly humming and binding the chain. "It's a spell to increase your personal charm and charisma. Right, Jenna?"

She nodded as she tied off the final knot. She looked up into Pecks' eyes. "This will make strangers trust you," she said. "It will make crowds listen to your words. It will make your words be remembered and heeded. It will make you stand out as special. It will make them love you." She paused. "Do you consent, John Pecks? In exchange for money, will you take this spell?"

"Oh, yes." Pecks' eyes shone, mouth hanging open in eagerness.

Jenna nodded. She straightened, taking a deep breath—

"Arrgh!" Pecks suddenly kicked out to an earsplitting yowl. Jenna's cat, barely visible in the shadows, jumped back, screaming, from Pecks' lashing foot.

"Goddamn cat!" Pecks' breathing was sharp and labored, his face a rictus of loathing. "Goddamn cat, where'd *that* come from?!"

"Here, sir!" Patrick hurried to snatch the animal up, but it spat at him and streaked away, leaping up and out of one of the empty windows, disappearing into the night. Patrick craned over the sill to make sure it had really left and breathed a sigh of relief.

"It's gone, sir." He turned back and faltered at the scene his flashlight revealed. Pecks, still tied to Jenna, was breathing hard and hadn't noticed Jenna had gone rigid, her face a frozen mask as she stared at Pecks through eyes that seemed—Patrick's flashlight shook—completely *black*, no whites or irises at all—

Patrick leaped forward, but too late: Jenna's hands had already swooped like claws, to wrap around Pecks' wrists. She yanked him close and whispered, whispered and whispered, until the indistinct phrases scuttled around the ruined mill like rats and the flowers glowed like neon stars—

Then, abruptly, darkness and silence fell, broken only by Pecks' and Patrick's sharp pants.

He had fallen to his knees, Patrick realized, dropping the flashlight. He groped around for it and switched it on again. Its beam revealed Pecks, also on his knees, gasping for air in the middle of the ruin.

"Sir? Sir!" Patrick hurried to haul Pecks to his feet. "Are you all right, sir?"

"I'm fine." Pecks coughed.

Partially reassured, Patrick looked around for Jenna, but she was nowhere to be seen. Nor, Patrick saw in increasing alarm, was Robin. "Robin? Robin!"

"I'm here." Robin appeared in the doorway. "Apologies," he said, lounging in. "I had to see Jenna off." He peered at Pecks. "How are you feeling, sir?"

Pecks breathed hard for a moment, his head bowed. Then he looked up with a long, slow smile that lit up the dark old mill.

"I'm fine!" he said, and a sense of bliss and wellbeing suffused Patrick at those words. "This is the best I've ever been!"

"Wonderful!" Patrick grinned. Indeed, he couldn't stop grinning as Pecks' happiness flooded his being. He sprang smartly back as Pecks leaped up.

"I see the spell worked," Robin said dryly.

"Of course it worked!" Pecks practically danced toward the door. "I'm ready to win this election right now!" He pumped his fists, shadowboxing.

"Of course! Of course!" Patrick gave a little skip, following Pecks out. Robin trailed after them with a silent, shadowed smile.

~ * ~

The next few weeks were among the most energetic and productive of Patrick's life—or, rather, of Pecks' life. He streaked through his campaign like a blazing comet, and not only Patrick but everyone else thrilled to be near him.

On Robin's advice, they sent Jenna her payment immediately. "If you don't make the exchange," Robin said, "the effects of the spell won't last. And pay in full. Trust me, *pay in full.*"

So they paid. As Pecks said, it was well worth it: with Pecks' charm and confidence constantly at full meridian, the campaign went four times as well.

Patrick practically danced every time he saw Pecks' polls. With the spell, Pecks could now persuade his campaign workers and volunteers to work twice as hard. His every public appearance was a roaring success. His TV interviews all went beautifully, and the Internet reacted positively to his every statement. It all had an effect: his numbers soared.

"I think it's time for another campaign rally," Pecks said mid-July. He and Patrick stood looking at a graph comparing his numbers to Woodley's. Pecks linked his hands behind his back and chuckled with pleasure. "Let's give this charisma spell a live audience."

"Good idea, sir." Patrick checked his calendar. "When were you thinking?"

"End of August." Pecks winked. "I guarantee I can get a venue." He and Patrick both laughed: no one had refused Pecks anything since Jenna's spell.

Best million dollars anyone ever spent! Patrick left the room with a spring in his step.

Preparations for the rally soon consumed the Pecks campaign. Patrick worked around the clock, facilitating preparations and communicating Pecks' requirements. Time flew by.

The day before the rally, Patrick bustled past Pecks' office door, arms full of equipment, and almost ran into Robin, just emerging from the office.

"Oh—sorry." He stepped back, cradling the laptop. Robin just smiled, closing the door behind him. "Were you with Pecks?" Patrick was surprised: Robin didn't usually meet with Pecks without Patrick in attendance.

"Oh, yes." There was an odd gleam in Robin's eye. "We were just discussing payment for my work in his campaign."

"Well, you certainly deserve it," Patrick said, only slightly grudging. He still didn't like Robin, even after all this time, but had to admit he'd done amazing work. "You connected us with Jenna

Marten, after all. Has she been in contact?" he asked curiously.

Robin shook his head. "Elections don't interest her much, I fear."

Patrick laughed in exultation. "How can she not be interested in this?"

"Well, tonight should be *very* interesting." Robin's grin widened. "Fascinating, in fact. I'll see you then."

He strode off down the hall, with only a faint whiff of evergreen to mark his passage.

~ * ~

Patrick smiled, pleased at the size of the crowd: almost a thousand state voters, all packed into the flag-hung auditorium. He electronically contacted the tech, with orders to make a minute adjustment to the PECKS FOR AMERICA phrase projected onto the screen behind the podium. There. Perfect.

Robin stepped up beside him. "Is everything ready?"

"Yeah, I think so." Patrick spotted some campaign workers in the wrong place. He frowned at them and made *move away* gestures. "Did you see Pecks?"

"I was making some last-minute arrangements." Robin paused. "Patrick—you'd do anything Pecks told you, wouldn't you? You would obey his wishes?"

"What?" Patrick was only half-listening, keeping one eye on his watch. "Oh, yes. Of course I would." Any minute now…

"Yes," Robin purred. "Of course you would."

Patrick looked at him. "What…?"

At that moment, the lights dimmed, the auditorium hushed, and Ellen, another campaign worker, stepped out onto the podium, perfectly coiffed and dressed. "Ladies and gentlemen!" she said into the mic. "I'm so pleased to see each and every one of you! Tonight we come out in support of John Pecks, future state Senator…"

Patrick tuned out most of her welcome speech, watching the shadows where Pecks would emerge. Robin stayed beside him, an elegant shadow of his own.

"…And now, without further delay, please welcome John Pecks!"

The sound system blasted patriotic music, the lights blazed brighter, and John Pecks stepped out of the shadows into the spotlight, waving. The crowd went wild, cheering and clapping and waving signs. Patrick joined in the applause, a grin taking over his face. *Yes,* he thought, *we made it this far.*

"Thank you, thank you!" Pecks stood full square in the spotlight. "I can't tell you how happy I am to see you all. Are you ready for an amazing campaign rally?"

"YES!" Patrick jumped a little at just how loud and emphatic the audience's reply was.

"So am I!" Pecks cried. "This campaign has been one long struggle, but you people make it all worth it! Yes—*you* people!"

"Yes! *Us!*" A spontaneous cheer ran through the crowd: every eye shone in brilliance, fixed on Pecks.

"I am going to be a Senator *for* you! Not just representing you; *for* you—"

"Yes! For US!" Another enormous cheer. A wave of restlessness ran through the audience.

"Under my leadership, this great state—"

"Yes! Great STATE!" Another wave of movement, larger and stronger than before. For a moment, Pecks faltered, smile slipping.

"We will see a new era," he continued. "One of prosperity and equality for all. Healthcare—"

"YES! *Healthcare!*" Patrick could practically smell the sweat and heat of the crowd. Every face bore the same wide, mad grin. A chant swelled: "*Pecks...Pecks...Pecks...*"

Patrick frowned. "Something's wrong," he murmured to Robin. "I'm getting security." He reached for his phone—only to have his hand freeze in midair. He strained but couldn't move it. In fact, he couldn't move at all. He was a standing statue next to Robin.

A long, graceful hand alighted on his shoulder. "Oh, no," Robin murmured in his ear. "Don't go, Patrick. This show's just getting started."

"Yes, state healthcare will be perfect under my leadership!" Patrick could see the sweat on Pecks' face, even over the moiling crowd. "I will be a Senator for the people, with your welfare constantly—"

"*Pecks...Pecks...PECKS!*" The chant grew louder. Everyone leaped to their feet, and motion ran through the crowd like a current. Even security officers and campaign workers gazed at Pecks with hungry eyes and chanted, waving their arms. Only Patrick and

Robin seemed unaffected, a lone, unnoticed island in the rising sea of violence.

"Sir! *Sir!*" Patrick screamed or tried to. He couldn't speak, couldn't move, as Pecks continued his speech, caught up in his own spell.

His own spell...

No! Patrick howled silently as the wave of rallygoers broke, sweeping toward the podium.

"PECKS! PECKS! PECKS!" People screamed out the chant, throwing themselves onto the platform. "PECKS! PECKS! PECKS!" They bellowed as they reached Pecks. "PECKS! PECKS! PECKS!" The horrible chant didn't stop even when Pecks broke off, mouth falling open, eyes going wide. It didn't stop even when he began screaming, trying to fight his way off the podium, through the roiling mass of people who surged forward, pouring over him, eyes crazed—

Robin let out a long, low whistle. "I'm impressed," he said to Patrick. "They didn't take long to go completely mad, did they? Jenna is certainly skilled."

A silent scream tore Patrick's throat as the first bloodstains appeared, spattering the adoring, seething throng that now loved Pecks so much they could not stop themselves from tearing him apart. Patrick shut his eyes, the only movement he was capable of.

"If only," Robin continued in regretful tones, "Pecks hadn't kicked Jenna's familiar. The one thing she couldn't forgive. Still," he added more cheerfully, "Ms. Woodley should be pleased. I'd say I fulfilled *my* half of the bargain."

Patrick's eyes flew open, even as he was forced to take in the carnage once more. Robin had had a bargain with Jenna, an exchange of favors, one he'd used to enlist her services. But what if he'd had *another* bargain...one he'd used his bargain with Jenna to fulfill...

Oh my God.

"Well, time to go, I think." Patrick swiveled helplessly around to face Robin. Now that he'd set aside his glamour, Robin glowed with inhuman beauty, eyes slit-pupiled like a cat's, ears pointed as daggers. "Pecks promised you to me, you see, just yesterday, as payment for my services. And you said you would obey him." He grinned, bright and sharp. "So come along."

And Patrick, caught in the spell, followed Robin from the auditorium, while behind them the first screams of realization and horror rang out and the terrified murderers reeled from the blood-soaked podium.

~ * ~

It was a peaceful, starry night. Jenna had finished her sewing and stolen away into the forest, her cat, Gompers, a soft shadow at her side. She now sat on a log and watched her familiar prowl around the clearing, careful to avoid the circle of wrinkled mushrooms. At Robin's silent approach, she looked up but didn't rise.

"Hello, Jenna." She nodded, and looked curiously at the silent, expressionless figure trailing behind him. Only Patrick's eyes were alive, darting to and fro, lit with helpless terror. He stared at Jenna, pleading with her in silence.

She raised an eyebrow at Robin. He grinned. "Pecks' payment to me," he said. "Not a wonderful personality, to be sure, but my Queen has many uses for a man of Patrick's energies and talents." He gave a happy sigh. "This has been a most satisfactory operation. A mortal prize, a bargain with soon-to-be Senator Woodley, my Queen's orders fulfilled…She was most emphatic Pecks not win, you know." He inclined his head to Jenna. "Of course, I give you full credit for your part. That was most cunning: strengthening the charm spell, giving Pecks *too much* of what he wanted. Very clever."

Gompers leaped onto the log and leaned against Jenna, purring. She scratched his ears and gave Robin a glower of deep suspicion. He widened his eyes. "What? You don't think I *arranged* for Pecks to kick poor Gompers, do you?"

She folded her arms, still glaring. He grinned. "Be cheered, Jenna: at least our own bargain is now fulfilled. I have no further claims on you." His eyes gleamed. "Not *yet*, anyway."

She waved a dismissive hand, rolling her eyes, and gathered Gompers into her arms. She rose to her feet and stood back as Robin led his captive into the circle of mushrooms. Robin turned back to her and gave a long, flowing bow. "Good night, sweet Jenna. Till next we meet."

She bowed back and watched as, in a flash of green light, the two figures vanished. Then, still cradling her familiar, she flitted away, back into the owl-winged shadows and the brilliant dark.

~ * ~ * ~

Rose Strickman is a fantasy, sci-fi and horror writer living in Seattle, Washington. Her work has appeared in anthologies such as *Sword and Sorceress 32*, *UnCommon Evil* and *Nightmare Fuel*. She has also been published in several e-zines, and has self-published several novellas.

Visit her author's page: www.amazon.com/author/rosestrickman
You can also follow her at: www.facebook/rose.strickman.3/

Breaking Down a Cursed Sandwich

Ray Daley

I couldn't believe my eyes, when the note dropped into my lap from above me. The flat door was closed, locked in fact. Deliberately, so I had no distractions from my writing. I'd only done it because I had been finding it impossible to get going recently. It was almost as if...

I had been having what I had thought to be a run of bad luck today. Milk seemed to be spoiling faster than normal, literally a matter of hours before it went off. My washing machine had overflowed twice in the last few hours as well. I opened the note and read it.

YOU HAVE BEEN CURSED. DO NOT ATTEMPT TO SEEK HELP. THIS CURSE WILL WEAR OFF IN THREE DAYS.

Okay. Cursed, eh?

A curse would account for why I'd dropped both of my last two meals on the floor for no apparent reason. So, who had cursed me, and more to the point, why? I looked up and saw nothing but the paint flaking on the ceiling above my head. Where in the hell had that note come from?

At that point, another note dropped out of the air into my hands.

SHUT UP AND STOP OVERTHINKING IT. YOU'RE CURSED, I DID IT, AND I'LL EXPLAIN WHY IN THREE DAYS. JUST WAIT FOR THE DAMN PHONE CALL, OKAY?

I guess that was me told then. I had to live with dropping crockery, tripping over carpets, and stubbing my toes on anything and everything for the next three days. I stopped eating food at home completely. In fact, I left the house immediately and went to check into a hotel.

~ * ~

After I'd checked in, I didn't leave the room once. Fortunately, I'd had the good sense to have all my calls forwarded to the hotel room.

Checking in was interesting. My credit cards didn't want to go through. Not any of them.

I smiled at the receptionist. "Okay, this will sound crazy, but I've been cursed. Which is probably why you can't get my cards to work. I'll whisper a web link to you, you can access my PayPal account and bill me from there, okay?"

She brushed invisible lint off her blouse and adjusted her name badge. *My name is Stefanie.* She said yes; it was crazy, but she took my details and billed me online. Not that the curse didn't try to waylay me there too. Their computer crashed (twice) and it plunged the entire hotel into darkness for over an hour, during an apparent freak power cut. Stefanie just switched on a flashlight she kept behind the counter as I waved, smiled and said: "I told you; I'm cursed!"

The power came back, and they eventually received my money. I took no chances and walked to my room, up the stairs. I didn't fancy several hours stuck in a dark lift with complete strangers, screaming their heads off. I'd asked for a room with a standard key, so she'd given me a room on the very top floor. I knew any electronic door card would have proved to be as useless as my credit cards had been.

The room was nice enough, for one holding a cursed man. The television was stuck on the religious channel. The taps in the bathroom all dripped non-stop, and the door couldn't be fully closed. So, I had that to put up with when I wanted to sleep. Any food I ordered via room service took at least an hour, and was always cold by the time it reached me. I explained my curse to the concierge, a miracle worker named Bob, who was used to dealing with all kinds of problematic guests.

Bob just gave me a jovial smile. "I can have a microwave oven placed inside your room to reheat the food, sir!"

I immediately saw all kinds of potential problems from the curse there. It'd probably blow up, catch fire, or irradiate me in the process. Probably all of the above, knowing my current state. "No, have it kept on the other side of the hall. Room service can knock, reheat the food, then I can take it once it's cooled a little. So, I don't burn myself."

~ * ~

I was able to sleep. Of course, the curse had its fair share of things to say about that small matter. Like how the mattress was infested with bedbugs. The replacement mattress had several springs sticking through. The sheets they'd given me were coated in, well, dried sperm by the look and smell of it. And the new sheets they gave me had been starched strongly enough for someone living in the deepest circle of hell. But I slept, eventually.

And I was able to shower. Albeit in scalding hot or ice-cold water. Not once was I able to have a nice shower, it was mostly jumping in and out of the water, and slipping all over the bathroom floor. At least I didn't fall and break my neck, I'd thought ahead and placed fluffy towels all over the tiled floor.

It was a thoroughly miserable three days I spent in the Grand Hotel. Nothing but the religious channel to watch, not just one but four Gideon bibles in my bedside drawer to read. All printed in Italian, I hasten to add. At least I had Bob at my beck and call, ensuring I wasn't dead, or otherwise horribly cursed each morning. He kept me fed, watered and generally sane. He even had one bell-boy read the newspaper to me each day, so I didn't get horrible paper cuts, and on the final morning, the phone rang.

I just sat there on the bed, staring at it.

Then a note dropped from the ceiling, into my lap. THE CURSE IS OVER, SHITHEAD. ANSWER THE DAMN PHONE, IT'S ME.

I picked it up. "This better be the most amazing explanation ever, or I'll go crazy at you."

It was a female voice. "Watch."

Another note dropped into my hands. STOP WITH THE THREATS. I CAN CURSE YOU WHENEVER I LIKE, FOR AS LONG AS I LIKE. UNLESS YOU WANT TO LIVE THE REST OF YOUR LIFE IN THIS MISERABLE HOTEL, I SUGGEST YOU SHUT THE HELL UP AND LISTEN TO ME?

"Okay. You've got my attention. Go ahead, I'm listening."

"Good. I'm sending you an address. Come here right away, and I'll explain everything."

If you guessed another note dropped into my hands at that exact moment, score all the points in the world.

Stefanie was waiting to check me out in the lobby. Of course, there were surplus charges to pay on my bill. Ripped sheets, a blocked toilet. My credit card went through the first time, as Concierge Bob hailed a cab for me. "Best of luck with the curse, sir. We're always ready to serve you here at the Grand, if you're ever in need again."

~ * ~

In hindsight, I should have walked. The address was a mere three streets away, a fact I didn't realise until the taxi driver pulled in. I only had to pay the service charge on the meter. Again, my credit card worked perfectly, at the first time of asking. He'd even dropped me right outside the door, too.

By the time I had turned around from the taxi, the front door was already open. She was standing there, just waiting for me. "Why did you take a taxi? If you'd asked Bob, he would have told you to walk here, you idiot! You could have saved yourself some money! Come on inside then, Andy. It's time I explained all this to you."

I wasn't at all surprised to learn she knew my name already. Of course, she did.

"Take a seat, love. Tea, with milk and three sugars, because apparently, you crave diabetes? So, I suppose you want to know how and why I cursed you?"

I nodded. "For starters, yes. That would be nice." I settled myself in, I had a feeling this was going to be a long story.

She smiled. "I'm Aggie." Then she put a local phone book on the table between us and opened it. I could see she had circled one name. It was mine. "I picked your name entirely at random, Andy. I'm a witch, you see. Don't say anything silly, like witches don't exist, okay?" She snapped her fingers, and a note dropped into my lap.

ANDY, DRINK YOUR TEA BEFORE IT GETS COLD. OF COURSE WITCHES EXIST.

They bloody well did now, apparently. I took a drink of my tea. Sweet and hot, just the way I liked it.

"So why did you pick me, Aggie?"

She smiled again. "I'm looking to go into business, Andy, and I need a partner, someone who'll invest in me. Someone who has seen my skills in action and knows that; not only do witches exist, they can and will curse people, for financial compensation."

I rubbed my chin. "It's an impressive pitch, Aggie. If this was

Dragon's Den, I could hardly say no. So, how is it done then?"

Aggie snapped her fingers. This time, it wasn't a note which fell into my hands. It was a colour photograph. Of me, sitting on my sofa in my living room, shortly before the first note had dropped into my lap. "It's done with magic, Andy. Much like that photograph. I could probably explain it to your satisfaction if you had a hundred years or so to spare. Let's just go with '*It's magic!*' and accept my word I can repeat it at any time, and at any distance too. You know it works. You've seen the after-effects up close and personal. All I need is ten grand, Andy."

It was a lot to ask. I had the money, and then some, but it's not every day a little old lady like Aggie asks you to lend her ten thousand pounds to fund her magical cursing business. Right now, in my head, I could hear Duncan Bannatyne saying, "I'm out!" in his thick Scottish accent. I took another gulp of my tea. No, it was still excellent. "Can I ask about the delivery method, Aggie?"

She nodded. "Look at the picture, Andy. All the information you need is right there in front of you, dear."

I gave the photograph a quick once over, then a second, closer examination. Okay. I could see me, a newspaper, the sofa, my TV remote, a cup of tea and a sandwich.

"The tea?"

Aggie shook her head. "A witch I may be, but I'm not a heathen, Andy. I couldn't, in all good conscience, curse a cup of tea. It's simply not cricket, dear."

Okay, strike the tea then. What else did I touch a lot, that would stay with me for at least three days? I was up and down from the sofa all the time, so if that had been cursed, it would have been giving me constant small doses every time I sat on the damn thing. Likewise, the newspaper and remote. Which left me with…

"Bingo, Andy."

"The sandwich? Did you curse a damn sandwich? How did you know I'd be eating a freaking sandwich?"

Aggie gave me a broad grin and snapped her fingers again. Nothing dropped out of the air this time. Instead, a saucer appeared on the table in front of me. And if my nose was anything to go by, it had a delicious beef sandwich with horseradish on. "The best, most powerful witches have a gift called second sight, Andy. You like your conspiracy theories; you've heard of the CIA remote viewing program?"

I had. I loved a good whack-job conspiracy theory! Remote viewing was done by witches? Was that what Aggie was trying to tell me?

Aggie laughed out loud. "I can't read minds, but I can certainly read your face, Andy. Witches are not responsible for remote viewing, dear. At least not all cases of it. Definitely, over fifty percent of them are witches though, even if the people involved don't know they *are* witches."

"What about the men, Aggie?"

"A bunch of warlocks, probably."

I could tell she had seen the opportunity to tell that joke coming from several sentences away and had leapt on it like a jungle cat. If she ever decided she couldn't cut it as a witch, she certainly had a natural talent for stand-up comedy. It was clear to me Aggie was powerful, as magical users went.

She could create something from nothing, she could see things over long distances, and she had curses which actually worked. She was the real deal, an honest-to-goodness witch who needed ten grand. Ten grand which I could give her, after a little bit of insurance was set up to cover my outgoings.

~ * ~

Suffice to say, we immediately went into business from that point. Aggie had plenty of potential clients lined up, all wanting to curse people for various reasons. Neither of us cared why, as long as the client could pay us in cold, hard, cash. I made my initial investment back, then ten times over that. The money kept rolling in. At least for the next three years.

That was how long it took me to break down a cursed sandwich and work out exactly which of the ingredients was cursed. Aggie had done a good job at our initial meeting, throwing me off the scent with that horseradish. The sandwich she'd cursed me with had had French wholegrain mustard on it.

And that had been the key to Aggie's success. In hindsight, I realised the answer to "which ingredient of a cursed sandwich would you actually curse?" is "all of them". That was when I finally decided to set up shop for myself.

Aggie didn't need second sight to see that one coming either.

The day I finally worked it out, a note dropped out of the ceiling into my hands.

Best of luck in the new business, Andy. There's more than enough room for both of us. Aggie.

I wasn't greedy. Enough people had seen me with Aggie to know who I was, via the grapevine. We had never needed to advertise, we got all our business by word of mouth, people referring us to their friends and sometimes even their enemies.

Folks are odd like that.

I once met two clients, ten minutes apart. Each was cursing the other, and both had been referred by the same mutual friend. "So, Bill, was it? I understand you're a big fan of artisanal foods? I'd like you to take a sniff of this delicious imported French wholegrain mustard. It's produced specially for our cursing needs in the interest of Anglo-Franco relations."

Obviously, I hadn't gone straight across to France and met with Aggie's supplier there. Oh, no. I was subtle. I met a man who knew a man, who drove a van for the man who supplied Aggie. I also found out that man didn't just make mustard either. Horseradish, vinaigrette, French dressing. All types of cursed condiments, with a personal guarantee they'd remain in the gut of their victim for a minimum of three days.

He could make them stronger if I wanted them like that. Or weaker too. Both two and one-day versions of those cursed comestibles. I've got him on speed dial now, for all of my personal cursing needs.

Yeah, be an angel. Make sure that bread delivery is on time this week, won't you? You've heard about my research into cursed flour, you say? I suppose we could discuss that another time.

It's a nice life I've got now, in the cursed sandwich game. *Just don't give me any sauce, okay?*

~ * ~ * ~

Ray Daley was born in Coventry and still lives there. He served 6 years in the RAF as a clerk and spent most of his time in a Hobbit hole in High Wycombe. He is a published poet and has been writing stories since he was 10. His current dream is to eventually finish the Hitch Hikers fanfic novel he's been writing since 1986.

Tweet him @RayDaleyWriter

Payback's a Witch

Harriet Phoenix

"There's an art to cursing," Briony announced. "And I don't like to brag, but I am an artist."

She quirked an eyebrow at the audience. In the glare of the stage lights, she couldn't see the rows and rows of spectators in their plush red seats, but she could feel the weight of their stares. The hundred or so watching in person (not counting the stage technicians and camera crew), and the hundreds watching the livestream broadcast. The untold thousands who'd watch for years to come. It was *happening* for her. Finally.

"Oh, who am I kidding?" She threw her arms out. "I LOVE to brag!"

The audience chuckled, and Briony dipped her head to add just a touch of self-deprecation. Arrogance was fine; getting carried away was not. Image, that was the thing these days. Every factor of her appearance was carefully chosen to project the witch of contemporary times. Red hair teased into wild waves, but held back in a clasp. All-black clothing, but in the form of jeans, zip-up boots and a button-down shirt. Simple silver jewellery; Claddagh ring, pentacle necklace and stud earrings. The classical witch, brought up to modern sensibilities. Putting the mage in image. Hmm, not bad. She made a mental note to use that for something and went on with her HEX Talk.

"They say things used to be simpler in the olden days, and I'm here to tell you that it's true. Our foremothers in times past had a much easier job than we do today. It's no longer enough to turn your cheating boyfriend into a frog or sour your neighbour's milk because he let his dog do his business on your lawn. Audiences these days have been raised on a diet of Harry Potter and Buffy the Vampire Slayer, and they are *far* harder to impress. They are *jaded*. And that, sisters, means we need to up our game.

"The key is to recognise cursing for what it is; *communication*. It's easy to get caught up in spreading misery and mayhem, and forget you're also supposed to be spreading a message: 'You have irked me, mortal.'"

Another chuckle, noticeably louder and more appreciative than the first, ran through the audience. Always good to unite your audience with something everyone could agree on; yes, Briony, you're right! Mortals *are* irksome!

"If we look at historical examples, we can see cursing is, at its heart, a form of social conditioning. We've all heard the tales in which a humble traveller, mistreated by their hosts, turns out to be a witch in disguise, who punishes the transgressors with obliteration. Or the so-called "fairy tale" of the gold and toads, where one sister is rewarded for her kindness with riches, while the other is punished for her rudeness with toads. In this case the curse is used to affect not only the recipient, but the greater community; obviously if you met someone who rained gold or toads whenever they spoke, you'd want to know how that happened, and so the lesson about minding your manners spreads…as do the toads.

"Now, how do we achieve this in society today? Let's look at some case studies."

~ * ~

She'd thought she could handle it. But, watching the figure onstage as she preened in the spotlight, Amethyst was shocked by the smouldering burn of hatred she felt. Shocked, but not surprised.

Two years.

Over time, she'd come to view the rancour she felt as a living thing, something nasty held in her mouth where it had no desire to be. A trapped creature that struggled and kicked. Something small, and slimy, like a frog. One of those jungle tree frogs with the poison skin that burned her tongue and her palate as it fought against the barrier of her teeth.

Two years.

She watched the figure of Briony Merryweather as she strutted underneath the giant sign of the now-legendary HEX Talks logo, *the* symbol of the modern magical community. Every witch worth her circle-purifying natural sea salt dreamed of one day standing under that sign to deliver a lecture. It was a mark of excellence, of substance, a sure sign you'd *made it*.

And they'd let *her* in. For a moment, the Frog of Rancour battled the nausea that threatened to crawl up her throat.

"First, let's examine the case of the bullying office manager," the figure onstage said. "In this case, an administrative officer had been promoted and instantly showed her true colours as a sadistic tyrant. Not just a tyrant, but a *lazy* tyrant who started taking credit for her subordinates' work. We've all met the type, I'm sure. A clear drain on society, just begging to become an example. But how to go about it?

"The key to formulating a suitable curse for this individual lay in realising *exactly* the lesson they needed to showcase for those around them. You see, this person seemed to think being promoted above her colleagues meant she no longer needed to care what they, or anyone, thought of her. I set out to show her how wrong she was."

Amethyst's breath caught. *No*, she thought. *She isn't...*

Her hand crept up to the burns that stretched along the left side of her face. For two years, her mother had begged her to accept a healing ritual, had even resorted to sneaking into Amethyst's room at night with a salve she'd made, a salve meant to heal not only her scars but to seep on through her skin and heal her psyche as well.

But Amethyst hadn't been there. She'd pulled a sneaking act of her own, creeping out with her scrying stone as she'd done night after night, searching for the name of the one who'd torn the heart out of their family.

Briony Merryweather.

She watched as the figure onstage called up a diagram of a pentagram, with arrows marking the placement of the various accoutrements of the spell; orange and yellow candles, a moonstone, incense.

Exactly as I saw it.

"I always find a twist of irony to be a vital ingredient in any curse. This person thought she'd escaped other people's opinions, so I made them inescapable. Once I'd enacted this curse, she heard anything and everything said about her, by anyone, anywhere, as if they'd spoken into her ear."

The Merryweather woman waited as the hushed crowd fell to whispering among themselves. The true horror of such a curse seemed to unpack itself in everyone's minds. Amethyst, who had already unpacked the horror for herself months earlier, sat rigid, hands squeezed together in her lap.

But she wasn't there.

Instead, she was in her sisters' Volkswagen. Aster, the oldest, was at the wheel, while Athena had the shotgun seat. Amethyst was the youngest, and she had the back. The sisters had been heading to a circle with their cousin's coven for Beltane. Nothing exciting, but it was a chance to go somewhere new, meet some new people.

The little car was full of chatter as Aster pulled onto the motorway. The two older girls had been speculating about the friends their own age their cousin might have, specifically boys, while Amethyst just wanted to make some new friends. She and her best friend had been fighting a lot lately, never over anything important, but *all the time*, and deep down she wondered if the problem was that they'd outgrown each other. Or maybe they'd just spent too much time together, but either way it couldn't hurt to widen her social circle. Maybe, if they both spent some time meeting new people, whatever rift had come between them would find a way to heal. It would be tragic to grow apart after being friends for so long.

It was odd, now, to think what had once counted as a tragedy.

It had begun with a tingle in her head. A tingle like a nettle sting, many-barbed and poisoned and *alive*. She twisted in her seat, trying to find where it had come from.

"Ames?" Athena called. "Something wrong?"

"Did you *feel* that?" She called back.

"No. What did it feel like?" Her sisters exchanged a look of worry. Amy was the sensitive one; she felt things the others had to search for. She was the one who carried hex bags for protection, whose bed was surrounded with chunks of her namesake crystal to keep spirits and psychic influences from preying on her as she slept.

"I think it's a...curse..." The words had barely left her mouth when a blue Lexus lurched across their lane, clipping the Volkswagen's bonnet and sending them into a tailspin. She remembered thinking, *that's it, that's the one*, as if it still mattered, as her sisters screamed and the world turned to screeching metal and breaking glass.

She shook herself out of her memories, or tried to. She wasn't sure she'd ever left that moment, not in the months she'd scried for the blue Lexus and the curse that felt like nettles. The information she had was vague, so she'd turned to more mundane means of gathering data; trawling through news articles and accident reports, pouring anything she learned into yet more scrying. She'd attended the funeral of the woman in the blue Lexus. No other witches were there, but she'd heard enough about her behaviour in her final weeks to get an idea of how the curse worked. But where did it *come* from?

Her mother had begged her to let it go. She'd lost two daughters already, she'd said. She couldn't bear to lose another. Her coven leader had told her to let nature take its course; the Threefold Law would catch up to the caster of that curse in its own good time. Everyone had piled on, telling her to let go of anger and let herself heal.

She hadn't listened to their hollow words. None of them had been there. They didn't believe there really had been a curse; none of them felt the things she'd felt. She could see it behind their eyes, their secret conviction she'd made it all up, invented a curse so she could have someone to blame for a tragic accident.

So, she'd kept going. When her mother hid her scrying crystal she'd turned to rituals, any she could find online and many more she'd invented herself. She'd consulted oracles, trafficked with spirits, travelled in higher planes, never losing sight of that tenuous trail from the nettle curse to whoever had cast it.

And then, finally, a name.

It was so much easier after that. The name led her to a social media profile which she'd relentlessly stalked. She created accounts specially to post comments meant to engage with her target, flatter her, and ingratiate herself with the community of followers. She'd befriended some, or pretended to, and it was from one of them she'd scored the link to a special access site that let her buy the ticket to tonight's event weeks in advance.

Her family thought she was going to a concert. They'd been pleased.

"So simple, isn't it?" The Merryweather woman smirked, enamoured of her own cleverness. "She found herself constantly harassed by the bad opinions of those she'd been bullying, unable to escape their jokes, their nasty nicknames and complaints about her behaviour. Call someone incompetent for her own screw-up? She heard everything her subordinates have to say about it. Cut someone off in traffic? Hear them call her a moron. She became erratic and paranoid, screaming abuse at people and lashing out in public. And best part? The effects of the curse are cumulative, because the more extreme her behaviour became, the more people spoke about her and the worse the things they had to say. Soon her bosses were talking about how unstable she'd become, which only made her more paranoid. The whole thing came to a head when she was put on administrative leave and had a meltdown in the foyer of her office building.

"Now, the nuts and bolts of casting this curse were complex, and figuring them out required…"

Wait. What? That was it? That was all she had to say?

The Frog of Rancour thrashed on Amethyst's tongue and she found herself rising.

~ * ~

This was everything Briony had dreamed it would be. She revelled in the audience's hushed awe as she explained how she'd worked out the curse.

The only problem was the nagging fear someone would realise exactly *how* she'd come across this example-waiting-to-happen. If word got out she'd been forced to take a mundane data entry job to make ends meet, actually found herself at the mercy of one of the mortals she was born to subjugate…oh, but she'd put her in her place, hadn't she?

"That's NOT what happened."

The voice was quiet, but carrying. Briony heard people shifting in their seats, trying to find the speaker.

Briony stumbled over a word, unsure of what to do. She decided to ignore it and turned back to her diagram.

"Tell the truth, Merryweather! Tell them what really happened!"

People were truly looking around now, and two technicians and a cameraman swung around, finding whoever was calling out from the audience. Peering out, Briony saw the figure of a girl in her late teens standing in the middle of the audience. The left side of her face was badly mottled and scarred, but it was the expression on her face as she stared up at Briony that terrified her to the very soul.

"Um, it appears we have a, uh, heckler," she faltered. "I'm sorry, folks, usually our audiences here at HEX Talks have a little more…"

"If you're not going to tell them, I will." The girl stood so still as she spoke Briony almost couldn't see her shaking with rage. "Because the story didn't end there, did it? Your office manager didn't just have her breakdown and vanish. No, she ran outside and got in her car, trying to escape all those voices you made her hear. She drove right out onto the motorway.

"But she really wasn't okay to drive, was she? Not with all those voices buzzing in her ear about how *unstable* she was, how *erratic*. She hit the central barrier and flipped her car and *died*, Merryweather, were you going to mention that?"

The girl paused as a susurration passed through the audience. Briony swallowed, feeling the cameras on the girl, and herself.

"I am not responsible," she croaked. "For the bad decisions other people…"

"But that wasn't all," the girl cut across. "Because first she hit another car. A car with three people inside. Three sisters. That car went into a tailspin and ended up in front of a lorry that couldn't stop in time. The two girls in front died instantly."

The audience was silent. Briony couldn't remember how to speak.

"The thing is, though, Merryweather?" The girl's tone was lighter now, almost chatty. "The thing is, I actually agree with you. No, really, I do!"

She stared straight into Briony's eyes with her Basilisk stare.

"Some people are just *begging* to become an example."

~ * ~

She hadn't known she was coming here for payback. It wasn't until the bragging had started that she'd realised. But how to do it? No one as accomplished at cursing as Merryweather would go anywhere without protection. Certainly nothing a novice like herself could get past.

So she couldn't curse the woman herself. But what?

And then, as she'd flung her accusations at her sisters' murderer, it had come.

Sensitives weren't usually curse-casters. But Amethyst had the power of two years' raw fury building inside her, and she reached deep inside to fling it all out in a single word of power as she pointed…not at the woman, but above her.

"BRISEADH!" *Break!*

The enormous HEX Talks logo above Merryweather's head juddered, suddenly far too heavy for its supports. A loud snap of many lines breaking at once rang through the space and the sign fell, twelve feet, onto the woman transfixed beneath it, and burst.

People screamed. A hundred people stampeded for the exits and the cameras, still recording, stood abandoned as people ran away from the many small, brightly coloured shapes that squirmed and hopped their way out of the wreckage of the sign. Of the woman buried underneath it all, there was nothing to be seen.

Amethyst fought the urge to slide to the floor. Suddenly the last two years seemed *very* long, and without the rage that had fuelled her she was exhausted. But she stumbled her way up and onto the stage, stepping carefully towards the writhing mound of tree frogs. She nudged them gently aside with a trainer until she found a hand with a Claddagh ring.

She stood for a moment, glaring at the hand. Then she pulled her jacket sleeves down over her fingers, grasped the wrist, and pulled.

It wasn't easy; people are heavy, after all. But finally, the woman came unstuck from the mound of frogs. When the head emerged, Amethyst seized the hair and pulled that too. Finally, the woman was free of the frogs and the wreckage of the sign. Amethyst rolled her onto her back and crouched over her, staring down at the woman she'd hated for so long. She certainly struck a pitiful figure, pale and sweaty and battered, shaking and moaning from the frogs' venom.

She had it coming. She was a bad person, who did bad things and then bragged about it.

Amethyst reached out and carefully wiped the slime off the pentacle at the woman's throat. Then she took it between her fingers and closed her eyes.

"Glanadh," she whispered. "Glanadh, glanadh." *Cleanse, cleanse, cleanse.*

She pressed the pentacle to Merryweather's forehead and sent her will through it. Merryweather twitched and groaned, then twisted to the side and vomited thoroughly onto the stage. Amethyst stepped backwards out of the way and Merryweather's gaze flickered up towards her. Amethyst looked into the eyes of the woman she'd wanted nothing more than to crush.

"Do better," she said. "*Be* better."

The studio was empty; everyone had fled. She turned her steps towards the nearest exit and started walking.

The frog was free.

~ * ~ * ~

Harriet Phoenix is a Creative Writing graduate and longtime nerd, currently residing in Wiltshire, UK. She's wanted to be a writer since she was old enough to understand that books are written by people, and her short fiction has appeared in The Screw Turn Flash Fiction Competition 2020, the Riptide journal and in Swindon Writing. Find her at harrietphoenix.com.

More Great Anthologies from WolfSinger Publications

Time Capsules – edited by Carol Hightshoe

Time Capsules—history and mystery—a gift or a message from the past to the future.

Messages that can easily be misunderstood.

What were the reasons for passing along a pair of pink, fuzzy handcuffs?
A glass vial containing a perfect dandelion puff?
A Japanese Katana?
A red and blue scarf?
A wooden spoon?
What magic do these items contain? What stories do they tell?

From the past to the future. Mysteries and meanings abound within these pages, as well as reminders of the things people find precious. What will you find?

Crunchy with Ketchup – edited by Carol Hightshoe

It has been said that one should never meddle in the affairs of dragons—for you are crunchy and taste good with ketchup.
Come enter the dragon's lair.
Take your chances with other would-be heroes and heroines who decide to face off against one of the biggest, baddest predators ever.

Witness a dragon civil war.
Hear the true story of the Battle of New Orleans.
Find out what it's like in the belly of a dragon.
Discover why cats can spell disaster when stealing a dragon's egg.
Meet a group of dragon riders who protect us from nuclear devastation.
Follow legends of modern dragons, only to find something very unexpected.

And more…

Crunchy with Chocolate – edited by Carol Hightshoe

It has been said that one should never meddle in the affairs of dragons—for you are crunchy and taste good with chocolate.

Come enter the dragon's lair and roll the dice. Within these pages you will still meet some of the biggest, baddest predators ever—but if you are lucky, you will also discover some that have a sweeter side.

Meet a dragon with a soft spot for hard luck cases and another who is a hopeless romantic.

Enjoy a musical battle between a dragon and the specter of one of the greatest guitarists to ever play.

Meet a dragon in trouble with other magical creatures because he enjoys hanging out with human children.

Join a mother and daughter and their teams of dragons on a dangerous cross-country race.

Reconnect with an imaginary friend—who is not so imaginary and escape the isolation of the pandemic.

And more...

So enter in BUT tread carefully—remember you are crunchy and taste good with chocolate.

Cat Tails: War Zone – edited by Rebecca McFarland Kyle and Dana Bell

Cats have been our companions since long before they graced the temples of Ancient Egypt. In addition to being members of our families, they have also stood with us through difficult times. From keeping pests and vermin away from our food stores to providing a comforting paw when we have been wounded; cats have been our sidekicks and friends in many different battles.

Cat Tails: War Zone contains twenty-five stories from Ancient Egypt to the far-flung future, about some amazing cats who have served as compatriots during war times. But beware, for they can also be tricksters sent to teach lessons.

The real heroes are the volunteers of SHADOW CATS, an Austin, Texas-based rescue that has saved the lives of 9,000-plus cats since 1997. Trappers, veterinarians, nurses, and adoption social workers volunteer to trap, neuter and return ferals, provide care for ill, injured and behaviorally challenged cats, find perfect adoptive parents, educate on proper feline care, and advocate for real change in communities.

Proceeds from this book will continue their efforts.

Love 'em, Shoot 'em – edited by Dana Bell

One should never be afraid to love or shoot the one they care about. A famed markswoman once said that. Or so it's claimed.

Imagine a town with a dog sheriff from another planet.
A zombie attack clean-up woman.
An attractive alien who likes to play love goddess.
A magical concert with dead musicians that gets out of hand.
Or those of the old west who meet aliens.
Those from the far future hunted for not volunteering to die.
A woman who learns a lesson with a twist during war time.
And more…

Come along with our writers and travel the diverse trails of their tales, of loving and sometimes shooting, in these pages of Love 'em, Shoot 'em.

Extinct – edited by Dana Bell

What if those ancient creatures so beloved in fiction, myth, and science had not disappeared? What if they were real? What might have been developed to handle them, and how might man have felt about the thundering giants in yesterday's, today's, or tomorrow's worlds.

Imagine a sanctuary established for dinosaurs that displaces humans.

What if Raptors were used on a distance planet as scouts for the new colony?

Could Dodo birds have left a record about what happened to them? Dragons helping settlers? Inconceivable!

A conqueror learns a hard lesson from a goddess and two children create their own 'monster'.

Lovely, unique, tales of lumbering giants of old, ancient rulers of the skies, and many others once thought to be myth or legend appear here in Extinct?

Tales From the Fluffy Bunny – edited by Carol Hightshoe

Welcome to the Fluffy Bunny

We welcome everyone—especially those with a story to tell. Adventurers, mercenaries, guardsmen, merchants, noble and peasant. Whoever. If you have a tale to share, then come in and have a seat. First drink and a hot meal are on the house.

What's a tale without an audience to appreciate it? So, even if you don't have a tale to share, come in, pull up a seat and enjoy these 17 tales of how a warrior or their weapon earned their name.

Visit us at www.wolfsingerpubs.com for more information

www.ingramcontent.com/pod-product-compliance
Lightning Source LLC
Chambersburg PA
CBHW070927260626
47162CB00007B/2826